I0760622

HUNTED BEAST

K. LORAINE

USA TODAY BESTSELLING AUTHORS

MEG ANNE

This book is a work of fiction. The names, characters, places, and incidents are products of the author's imagination or have been used fictitiously and are not to be construed as real. Any resemblance to persons, living or dead, actual events, locales, or organizations is entirely coincidental.

ISBN:

978-1-961742-28-4 (Paperback Edition)

978-1-961742-29-1 (Hardback Edition)

No artificial intelligence was used in the creation of this work of fiction.

Permission requests can be sent via email to: authors@themategames.com

Edited by Mo Sytsma of Comma Sutra Editorial

Cover Design by CReya-tive Book Design

Photographer: Wander Aguiar

Model: Matheus M.

For the ride or dies who know where all the bodies are buried and never hesitate to pick up the shovel.

"Are you saying you wouldn't fight for me?"

"Darling, I would burn this world for you."

— SCARLETT ST. CLAIR, A TOUCH OF RUIN

HUNTED BEAST

AUTHORS' NOTE

Hunted Beast contains mature and graphic content that is not suitable for all audiences. Such content includes scenes of emergency birth control, somnophilia, drugging and drug use, mentions of mental illness and more. **Reader discretion is advised.**

As always, a detailed list of content and trigger warnings is available on our website.

SESSION TRANSCRIPT: NOVEMBER 9TH

Dr. Temperance: Are you recording this?

Dr. Masterson: Of course I am. I record every session.

Dr. Temperance: But I'm not one of your patients. This isn't technically a session.

Dr. Masterson: So? The best way to learn from conversations is to play them back and listen to the important parts.

Dr. Temperance: All right, then. You wanted to discuss the progress you've made so far with your subject. Tell me what you've found.

Dr. Masterson: Very little so far.

<<pocket watch clicks open and closed repetitively>>

Dr. Temperance: *hums* Well, that's not very encouraging, is it?

<<pocket watch clicks open and closed repetitively again>>

Dr. Masterson: Still carrying that old pocket watch, I see.

Dr. Temperance: Still judgmental as ever, I see.

Dr. Masterson: *laughs* It's my job to probe, no insult intended. Have you had a chance to look over Miss Moore's file?

Dr. Temperance: You mean the one I started when I recommended her to you? Yes, I've flipped through it. Hypnosis was an interesting choice. Usually that's not recommended with trauma such as hers. Especially not for a powerful psychic. You could've been hurt.

<<high heels clicking on hardwood floor>>

Dr. Masterson: She has no idea of the scope of what she is. I'm trying to help her unlock it.

Dr. Temperance: Is that wise? Given what we assume about the nature of her *clears throat* screams.

Dr. Masterson: If she doesn't understand it, she's more likely to use it carelessly. Just like Tor and the rest of them.

Dr. Temperance: You think they're reckless?

Dr. Masterson: I think they don't realize they're villains.

Dr. Temperance: What villain isn't the hero of their own story?

Dr. Masterson: My point exactly. In fiction, heroes are reckless. True villains are strategic.

<<rustle of clothing>>

Dr. Temperance: Wait, that's your treatment plan? You're encouraging them to be villainous?

Dr. Masterson: Given their predilections, I think it the safest course forward for all involved. Wouldn't you agree?

<<pocket watch clicks open and closed repetitively>>

Dr. Temperance: *hums* Let them out to play so we can harness them. Get them on our side to save the rest of the world from their power.

Dr. Masterson: Exactly.

Dr. Temperance: It's brilliant. Devious, but brilliant. This is the sort of thinking that gets your name in books.

Dr. Masterson: *tittering laugh* I'm glad you approve of my approach.

Dr. Temperance: That's not all I approve of. Have I told you how fit you look today?

<<footsteps on hardwood>>

Dr. Temperance: You're blushing, Doctor.

Dr. Masterson: Nathaniel . . .

Dr. Temperance: Lizzie . . .

<<rustle of clothing>>

Dr. Temperance: *voice low and seductive* I don't think we need to record this part.

<<static>>

End of transcript.

CHAPTER ONE

DAHLIA

I never wrote baddies like these. Sickeningly sadistic with murder in their eyes, sure. Blood dripping from sharp teeth, absolutely. But the smell of them? That was something I couldn't capture or even imagine. Rot and death, putrid, and somehow acrid like sulfur all at the same time.

My brain couldn't even supply names for all the creatures converging on the door. And the ones I did have . . . Let's just say if I wasn't already in the supernatural equivalent of a mental asylum, I would have booked myself a one-way ticket.

Tor stood in front of me, the muscles in his back and shoulders rippling and growing as I watched. He was shifting.

Shit.

Blood sprayed across the demon's twisted face, and Tor let out a vicious howl that was so loud my ears hurt. It took everything in me not to cower on the floor behind him. The demon disappeared from my vision, the sound of him crumpling to the stone causing me to look around Tor's huge body.

"T-Tor?"

I had to blink twice before my brain accepted what my eyes were seeing. Tor was . . . he'd just . . . Fuck, that guy didn't have a head anymore. Tor just lobbed it at the creatures in the doorway like he was participating in a macabre version of bowling. Or maybe soccer.

Gag. I was never going to be able to sleep again.

My Viking mate, the man who'd just claimed me as his, treated me like his most precious gift as he'd taken my virginity, turned to face me. His formidable build twice as large as normal, he stared at me, eyes gone fully black, horns curling from his forehead, cheekbones sharp enough to cut glass.

I swallowed. This wasn't *my* Tor. This was my Beast, and with the barest of nods, I set him loose.

His lips curved up in a wicked mockery of a smile as he turned back toward the monsters too stupid enough to realize that death was coming for them. I'm not even sure I blinked before he had two more of the fiends torn into pieces.

He could destroy them all—and likely would. If I'd learned anything in my research about animals and their mates, I knew he would protect me to the bitter end. Presumably *their* bitter end.

It seemed the monsters were on the same page as me because they were no longer fighting each other to get in the room, but to get out. All but one tiny man with a rusty red cap were pushing their way back to the hallway. With his matted gray beard, the guy looked a bit like the scary version of a Keebler elf.

An alarm blared, causing Tor to release a bellow as he reached for the small man who darted toward the doorway. But without warning, the heavy slab of metal slammed shut, locking with an audible click.

A robotic voice followed over the hidden speaker somewhere in the room. "Attention, this is a lockdown. There has been a security breach. Remain where you are until the all clear is sounded."

Oh dear God, we were locked in here.

The elf-like man froze, a string of unintelligible curses leaving him as his shoulders slowly dropped. Not in defeat, I realized, but acceptance.

Removing his hat, he let the long, pointed end drag through the pool of blood on the floor as he turned to face my beast. The act must have triggered something in my memory, because my fae lore came back to me in a rush, providing me with a name for the creature.

Redcap.

Oh fuck.

With a scream, he bolted for Tor, climbing him so fast I could barely see him. Talon-like claws dug into the flesh on my mate's shoulders, cutting through the scales he'd sprouted like they were butter. Either his claws were really that sharp, or the scales were just for show. I didn't give it any more thought as blood spilled down Tor's back in thick rivulets.

He let out a rage-filled snarl, gripping the murder goblin with both hands and prying him off, the claws ripping muscle down to the bone.

I winced, hoping the magic that turned him into the beast would also help him heal because my first aid knowledge was limited to one afternoon of CPR. And I was pretty sure shouting for someone to call 9-1-1 while I checked that his airway was clear wasn't going to do anyone any good.

The creature clawed at Tor's hand, which was now wrapped around his throat, his face going purple from lack of oxygen. As I watched, my kind, caring Viking squeezed hard enough the goblin's eyes bulged and eventually exploded from the pressure.

But the part that sent chills down my spine? That came after, when Tor laughed.

Vicious didn't even begin to describe my mate. Sadistic, maybe. Brutal for sure.

He was *playing* with the goblin. Taking his time, like a cat with a mouse.

Bile crawled up my throat as Tor let the now limp body fall to the floor. I couldn't even muster the beginnings of a protest before he brought his bare foot down and stomped on the redcap's head until it was nothing more than a pulpy mess smeared into the concrete.

I couldn't help my whimper as I finally gave in and cowered in the corner. I was surprised I hadn't vomited yet. Yay me.

Tor turned around, his breaths heaving, body covered head to toe in blood and . . . other things. A shiver raced down my spine as he trained his gaze on me. There was no recognition there, only a terrible thirst for violence.

He stepped toward me, and my protective instincts overrode all other thought. A scream ripped out from deep within me. Not one of those horror movie scream-queen situations, but the same mind-melting wail I'd let loose twice before. Both times with deadly effect.

It was the only defense I had, the only thing that would shake him out of his bloodlust.

My wail was all I heard as Tor stopped, anguish rippling across his face, clawed hands coming to his ears. His mouth opened on a pained groan, his void-like eyes locked on mine as my scream went on and on until finally, he dropped to the floor.

One more unmoving monster among the remains of the others.

I couldn't move, couldn't get my limbs to unlock so I could check and see if my mate was still breathing. I couldn't do anything because, just like every other time I used this particular party trick, as soon as my shriek subsided, I blacked the fuck out.

CHAPTER TWO
HOOK

Generally speaking, I quite enjoyed being an instigator of chaos. What were rules and laws besides challenges begging to be broken? Unfortunately, chaos breeds danger, and it would seem I'd been a mite too cocky this time. Every step I took toward Dahlia's cell was met with some degree of violence I had to use my power to repel. At this rate, I would be drained and useless to her by the time I unlocked the bleeding door.

The door in question was only twenty paces away, but it felt like miles. Mainly due to the creatures I'd unleashed that were busy pummeling each other as a means of venting their frustrations. Okay, it might be because I'd *influenced* them, but it amounts to the same thing, really. And it's not like it took much more than a little nudge to convince them to give in to their natural impulses.

Pain blossomed across my jaw as an absolute twat of a goblin hit me with an uppercut I hadn't seen coming. The cheeky fucker might've been short, but he was strong. I snarled in his general direction before kicking him square in the chest with a booted foot and sending him flying.

"Well, Cas, you wanted a distraction. You certainly got it," I muttered to myself as I wiped at my lower lip.

Without warning, a scream pierced the air, muting all other sound. In less time than it took to blink, the grunts, growls, and smacks of flesh meeting flesh were absolutely overwhelmed by the wail, reducing the scenes around me to a series of silent vignettes. I'd never been particularly sensitive to loud noises—pirate ships weren't known for their quiet solitude—but this went from shrill to agonizing, the sound so powerful my ears rang and I fell to my knees. So did all the creatures in front of me, blood trickling from their ears.

"Fuck," I groaned as the ringing in my ears intensified, accompanied by a blinding pain in my head. I couldn't focus on anything with the way it felt as though my brain was currently leaking out of my ears.

Stop. Goddess, please stop.

There was no way to know if the plea left my lips. I couldn't hear anything beyond the echo of the scream and the roar in my ears. And then silence.

I couldn't tell if it was because my eardrums had ruptured or if the scream had stopped, but my money was on the latter since my brain didn't feel like it was melting any longer.

It took another couple of seconds before I could manage to do more than blink. As I pushed myself up to standing, I took in the carnage around me. All the creatures who'd been in front of me were still on the ground, either moaning or out cold. The ones behind me fared little better, though they at least seemed to be moving. Some going so far as to help others up.

It was an odd scene all around, given that they'd all been at each other's throats less than a minute prior. My stomach rolled like it had the first time I'd been aboard ship and hadn't yet gotten my sea legs. Lurching to the side, I vomited spectacularly until I couldn't bring anything else up.

"Bloody fucking hell, what did that?"

As much as I wanted answers, I also knew I needed to get to

Dahlia. If the scream had been enough to bowl me over, she had to be in even worse shape. Especially since it seemed to have been at its zenith near . . . Wait.

Had that scream come from her cell? Had it been her? Or the beast I'd accidentally locked her in with?

Plucking the skeleton key free from my pocket, I made my way as quickly as my shaky legs could manage while the worst of the creatures were still knocked out. I had to stop once to swallow back another wave of nausea, but I soldiered on like the hero I was. This was my doing. I needed to see her safe while also escaping notice myself.

Soft sounds came from the downed baddies near her door, the knowledge they were rousing spurring me forward. Key in the lock, I twisted until the heavy bolt disengaged and I was able to shove open the slab of metal.

She was curled up with her head in her hands, naked, trembling, covered in blood and ichor. That should have been enough to terrify me, but it wasn't the only alarming thing in this cell. Dahlia wasn't alone. The Beast was unconscious in front of her, blood trailing from his ears and nose, claws stained red from what could only be the remains of the adversary unfortunate enough to be locked in here with them.

"Dahlia, are you all right?"

She didn't so much as flinch to show that she'd heard me.

I took a tentative step forward, eyes shifting to track the man on the floor. He didn't register my presence either. Encouraged by that bit of news, I moved more quickly, crouching down so my face was level with hers. "Darling, we need to go."

She was babbling beneath her breath, the same nearly incoherent string of words. "I had to. Had to. I . . . I . . ."

Reaching out, I gently took her face between my palms and forced her to look at me. Her eyes were unseeing pools of gray until she blinked a few times and focused on me.

"C-Caspian?"

"Yes, sweet girl. It's me."

"Wh-what happened?"

Swallowing hard against the lump of guilt in my throat, I forced out, "A prison break. Come along. We can discuss more later. We need to get out of this place."

I held my hand out to her, but she was slow to reach for me. It was obvious she was trying to piece together what had happened. Already, panic was returning to her features.

"Just focus on me, love. We can worry about the rest once we're safe."

Normally, I'd have taken any opportunity to ogle her naked body, but right now, all I saw was a terrified woman I needed to help. So I snagged the rumpled sheet off the bed and wrapped it around her before tucking a lock of hair behind her ear and whispering, "I've got you."

"Tor," she whispered, her eyes darting to peer over my shoulder.

I stood, blocking her view. "He'll be fine. We both know he'd be in agreement with me about getting you out of here, so let's do that, shall we?"

She nodded slowly. "Okay."

"Eyes on me, sweet girl. Don't look anywhere else, understand?"

Doing as she was told, she let me lead her out of the cell, over the mess of body parts and entrails, and out into the hall.

It was a miracle she didn't try to look down. If she'd been a bit more lucid, I doubt I'd have gotten so lucky. As it was, I knew I'd have a lot to answer for once she returned to herself fully. Unless she didn't put it all together. I hoped fate would smile upon me and I'd be spared her ire.

Unfortunately for me, the jig was up the moment I used that blasted key to open the locked door that would get us out of No Man's Land. I felt her stiffen next to me, heard her soft gasp. She was too smart for her own good.

Not giving her a chance to ask the question building behind her lips, I pulled her through the door and then slammed it shut, relocking it behind me.

The sound of running footsteps had me moving protectively in front of her.

"Dahlia? Where is he? Did he turn? Are you hurt?" Bruno, the Beast's pissing keeper, came barreling at us, ignoring me completely.

"He t-tore them to shreds. He wouldn't . . . couldn't stop. I . . . I think I killed him." Fuck me. The way her sweet voice trembled made my heart do things it'd never done before.

"Where?" Bruno asked.

She waved a hand at the door behind us. "In there. He took us to a cell." The words were sleepy and uncertain, as if she was recalling a dream that was already fading from memory. "He . . ."

Bruno reached out and grasped her gently by the biceps. "Dahlia, I need to know. Did he turn?"

"Y-yes."

Something in the man's eyes snuffed out. It wasn't until I heard the despair in his voice that I realized it had been the final shreds of his hope.

"Fuck. The final petal." Bruno's attention snapped to me, his gaze narrowing. "Get her somewhere safe. I'll deal with Tor."

I'd well and truly fucked up. This was far worse than anything I'd intended, but there was no chance in hell I'd say anything. A curt nod was all I offered him as I tugged Dahlia away, running through the halls.

"Come to my room, love. You shouldn't be alone. We can get you cleaned up and find something for you to wear."

I hadn't made it up two stairs before that Scottish dragon called her name. And right on his heels was Cain. Goddess, they just kept showing up, like scurvy or the pox. The second those blazing blue eyes locked onto mine an echo of the pain I'd felt last time we'd been alone rippled beneath my skin. A shudder worked its way along my spine. I didn't have the name for whatever it was he'd done to me, but I sure as shit didn't want to experience it again. Best to keep my distance...for now.

"Kai?" Dahlia's surprise pulled me back to the present.

"Are you hurt? Where are your clothes?" he asked, ripping his shirt off and bodily pulling it over her head. She dropped the sheet and wove her arms through the holes, immediately moving to curl herself around his hulking form.

He held her protectively, one hand cupping the back of her head as he dropped his lips to her ear. "I've got you. You're safe, gem."

I couldn't help the glower I tossed his way. I was the one who'd rescued her. Why was he getting the cuddles?

"What the hell happened to her? Why is she covered in blood?" Kai barked, an accusing glare leveled at me over Dahlia's head.

"It's not my blood," she whispered, her face still tucked into his chest.

"Then whose is it?"

"Tor . . . he killed them."

"Killed who? Where were you?"

"Yes," Cain snarled softly, his burning stare making me flinch. Given the smirk that immediately curled his lips, the fucker clocked the involuntary move. "Where were you, Hook? How was it that you came to find Dahlia when we searched everywhere for her?"

"No Man's Land. Tor took her there," I blurted like the absolute git I was.

Kai and Cain exchanged dark looks at the mention of the Novasgardian, then pinned me with their attention once more.

"How did you get in?" Kai asked, but before I could answer, Cain put himself in front of Dahlia and forced me to stare directly at him as Asshole growled at my feet.

"And if you were there, how the fuck did you get out during a lockdown?"

I was caught, the noose around my neck tightening as Dahlia outed me.

"He has a key."

"Does he really?" Cain practically purred. I could take a lesson from the bastard when it came to making innocuous comments sound menacing. "How convenient."

"Well, you see, the thing is—"

An alarm blared through the estate, halting all conversation.

"What is that?" Dahlia asked, fear in her question.

"Fire," Kai rumbled. "I can smell the smoke."

Ah, saved by the bell. Fate *was* shining upon me.

CHAPTER THREE

KAI

"Now there's a fire?" Dahlia asked, her exasperated tone betraying how shaken she really was.

"Someone was intent on causing mischief tonight," Hook muttered.

"Yes, someone," Cain said, one of his brows lifting as he pointedly stared at the pirate.

"Oh, come off it. I'm here, aren't I? How could I possibly have started a fire?"

"At this point, I wouldn't put anything past you."

"Well, it's nice to know you've stopped underestimating me."

Cain's lips curled into a dark smile. "That would require me to estimate you at all. And I don't. You register in my thoughts about as often as a gnat."

"Enough of this. We have to get out of here before we get up close and personal with the flames. I may be fireproof, but the three of you are decidedly not." I snagged Dahlia by the wrist and tugged her behind me, resisting the urge to throw her over my shoulder and race as fast as my legs would carry us. The only thing truly stopping me was her newly acquired mate bond. Speaking of . . .

"Where is Tor? You mentioned he was with you."

No need to let on that we'd already known that and it was the main reason we'd come running.

Dahlia blanched, which was hardly the reaction I'd expected when inquiring about her new mate. Perhaps she wasn't happy about her new status. Perhaps he forced her . . .

My dragon clawed at my chest, practically shouting in my head, *"I told you so."*

"Right. We'll talk about it when we're safe."

"Where are you taking me?" she asked, her steps unsteady and a bit clumsy as she followed me.

"We need to get out of the building."

"Are you really so sure outside is the safer option?" Hook asked.

"Safer than a building on fire?" I countered.

"Have you forgotten the serial killer roaming our woods?"

Dahlia froze at the mention of the Ripper.

"We'll go to my tower," I decided. "It's far enough from the main residence and defendable if anyone unwanted tries to get to us there."

A haunted look crossed Dahlia's face, there one moment and gone the next.

"Lass?"

She shook her head as Asshole pawed at her foot, begging for attention. Bending down, she scooped him into her arms, and the ball of fluff licked her face enthusiastically. Lucky son of a bitch. "It's fine. Let's go."

I'd let her think the matter was dropped for now, but I'd make her admit what was bothering her once I knew she was safe. Sooner rather than later.

As we followed the crowd outside, I kept a close watch on Dahlia. Her posture was all wrong, the energy surrounding her not that of a happily mated woman, but a tormented one. My protective instincts were on high alert with every passing second, hammering home my earlier suspicion that she'd been forced.

I'll kill him.

"Dragon, we need to move faster. She's hardly wearing a stitch of clothing and has another man's cum dripping down her thighs," Cain snarled, grabbing me by the elbow in a move far too bold.

Hook and I both faltered at that. My eyes darted to Dahlia, but she'd ducked her head and was currently using her hair as a shield. If we weren't in the middle of fleeing, I'd smack the prick upside the head for embarrassing her.

"That door, just up ahead. Key is behind the—"

"Third brick from the keyhole," Hook finished, darting ahead to grab it.

"How did you know that, Cas?" Dahlia asked.

He shot her a patronizing glance. "Pirate."

"Right, that explains everything," Dahlia grumbled.

"Of course it does. They're the original blackguards and the definition of morally bankrupt."

"Hey now," Hook said, glancing over his shoulder as he unlocked my tower.

"Am I wrong?" Cain taunted.

"Well, no . . . but it just sounds ugly when you say it."

"Nothing sounds ugly when I say it."

"Are ye quite finished? We should get upstairs," I interrupted, staring daggers at Cain as he leaned against the stone wall with an impassive expression.

Asshole growled at me, not liking the way I was assessing his master. Maybe he could sense the predator lurking beneath my mortal facade. If so, he was a damn sight more clever than I gave him credit for.

"Dinnae fash yerself, pup. Your master's just fine."

Cain's gaze flicked between his dog and me before he quirked a brow. "Of course I am. You're not the only one with fire, dragon."

Hook had already started up the staircase, so I urged Dahlia forward. She was unusually hesitant, her shoulders stiff, the pulse in her wrist faster than I'd like. Almost like she was frightened.

"What is it, gem?"

She peered into the stairwell and heaved a sigh. "I'm just checking."

"There's nothing here, baby doll. I promise. Go on up." His voice was noticeably gentler than it had been up until now, and even Dahlia seemed startled by the shift. As if realizing what he'd done, Cain scowled and added, "Take a picture, it'll last longer."

"Wow, just when I think you've hung up your alphahole spurs, you prove me wrong."

"I don't wear spurs. What do you think I am, a cowboy?"

"No one knows what you are. Including yourself. Isn't that why you're here? God, get over yourself, Cain." She huffed and pulled her wrist free of my grasp before stomping up the stairs.

"Do you get off on being an arse?" I asked him.

Smirking, he shoved off the wall and strode past me toward the staircase. "It got her up there, didn't it?"

"I'm not sure you should count that as a point in your favor."

He shrugged. "Maybe the two of us are playing different games."

I pondered over his meaning as I climbed the stairs behind him. Whatever the game, I wasn't keen to lose.

When we reached the top, Dahlia paced nervously in front of the window while Hook was lowering himself to my nest. Right beside the pillow Dahlia had marked for me.

My dragon snarled in pure possessive rage. Hook's eyes went wide as I launched myself across the room and snatched the pillow up before he could defile it with his own scent.

"Mine," I growled, not fully aware that I'd lifted it to my face until I caught the delectable aroma that was all Dahlia. Her eyes met mine over the pillow, her cheeks flushing pink as I smirked and took another, much longer whiff.

"You dragons really are a bunch of possessive fuckers, aren't you?" Hook asked with an uncomfortable laugh.

"You have no idea." I tucked the pillow away on top of my pilfered bookshelf next to the stack of Ruby Spector novels I'd special ordered. Then, once I was sure my treasure was safe, I turned to Dahlia and leveled my gaze on her. "All right, lass. We're out of harm's way. Tell us what happened."

My dragon stirred, readying us both to take down the monster who hurt her if she said the word. Tor may be the closest thing to a friend I had in this place, but I wouldn't hesitate to destroy him if he harmed so much as a hair on her head. I'd slay my own sire to save her.

"It happened so fast. All of it."

Cain glowered from where he was sitting on the windowsill, but he didn't say anything. Neither did Hook, for that matter. Which was rather uncharacteristic of the self-important fuckwit.

"One minute I was rushing to tell Doctor Masterson about what the ghost told me. The next, Tor had me over his shoulder and on the way to No Man's Land."

"What *did* the ghost tell you, by the by?" Hook asked.

She swallowed nervously, her tongue darting out to wet her lips. "That the Ripper was after me."

Great. But that was a problem for another time. Right now I was more concerned with something else. "Dahlia, I need to know one thing before you go on," I said, unable to stand not knowing.

Wide, questioning eyes locked with mine as she waited for me to continue.

"You were with him. You bonded. Did he force you?"

She gasped. "How did you know?"

Rage had me ready to tear his head from his shoulders. Cain shoved to his feet Asshole a symphony of furious growls as he paced in circles around him. Hook followed suit, standing as well. Apparently I wasn't the only one ready to go on a murder spree to defend her honor.

"Where is he?" It took everything in me to keep my voice low and controlled.

"He's where I left him. Kai, how did you know I accepted the mate bond?"

"Dahlia, I need you to tell me if he forced the bond on you. I have to know."

Shaking her head, she pressed a palm over her heart as she addressed us all, finally seeming to realize the fuse she'd lit with her words. "No. No, it's not what you're thinking. I *asked* him to claim me. Nothing was forced."

"Then why the hell isn't he with you now?" Cain snarled.

"The creatures came after us, and he turned to save me, then the lockdown happened. He couldn't help himself. With no one to stop him, his beast was in control. I was afraid." Fuck, I hated the wobble in her voice. "I . . . I screamed until he was unconscious."

"Bloody hell, that was you?" Hook whispered.

Dahlia nodded, looking guilty. "I think I killed him."

"You'd feel it if your mate died, baby doll." Cain's voice was strangely hollow. Like he knew from personal experience.

My mind was still caught on another detail. "Gem, when you say his beast was in control, do you mean he transformed completely?"

She nodded. "Horns, scales, the whole nine."

Fuck.

Fuuuuck.

"The last petal," I groaned.

"Bruno mentioned that too. What are you guys talking about?"

"His curse. Every time he turned, a petal fell. It was a countdown of sorts. A way for him to keep track of how long he had before he passed the point of no return."

"How . . . how do you know that?" she asked.

"Because I gave him the tattoo. He wanted a way to track its progress."

"Wait, so you're saying he's what . . . stuck like that?"

Blowing out a heavy breath, I nodded. "I'm afraid so. It's why he'd been in all those extra sessions with Bru and the doctor. He was trying to work on his control so he could prevent it. So he could be with you, but I guess the threat to his mate was too much for him."

"No," she whispered. "No, you can't mean that. He . . . he'll never be himself again?"

"Typical," Cain huffed.

"What was that?" Dahlia shot back.

"Your handsome prince lost his shine, so you're distraught. You only want him when he's pretty. Now you're horrified to be mated to a beast. Fucking typical."

Dahlia went from heartbroken to enraged in an instant. "How fucking dare you."

"You're the one that said it, sweetheart. I'm just calling a spade a spade."

"I did *not* say that. You put words in my mouth."

She lunged for him, but I caught her around the waist and pulled her to my chest. "Easy, gem. He's trying to rile you and you're letting him."

"He's a cunt."

"Aye, he is."

"Mmm, I like it when you talk dirty, love. Keep telling Cain what you think of him." Hook smirked and waggled his brows.

"Stop trying to influence this conversation, pirate. You're shifting the focus off the real issue," Cain snapped.

"Which is?"

"The fact that you're the one responsible for this."

"I have no idea what you're on about. I certainly didn't turn Tor into a beast." Hook backed away and pretended to busy himself by browsing my hoard. If he touched a single item, he really would need a hook for a hand when I was through with him.

"So it's all mere coincidence that you just so happen to have a key to the place where the prisoners broke free? When, as far as we know, there's never been any kind of breakout before today?"

"To be fair, you don't *know* much of anything."

Cain only held Hook's stare, silently demanding an answer.

"Come now, none of us are prisoners," Hook said, but he was lacking some of his usual swagger.

"What were you doing in No Man's Land, Caspian? No one goes there willingly." Cain took a menacing step toward him, his blue eyes blazing.

"Dahlia did," he said almost defensively as he stepped back. Remembering the state I'd found Caspian in the last time Cain got his hands on him, I didn't blame the man for wanting to stay out of the southerner's range.

"Technically I was taken there. Thrown over a shoulder and absconded with."

"Okay, fine. Tor, then. Which still makes your theory moot. People have and do go there willingly, so why not me as well?"

"Because you're a sneaky little fucker, and you don't do anything without an ulterior motive."

Dahlia wriggled out of my hold and approached the pirate, her fingers working the hem of my borrowed shirt like it was her lifeline. I had to admit, I liked knowing I could bring her comfort during a time like this.

"Cas, did . . . did you do this?"

He met her imploring gaze, opened his mouth, closed it, and then swallowed before looking away. It was as good as an admission.

"But . . . why? What good could possibly come out of releasing those . . . monsters?"

Floundering for the briefest moment, he searched the space above her head as though he could pluck an answer from the air before his mask slipped into place. "For you. I did it for you, darling."

"Me?"

"You're too precious to be in No Man's Land. I was merely trying to cause a distraction so I could break you out."

The sincerity in his tone was overly done and achingly false. Like a cake with too much icing. "What a load of horse shite," I spat.

Hook's jaw clenched, a muscle low in his cheek pulsing for a few beats before his lip curled in an ugly sneer. "Fine! I was fucking bored, all right? Are you happy now?"

"You were bored?" Dahlia's voice was a low warning. "Bored? You just decided it would be fun to let dangerous, unpredictable psychopaths who thirst for carnage out to play because you were bored?" She was yelling now, her body trembling.

Hook's eyes widened in surprise at her response, but me? I had to adjust my thickening cock at the sight of her coming into her own and handing him his arse.

"Do you have any idea what you've done? Tor is *stuck* in his beast form because of you."

The pirate inspected his nails as if he couldn't be bothered. "Well, perhaps I did you a favor. It was bound to happen sooner or later. I just helped matters along."

For a second I thought she might slap him, but instead her eyes narrowed and her hands balled into tight fists at her sides. When she spoke, her voice was low and cutting, her pain and anger bleeding through her words. "He has a family, Caspian. A twin, a niece, a father and mother. People who love him that he may never be able to see again. One impulsive decision destroyed a man's entire life. No, not just a man, an entire family. How does that not bother you?" She shook her head and took a step away from him. "You play a big game, with your charm and your flirty banter, and you use your handsome looks to trick everyone into believing you're harmless. But you're the biggest villain of them all. You're heartless and cruel. You disgust me."

"Dahlia . . ."

She backed away even further. "I think you should go."

"What? You can't be serious. There's a serial killer out there."

Her voice was ice when she responded. "For all we know, you're the Ripper."

"He's not the Ripper. He'd never fly under the radar this long. The ego on him is big enough to sink a ship," Cain muttered.

"Well, he sure fooled me."

There was a flicker of emotion on Hook's face before he hid it away once more. "You want me gone? Fine. I was getting bored with you lot anyway. Better watch out, I might be liable to do something reckless and impulsive again," he said, waving his hands around sarcastically.

"Haven't you ruined enough lives for one day?"

This time Cas met and held her gaze. "Maybe I have."

And then he left.

CHAPTER FOUR

CAIN

Once it was just the three of us, Dahlia seemed to deflate a little. She wasn't the only one affected by Hook's absence. I was loath to admit it, but my verbal sparring match with him had been a distraction tactic. The revelation about the origin of that scream and the fact that it came from Dahlia had left me shaken to my core.

As soon as that unearthly wail pierced my ears, an infernal buzzing had taken root in the back of my mind. The more I tried to ignore it, the worse it became, almost like a relentless knock on the door.

Dahlia's scream meant something. I was sure of it. I also had zero interest in finding out *why* I was sure of it. I didn't need any more ties between the two of us. I was too busy severing the ones we already had, though I suppose she and Tor had taken care of that.

"Are you sure I didn't kill him?" Dahlia asked in a soft voice. It took me far too long to realize she was asking me.

"He's your mate, isn't he?" I spat.

She flinched at the vitriol in my tone. Kai glared at me, taking a protective step closer to her. Somewhere between searching for her and coming up here, he seemed to have lost his anger at her new status. Not me.

Without Hook as my verbal punching bag, my fury was aimed at its true target.

She betrayed me.

She chose him.

Asshole let out a grumbled whine, leaning his body against my ankle as though reminding me she couldn't betray me because we'd barely interacted by my own doing.

"Why are you mad at *me*?" she asked, staring me down instead of cowing to my anger.

My traitorous dick perked right up at the fire in her, at the challenge she presented. She reminded me of the woman in my spotty memories. They didn't look alike, but they fought me exactly the same way.

"Because if you could simply keep your legs closed, we wouldn't be in this mess."

"What *we*? You and I aren't anything, remember? Which means this *mess* doesn't concern you. Feel free to fuck right off."

I was about to give in to my urge to collar her throat and shove her against a wall so I could teach her a thing or two about respecting me when Kai got between us both.

"All right, that's enough. You didnae kill him, lass, but your scream was so powerful we all felt it."

"You did? But how are you . . ."

She didn't need to finish the sentence; it was obvious what she was asking.

"Because we were far enough away," Kai answered.

"The last time I screamed like that, everyone around me died. I saw the video." Her voice was haunted, and my blood turned to ice.

"But they didn't die, remember? Kiki is still alive. Everyone is."

Dahlia rubbed at the center of her forehead like she was fighting off a headache. "It's all such a jumble. I feel like my brain's trying to protect me, but it's just making things worse."

A pulse of relief momentarily silenced the persistent buzz. I'd forgotten that she'd mentioned her scream to me before. Twice, actually. First when she introduced herself in our group session, and again when she told me the story of the ritual her cunt of a father forced her to participate in. Perhaps that's all this was. My foggy brain attempting to connect the dots.

"It's not normal, is it? To scream like this. It's like a myth or legend or something. No one can knock people out with the power of their voice alone." She paced back and forth, almost talking to herself instead of the two of us. Asshole followed, constantly at her heel.

A word hovered at the periphery of my mind, just out of reach. I was only distantly aware of the conversation taking place around me as I chased after it.

"Well, you also see ghosts, so I'd remind ye that normal is relative. It's also a bit of a dirty word around here."

Dahlia paused in her pacing, shifting topics. "Do you think the ghost's warning was wrong? Since Hook was the one who orchestrated the attack?"

Kai sighed heavily. "I think the two are nae connected."

"So the Ripper *is* after me."

"It's very likely. He hunts powerful supernaturals. Almost like he's collecting them."

"But I'm barely a supernatural. All I do is see ghosts."

And scream so loud you can take down a room filled with out-of-control creatures.

A shiver racked my body as the memory of her cry chased through my head again. I'd heard it before.

The word hit me out of nowhere, and I blurted, "Banshee."

Before I even registered what I'd said, I was pulled headlong into a memory I wished would have stayed buried.

"Wife, you can't stay angry with me forever. One of these nights, you're going to get lonely and remember exactly why we are so perfect for each other." I stood in the doorway of the night garden I'd created just for her and waited for a response.

She ran a fingertip over the cascade of night-blooming jasmine that crept up one wall and sighed. "You underestimate me, my lord. I am a woman. I can stay angry for an eternity."

I had no doubt she was right. In the course of our tumultuous six-month marriage, her temper had proven to be as unpredictable as my brothers'. As I'd predicted, all that fire burned hot in the bedroom. We were more compatible than I'd ever hoped, and the path from hate to love had been an easy one for her to travel.

But now she wanted something from me I could never give her, something I'd sworn I would never do.

"I cannot stay here any longer, husband. I'm a creature of life and light, not darkness and death. Can't you see how I'm withering? I feel like a narcissus struggling to bloom in the dead of winter."

"My love, ask of me anything else and it is yours."

"I want a child, husband. Your child. Please."

The weight of my promise, along with her plea, melted my ice-cold heart. She alone could warm me. My bride had me wrapped around her finger, and I doubted she knew even a fraction of the power she held over me.

"It is not possible. Let go of this and just allow yourself to be happy being mine."

Her face fell, the defeated slump of her posture making me ache to hold her. "All I've ever wanted was to be a mother. You've already taken so much from me. Please don't take my dream."

"Is a lifetime spent at my side not dream enough?"

"Perhaps, if I spent more than nights in your bed."

"Nights filled with pleasure," I reminded her, but her lips did not so much as twitch in a smile.

"Be that as it may, when the morning comes, you are off doing whatever it is you do, and I am alone. It's not enough. I cannot live only for our nights. It's a half-life, at best."

Agony ripped through me. These feelings she evoked in me were unfamiliar and frustrating. Until her, I hadn't known the pain of longing or the emptiness of unrequited love. I'd walked through millennia without her, but the moment fate had shown her to me, everything changed. I'd moved mountains to have her, bargained with the Fates using the only thing I could to ensure she was mine. And still, I was losing her.

"You can't know how your words wound me, wife."

She turned haunted gray eyes on me, and my heart lurched. "Are you so sure? Every time you leave our bed, your absence cuts like a knife. Soon I'll bleed out from loneliness and your abandonment."

Her grief wrapped around me like Death's own shroud. This was not the game of a bored housewife. She meant every word. Had I really come this far only to lose her now? I couldn't bear it. All I wanted was her happiness. It fed my own.

"Okay."

She blinked. "Okay?"

"Okay, we can try for a child." Even as the words left my lips, a chill of foreboding slid down my spine. One did not cross the Fates without dire consequence. I could only pray they turned a blind eye our way.

Thankfully her joy was infectious, and it chased away the doom and gloom crowding my mind. In a rush, she came to me, wrapping me in her embrace and whispering, "Thank you."

Hours later, I lay in bed with my wife curled into my side. Even in sleep she wore a faint smile. She was certain our efforts had been successful, and I didn't know if I prayed for her to be right or wrong. Anxious energy flowed through my every cell, keeping me from slumber. Not wanting to wake her with my restless tossing, I climbed from our bed, dressed, and made the unconscious decision to go to my office. There was always work to be done. The business of souls was never-ending.

As I pored over my books, the atmosphere in my office shifted from comfortable to oppressive. I felt the presence before I turned around and spotted her. A banshee, her eyes milky white, mouth gaping as she pointed to the portrait of my love sitting framed on my desk.

"No. You can't have her," I whispered fervently. "You won't."

Without looking at me, she released an ear-splitting scream, and intense pain filled my head before I lost consciousness.

CHAPTER FIVE

DAHLIA

"I'm sorry, can you repeat that? Did you just call me a banshee?"

Cain was still staring at me, but his eyes were unfocused, telling me he didn't actually *see* me at all. Whatever was going on in his mind right now had his full attention.

"Cain? Cain!" I finally shouted, frustration boiling my blood.

He blinked a few times and seemed to come back to himself, a rare glimpse of vulnerability flashing across his face before his arrogant expression returned. "There's no need to shout."

"What do you mean 'banshee'?" I demanded.

"What about it are you struggling with?" he shot back.

"Um . . . all of it."

"I thought you were a writer. Aren't you supposed to know about these sorts of things?"

The absolute fucking audacity of this guy.

"Dude, go fuck a pine cone."

"I think I'll pass, thanks." Cain settled in a well-worn velvet wingback chair near one of the narrow windows of the tower. He patted his knee, encouraging Asshole to come to him, frowning when it took the sweet dog a moment to acquiesce.

Kai tugged me into his hold, as though he sensed I was about to become a murderer myself if Cain continued to goad me. "He's right, gem. That scream, the things you've said you've done, it tracks. I've never witnessed a banshee, but I've heard tell of them often enough."

I let out a nervous laugh. "I'm not a banshee. I'm a ghost whisperer."

"Lore has it that they walk between the veil of the living and the dead, a messenger of sorts. It explains why spirits are drawn to you. Why your scream is so powerful. And with what we know of the part you played in your father's cult, it stands to reason that you'd be marked by death."

"But aren't banshees ugly and scary wraiths? You know, long scraggly hair, gaping maws, white shrouds, the whole nine?"

"Can confirm," Cain muttered, fingers stroking behind his dog's ears.

I glanced down my body. "I'm hardly a wraith. Something tells me they aren't much for conversation either."

"They mostly stick to the screams," Cain agreed.

"So there you have it." I pointed to myself. "Not a banshee."

"You could be a hybrid of sorts. Maybe you inherited the ability from your mother." Kai was offering suggestions, but it was obvious he was rifling through his memories and only half aware of what he was actually saying. "They're so rare, though, long believed to be extinct. I didn't even think they could reproduce, since they're generally thought of as belonging to the afterworld."

"Are you telling me my mommy was a mummy? What part of that exactly is supposed to make me feel better?"

The joke fell flat, though I was still a little proud of my ability to make one in the face of everything that had been dumped on me in the last few hours.

"She's something—and she's clearly dangerous," Cain grumbled.

"News flash, Colonel Sanders. Everyone here is dangerous. That's why they sent us to this place." His eyes flashed with anger at my jab, but dammit, he had it coming.

Kai kept talking as though Cain and I hadn't said a word. "They also dinnae tend to be known for screaming on the defensive. Banshees foretell the coming death of a person or family member. They don't kill or incapacitate with their screams."

Cain made a sound of dissent. "That's not strictly true."

"And yer an expert now, are ye?" Kai asked.

"Yeah. How come you suddenly know so much about banshees when you can't even remember your own name?"

His expression darkened. "Because I've seen one firsthand, and she nearly took me out."

Kai finally gave him his full attention. "She screamed for you?"

Cain nodded, eyes dark with what could have been grief or indigestion. It was hard to tell with the grumpy bastard. He didn't show emotions like normal folk. Unless he was stoned off his ass.

If I was a banshee—or banshee-ish—did that mean I'd heralded Tor's inevitable death? Had I somehow cursed him . . . more? Double cursed? Was that a thing?

"I thought you couldn't remember your life," I finally forced out as I left the comfort of Kai's embrace and curled up in the nest of pillows and blankets in the corner.

Bright blue eyes met mine from across the room. "I've been remembering in bits and pieces. Not enough to make sense, but enough to know what your scream can do. It's a sound I never want to hear again."

"Who died?" Kai asked.

Cain shook his head, his gaze shuttering. "I don't know."

Somehow the words rang false. Maybe he didn't know for sure, but I was willing to bet he had a good idea. But I couldn't worry about deciphering the mystery that was Cain Alexander—if that was even his real name. I had more than enough unanswered questions of my own.

I may or may not have killed my mate. I may or may not be on the

Ripper's hit list. I may or may not be a banshee, or part banshee, or just banshee adjacent. I could still see ghosts and was pretty sure one was fucking with me. I was no closer to understanding what the hell I was supposed to do with these so-called gifts of mine. As far as I could tell, they were nothing more than burdens.

My eyes dropped to my legs and the splashes of dried blood that were flaking on my feet and shins. I shuddered and forced myself not to think about the massacre Hook caused. Or that I was sore in places I never even felt before today. All of this . . . everything . . . was too much. My poor heart ached, but there was no time to grieve Hook's betrayal or the loss of Tor's humanity. No time for anything more than taking events at face value and moving on.

"Is this why he wants me?" I whispered, mostly to myself.

"Who?" Kai asked, kneeling in front of me.

"The Ripper. The ghost warned me. They say he's collecting us, stealing power. Is he up to more than just sating his lust for death?"

Cain snorted. "Of course he is. Murder involving supernaturals is rarely as simple as killing for the sake of killing. He'll get something out of it, but the victims have all been powerful beings rather than humans with no preternatural strengths. He's taking souvenirs, collecting pieces. It sounds like death magic to me."

"Are you an expert on death now as well?" I asked.

He looked surprised by his own outburst. "It seems like it. Fuck, I need my damned life back. When I find out who stole my memories, I'm going to send them straight to hell."

A new question occurred to me as Kai stood to his full height. "Why do you think they were taken?"

"Your guess is as good as mine."

"You probably knew something they wanted hidden," Kai said.

"Do you think it was the Ripper who took them?" I asked.

"Why wouldn't he just kill him instead?"

"Perhaps I can't die." Cain's words were a little bewildered, as though maybe he just realized he was doomed to live a life with spotty memories forever.

I couldn't help but think that if Tor were here, he'd offer to help Cain test the theory. Caspian too. I could hear Tor's voice clear as day. *"I'll be glad to help you find a definitive answer to that."* The low rumble of his voice in my mind hurt, and I had to forcibly shove it away, locking both him and Cas into a box in the back of my mind. I couldn't worry about them right now. Later, when I was alone, maybe I'd deal with what I was feeling.

Or maybe I'd just live in denial forever. That seemed easier.

Kai made a considering sound and shook his head. "The Ripper deals in parts. Memories don't seem like his game. My gut tells me he's not involved." Kai made an annoyed sound, eyes trained out the window at the courtyard below. "What the fuck is happening now?"

Cain and I both got to our feet, Asshole yipping and bouncing in agitated circles between us.

"Quiet, Asshole."

The puppy harrumphed and sat down, as if he was annoyed with his human for not understanding what he was trying to convey.

"What's going on, Kai?" I asked, trying to see past his broad frame.

He turned toward me, face drawn and pale. "It's Dr. Masterson. I think she's been killed."

"I NEED A HEALER OVER HERE!" Dr. Temperance shouted as we came out of the tower and raced toward his blood-soaked body.

"What happened?" Kai shouted, racing ahead. With his long legs and speed, he zoomed off, the first of us to reach the small crowd that had gathered on the lawn just outside Blackwood's main entrance.

I'd fallen behind, of course. Running really was the devil. I wasn't dressed for high-intensity exercise. Kai had loaned me a shirt and a pair of his sweats from the stash he kept in his tower, but I still didn't have a bra. Let me tell you, running with the wrong bra—or none at all in my case—with tits like these was a no-go. The rocky terrain bit at my bare feet, and it was all I could do not to cry out when a sharp piece of gravel stabbed my heel. Despite my effort, I whimpered.

Cain was near enough to hear me, and he turned back and scooped me up in his arms without so much as a "how do." I'd have been less stunned if Kai or Tor were the ones to execute the maneuver, but coming from Cain, it was about as shocking as the pixie orgy. He wasn't gentle or kind. Cain was an enigma, not to mention he wasn't built like a gladiator. The man, while tall and striking, was much leaner.

"You're stronger than I thought," I said, gaze trained on his tightly clenched jaw.

"And you're as soft as I remember."

Not prepared to deal with the flutters that set off, I forced a smile. "Just consider me your very own Pillsbury Dough Gal."

"Don't say things like that about yourself," he grumbled.

"What? I like being huggable. I'm not down on myself about it. I love these curves even if they give me trouble sometimes."

He didn't respond, but his arms tightened around me just a fraction before we caught up to Kai and the others. He set me down without a word as we took in the chaos before us.

Dr. Temperance had laid Dr. Masterson down on the lawn. There was blood everywhere. Her injuries were clearly not the work of the fire. It looked as if she'd been shredded. There were big gaping wounds across her abdomen, and it was impossible to tell if the slashes were caused by a knife or claws. The way her eyes stared off into the distance, sightless and vacant, opened a pit of dread in my gut. She was gone. A healer wouldn't help now.

"What the bloody hell happened, man?" Kai asked again, standing over Dr. Temperance.

"I was with her when the lockdown happened. She sent me to make sure residents were returning to their rooms while she dealt with the breakout in No Man's Land. She was . . . God, she was supposed to join me once she'd finished. Wh-when she didn't come to me, I went to see if she needed help since the orderlies seemed to have things well in hand." He paused for a beat and drew in a shaky breath before he could finish. "I found her in her office. There was so much blood."

He was right. Her clothes were drenched, stained a deep crimson, and so were his hands and sleeves from where he'd clearly tried to stop the flow.

"Hang on, Lizzie. Someone will help you," he whispered, kneeling at her side as he rocked back and forth.

"Is she . . .?"

I couldn't finish the sentence. In my gut I already knew the answer, but I needed it confirmed before my brain could accept it.

Before anyone could speak, she sucked in a rattling breath, eyes gaping wide.

"Lizzie? Oh, Lizzie." Dr. Temperance pulled her into his arms, heedless of her wounds.

She let out a wheezing gasp, more blood spurting out of the wound we hadn't noticed along her back.

"Careful!" Kai admonished.

"Sorry, sorry, I—" the handsome doctor rambled, easing her back down. "I'm just so relieved. My God, Lizzie. I thought I'd lost you."

"I knew it," I muttered under my breath.

"What?"

"Those two are fucking."

"How? I don't see it," he whispered.

"Body language. You're not paying attention to the right things."

Cain made a soft noncommittal sound while Asshole growled and sat right between my bare feet, his fur tickling.

"Lizzie, darling, did you see who did this to you?"

Dr. Masterson's eyes fluttered closed, brow furrowing as she let out a soft, pained noise. "No. It came out of nowhere. I couldn't find my key." She took a shallow breath. "Came from . . . behind me."

"Was it the Ripper?" a little witch I'd spoken to once before asked from our left.

The crowd that had gathered looked worse for wear, some soot-streaked, others bruised and bloodied, and I wondered if there'd been a frantic stampede after Kai got us out.

Dr. Temperance looked her over, then relief crossed his face when a healer came busting through the gathered people. "Step aside, Doctor. I need to see to her wounds."

"Look at her. It was definitely the Ripper. He slashed her to ribbons!" someone in the crowd called.

"No, it's too sloppy. The Ripper is precise. Methodical. He wouldn't have left her alive," someone else said.

"It doesn't matter who the culprit is. Right now we need to focus on getting her patched up," the healer said decisively. "You there," she said, looking to Kai, "I need your help to carry her to the healing ward. Careful now, she's fragile."

"I'll help," Dr. Temperance said.

Kai took Dr. Masterson's ankles while Dr. Temperance gingerly lifted her by her shoulders. She whimpered, but her eyes didn't open as they carried her away, leaving a bloody patch on the lawn I couldn't tear my gaze from.

"She should be dead," Cain murmured.

"What?"

"That bloodstain. She's lucky to be alive. Doc got her help just in time."

"I thought she was dead," I admitted. "Wounds like that . . . She didn't even appear to be breathing."

We held each other's eyes, the events of the last few hours stretching out between us. My gaze traveled across the groupings of residents and orderlies scattered around the grounds, stopping on a lone figure near the outskirts of the vast lawn.

Caspian.

He leaned against a battlement wall, and I could feel his attention trained on me even if I couldn't make out his expression from this distance.

I wasn't buying his excuse for the mayhem he caused tonight. He started a riot just because he was bored? More like he'd been jealous that I'd been with Tor. But that was no excuse for what he'd done. The consequences had quite literally been fatal.

I suppose we could argue that the Ripper would have struck either way. But the breakout? Tor falling victim to his curse? The fire? Those would have likely never happened were it not for Cas and his mischief.

I needed to get out of here.

Turning on my heel, I headed toward the main house, desperate for some time to myself where chaos was only in my head and not swirling around me in a sea of testosterone-laden angst. But two steps in, I was yanked back against Cain's solid chest.

"Where do you think you're going?" he snarled.

"To my room."

"No you're not. They haven't sounded the all clear. You're staying right where I can see you."

I met his glare with one of my own, but I just didn't have the energy to fight with him. I was tapped out. Emotionally and mentally spent. I'd gone from ghost attack to losing my virginity to absolute fucking bedlam in a matter of hours. It was more than any one person should have to deal with in a week, let alone a single day.

"Fine," I gritted out, plopping down on a low stone wall nearby. "But I get to hold the dog."

As though he understood me, Asshole jumped onto my lap and made himself comfortable.

Cain glowered, but didn't pluck him out of my hold. Instead he stared down at the dog and took a seat beside me, muttering, "Little traitor."

CHAPTER SIX

KAI

My fingers itched for my sketch pad as I trekked across the courtyard. The sun was just beginning to rise, soft purples and pinks streaking across the night sky, almost like little drops of watercolor working their way across a canvas. It was moments like these I wanted to capture and save forever, especially when my gaze swept over the horizon and I finally found the treasure I'd been searching for.

Dahlia sat on a low rock wall with Cain's tiny dog in her arms. She was as beautiful as ever, especially clad in my clothes, but there was no missing the signs of exhaustion. Her gaze was distant and unseeing, her fingers playing through the puppy's fur an unconscious act, her posture curved in and protective. And all the while, that Southern Kentucky fried arsehole sat within reach but did nothing to give her relief. The last few hours had been hell for her; the least he could do was offer some respite in the form of his shoulder.

"What the hell are you still doing out here?" I barked.

Dahlia's head snapped up while Cain's eyes narrowed in annoyance.

"What exactly did you expect us to do?" he asked. "They haven't given the all clear yet."

"Well, you have eyes in yer head, don't ye? She's so tired she cannae see straight, and you're . . ." I couldn't finish my tirade. I was too frustrated. "C'mon, gem. If this wanker's nae gonna make sure you're comfortable, I will." I'd sit on the cold ground and cradle her against me until the all clear if need be, but I certainly would do a damn sight better than leaving her to perch on a fucking rock wall while I sat like some gargoyle.

She set the dog down and started to straighten just as a familiar voice behind us called out, "All right, everyone, the coast is clear. You're all safe to return to your rooms."

Dahlia let out an exhausted whimper at Joffrey's announcement. "Finally. I need a shower more than I need coffee. That's saying something."

Instead of letting her take one step, I scooped her into my arms and held her tight, eyes flashing danger at anyone who looked at us wrong. She may not understand the connection between us, but I'd been on edge since the moment she was claimed by Tor. I couldn't deal with her being away from me a second longer. My dragon wouldn't be able to handle it either. He was restless, desperate to have her secreted away where she'd be safe.

"I could say something like, *'I can walk, you don't have to carry me,'* but I'm not going to. I'm temporarily lowering my feminism flag."

She nuzzled her face into my chest and inhaled deeply, a sated sigh leaving her.

"Mmm. You smell so good."

A swell of pride washed over me, and my dragon tattoo moved along my skin, a skittering sensation I couldn't ignore. He settled his snout directly under her cheek and stayed there, content for the first time in hours.

With my shirt covering him, she couldn't have known she was basically snuggled up against him, but she let out a happy murmur that echoed his. I'd spent so long fighting my beast, seeing him as nothing but a monster, but in this moment, he was my ally. The first part of me that resonated with Dahlia. Without my dragon, I'd have no need of a mate. Mates weren't guaranteed for the fae; they were gifts. Dragons were another story. Or so the legends went.

When we reached her door, I all but kicked it open and strode inside, taking her straight into the bathroom.

"Shower or bath?" I asked, gripping the edge of her borrowed shirt and tugging it over her head after she raised her arms on autopilot.

"Bath. I can't stand long enough for a shower. I'm so tired."

I tossed the shirt on the floor and leaned past her to draw the water. As I moved back into position, I let my lips graze her bared skin. I didn't linger. This wasn't about seduction; I just needed a taste of her. Dragons and fae alike were creatures who craved touch. I needed her skin on mine like I needed air.

"Sit there, lass. I'll help you in when it's ready."

She leaned up against the counter, and as I poured sweet-smelling bubble bath into the water, I heard the rustle of her pants as they hit the floor. Knowing she was nude behind me sent a ripple of desire through me, but I caged it, fully aware she wasn't ready for me. Not yet.

An unexpected giggle had me turning to face her. "Something amusing you, gem?"

"I had a fantasy that sort of started off this way," she murmured, her eyes warm with remembered passion, cheeks slightly flushed.

"Want to enlighten me?"

Those cheeks turned crimson, and her gaze flitted away. Oh, now she thought she'd be shy? We'd see about that.

I held out a hand, waiting for her to take it before tugging her close and leaning down to her ear. "I love a good spicy scene. Especially if it's one of yours."

The way her breath caught before I helped her into the tub had my cock stirring. I needed to settle down before I forgot myself and asked for too much from her.

"There's no such thing as too much. She belongs to us."

I ignored the persistent voice of my dragon. If he had his way, I'd have bypassed the bath entirely and flung her on the bed before I nailed her to it with my dick, effectively erasing all traces of Tor's scent from between her thick thighs. Goddess help me, I had to reach down and palm my aching length to relieve some of the pressure before I started humping the side of the bathtub.

"Lie back and let me wash you," I murmured, soaping up a washcloth and running it along her skin.

"Mmm, this is way better than my fantasy."

"Aye? I'll continue, then."

And that's exactly what I did until every inch of her skin was clean and smelled of nothing but the jasmine-infused soap.

"If you tell me where to look, I can grab you something to wear to bed."

She glanced coyly over her shoulder as she finished wrapping herself in a towel. "Do you really need my help, Sticky Fingers? You sure seem to know your way around my room with the way you keep stealing my things."

I laughed. "I see you've got your second wind."

"Maybe."

"Grab your hairbrush, you pretty menace. I'll pick out something for you to wear."

Moving to her dresser, I opened a few drawers before finding something suitable. Despite her accusations, I never mindlessly rifled through her belongings. I only took objects that smelled of her or were obviously preferred by her. It was never about stealing. It was about claiming a small piece of her.

When I turned back, she had the brush raised like she was going to take care of the damp, snarled locks herself. "I don't think so, gem. Give it here." I held out my hand and waited for her to deposit the brush. "Sit. I'll care for ye. Once this is done, you can dress."

"You're getting off on this, aren't you?" she asked as she did exactly what I told her.

The bristles ran through the thick length of beautiful white-blonde as I hummed an affirmative noise. "I like taking care of what's mine."

Except she wasn't mine. Not if the mating between her and Tor meant anything.

"*She smells like ours.*" My dragon's voice was a whisper in my mind as he shifted along my skin.

"Tor's not going to like that."

"What was that?" Dahlia asked, causing me to inwardly curse my carelessness. I hadn't realized I'd spoken out loud.

"Erm, your mate. He isnae going to be happy I washed him off you."

She made a soft sound. "You're probably right. He definitely didn't like when I showed up smelling like you. I can't imagine he'll be happy that all trace of him has already been removed." She stiffened suddenly, jerking the brush from my hand with the unexpected movement. "Oh God. Oh *God.*"

"What is it? Did I hurt ye?"

I couldn't be sure my words even registered as she stood and began pacing.

"I am so fucking stupid. How could I be so stupid?"

"What are ye goin' on about, lass?"

She spun to face me, her voice tremulous and high-pitched. "You washed him off me. Off. Me."

My eyes narrowed in confusion as I nodded. "Aye, I did. Did you want to keep it?"

"He fucked me without a condom. Shit. Fuck. Shit. He probably filled me with his giant Viking babies, and I just *let* him do it because I was the stereotypical clueless virgin heroine who was hypnotized by his dick. He dickmatized me. Goddammit. This is just great. Juuust great. I'm not ready to be a mom. I'm here trying to figure out the fucking ghost problem, and there's a murderer on the loose, and, you know, I'm pretty sure three other hot men want to put their big-headed babies in me too. I can't deal with this right now. God, his spawn will probably kill me—or at least ruin my vagina. I'm basically keeping myself together with duct tape and string as it is. How can I be responsible for a tiny human? I can barely be responsible for myself."

I had to stop her before she made herself pass out.

But she didn't give me a chance. She kept going, hands flailing as she chastised herself. "I'm so stupid. I should have reined in the hormones and made him at least pull out. Fuck. Is there somewhere I can get a Plan B?"

"What's Plan B?" I asked when she paused to suck in a ragged breath.

"Emergency contraceptive. You know, sort of like birth control for after the fact?"

"So it's something we could get at a chemist? I could try to get outside and find it for you, but it'll take me at least until tomorrow."

She shook her head emphatically. "No, that'll be too long. It won't work by then. Oh God. I'm going to kill Tor if he knocked me up."

"Hang on, lass. I have a solution if you're willing."

One brow arched as she assessed me, waiting for me to continue.

"It'll be a bit . . . painful."

"As painful as pushing an entire child out of my body?"

"I cannae say, having never experienced that, but I suspect not."

"Sign me up."

It took me all of five minutes to collect my kit from my room. Dahlia watched with wide, curious eyes as I started setting up my supplies on her desk.

"What is that?"

"My kit." I busied myself with sterilizing my materials, forcing my gaze to stay focused on the task at hand and not the beautiful woman near me.

"As in your tattoo kit?"

"Aye."

"Why did you go get that? I like ink on you, but not on me."

"Ah, but this is magic ink."

"Magic ink?" she repeated dubiously. "Why do I feel like you're teasing me?"

I chuckled as I poured the black liquid into small disposable cups. "You're thinking of tattoos in the traditional sense. The ones I do aren't like that. Mine are infused with magic."

"What do you mean?"

"Once I'm finished, you're not going to see the spell I'll etch into your skin, but it'll be no less effective."

"That doesn't make sense. I can see Tor's tattoo. Yours too."

"Different spells, gem. Yours will serve a different purpose than Tor's. His was more like an hourglass keeping time. Yours will prevent you from getting pregnant and will have a time limit attached to it."

"How can a tattoo I get inked into my skin have a time limit?"

"Well, I'm assuming you might want to have children one day?"

"Possibly?"

I laughed at the uncertainty of her answer. "Well, just in case, I'd rather not permanently neuter you. That's why the spell will only last for six months. After that, you'll have to decide if you want to sit for me again."

"Okay, so just to be clear, you're going to give me a magical, temporary, and invisible tattoo."

"Exactly."

"I really feel like this is some sort of practical joke."

How could I prove this to her?

My dragon tattoo shifted until his head poked out of the collar of my shirt, almost mocking me for my stupidity. Pulling my shirt over my head, I turned to face her so she could take him in.

"Is this proof enough, lass? He's bound within the constraints of the ink."

"You did that to yourself? How?"

I smirked. "Patience. But I didn't put him where he is now. He was a tiny wee thing on my thigh until the magic took hold and he grew."

"Sort of like those toys that expand when put in water."

My dragon huffed in annoyance. He did not appreciate being compared to a child's novelty item.

"Careful, or he'll have me showing you exactly how unlike a toy he is."

Her wicked grin did things to me. "Toys can be fun, though."

Right. It was time to get her taken care of before I became the problem and not the protection. Because if Tor hadn't already planted his seed inside her, I would.

"Focus, gem. You're a terrible tease."

She heaved a sigh. "Okay, fine. So you're going to give me a birth control tattoo that lasts for six months. That's great for future me, but what if I'm already pregnant?"

"You misunderstand. This will ensure that nothing will be able to take root in your womb. So even if you are, it won't be able to survive by the time I'm finished."

She bit down on her lower lip, seeming to weigh that in her mind before she released a heavy breath and nodded. "Okay. Let's do it." She was fucking adorable when she sat on the bed and rolled up her sleeve, oozing determination.

"That's not where it goes."

"Uh, okay. I didn't realize there was a special place you had to put the magic."

Releasing a low chuckle, I reached out and touched her sternum before dragging my finger down her body until I found her pubic bone. "The spell will be most effective if it is housed over the part of the body it is designed to protect. That means aside from me branding you from the inside, the best place for this will be right here."

"That's . . . um . . . very intimate."

"Lass, I've buried my face in your cunt until you soaked my lips in your cum. I think we're a bit beyond that."

Her cheeks were crimson as she sputtered, "Well, when you put it that way."

"Lie back on this for me, my beautiful girl. I need to be able to see all of you." I draped a towel on the duvet and waited for her to do as she was told.

She raised a brow. "Why do you need to see my pussy to tattoo Madam Foops?"

"I beg your pardon?"

"You know"—she reached down and grabbed the swell of her lower belly—"the FUPA. She's not going anywhere. She deserves an honorific."

"Ah, you mean my perfect hand hold? I do love her. But she's not getting the ink."

Her eyes widened. "Then where?"

"You'll see."

She sat up. "Wait a damn second! I did not agree to you tattooing my labia!"

"Relax, gem. My mark will go here." I rested my fingers just above the juncture of her thighs.

"Oh God, that is going to hurt like a motherfucker."

"I did warn you."

Reaching up to her waistband, I dragged the sweats she wore down her legs, baring her curvaceous lower half to me inch by inch. God, she was a vision. I'd dream of her tonight, no question.

With one hand, I grabbed my straight razor from my kit. You would've thought I'd bitten her with the way she tensed.

"What the fuck do you need that for, Sweeney Todd?"

"You've never watched someone get tattooed before, have you?"

"Just when I walked in on you."

I worked hard to keep the laughter from my voice as I explained. "You have to prep the area first." I waved my razor slightly to help convey my meaning.

"And by prep, you mean shave."

I nodded. "Quite so. Even the smallest hair can interfere with the ink. The skin must be completely smooth."

"I can do it."

"Not as well as me."

"You aren't shaving my lady business, Kai."

"Yes I fucking am."

Her breath caught, just the tiniest hitched gasp, but I knew my determination affected her.

"Oh God. Okay, but don't cut me."

My stare was hard when I lifted my gaze to hers. "I'd rather raze the world to nothing but cinders than hurt you."

Her throat worked as she took in my vow. "I trust you."

My dragon fucking preened at that.

"Good. Now part your thighs for me."

She did, and fucking hell, her cunt was already glistening. A triangle of blonde curls may have covered her plump lips, but there was no disguising how turned on she was. Even if I couldn't see it, I'd have been able to scent her arousal. It was going to be a herculean effort not to taste her before my job was done.

Carefully, I set down my razor and grabbed the tin of shaving balm, scooping some of it out with my fingertips. Dahlia sucked in a breath when I worked the balm into her swollen flesh.

"If this turns out to all be some sort of elaborate ruse, I'm going to be so pissed."

My grin was pure dragon as I shot back, "You and I both know I don't need a ruse to get my hands on you, gem."

"True, but if I develop a shaving kink because of you, we're going to have words."

"Does this make you want to come? Is it the risk or the intimacy?"

She squirmed. "Maybe both?"

"That's a good answer," I murmured, wiping my fingers clean on the towel I'd set out for that purpose. Grabbing my razor once more, I added, "Now stay still so we can get to the good part."

CHAPTER SEVEN

DAHLIA

My breaths sawed in and out of my lungs as I tried like hell to calm myself down. Kai was holding a fucking straight razor and staring at my feminine wilds like he was setting about his life's work. Yes, I said wilds, deal with it. I've never had a reason to ladyscape before, okay? Except that one time, but that was different. She didn't need a weapon to get the job done. I was understandably nervous.

"Wait," I blurted, panic winning out as he closed in.

Kai's violet eyes lifted to meet mine. If the razor hadn't still been clutched in his steady hand, this would have been a way sexier visual.

"You've done this before, right?"

His lips cocked up in a smirk. "You're in good hands, gem. I promise."

"So you've done this a lot, then?"

"Enough to know my way around."

Jealousy flashed hot and unwelcome at the thought he'd had more than me in this vulnerable and somewhat precarious position. I was a fucking hypocrite, but I couldn't control my emotions.

He must've sensed my discomfort because he laughed. "I'm a tattoo artist, lass. I do this all the time. Maybe not this specific spell, but whenever I work, a body is just a canvas."

Swallowing hard, I gave a tight nod. "Good. That's good. I'd really like to keep my vulva intact, and knowing you haven't mutilated anyone else doing this makes me feel better."

Flashbacks to my one and only bikini wax session had me desperate to hide myself from him, even though I knew shaving wouldn't hurt if he did it right.

"Just breathe, gem. This is the easy part."

"Tell me that when I'm the one holding a knife to your balls."

He chuckled, and his warm puffs of breath tickled my sensitive flesh, sending a whole different sensation up my spine.

There was no way I was getting through this without embarrassing myself.

My thighs trembled as he settled in and began slow drags of the blade over my skin, one after the other, at the top of my pussy. His attention was focused solely on his task, his brow furrowed as he worked. When he'd finished the top where the tattoo would go, he surprised me by continuing lower, the flash of the razor in the light as he adjusted my position, making my heart race.

"Wait a second. Aren't you done? The tattoo isn't going there." Was I embarrassed by the high-pitched squeak in my voice? No. Not at all.

He broke concentration to cast that devastating gaze up my body, and then he offered me a panty-melting grin. "What can I say? I'm a perfectionist."

"This is payback, isn't it? For the pillow?"

"Payback? Why would you think that? The pillow is the best gift I've ever been given. I can't wait to bury my face in it at night."

Sure strokes along the outside of my pussy did the opposite of scare me now. Somewhere along the line, I went from apprehensive to aroused. Oh God, he'd see. There was no hiding my wetness from him when he was removing the only thing that could cover it up.

I kept waiting for Kai to call me out, but other than a sharp inhale, he remained as steadfast as ever. A professional through and through.

"There, that wasnae so bad, was it?" he murmured, cleaning off the blade and setting it aside.

My heart was still racing, but I'd be an absolute fucking liar if I said I hadn't enjoyed every second of that. His furrowed brow. The intensity of his gaze. The total fucking competency of the act. My lady boner was raging. Quite literally.

He grabbed me by the thighs and tugged until my legs hung off the bed, my mons fully displayed for him. "Now, ye may want to squirm. Don't. Feel free to make as much noise as you need. I'll be as quick as I can."

Oh God. We still had the tattoo to get through.

The thought of pain was enough to send my arousal fleeing. Which was a bit of a relief because I wasn't sure how I'd survive him being that close and not doing anything to help me out with it.

He wiped the area down one final time before grabbing his tray of tools and magic ink. I wasn't really sure what made it magic. It looked like regular black ink to me.

I got my answer a second later when Kai pricked his finger with a fresh needle and added a drop of his blood to each tiny container of ink. The obsidian liquid turned a smoky color. Shimmering and diaphanous. It almost looked like he'd found a way to trap mist in a bottle. I didn't have long to appreciate the magical transition because the buzz of his gun turning on pulled my attention.

"Ready?"

"No?"

He chuckled, one hand clasped around my thigh, holding me in place. "Here we go."

I flinched when the vibration hit my skin, rushing through my whole body and making me tense. Each breath was a tight drag as he worked, my pulse pounding in my ears as the unusual sensation eclipsed everything else around me—until he began moving the needle across my flesh. Then I felt the pain, a stinging burn accompanying the vibration. It was both better and worse than I imagined. I'd been told before that getting tattooed felt a bit like having a sunburn. Whoever said that was a goddamned liar. This was awful, but not unbearable. Just when I thought I couldn't take anymore, he would pause and give me a moment to compose myself.

"Breathe, gem. You're turning purple."

Oh shit. I was holding my breath. I exhaled and trained my eyes on his as he waited for me to give him the go-ahead again. His large palm shifted to my inner thigh right over where my panty line would be if I wasn't bare ass naked.

His thumb brushed my freshly shaved lips, and I sucked in a gasp as he continued the soothing strokes.

"Wh-what are you doing?"

"Distracting you."

"I thought I was just a canvas."

"You could never be *just* anything."

That thumb pressed between my folds as he widened the spread of my thighs and opened me to him. He returned to his work, the needle dragging across my body the only thing I could focus on. Then Kai's thumb grazed my swollen bundle of nerves. The groan I released when he circled my aching clit was obscene, but the sensation overload was quite possibly going to kill me.

The pain was acute, but so was the pleasure. My mind couldn't fully focus on either, which forced me to exist in a weird sort of limbo. I guess that was the point.

"Nearly there," he bit out, his voice a dark rasp.

"God, yes." I was nearly there. So close I could see the shimmering edge of orgasm on the horizon.

"I meant me, gem. I'm almost done."

"Yeah," I said, my voice more breath than anything. "I knew that."

His hand left my thigh, and I almost protested because I really didn't want his thumb to go anywhere. But then his fingers slid across my wet flesh before he sank one inside me. "Fuck, you're soaked."

"What were you expecting with all the rubbing and vibrating going on?"

"Does my treasure like a little pain with her foreplay?"

"You can keep the pain, but I'll take the touching and vibrating all day long."

"Noted."

His finger slowly pumped in and out as he etched his spell into me, and it was the strangest thing, but I knew the moment he was finished. The magic rushed across my skin like a strong wind. It was there and gone in a moment, but the silence that followed when he switched off the tattoo gun proved I'd been right.

It had been nearly impossible to keep myself from moving against Kai's hand, but now that the tattoo was finished, I didn't waste any time rolling my hips into his touch.

Only for him to pull his fingers out.

My whimpered protest was largely incoherent.

"Wha—but . . . Wh-why are you stopping?"

"I'm not stopping. Not unless you want me to. I'm taking every damn thing you'll give me. I didnae think it would be so hard for me to see you mated to him, gem. But it is. It's driving me mad knowing you're his when you should be mine too."

"Kai," I whispered, scooting back on the bed so I could see him better.

I watched him clean up his kit and knew this was the moment I had to decide if it was solely going to be Tor or if we'd be a unit.

You made that choice the second you let him take care of you in the bath.

Tor may have "claimed" me first, but I'd always been drawn to all of them. Hadn't that been part of the conversation we'd had before completing our bond? That I belonged to him, but them as well? My sensitive dragon. That sneaky fucking pirate. Broody Cain and his sweet dog. And my tortured Viking.

If I denied Kai, I'd be denying something bigger than attraction or lust. I'd be denying fate, as corny as it sounded.

"Do you want me to leave, gem?" Kai said as he stood over me, his erection visible from behind the dark gray joggers he wore.

"That's the last thing I want, Kai. I don't ever want you to leave."

He stepped closer but didn't join me on the bed. Instead he let his fingertips stroke along the inside of my thigh. "Are you sore?"

At first I thought he meant from the tattoo, and I shook my head no, only to realize he was referring to something else.

Cheeks burning, I had to stop and do a mental inspection.

Was I sore? I'd been so distracted by everything else happening around me that I hadn't really had time to think about the damage Tor's monster dick had done. Kai's finger slipped inside again, first one, then two, and there it was, the stretch and burn.

I didn't quite wince, but there was a definite hitch of breath. "Maybe a little," I admitted, worried that he'd stop when all I wanted was for him to continue.

"Too sore?" he asked, arching a brow while his fingers continued to pump in and out.

"No."

His grin was the most beautiful thing I'd ever seen. "Good."

"God, Kai. I need you. Either make me come or make me yours. Your choice."

"Does it have to be a choice? Personally, I'm a fan of both."

"I love a twofer."

God, what the fuck was I even saying? This man could get me to sign over the rights to my unborn children, and I wouldn't even blink. Kiki would kill me if I didn't jump all over his dick right now.

For science.

Someone needed to find out what that dragon peen could do. The ridged, *tattooed* dragon peen.

God, that made my fanny flutter.

"I felt that," he growled. "What are ye thinking?"

"I want to know what it feels like to be fucked by a dragon."

The sound that left him at that was part growl, part roar, and all primal male pride.

"Get on your knees."

I think I might have made some kind of grunty, happy noise as I worked to get into a kneeling position.

"Not like that. Turn around and bend over. I want every inch of your perfect arse on display for me, and I need to see the puffy lips of your shaved cunt peeking out from between your thighs."

"Jesus, where's my notebook? I need to write that line down."

"Dahlia . . ."

I glanced over my shoulder as I got into the exact position he asked for.

"Shut the fuck up and take this dick like a good girl."

Oh God, that hit so different in real life. In a really fucking good way. I could feel arousal dripping down my thighs.

I kept my lips sealed and my eyes trained on him as he dropped his pants. Holding my stare, he took himself in one hand and gave his thick length a few cursory strokes.

Tor was big, but Kai was girthy AF. Like a can of Coke. Jesus. Maybe I needed to stop doing Kegels and start doing stretches?

He closed the distance between us, his body heat sending a thrill through me. I wanted us as close as physically possible. Right fucking now. When the slick tip of his cock pressed against my opening, it took all I had not to beg him to sink deep. In fact, I tried, but his big palms held my hips still, keeping me from doing just that.

"I'm in control right now, gem. Not you. You'll take what I give you."

I bit down on my lower lip and nodded. Apparently, I'd taken his order to heart. I wanted to know what it was like to have Kai fucking own my pussy.

His fingers dug in deep as he sank inside me until I moaned. He wasn't giving me everything he had yet, but oh God, the ridges. They were perfect. Rubbing just right, making me see stars as he worked to stretch me out to take the rest of him.

"You look so damn perfect writhing on my dick, just like you were meant to."

Remember the fanny flutters? Yeah, they were back.

"Goddess, yes. Squeeze me like that again."

Maybe the Kegels weren't a bad idea after all. He all but purred when I gripped him with my inner walls. But I stopped teasing him as soon as he pulled back and sank in deeper. The feel of him filling me so full took my breath away.

As tight a fit as it was, it also felt like I'd been made for him and him for me. I needed more, and before I spoke up to tell him, he slammed home, rutting into me with long, hard strokes. I cried his name, begged for it, moaned some kind of gibberish, and I never wanted it to end.

I existed only for this. Only for him. I had no purpose beyond this moment. And let me tell you, I was so fucking okay with that.

Kai leaned over my back and wrapped one large palm around my throat before lifting me until I was kneeling, my body flush against his as he pounded up into me. This angle wasn't as deep, but the hand necklace was perfection.

"Do you like this? Are you my good girl who needs me to choke her?"

Having never been a good girl or choked before, I did what any questionably sane woman in my position would do.

"Hell yes."

His chuckle rolled through me as sweet as the tattoo gun's vibrations, lighting me up just as his fingers started to squeeze.

Trailing his other hand across my front, he stopped when he reached the place where my tattoo hid. "One day, when this expires, I'll leave more than my cum inside you, gem. Understand? I'll make you mine in every way I can. Take every hole. Fill you with me."

"Yes. God. Yes, Kai."

"I want you covered in me until you can't remember where I end and you begin. You are mine, Dahlia."

"Yes," I panted, little spots dancing in my periphery as his grip on my throat tightened and his thrusts turned almost punishing.

He toyed with my clit in sync with those deep rolls of his hips, and I knew I wouldn't last much longer.

"Please," I begged.

"Please what, my treasure?"

"Let me come."

"You need my permission?"

He slammed home again and again, those ridges stimulating my G-spot and his grip tightening as my orgasm began to crest.

"Yes."

"Come for me, then. Come all over my cock until you're dripping down my balls and making a mess of the floor."

"Oh God."

With his lips right at my ear, he breathed, "My name is Malakai."

And that's when I came.

My orgasm must have triggered his because his pace faltered, and he drove into me twice more before shouting my name. My orgasm reached new heights, and I could feel each hot pulse of his cum as he came with me. Without warning, he pressed his open mouth against the back of my neck where it met my shoulder and bit down. Pressure mixed with the sharp sting of pain, but all of it only spurred me on. He was making me his, just like he promised.

He slid out of me before I was ready, the warm collar of his hand leaving my throat as he pushed me back down on my hands.

"K-Kai?" I stuttered, not wholly coherent yet.

"Shh, I need to taste us."

Did he mean what I . . . Oh Jesus, he did.

His face nestled between my legs, he licked his way inside me, savoring our flavor. All too soon, he was gone, flipping me onto my back and crawling over me. With one hand, he gripped my chin, and I instinctively opened for him to kiss me. Never in my wildest dreams would I have thought I'd experience what happened next. Kai spit his cum into my mouth, watching me intently as he did so. Then, with a grin, he said, "Be my good girl and swallow."

I did and then opened my mouth to show him.

Like I said, the guy could talk me into anything.

"Perfect," he breathed. His gaze trailed from my eyes to the place he'd marked me, fingers following soon after as he traced the spot. Then his dragon tattoo slithered across his skin, stopping when the head was resting over his heart, those violet eyes locked on mine.

In a voice I'd never heard from him before, he said, "You're mine now."

CHAPTER EIGHT

TOR

Icy water splashed into my face, snapping me back to consciousness with a feral snarl.

"Good, you're alive."

My gaze lasered in on the man with a bucket in his hand. A warning growl slipped free as I marked him for death.

"Not so fast, mate. Feel those chains around your wrists and ankles? You're not going anywhere."

With a fierce bellow and all the power I possessed, I yanked on the shackles, but the cuffs bit into my skin and stopped me from killing him. Lucky prey.

As soon as I got free, his luck would run out.

"Stop staring at me like I'm a bunny you intend to hunt. If it weren't for me, you'd be at the bottom of the lake right now. The higher-ups wanted to kill you after what you did."

What I did?

"They'll be cleaning up that solitary cell for weeks. Might never get the brains out of the masonry."

Foggy bits of slaughter flashed through my mind. A head torn from its body. Another enemy crushed beneath my foot. Blood and gore splashing across my skin.

A grin tugged at my lips as pride and pleasure washed through me.

"Christ, you're terrifying like this."

The little man was afraid of me. Of course he was. He should be.

I yanked on my chains once more. I needed out. I had to get to . . . something.

"You have to stay here until I can find a way to break your curse, Tor. You're a danger to everyone around you right now. Not even my binding magic can hold you."

A bone-rattling roar escaped me. He couldn't keep me here.

"I'm sorry. I know you only did it to protect her. Nothing else would have set you off. You proved time and again that she was your last remaining trigger. I wish . . . I guess it doesn't matter what I wish."

He continued to utter meaningless words, but they didn't matter. All the air left my lungs as her name came rushing to me.

"Dahlia."

The man's eyes widened. "She's safe. She's with them."

No.

Mine.

My mate.

She should be with me.

I tugged at my bindings with renewed fury. I needed to find my mate. To protect her. I belonged by her side.

"Tor . . ." The man backed away, but I continued yanking my chains hard enough blood dripped from my wrists.

They wouldn't keep me from her.

Nothing would.

I would kill anyone who tried.

Tilting my head back, I unleashed the rage pumping through my veins and roared my unholy vow to the heavens.

None would be safe until I had my mate.
And I would start with this one.

CHAPTER NINE
HOOK

Dahlia may be cross with me, but she'd get over it. Especially once she got the full Caspian Hook experience. I could be a swoon-worthy, dashing love interest. No one could resist me for long.

But on the off chance she still didn't forgive me, I'd simply sprinkle in a little fae magic for good measure. Something about the thought didn't fill me with confidence like it should have. If anything, it left a decidedly sour taste in my mouth.

My steps faltered as I pondered the new occurrence. I'd never hesitated to use my glamour when it suited me in the past. Why would ensuring my return to Dahlia's good graces be any different?

Answer: It wasn't. I was just tired.

We'd see to that soon enough. Hands laden with my peace offering, I ascended the stairs and then strode confidently to her door. I knew how this would go. She'd open for me, give me a dubious once-over and pretend I didn't affect her knickers, then I'd present her with the pastries and coffee with an air of humility as my roguish charm did the rest. It was a perfect plan.

Filled with confidence once more, I hustled down the hall until I was outside her door. Taking a deep breath, I arranged myself so I displayed my full knicker-destroying potential. Eyebrow cocked, chin up, head tilted just a hair to the side to showcase my devastating dimple. I knew how to work a room, and I knew she loved my swagger.

Of course, I didn't have a free bloody hand, so I had to give the door a less-than-charming kick instead of the confident rap of my knuckles I'd wanted, but we take what we can get.

Smile in place, I waited for Dahlia to greet me.

And then waited some more.

I knew she was in. I'd been camped out in the dining hall all morning and afternoon, waiting for her to appear. Thus my gift selection. I'd seen the woman worship her morning pastry and coffee like a devout nun at the most sacred of altars. Just like I would when I got between her thighs.

Whoa there. Reel it back. Focus.

She hadn't answered, so I kicked the door once more, this time with a little extra annoyance.

"God, fine, I'm coming." Her frustrated and surprisingly tired voice filtered through the wood.

All right, Hook, this is your moment. Seduce her, but look repentant. Give her the smolder but promise her the world all in one look. Shoulders back, playboy turned up to a respectable seven, and—

The door opened partway, revealing most of her. "Oh. It's you."

I fucking wilted.

Definitely still mad, then. All right, time for plan B.

Letting some of my fae power ooze into my words, I held up my treats. "I came to apologize. You know you want to let me inside."

She crossed her arms under her delectable chest, and it took everything in me not to glance down and fully appreciate the picture she presented in her oversized jumper and tiny shorts. Still, my cock took notice.

"Do you even know what you're supposed to be sorry for?"

I scoffed, rolling my eyes. "Yes," I blustered, because I did *not* actually know what could constitute such a lengthy run of ire towards me. Tor wasn't dead. The big Viking would be fine. And she couldn't possibly be mourning for those other bastards. If anything, I did the world a favor by ensuring they were wiped off the face of the planet. How many lives were saved by ridding them of theirs?

"Tell me."

"I . . . well . . . I'm sorry you thought I was—"

"Wrong."

"I apologize if—"

"Try again."

I sighed. "Dahlia, I am genuinely sorry I did . . . something that upset you."

She let out an exasperated sigh and started to shut the door in my face.

"Wait!" I cried, shoving my boot in the doorway before she could shut me out. "I brought you these."

I was more than a little shocked when the door fully opened and Kai loomed beside Dahlia, naked as the day he was born. My eyes immediately moved behind them to the rumpled bed. The rumpled bed with its evidence of not one but two occupants. The rumpled bed that I was sure reeked of both of them.

Is that a . . . cum stain?

"Thanks, we're starving. It was a long night. Who knew claiming yer mate would be such hungry work?" he mused, snatching the bag and coffee from my hands and leaving me gaping after him.

"Goodbye, Caspian," Dahlia said, her gaze stone cold as she shut the door in my face.

"Claiming yer mate?" I grumbled in an affected Scottish brogue. "I wouldn't bloody know how hungry claiming her would make me because I haven't had the chance!" I stalked down the hall toward my room, but not before calling back, "And that extra toffee nut latte and pain au chocolat was for *me,* you scaled Scottish scoundrel."

My pique only grew as I stormed into my room, my mind filled with images of Kai bending Dahlia into all sorts of delicious pretzels.

Kicking the door shut behind me, I vented my frustrations aloud.

"How the bloody hell was I supposed to know a bit of innocent hijinks would cause the lout to fall victim to some pansy-arsed curse?"

I tossed myself onto the bed, one arm draped over my eyes as I bemoaned the coarse and unwarranted rejection I'd just received. I should be cross with her, not the other way around. She'd just humiliated me.

Except instead of visions of her crawling to me with an apology on her lips, I saw that dragon having his way with her again. I wanted that. I deserved it. She would have been mine if I'd continued my pursuit in earnest rather than let those villains weasel their way into her heart.

Now she was mated to two of them. Not just fucking them, but bound to them.

"Arg!" I growled, ripping my pillow off my bed and smothering my face with it to muffle my enraged cry. No one needed to overhear me losing my proverbial shit.

I was not the one who got bested.

I was not the one who lost the girl.

I was the one who stole her from her man and then kicked her out of my bed.

Everything was backwards and wrong. Worse, I didn't think Dahlia was throwing some sort of tantrum. She was truly fed up with me. Possibly for good.

What the hell was I supposed to do with that?

Did I . . . Oh, bloody hell, I cocked it all up. It was me, wasn't it? I was the problem.

To be fair, that was usually the case. I'd just never cared until now. As long as I got what I wanted, why did the rest matter?

Except it did. This time, it fucking mattered, and I couldn't understand why.

This wouldn't do.

Captain Hook could *not* lose.

I'd lost too much already. My ship. My crew. My home.

I refused to add Dahlia to the list.

"Do you hear me, darling? I refuse!"

I stood and strode to the mirror on my wall, raking a hand through my hair as I made a promise to myself.

"I'll have her. Mark my words, Dahlia Moore will be mine if it's the last thing I do."

SESSION TRANSCRIPT: NOVEMBER 23RD

<<shuffling papers and chair squeaks>>

Dr. Temperance: *clears throat* Uh, right. Okay, I think we're rolling now. Yes? Brilliant.

Cain: You sound really confident there, Doc.

<<dog yips>>

Dr. Temperance: Do you mind? These are Italian leather.

<<dog growls>>

Cain: C'mere, Asshole. You sit with me. Leave the doc's shoes alone.

Dr. Temperance: Thank you. Now, where were we? Oh, right. This is Dr. Nathaniel Temperance, standing in for Dr. Elizabeth Masterson. The date is November twenty-third at . . . eleven-oh-seven a.m.

Great, now that that's out of the way. Why don't you tell me a bit about yourself, Cain?

Cain: *dark chuckle* You didn't read my file, did you Doc?

Dr. Temperance: Erm . . . things have been a titchyroo hectic around here. But I always prefer to hear things from the horse's mouth, as it were, so even if I had, I'd still begin our time together with you filling me in.

Cain: Here's what I know. I blew up a hospital ward and woke up here. I only remember slivers of my life, but from what I've seen, I think I'm a real piece of work.

Dr. Temperance: *hums musingly* How do you mean?

Cain: Well, for starters, I'm married, but I don't think she wanted me.

Dr. Temperance: Ah, like an arranged marriage?

Cain: Something like that.

Dr. Temperance: And you feel guilt about this?

Cain: No. She was mine.

Dr. Temperance: Cain, please extinguish the fire on the couch.

Cain: What? Oh fuck.

<<pats cushion>>

Dr. Temperance: Let's go back to the hospital. Do you recall what brought you there?

Cain: No.

Dr. Temperance: I have a suspicion.

Cain: How the fuck could you know why I was there?

Dr. Temperance: Because I was as well. I saw you standing outside of her room.

<<dog growls>>

Cain: What? Who's room?

Dr. Temperance: Dahlia's, of course. I was her attending physician that night.

<<silence>>

Dr. Temperance: Cain? Are you all right?

Cain: I was there for her?

Dr. Temperance: It looked like it. Would you like to hear what happened?

Cain: Is the pope fucking Catholic?

Dr. Temperance: *chuckles* Well, it's not a pretty story, but here's what I know. You snuck into the ward without permission and refused to leave the station you'd taken up outside her room.

Cain: Did she see me? Did she know I was there?

Dr. Temperance: No. Dahlia was heavily sedated due to the traumatic incident she'd just been through.

Cain: And?

<<clothes rustling>>

Dr. Temperance: Security finally had to escort you off the premises. But you wouldn't be swayed. You fought them until I had no choice but to administer a strong sedative. You woke much sooner than we expected, likely due to your supernatural immune system, which we did not know to take into account at the time. When you returned to Dahlia's room and found her missing, you had a rather . . . erm, strong reaction.

Cain: I blew up the fucking ward.

Dr. Temperance: You blew up the ward.

<<dog whines>>

Cain: It's okay, buddy.

Dr. Temperance: Now, why do you think that was? That Dahlia would be such an explosive trigger for you?

Cain: *snorts* Explosive? Really? I didn't take you for a jokester, Doc.

Dr. Temperance: Answer the question.

Cain: *heavy sigh* I'm not sure.

Dr. Temperance: Perhaps you should spend some time reflecting on why. Isn't it interesting that you both ended up here? That the two of you must have some sort of link prior to your arrival at Blackwood, yet neither of you seems to recall it?

Cain: That's one word for it.

Dr. Temperance: Well, what word would you use?

Cain: Fucking convenient.

Dr. Temperance: That's two words.

Cain: She's . . . fuck, Doc. She's not mine.

Dr. Temperance: Your reaction says something very different.

Cain: What are you implying?

Dr. Temperance: I'm not implying anything. Merely making an observation.

Cain: It doesn't matter. I can't have her anyway. The Viking claimed her.

<<clothes rustling>>

Dr. Temperance: What?

Cain: You heard me. They're mated. It's out of my hands now.

Dr. Temperance: That changes things. I'm sorry, Cain, but I'm going to have to cut this session short. If the Beast is mated to her, I'll need to ensure he's being securely held for the safety of everyone here.

<<paper rustling and chair squeaks>>

<<static>>

End of transcript.

CHAPTER TEN

DAHLIA

"What do you mean he tattooed your pussy?"

Curling my legs beneath me in my chair, I cocked a brow and held Kiki's incredulous stare while twisting my hair into a bun. "What part are you struggling with?"

"The part where you let a hot dragon man shave you bald and then tattoo you. You don't get tattoos. You barely leave the house." Kiki's whisper spoke volumes. She was so close to the camera I could see the reflection of the screen in her glasses.

"I get them when they are magic-infused birth control."

She shook her head, her expression so disappointed she reminded me of a disgruntled school marm. "I can't believe you, of all people, turned out to be an absolute virgin stereotype. You literally write these scenes. You know about condoms, or hell, the importance of pulling out, but noooo, you just went ahead and let the sexy Viking man pump you full of his sexy Viking sperm."

My cheeks burned as a vision of Tor doing exactly that washed over me, followed by Kai wrapping his hand around my throat as he did the same.

"That's why I got the tattoo. Are you even listening to me?"

She sat back in her chair, crossing her arms over her chest and huffing. "You get to have all the fun, and I'm stuck here with the typos and dangling modifiers."

"Yeah, well, next time you can be the one to hallucinate in public and be shipped off to the asylum for some much-needed therapy, and I'll stay home."

"If by therapy you mean getting my insides squeegeed by a massive dick, then sign me the fuck up."

"You're not even going to answer my question, are you?"

"Which one?"

I sighed. "How am I supposed to choose? They both marked me."

"I thought the point was that you weren't going to choose. That's what you said to Tor, and to me the last time we talked. And it doesn't seem like Kai was all that concerned with Tor getting to you first, so I'm not sure I'm understanding your moral crisis."

"It's not a crisis. It's fear. They might say they're fine with it, but you didn't see Tor. He's not himself any longer. He's primal. The two of them sharing me isn't something I think will be workable long-term."

She tutted, shaking her head. "First rule to avoid a miscommunication trope. Let them decide for themselves."

"And what do I do in the meantime? Cross my fingers and toss up a prayer that no one dies before they get their poop in a group? Can't see that working out for me."

Not that it didn't hold some serious appeal.

"Or you just lie back and enjoy the ride."

"Maybe someone knows where I can find a magic lamp."

"What?"

"You know, one with a genie. If dragon shifters and vampires are real, why not a big blue guy with a thing for cuffs and tiny houses?"

"What time is it there? Are you delirious?"

"Um . . . around two, I think? We don't really keep track here unless we have a session, and with Masterson still in the hospital, I'm not sure when those will start up again. I've just sort of been hiding out in my room and avoiding everyone." I cast a quick glance at my bedroom door, the darkness creeping in from underneath reinforcing that most residents were in bed.

"Why would you do a stupid thing like that?"

"It's basically my default state. Are you kidding?"

"But . . . dragon dick."

My heart fluttered. No, that wasn't my heart. That was my pussy. "It's ribbed."

"Of fucking course it is. Next you're going to tell me it vibrates."

"Nope. Think that one still only happens in books. Or with batteries."

"Can't win them all, I guess. Maybe you *should* look into that genie. You're clearly suffering."

"Your sarcasm is noted."

"Good. So, you've got dragon dick and Viking dick. What's the problem? You can't really be calling me to complain about getting so much dick you can't walk straight."

She wasn't wrong, but I couldn't resist messing with her. "Why does it sound like you're jealous?"

"Bitch, because I am. I haven't gotten fucked since Miss Muffet sat on a tuffet. Or maybe Easter two years ago, which is basically the same thing."

A sudden shiver worked its way down my spine out of nowhere. Trying not to overthink it, I snagged the throw at the end of the bed and wrapped it around my shoulders like a cape.

"So call up that one guy. What did you name him? The Clit-meister? No, wait . . . Grand Master of Orgasms?"

"Pussy president."

"That's right. You were going to help him christen his big white house."

"Stop trying to distract me."

"The guy's name was Ransom. He was a cowboy. A *billionaire* cowboy. He was practically made for you."

She waved a dismissive hand. "Nope, he was too hung up on his ex. You know I don't play second fiddle to any woman."

"And this is why you're celibate."

"Says the woman currently turning herself into a stuffed animal. What is wrong with you? Did the fire go out or something? Why are you wearing your pillow like a hat?"

"This is how I know you're not my real friend. If you were, you'd ignore this." I gestured to my attire as a shiver rippled across my skin.

"You also say real friends are supposed to understand each other no matter how much food is in their mouth or how hard they're yawning while trying to finish their sentence, and still, you have yet to master that skill, so . . . I win."

"These are not remotely the same things."

"Dee, come on. Something is clearly going on. Are you okay? Do you need me to page the hot doc? Or your dragon? You look like you're on the verge of tears or something."

I couldn't tell her what was wrong because I didn't know. My heart raced as a sense of foreboding filled the room.

No. Oh no. Not again.

"Keeks, I think I should head to bed."

"Nope. No way. Don't you dare hang up on me mid-freak-out. This is my time to shine, boo."

Without warning, a knock rattled my door, ripping a terrified squeak from me. I slammed the lid of my laptop closed, effectively hanging up on Kiki so she wouldn't have to witness my downfall.

It still hadn't clicked that the knock came from *outside* my room. I was too caught up on the part where I was pretty sure my malevolent ghost friend was kicking off their comeback tour.

Breath sawing in and out of my lungs, I clutched the arms of my chair as I turned around just in time to see the door jostle. The knob turned, but thankfully it was still charmed, and the lock held fast.

Another shake of the wood accompanied a loud thump, and I

couldn't do a damn thing to keep myself from whimpering. The spirit was tormenting me.

I knew it was only a matter of time before it made its move, and I didn't even have the benefit of being able to see it to try and counter its attack.

This time a soft electrical hiss was my only warning before my doorknob glowed an eerie and oddly familiar shade of blue seconds before crashing open.

"Dahlia!"

"Cain? What the fuck? Why are you breaking into my room?"

"Why the fuck are you squeaking like a damn scared kitten? I knocked. You're lucky I did that much."

"As opposed to melting down my door to bypass the magical lock?"

"Precisely."

"You need help. You do realize that, right? I'm told it's a crucial first step."

"Ah, but that would mean I think there's something wrong with me. I've yet to subscribe to that theory."

Asshole stood on his hind legs, pawing at me to pick him up. I scooped the fluffball into my arms and instantly felt better at the contact. There was just something about a puppy.

Instead of chastising me for touching his precious pup, Cain's brow furrowed. "Where did you get those bruises?"

"What bruises?"

"Those ones," he said, pointing to my legs.

Oh, dear lord. Did Kai leave marks? Or Tor? That would be just my luck.

I glanced down, finding what could only be described as fingerprints dotting the front of my left thigh. It's as much as I'd expected, but the placement made no sense. Neither did the size. They weren't much larger than my own fingers. Kai and Tor weren't small men. They towered over most of the creatures at Blackwood and could easily wrap my entire hand in one of their palms. If the bruises were from them, the purple dots would be on the sides of my leg. And they certainly wouldn't look fresh.

"Um . . ." The unease that had been brewing before Cain busted open my door returned with a vengeance.

Either sensing my distress or picking up on the same unearthly vibe as me, Asshole began to growl.

"Dahlia," Cain whispered, his voice tight with tension. "Whatever you do, don't turn around."

CHAPTER ELEVEN

CAIN

Twenty minutes earlier

There was something about the quiet hours between midnight and dawn. It was a time for sinful deeds and carnal delights, but for me, this was my only opportunity to gather my thoughts and try to make sense of the jumbled memories I'd unlocked. Flipping through the pages of my leather-bound journal—a gift from Dr. Masterson—I was attempting to chronologically organize the scraps of my past.

It didn't take long for me to understand one core truth about myself. I despised not having answers. Especially about my own past.

Blowing out a frustrated breath, I reached for my highball glass and took a long, slow sip of my bourbon. Fuck, a good batch was a beautiful thing, and I'd hand it to Blackwood, they kept the finer things on hand for those of us not trapped in No Man's Land.

A sharp yip escaped at my feet as Asshole played tug-of-war with my shoelace. The little shit loved destroying my shoes. It seemed to be his favorite pastime.

"Asshole, leave it. That's not for you. If you're a good boy, I'll steal one of Hook's boots for you."

The little ball of fur gave a disappointed huff, but did as I bade and curled up, his chin resting on the toe of my shoe.

Turning the page, I found a blank one and scribbled down the remnants of what could have been a dream or a fragment of memory. Since it was impossible to know, I couldn't risk allowing the details to slip away.

The only sounds in the room as I jotted down my recollection were the scratch of my pen on paper and Asshole's tiny snores. All I remembered was walking through a manicured garden under the cloak of the night sky, the stars creating a canopy overhead. I was searching for something, but couldn't pinpoint what it was. As I passed a row of trees, a soft thud stopped me in my tracks. The ripe red fruit split open upon impact, releasing its sweet scent. Reaching out, I picked up one of the halves, bringing it to my face and inhaling deeply. Something about the smell had me rock hard and aching, and without warning, I buried my face in it and sucked up as much of the juice as possible until all that was left dripped down my chin.

"Fuck," I muttered, setting down my pen and adjusting my straining dick. "Turned on by a bit of fruit? What the fuck is wrong with me? Do I need to add sitophilia to my growing list of depravities?"

Perhaps I should return to my room and relieve the ache that recollection had created. Or, hell, I could just do it right here. No one was around.

The scent from my memory lingered in my nose, reminding me too much of the woman I'd been trying to avoid. The one I told myself I shouldn't keep picturing as I pumped my cock until I came all over myself most nights when sleep eluded me.

Taking a deep breath, I forced myself to keep my dick in my pants and not give in to my urges. Which ended up being a good call since not even seconds later, bright blue sparks burst from my fingers, setting the edge of my most recent journal entry on fire.

"Motherfucker," I hissed, snapping the book closed and extinguishing the flame.

Asshole perked up, shot me a dirty look, then went back to sleep.

Where the hell had that come from?

I was no stranger to unprompted bursts of my power, but that was usually in response to an extreme emotion. Generally anger. But I wasn't angry right now; I was pent up. Maybe a little on edge. Jittery?

The more I tried to sort through the riot of sensation occurring within me, the less I could grasp it. Something just felt . . . off.

A low groan came from just outside the study a moment prior to the door flying open as two figures tumbled in, hands pawing at each other, the scent of sex already following in their wake.

"Fuck, you're a temptress," the man I now recognized as Kit said, his voice breathless and hungry.

"I'm a vampire. It's in my blood."

Sorcha Blackthorne was fucking Kit? That was an interesting development.

"You can tempt me anytime, my dark and twisted queen. So long as you're willing to deal with the consequences of your actions."

"Does it seem like I lack follow-through?" she asked in a throaty whisper.

Kit's soft grunt made it more than clear where her hand had just snaked down to. "Fuck, baby. Bite me already. Stop playing with your food."

"Oh, now you're done with the poetic turns of phrase?"

"Your hand is on my cock, and you're expecting sonnets?"

"Men. All the same in the end. I'd say I was disappointed, but . . ."

"But you know exactly how good I am, and you crave it."

"Yes. That."

He shoved her against the bookcase, two figurines crashing to the floor as a result as she sank her fangs into his throat, and he yanked her skirt up to her waist.

All right, it was time to make myself known. Enough was enough. If I wasn't getting any, neither would they.

I stood and stepped out of my dimly lit corner while obnoxiously clearing my throat.

"Do you mind?"

Kit paused in the middle of pulling Sorcha's thong down her thighs. "Oh, we have an audience. Goodie. I always perform best in front of a crowd."

Sorcha's gaze was so threatening I'd be afraid if I didn't know she wore baby pink lacy underwear. "Leave."

"I was here first, Blackthorne. You two need to better assess your surroundings if you plan to skulk off to fuck in communal spaces."

"If you want your head to remain attached to your body, I strongly suggest you heed my previous warning."

An electric surge sent a buzz through the air, causing the lights to flicker, die, and then come back on.

"Fucking poltergeists," Sorcha groused.

Before I had a chance to respond—to either her threat or the light show—Asshole gave a little yip and bolted out of the room.

Sorcha ran her palm down Kit's torso, heading south until he grunted, but her eyes didn't leave me. "Oh, look at that. You've lost your puppy." She smirked. "Fetch."

I glowered at her, but was already moving toward the door. It was unlike my furry shadow to leave my side, and his doing so now was troubling.

"Remember, the louder she is, the more likely she's faking it, Kit. This one looks like a screamer."

"Don't worry about me. I know my way around a woman's body."

Pausing in the doorway, I gave him a considering hum. "Do you? Or are you just so used to adoring fans that you've forgotten what a performance looks like?"

Asshole's frantic barks had me rushing out of the room and into the hall. I swear to the gods, if anything happened to the little prick, I would rain fire down on whoever deigned to hurt him. I caught sight of his fluffy white form as he ascended the stairs and headed down the hall.

"Asshole! Get back here!" I whisper-shouted.

Instead of heeding, he only barked louder.

"Quiet! What are you trying to do, get me thrown back in No Man's Land?"

His barks abruptly cut off and turned into a pained whine. My belly twisted at the sound. Oh, someone was about to know the extent of my wrath. Sparks flew out of my fingers as I took the stairs two at a time. No one fucked with my dog and lived to tell the tale.

But when I turned the corner, Asshole was alone, pawing at a very familiar door.

"Back away from the pretty girl's door, you tiny stalker. I know she smells like candy, but she's not ours to devour. Remember?"

Given the pang of denial my words sent through me, I wasn't sure which one of us that reminder was really for.

Not one to be denied, Asshole smacked the door again, still growling softly when I refused to open the door for him.

"It's not our room. I can't just—"

But then a very distinctive whimper came from behind the slab of wood, and my very logical explanation died a swift death.

Suddenly, I had no problem at all busting my way inside.

"Back," I ordered, my voice a dark growl.

This time Asshole was quick to obey. Probably because he knew he was about to get his way.

And that's how I found myself staring down the woman I shouldn't crave as a dark, angry spirit loomed over her. "Dahlia, whatever you do, don't turn around."

The black writhing mass was so close that if she turned to face it, I was horrified it would suck the soul right out of her. Smoky tendrils that resembled claws reached for her, and I could see the residue of where it had already tainted her on the exposed flesh of her thighs.

Unexpected terror had me in a chokehold as the darkness shifted, revealing a gaping maw that stretched open obscenely on a silent scream.

"Dahlia!" I shouted, but that was the only warning I could manage as the smoky claws solidified for the span of a heartbeat and sent her crashing out of her chair and straight into the corner of her dresser.

I reached for her but was too slow as she fell. The evil entity turned its furious energy on me, rushing toward me like one of those specters from a haunted house. I wasn't afraid; in fact, I felt a strange sort of kinship. This being had no power over me.

Just as the smoky form reached me, I held my blazing palms out, the shadows reflecting the light of my fire as the presence shattered, leaving no trace of its existence behind.

"Are you all right?" I asked once I was certain we were alone.

"I . . . I think so," she said, voice shaky.

The only reason I didn't help her to her feet was because Asshole was attempting to climb into her lap, furiously licking her face as if to offer his own brand of comfort.

"I'm lucky you were here to banish it, or whatever that was," she said, trying to twist away from the dog's incessant tongue bath.

"Don't thank me. Thank your fierce protector."

She glanced up from the puppy to look at me. "What do you mean?"

"He knew something was wrong. He led me straight to you."

Her expression morphed from strained to touched. "Aw, little guy, thank you. You are just the sweetest bodyguard a girl could ever ask for," she cooed as she pulled my dog into her arms and started raining her own set of kisses down on his head.

Like the Asshole he was, he basked in her praise, rubbing it in my face.

Aaand now I'm jealous of a dog.

She stopped petting the dog and lifted her gray eyes to meet mine, awe in her expression. "Cain, you banished it."

Uncertain why we were revisiting the topic, I nodded slowly. "Yeah, did you not want me to?"

"But that means you saw it."

"And?"

"I thought I was the only one who could. You saw it before I did. It only revealed itself after it shoved me."

I shrugged it off. I didn't have any answers for her. I barely knew myself at this point. "Lots of people here see and interact with ghosts."

"Cain, we both know that wasn't a regular ghost."

"Well, whatever it was, it's gone now."

Her eyes dropped, and she brushed her fingers over the bruises marring her skin. "They've never hurt me before. This is the third time the same one has come after me."

The way my rage bloomed in my heart all over again at the knowledge she was in pain should have given me pause. It didn't. Instead, all I wanted to do was make sure nothing ever touched her again.

"It sounds like you're being haunted."

She physically recoiled at my declaration. "That sounds . . . ominous. How am I supposed to defend myself against an evil spirit? It's not like I can count on you and your dog to swoop in and save me."

Yes, you can. I'll take you to my room and keep you.

My whole body stiffened at that thought. I couldn't do that. She wasn't mine. She was mated to Tor. Besides, I was already spoken for. My heart wasn't mine to give. It belonged to the woman in my dreams. The one filling the pages of my journal.

Shit, my journal. I'd left it in the study. I had to retrieve it before Kit and Sorcha spotted it and tried to use its contents as ammunition against me. Blackmail seemed right up their alley, and out of the two, I couldn't be sure the demon was the bigger threat.

Latching onto the excuse, I opened my mouth to say my goodbyes. But it turns out I didn't need to. Dahlia's phone rang, interrupting our conversation.

"Shit, I bet that's Kiki. She's got to be worried sick. I should take this."

"Of course. I'll leave you to it."

I forced myself to head for the door without looking back, but she stopped me with a soft, "Cain?"

Steeling myself to stare into her painfully familiar eyes, I turned. "Yes?"

"Thank you."

I gave her a curt nod before I adopted my indifferent prick persona. "Let's not make a habit of it."

CHAPTER TWELVE

KAI

"*Go to her. You know she needs you.*"

"Leave off, ye wanker. She's fine." Even as I said the words to my dragon, I knew they were a lie.

Dahlia was far from fine. She missed Tor. She needed him.

"She doesn't look fine. She looks like she needs her mate to remind her of what she still has."

He wasn't wrong. Even from my tower, I could feel her sadness. It didn't help matters that I could also track her path through the garden. Her shoulders were slumped, her steps slow and meandering. She looked lost, and it gutted me.

We're newly mated. She should nae have a cause to be so unhappy.

"She should still be in our bed. You never should have let her go."

"I couldnae exactly make a nest for us when she all but shoved me out the door."

"Because you didn't let me take over. I would have convinced her to spend the rest of her life with me between her thighs."

"You heard her as clearly as I. She had to work."

"Does that look like working to you?"

There was no need to answer; he knew he had me, and so did I. His presence in my mind was near constant now that I'd mated Dahlia. It wouldn't be long before the two of us became one, but the last time that happened, I ended up here.

Where would they send me if there was a next time? No Man's Land for the rest of my life?

It hardly bore thinking. My mate needed me; I couldnae allow anything to keep me from my place at her side.

My gaze raked across the grounds, assessing the surroundings for any possible danger to her. Blackwood had proven itself to not be the safe haven they'd promised, and as we'd just been reminded, a serial killer had us in his sights. If anything happened to her . . .

What the bloody hell is that fucking pirate doing now?

Hook stood in the shadows, staring after Dahlia as she wandered. He radiated desperation and a hint of madness as he watched her. Logically, I couldn't blame him. I'd be right there beside him had my position not changed in the last span of days. But I wasnae a logical creature at the best of times.

"If you kill him now, you'll spare her from future harm."

"I cannae go around murderin' people."

"When will you remember what we are?"

"A dragon? Trust me, I'm aware."

"Nae. A villain."

"Ahmnae a villain."

"Liar."

I wanted nothing more than to go to her and scoop her into my arms before sequestering us up here in our nest. But ours was a more complicated bonding than most. She wasn't solely mine, and she needed her other mate just as much.

If Dahlia was feeling even half of the pull to be together I was, then she must be in absolute misery being cut off from one of the men who'd set claim to her soul. I could not let her suffer. No matter how much I wanted to keep her all to myself. Her pain would become my own.

Resolved, I turned away from the window and set off to find the one person who might be able to give me some answers.

"Do you mind?" Bruno snarled as he opened his door.

My fist was still curled in the air from the pounding I'd given it. From the looks of things, I wasn't the only one doing some pounding. Oz's disheveled head was just visible behind Bruno, who was clad only in a blanket that barely stayed wrapped around his hips.

"Oh, I see. Tor's locked away, so you're off duty. Making the most of your vacation, are you?"

"I don't remember inviting you over, Malakai, so perhaps you want to get to the point before I slam this door in your face?"

"When are you going to get off your arse and fix him so he can come back?"

Bruno's eyes widened. "*Fix* him?"

"Aye. You heard what I said."

"There is no fixing him, Kai. He's lost."

"He cannae be lost."

"Yet he is and only continues to grow more so as the days pass."

"He needs his mate."

Bruno shook his head. "He won't even recognize her at this point. He'd tear her to shreds."

"Nae. He'd never harm her."

I said the words with conviction, but my conversation with Tor rang in my mind. He'd asked me to kill him so he wouldn't be able to hurt her. I'd given him my vow, but I wouldn't keep it until we'd exhausted all other options.

"Bru, you need to tell him," Oz said as he came up beside the man. Somewhere during my conversation with Bruno, the psychic had pulled on a pair of boxers.

"Tell me what?"

Bruno held Oz's obstinate stare before blowing out a heavy breath. "I never should have told you that."

"Technically you didn't *tell* me anything."

"No, but I let you touch me while it was weighing on my mind, which is basically the same thing."

Oz shrugged. "If you don't tell him, I will. Dahlia deserves to know."

That argument, more than any other, seemed to do the trick.

Bru's reluctant gaze returned to me. "There's been talk in the last couple of days."

Rather than demanding he get to the point, I simply crossed my arms and waited him out. Say what you will about dragons, but we could be incredibly patient when the need arose. Few species lived longer than us; time was always on our side.

"If he doesn't come out of his rage soon, they're going to put him out of his misery."

Ice raced down my spine. "What?"

"A Berserker locked in a blood rage like this is dangerous enough, but his curse means there's no hope. He's a beast with Berserker power on top. He can't be released, and they won't keep him forever."

"So they're just going to . . . put him down like a rabid animal?"

"It's mercy."

"It's execution."

"He will never leave that cell in his current state. If it was you locked in there, can you really say you'd want that? A lifetime spent in solitary confinement? Out of control. Alone with nothing but mindless rage as company? Your mate always just out of reach?"

Fuck, he was right. If Dahlia wasn't in my sight, I was itchy. I couldn't imagine what I'd do if I was locked away from her.

"You have to give him a fighting chance. I'm telling you, he will never hurt her. She's quite possibly the only one who can bring him back from this."

"We can't risk that, Kai. She's not a tool we can use to pull him out of this."

Oz nodded. "Dahlia has no idea what she's asking if she wants to go in there. You should be protecting her, not sending her to him like a lamb to the slaughter."

"Are you mated?"

Oz blinked, not expecting the sudden shift in conversation. "Um, no?"

"Then shut the fuck up. You don't know what you're talking about. There is nothing that woman won't sacrifice for him, not if there's a sliver of a chance she can help save him. Denying her, nae, denying *them* that hope is damn near the same thing as pulling the trigger yourself."

Oz swallowed, and Bru put himself fully between us as he leveled his stare on me. "I'll see what I can do. I doubt the powers that be will go for it, but you're right. Tor deserves a fighting chance, and Dahlia may be the only option. I'm assuming you'll want to be there with her?"

"Obviously."

He gave me a tight nod. "I'll ask. That's all I'm promising."

"Good man." I backed away from the door and gave him a pointed look. "Carry on with whatever it was you were—"

"Fucking. We were fucking," Oz called.

Bru's ears went pink before he closed the door in my face.

"We should be fucking."

"Haud yer wheesht," I grumbled, annoyed that the dragon was right. We *should* be fucking, and instead I had a mate who was all alone with a pirate stalker and no one watching over her.

I could fix that.

In fact, I would. We'd been apart too long. I'd given her space to work as she'd requested, but now she was all mine. It was time for her to STFDATMDLAGM.

Sit the fuck down and take my dick like a good mate.

CHAPTER THIRTEEN

TOR

"Subject is still showing no signs of improvement. Continuous agitation and displays of aggression are the norm, and all attempts at sedation have been unsuccessful. As of today, the subject has ripped his chains free of the wall three times and harmed twice as many orderlies. Despite his handler's assertions that access to his mate might be required, I will not risk any more of this facility's residents or staff."

The doctor's voice cut through my haze of fury, pulling my attention to where he stood behind the window.

I grunted as I struggled against my chains. My throat burned with thirst, my stomach ached with hunger.

"We've resorted to a drastically restrictive diet in order to weaken and subdue him in hopes he can be rehabilitated." The doctor paused, looking me over before raising his hand to his mouth again. "As it stands, if we do not see a marked improvement in the next forty-eight hours, we will have no choice but to resort to termination."

Their attempts to weaken me were working, but even in a weakened state, they were no match for me. And if they sought to end me, well, I'd never back down from a fight.

I'd never lose one either.

"Perhaps Miss Moore's presence, if from a distance, could offer some insight into the subject's mental state beyond his agitation. I am certain Dahlia would come if the opportunity presented itself. The question is, would she be safe from him if he broke free?"

Her name sent a bolt of longing through me. For one sliver of a moment, it was as if the clouds parted and the sun broke through.

Dahlia. My mate.

My voice was barely more than a guttural rasp. "Mine."

The doctor ceased his ramblings, his eyes sharpening with interest. "What was that?"

I had to swallow to force some moisture into my mouth before I could speak again. "Dahlia . . . mine."

"I can't let you see her, Mr. Nordson. Not if she's at risk. You'll hurt her."

Despair and denial burned in my veins, swiftly followed by my ever-present rage. I needed a target, or at the very least, some way to vent it before it consumed me.

"She's safe with Kai. He's taking care of her," the doctor said, his eyes gentle as he stared at me with pity. "You can't be with her like this. If you were in your right mind, I know you'd agree. She deserves more than a beast in her bed."

My fury sharpened, jealousy giving it teeth.

I needed to get free of this place.

I needed my mate.

For all the doctor's ramblings, few of the words made sense. What was clear, however, was that my time was limited and that if I had any hope of reclaiming my mate, I needed to convince them I'd been tamed.

What predator didn't know how to fool its prey?

For her, I would play this game. And once she was mine again, I'd slaughter them all and take her far away.

I ripped my chains from the wall with a roar that sent the doctor stumbling one step backward. He knew as well as I that the glass wouldn't hold me.

"Tor. Stop."

I didn't. Not until I was nose to nose with the barrier separating us. Then I raised my fist as though I'd smash the window. Instead, I flattened my palm and pressed it to the cool surface as I stared into his eyes.

"I . . . need . . . her," I growled. "Please?"

CHAPTER FOURTEEN

HOOK

"Come on, come on, it has to be here somewhere," I muttered, shutting the drawer I'd been rifling through and opening the next. Just because the good doctor was currently residing in Blackwood's medical ward didn't mean I had carte blanche to her office. If I was caught in here, it would be a one-way trip to No Man's Land for me.

Casting a glance over my shoulder, I let my gaze linger on the bloodstained wood floor. Technically Dr. Masterson's office was still considered a crime scene—if one subscribed to things such as police tape or badges lending someone an ounce of authority. I decidedly did not.

Slamming closed yet another dead end, I placed my hands on my hips and cast my gaze around the room. "If I were a head shrinker, where would I keep an enchanted compass that doesn't point north?"

I narrowed my eyes and scanned the desk, which was unfortunately pitifully bare. But that simply meant the drawers held all her secrets. Or perhaps her shelves. Was one of those leather-bound tomes a secret hidey-hole? I knew more than my fair share of heathens who carved out a pocket in their holy books to stow a bit o' rum.

"Caspian, you brilliant pirate," I congratulated myself.

Forgoing the desk drawers, I made a beeline for the bookcase behind her desk and trailed my fingers along the spines of every one of her leather-bound books so I could feel for the one that would surely be false. There was always at least one. Mine was *Winnie-the-Pooh*. What? I indulge in a bit of whimsy every now and then. Everyone should connect with their inner child.

"Ah-ha, found you, you scurvy-blind bastard." Hooking my finger at the top of the spine, I allowed myself a moment to bask in my brilliance. Sadly, any pride I felt at my discovery faded when I saw the title. "*Gray's Anatomy*? Really, doctor? It should have been *Fifty Shades of Grey* at the very least."

Although, I suppose there was something to be said about picking the most boring book in the lot to dissuade any potential sticky fingers. Too bad for her I was basically a criminal mastermind.

"Let's see what you're hiding in here, shall we?"

The large tome was still heavy, even if it wasn't being used for its intended purpose. I let it fall onto the desk, wincing at the loud thwack as it hit the surface. I had to hand it to the doctor, she'd done a bang-up job with this trickery. The first few pages were fully intact, but once I turned to page five, all bets were off. She'd carved a large well inside the book.

"What the devil?" I muttered as I stared at the contents. Instead of a collection of confiscated goods as I'd expected, it was a much more mundane treasure: tapes. Well over two dozen of them, all with dates on them in the doctor's precise scrawl.

I plucked one out at random, not able to make sense of whatever coding system she used to identify them. Smart enough to know that the contents of these tapes had to be worth a listen if the doc went to such trouble to hide them, I pinched the recorder from the front pocket of the lab coat hanging from the nearby coat rack.

"You really shouldn't just leave your things lying around, Lizzie. Someone might steal them," I tutted.

Popping a tape into the recorder, I pressed play and waited as the hiss began.

"This is Dr. Elizabeth Masterson . . ."

"Yes, yes, we know," I grumbled, fast-forwarding a few seconds before hitting play again.

" . . . I'm not avoiding her."

"Oh, hello, Viking. Fancy meeting you here."

Settling into the doctor's chair, I allowed the tape to continue playing.

"And yet you seem to be going out of your way to do so. I have personally witnessed you spot her walking into a room, only to turn on your heel and head the other way."

"She's not . . . she can't be mine."

My gut twisted at the despondency in his words.

"Why is that?"

"I'm a monster."

"Aren't we all, mate? Aren't we all."

"A monster wouldn't be this distraught over being what they are."

That doctor was actually pretty good at her job, now that I was listening to her work with others. But then, they actually needed her services. I was only here because I was on a mission to find the key to my glorious homecoming.

"I'll hurt her."

"How are you so certain?"

"My beast is too strong."

"Bo-ring," I sang, stopping the tape and replacing it with another.

Fast-forwarding through the introduction, I smirked when my own voice greeted me. Mmm, I certainly spoke with a very sexy timbre. I should speak to Dahlia about narrating one of her audiobooks.

"What can I say, Doc? The ladies love me. The lads too, for that matter."

Of course they do, you beautiful bastard. You're irresistible. Smirking, I hit fast-forward again, not needing to relive something I'd already sat through once, but I was curious if she'd said anything after I'd left.

"Subject appears to suffer from delusions of grandeur and narcissistic personality disorder. He has no respect for boundaries and continues to skirt the line of appropriate behavior. Despite several dosage adjustments, he can still access the full extent of his fae glamour, which makes him dangerous indeed. Recommend a covert detail watching him at all times."

"Spies? Really, Elizabeth?" I scoffed. "Also, they aren't delusions if they're true, are they? I take back every nice thought I had about you. You're a quack."

I tore the tape free and tossed it into the pile before snagging another. This time when the voice started speaking, I sat down and paid close attention. It was my darling. My Dahlia.

"Why do you need to know about that?" Dahlia hedged.

"Well, you call yourself a deviant. We need to address that. Our fantasies tell us a lot about ourselves. And part of your journey here requires that self-knowledge and acceptance."

"Oh, hell yes they do. Now we're talking." Spreading my thighs a little wider to accommodate my already thickening cock, I closed my eyes and listened intently.

"But it's . . . private."

"This is a safe space, free of judgment, Dahlia. For us to explore the depth of your power, we have to unlock you. All of you. I'm not here to shame you. I'm here to help you find yourself."

Dahlia's deep inhale was caught by the recorder, and I could so easily imagine the way she chewed on her lower lip while making up her mind.

"My fantasies tend to be a little, well, dark, I guess."

"Define dark."

"Oh yes, please do, Dahlia darling."

"Some might call them consensual non-consent." Her self-deprecating laugh was music to my ears. *"I blame it on being desensitized because of all the steamy scenes I write. Or maybe it's my fucked up childhood, now that I think about it."*

The doctor's hum of acknowledgment was all Dahlia got before she continued.

"Well, I guess if we're doing this, I'd better just dive in head first, huh? Rip the Band-Aid off and put the most fucked up one out there. Since you're not gonna judge me and all. It's not like you can lock me up and throw away the key. That already happened."

Hands pressed against my thighs, dick straining against my trousers, I leaned closer as if I could somehow draw the confession out more quickly. I do believe this is what they refer to as waiting with bated breath. The anticipation was delicious.

"There's nothing that turns me on more than the idea of waking up to find myself already being taken by a lover."

"Ah, yes, somnophilia. It's quite popular, I assure you."

"Isn't it rape?"

"It depends. Is this lover a stranger? Are they someone you desire? So many factors are important to consider with a fantasy like this one. Rape fantasies are not uncommon either, Dahlia. Fantasy is where we can safely work to heal our wounds."

"So I'm not an absolute freak for wanting the choice taken away?"

"Well, as you said, it's a form of consensual non-consent. So your choice was already taken into consideration ahead of time. It's merely the time and place that are out of your control. This builds the excitement. In scenarios such as this one, it's not the act itself that's reflective of your desire, it's the excitement and unpredictability. The unknown. That it could happen at any time, that your body is at the mercy of your lover's whims. It's a very attractive possibility for those who have to exercise extreme control over their day-to-day lives. A way of breaking the cycle and handing all of that stress over so they can simply exist and enjoy."

"But it's not like I could ever ask a partner to give me that. They'd

think I was damaged. They'd run so fast I wouldn't get a chance to explain."

"Not necessarily. This is why talking it through and understanding your desires and limits is so important."

"What would a conversation like that even look like? I can't imagine a scenario where that just comes up organically over dinner."

Dr. Masterson chuckled softly. *"You might be surprised. But you raise a great point. Let's practice. I will play the role of your future lover, and you will work on expressing your desires and limits to me."*

"You want us to role-play?"

"It's an excellent way to learn."

"Okay. Um . . . what do I call you?"

"Whatever name you wish."

"It's too weird to use someone I know."

"Then how about one of your characters?"

"Sure. We'll go with Fox. He's a pirate king with something to prove."

Oh-ho-ho. Seems that I left an impression. Excellent.

"Go on. Tell Fox what you want."

"Um . . . Fox, I want you to touch me while I'm sleeping."

"Touch you how? Be specific."

"Run your fingers over my body, under my clothes . . . between my legs. I . . ." Dahlia took a deep breath and blurted, *"I want to be used. I want to wake up choking on your dick, or being impaled on it. I want the choice of when taken away. I want to feel so desired that you couldn't wait and just had to take me right then and there."*

"Fuck me. As you fucking wish, darling." Why hadn't I sought out these tapes sooner? They were a fucking treasure trove of useful information.

"Dahlia, that was very good. It was honest and real. Now I want you to think about your limits. Is there anything in that scenario that would be unacceptable to you?"

"What do you mean?"

"Well, would you be okay with being drugged, for instance? That's a fairly common practice in CNC. It would render you unconscious for the

entire act, and you would not be aware until after the fact that you'd been taken sexually. Is that something you'd be interested in, or is that off limits?"

"No drugs. No . . . no bondage. I don't ever want to be tied down. I need to be aware when I wake up. I'd need to experience it and be able to use my safe word."

"Which is?"

"I don't know. I've never had a reason to use one."

"That's fine. For this purpose, we will go with 'red.' What would make you say it?"

"Violence, I suppose. I don't want to be hit. Or humiliated. I'm not into the idea of degradation."

"Very good. I think you've learned a lot about yourself today. About how your desires are not reprehensible but completely natural, and when expressed and explored in a consensual and safe setting, they can be very liberating and, dare I say, therapeutic."

"Sex therapy?" Dahlia laughed. *"Sounds fun."*

They changed subjects then, and I was no longer interested. It was a far cry from my compass, but even so, I'd gotten exactly what I needed.

Fairy dust and moonbeams, I was so turned on I couldn't see straight. My whole body lit up at the prospect of giving her what she wanted. Of sneaking into her room late at night, watching her sleep, taking her while she was lax and vulnerable, drawing a response out of her and making her cunt swollen and wet before she was even conscious. Oh yes, this was absolutely the sort of depraved fantasy I could get behind. And knowing it was one she was too afraid to ask for? That her precious mate would never have this part of her . . . that it was something only I could give her and would fulfill her deepest, darkest desires?

Sign me up.

CHAPTER
FIFTEEN
DAHLIA

In another life, if given the choice, I'd be a cat. Just lazing about in the sun while someone scratched my belly. Cats could be petty and mean just because they felt like it, and their owner would still keep the food dish full and welcome them with open arms and endless cuddles. That's what I call unconditional love.

As though reading my thoughts, Kai tugged my feet toward him and placed them in his lap.

"I'm wearing shoes, you weirdo."

He grinned and turned those purple eyes on me. "I don't care. I just need tae be touchin' you."

Shrugging, I went back to the notes I was making for my next few chapters, and he continued his sketching. Being with him was a beautiful sort of comfort. It would be even more wonderful if we weren't stuck in the dayroom at an asylum, but beggars can't be choosers and all that.

Pondering my next plot point, I looked around for inspiration, scowling the second my gaze found Hook. He was positioned directly across the room from me, his mermaid fan club at his feet, his expression broody and more than a little mean. Honestly, it gave me pause. Cas never looked mean. He was perpetually unbothered by everything going on around him. Aloof and carefree. Never broody. Never angry. It was part of the reason I was so upset with him. It's like he had no understanding at all about what he'd done or the consequences of his actions.

For the first time, I could actually see him as the villain the stories painted him to be.

I had to force myself to look away when his gaze found mine. As upset as I was with him, he still affected me. I didn't want him to see that in my eyes. So instead of allowing the pull between us to dictate my focus, I turned my attention to the vampire standing in a shaft of sunlight nearby.

"Kai," I whispered. "If Sorcha is a vampire, how can she stand there in the sun?"

"Magic, lass. She cannae go outside during the daylight hours, but within the walls of Blackwood, she's as safe as the rest of us."

"Huh. I didn't realize that was possible, but I guess it makes sense. Do they also prevent werewolves from shifting during the full moon?"

"We just call them wolf shifters, and they can shift whenever they desire. Although it is true they are a bit more feral during the full moon."

"The more you know," I mused, mentally picturing a shooting star darting across my mind.

My gaze lit on a barely visible spirit as he took a turn about the room. Old by the look of him, dressed in Victorian garb with posture that would make a clothes hanger jealous. He didn't see me, and I'd come to realize that was more common than not. He simply existed trapped in his own reality where no one else could.

"Are ye seeing a ghost?" Kai asked.

"How'd you know?"

"I pay attention. Your eyes get a faraway look in them."

I loved that he could tell. "He's just walking. Not a threat." Attention still on the spectral form as he strolled across the room, I let out a little gasp when Bruno marched straight through him, and the ghost vanished.

"What happened?"

"Bruno. He's probably all covered in ghost residue."

"Is that like slime?"

I shrugged. "Not sure. It's something only Cain can see. You'd have to ask him."

"Morning," Bruno said once he reached us.

"You're looking a little worse for wear, Bru. Had a late night, did you?"

"That's for me to know and for you to never find out."

I glanced between them, picking up on some sort of tension. It was always hard to tell here, though. Were people just on edge because it was Blackwood and they were always on edge, or if something had actually happened?

"Did you need something, Bru? Is Tor okay?" My heart did a little flip at the thought of Tor. Until now, I'd tried so hard to trust in the staff here, hopeful they'd help him so I could get him back somehow. Knowing they wouldn't let me see him was a pain that had only been eased by Kai.

"There's been a development," he answered, not really telling me anything.

"A good one?" I pressed.

"The doctor seems to think so. He's agreed to let you see him."

At first I was like a zombie, mindlessly parroting the words back. "He agreed to let me . . ." Then they clicked, and I was up out of my seat so fast every set of eyes in the room turned my way. Or perhaps that was because of my shouted, "Are you serious? I can see him?"

Bru's smile looked genuinely pleased for me. "That's why I'm here. To fetch you."

"Well, gem, what are ye waitin' for? Best we get going."

"We?" I asked, my stomach twisting nervously.

"Are you sure that's a good idea?" Bru asked, likely feeling the same sense of foreboding I was.

"There's no way in hell I'm letting her go to him alone."

"Your presence could be the thing to set him off. I know you want to protect her, but you might cause more harm than good."

"It's a risk we'll have tae take. I'm her mate. Where she goes, I follow."

Bruno's eyes widened. "What do you mean, you're her mate?"

"I said what I said."

"Surprise," I uttered weakly when Bru looked at me as if to confirm it.

He groaned. "We can't leave you alone for a minute. You're collecting mates left and right."

"Gotta catch 'em all." At their confused expressions, I blushed and shook my head, "Never mind."

"Did you mark her?" Bru asked, his focus squarely on Kai.

"Aye."

The pride in Kai's voice was unmistakable.

Bruno squeezed the bridge of his nose, looking beyond pained. "There's no way this ends well for us."

"Are you sure you should come with me?" I asked, hand pressed to Kai's warm chest.

"There isn't a scenario on this earth that would keep me from accompanying you. I made Tor a promise."

"You did?"

Kai nodded. "He came tae me once he knew only a single petal remained. He asked me to protect you from him if necessary. He knew it might come to this."

"I . . . really?" My belly swooped, and tears pricked my eyes. The move was undeniably romantic—and so utterly Tor.

"There's nothing we wouldn't do to keep you safe."

"As touching as this is, we need to shift and get you to him before it's too late." Bru's voice held an edge of urgency, snapping me out of the haze of emotion.

"Yes, of course. Let's go."

"I NEED TO WARN YOU, it's not pretty," Bru said, his voice tight as we stood in front of the blacked-out window of his cell.

"I don't care. I just want to see him."

Not unlike the last time I visited this ward, the air was thick with ominous tension. There was just something about this place that reeked of barely restrained violence. These cells contained the true monsters. The ones other supernaturals feared.

But even knowing that, I couldn't find an ounce of fear in my heart.

No matter what form he might wear, he would always be my Tor. The great big brute of a man with an even bigger heart. The one who needed only a single look to know that I belonged to him. His Kærasta.

Bru waved his hand in front of the glass, and it transformed from black to clear, revealing my mate's hulking form sitting despondently in the far corner. Knees pulled into his chest, forehead resting atop them, he looked so much like the man I fell for, save the horns and scales that went up his arms. Hair that was once golden and streaked with darkness was now pitch black and hiding his face.

"Tor," I whispered.

At the sound of his name, his head snapped up, and he found my eyes instantly.

No word in existence could encapsulate the raw emotion I found in his gaze. It was a mix of hunger, pain, longing, need, but more than anything, fury.

"Mate," he growled, his voice no longer my Tor's smooth timbre but the rough rasp of the Beast.

"I'm here." I pressed my palm to the glass, my heart breaking to see him like this. I turned to Bru, desperation filling my veins. "Can't you let him out? Look at him. He's wasting away."

"Fucking hell," Kai snarled, wrapping his arm around my waist and tugging me away from the barrier and into his hold.

I followed his gaze to find Tor standing at the window, his palms flat against the surface, midnight eyes trained on me. His bare chest was heaving, jaw clenched so hard I could see the muscles working along his neck.

"Mine," he growled again.

Tugging free of Kai's hold, I pressed my palms to the glass, mirroring his position so our hands appeared to be touching. "Yes, Tor. I'm yours."

I knew if I looked back, I would find conflict on Kai's face. It must cost him not to make a declaration of his own, but I could only assume he knew what damage it might cause in this tenuous moment.

A flicker of peace lit in Tor's eyes as his breathing evened out, and he watched me.

"Mine," he rasped, his voice more controlled.

"Yours."

He closed his eyes and took a long, shuddering breath. "Dahlia."

It was such a small thing. Just a single word. But it's what the word represented that almost brought me to my knees. He remembered. Somewhere in there, my Tor remained.

"Yes, Tor. It's me, Dahlia."

It could have been seconds or hours that we stood there locked in each other's gaze. If not for the sound of approaching footsteps, I don't think I would have ever looked away.

"Well, I think I've seen all I need to see," Dr. Temperance said as he joined our little group.

Tor growled low in his throat, but didn't move a muscle.

"What have you done to him?" I asked, whirling on the doctor. "He's gaunt. He looks like he hasn't eaten in days."

"We're only trying to save him from himself, Miss Moore. He's a danger to all of us if he doesn't get under control."

"Look at him now. He's not trying to hurt anyone."

"Yes, I know. Thus my earlier statement. You seem to be a calming influence on him after all. Still, you cannot be with him twenty-four seven. But you've given us something no one else has been able to."

"What's that?"

"Hope."

I glanced back at my mate, whose palms remained urgently pressed to the window in search of mine. "He needs me. And I . . . I need him too."

"I understand. For now, put your faith in us. I witnessed the same spark of humanity you did. Trust me when I say I want nothing more than to return your mate to you, but I'm afraid for now, visiting hours are over."

"But I just got here."

"Rules are rules, Miss Moore. You have your own work to do. And if I recall correctly, you skipped your session with me yesterday."

Guilt gnawed at me, along with the familiar taste of anxiety. I'd only just begun to trust Dr. Masterson; I wasn't prepared to start over with someone new. "I guess I forgot," I lied, my eyes never leaving Tor's.

"Not to worry. I took the liberty of rescheduling for you. Now, Bruno, if you would be so kind as to escort Miss Moore and Mr. Nash back to the main residence, I'll see to Mr. Nordson."

Bruno moved to take my elbow, but Kai snarled and pulled me into him once more. That was all it took for Tor to lose his hard-won control. He slammed both palms against the glass, hard enough to make the magically reinforced pane shudder.

Then he did it again. And again. All the while, his furious snarls filled the air. He was seconds away from snapping.

Panic coiled around my heart. "He just doesn't want me to leave. This doesn't mean he can't control himself. If you just let me stay a little longer . . ."

"No, Miss Moore. He's not ready for anything other than what you gave him. But I have much more confidence he can be reached, thanks to you."

With no other choice, I allowed Kai to pull me down the hall, but I didn't look away from Tor until the last possible moment. Just before I had to turn the corner, I shouted, "I'll be back. I promise! Just hold on for me."

CHAPTER SIXTEEN

CAIN

"Okay, Kai. Say 'purple burglar alarm.'"

I rolled my eyes at Oz's enthusiastic prompt, hating the lighthearted fun they were having at the table beside me.

"Purple burglar alarm," Kai said, all those rolling Rs tripping him up.

"Oh, for fuck's sake," I muttered, rubbing my brow. "At least give him something difficult like 'my Irish wristwatch was irrevocably broken.'"

"Me next!" Dahlia said, laughter in her voice.

"Okay, let's see," Kai mused. "Mrs. Puggy Wuggy has a square-cut punt. Not a punt cut square, just a square-cut punt." Unfortunately for him, he didn't make it through without laughing.

"You know what, if your tongue can't handle it, neither can mine."

"You little brat."

"You love it."

"Aye. I do."

Gods, I was going to vomit if they got any more sickeningly sweet.

"All right, Sorcha. You're up," Oz prompted.

"Fuck off."

"Come on, where's your adventurous spirit?"

"What about me screams adventure to you?"

"The part where you wanted to murder your husband?" Dahlia offered with a giggle.

"Ugh, fine, although how tongue twisters equate to adventure in your world is an absolute mystery to me." Sorcha cleared her throat and sat up straighter in her chair. "I am not the pheasant plucker, I'm the pheasant plucker's mate. I am only plucking pheasants because the pheasant plucker's late."

I wasn't going to last much longer. This group was ridiculous. But then Dahlia laughed and pointed at Oz.

"You haven't done one yet."

"Neither have you, Miss Perfect."

"You first."

Oz rolled his eyes. "Okay. Ready to be slaughtered?"

They nodded as the man stood.

"One sock cutter, he cut socks. Two sock cutters, they cut socks." However, the table erupted in laughter when instead of 'cut socks' Oz said 'sucks cocks.'

I was about point two seconds away from stabbing myself in the eye with a pencil just to have an excuse to be spirited away.

"It's a good thing we're all so skilled with our tongues. The Ripper won't dare harm any of us," Sorcha said, sarcasm dripping from her every word.

"There may be something to that," Oz said. "He's up and vanished."

"How can you say that?" Dahlia asked. "He just tried to murder Dr. Masterson."

"There's no way to know that was him."

"Oh, sure, because people routinely attack with vicious slashes like that. And it's totally common for multiple serial killers to use the same hunting ground."

"Statistically, I'm pretty sure that's true," Sorcha mused.

Dahlia huffed. "I'm just saying, you're all idiots if you think we've seen the last of him."

It took all my strength not to insert myself into the conversation so I could back her up. I even pushed myself out of my chair to go stand at her side for some godforsaken reason but stopped when the door opened and a group of newcomers swept into the room.

It didn't take more than a passing glance to know that pure power was rolling off one of them in waves. Or perhaps it was *all* of them.

The woman who led the pack was clad in skintight black denim, a black lace bustier with a blazer buttoned at the waist, and the most intimidating pair of thigh-high boots in existence. She was terrifying in her sensuality, and no one was immune.

At her side was a dark-haired male whose aura of danger matched her potent sexuality point for point. The term power couple was invented for people like them. He didn't walk beside her so much as prowl, and as soon as those silver eyes swept over mine, a sense of recognition passed through me. Not in the 'I've seen him somewhere before' sense, but more as in one apex predator recognizing another. Interestingly, an impossibly thin gold chain collared his throat and connected to her wrist.

Tucked between them was a woman who could only be described as a walking wet dream. I more than had my hands full dealing with my forbidden attraction to Dahlia, but even so, I couldn't help the way my cock stiffened in appreciation. She wasn't even my type with her extreme hourglass figure and pouty lips, sweet face that would make angels weep, and seductive sway of her hips. But I knew many men would fall to their knees for a moment of her attention.

It was a full heartbeat later that my brain supplied the answer to a question I hadn't consciously asked.

Succubus.

Two of them.

No wonder I was sporting wood for no damn good reason. And apparently I wasn't the only one.

"Christ, I don't even like women, and I'm hard," Oz grumbled.

Dahlia turned wide, lust-filled eyes to Kai. "What is happening right now?"

He leaned down to whisper in her ear, though given my proximity, I had no trouble hearing every word. "Succubus pheromones. dinnae worry, I'll take ye upstairs and care for you soon enough."

I swallowed back a growl. She was wearing a skirt. Why take her upstairs when she could be bent over right here? I could teach the dragon a thing or two. Fuck her so hard her tits popped out of the neckline of that flimsy shirt she was wearing.

"Merri, darling, tone it down. You're driving the locals wild," the woman with the dark hair said, her voice a seductive croon.

"Sorry, Auntie Lilith. I'm not doing it on purpose."

"I know, precious girl. That's why you're here, to help you learn control in a safe setting."

The red-haired bombshell nodded sullenly.

"Lilypad, I don't understand why *we* have to be here. Meredith is a grown woman. She certainly should be able to see herself safely here." The man chained to . . . Lilypad made his annoyance clear not with what he said, but his tone.

"Drystan, do not make me remind you of your manners."

The man sneered but remained surprisingly silent.

The woman, Lilypad, looked around the room. "We were supposed to be greeted by Dr. Masterson. Tell me, where is she?"

But before anyone could answer her, a tall, handsome man I'd never seen before walked in behind them.

Oz started to cough, much to Sorcha's amusement.

"Down, boy."

"But he's so pretty."

"You're taken, remember?"

Oz waved a hand. "There have been no declarations. Don't ruin this for me."

"Oz, you are a shameless slut."

"Don't slut shame me, husband killer."

"Attempted killer," Sorcha corrected with absolutely zero remorse.

"Lilith, what an honor to meet you," the stranger said as he approached.

The intimidating woman gave an irritated huff. "Yes, it is an honor for you. Where is Elizabeth?"

His eyes widened. "Oh, didn't you hear? Dr. Temperance sent word to *Iniquity*. She was . . . gravely injured in a terrible attack. She's recovering but unfortunately not well enough to receive visitors."

Lilith raised a brow, and no lie, a shiver of apprehension rolled down my spine. Here I'd thought the male was the dangerous one, but no . . . she was every bit as deadly as him. Perhaps more so.

"I see. And what about my ward? Have accommodations been made for her? She needs help, Doctor . . ."

"Swift. Oh, wait, no. My name is Taylor. I'm not a doctor. I'm Dr. Temperance's assistant."

"Well, Taylor, she nearly drained three patrons this week alone. It was . . . messy."

My attention went to the redhead, and I was nearly sucked into her gaze simply from eye contact alone. She dipped her head, breaking our stare, and the pressure in my skull instantly receded.

The bumbling idiot assistant nodded. "Yes, of course. Just because Dr. Masterson is out of pocket doesn't mean that work here has come to a screeching halt. If anything, we are busier than ever. Which is why Dr. Temperance flew me in."

Lilith held out a hand, palm facing down. "Well then, Taylor love, charmed, I'm sure."

The handsome assistant's swallow was audible even from here.

"Lilypad, stop playing with your food. He's shaking like a leaf and hard as a rock. Honestly it's humiliating. I am standing right here."

"I can't help it. This place is a veritable buffet of untapped potential." Lilith leaned in and sniffed Taylor. "Mmm, you smelled like trouble when you walked in. Always good to know I haven't lost my touch and that, as usual, I was right."

Oz elbowed Sorcha, whispering urgently, "Did you hear that? His name is Taylor Swift. That was a Taylor Swift joke. Lilith is a secret Swiftie."

I had to get the fuck out of here. The last thing I needed was a succubus, or succubi as the case may be, fucking with my willpower. I had ninety-nine problems, and a woman who answered to *Lilypad* was not about to be one. That spot was reserved for Dahlia.

Scooping Asshole up from where he was sleeping at my feet, I made for the exit, trying hard not to turn back and check if Dahlia was tracking my movements, but the powerful succubus snagged me by the elbow.

"Oh, hello. I didn't expect to see you here. It's been what, six, seven hundred years?"

"I couldn't rightly say," I answered stiffly, defaulting as always to deflection when I couldn't easily answer someone's questions.

She stared into my eyes until I squirmed under her scrutiny. "Hmm. I see. You certainly couldn't, could you . . . Cain? That is what you still go by in this realm, isn't it?" Her ruby lips twisted into a grin as her gaze landed on Asshole before she reached out and patted his head. "My goodness, this disguise certainly is precious. I see you're going for harmless this go round. Smart. Very smart."

Asshole let out a happy yip, tail wagging in delight. He seemed pleased by Lilith's assessment.

Tired of feeling out of the loop, I barked, "I'm sorry, do I know you?"

"Oh, sweetie. We go way back."

This response prompted a little growl—from the man at her side, not the puppy in my arms.

"Not like that, poppet. Don't get your knickers in a knot. Cain and I are just dear friends. He only has eyes for his soulmate, isn't that right?"

"Yes," I growled automatically. Not a second thought for my answer as my gaze went to Dahlia.

What the fuck?

Yanking my arm from Lilith's grip, I grumbled, "If you'll excuse me," as I left the room.

Lilith's voice chased after me. "It's good to see some things never change, Cain."

CHAPTER SEVENTEEN

DAHLIA

Who the fuck is this gorgeous creature, and why the hell does she have her hands on Cain?

Okay, where had *that* come from? Cain could do what he wanted. He hadn't made any declarations unless coming in his pants as he dry humped me counted.

I could practically hear Kiki purring in my ear: *It totally counts.*

She wasn't helpful. I didn't want to hear my truths right now. Not when jealousy burned through me like fire in my veins.

"Who is that?" I whispered as I watched their interaction.

"Lilith Duval, the original demon. Powerful succubus. She's the proprietress of *Iniquity*, a very popular club in London." Kai's palm slid over my nape, his touch soothing me.

"How does she know Cain?"

"How does anyone know Cain?" he countered.

Fair enough.

I was still frowning as my eyes shifted to the ridiculously handsome albeit very scary man standing possessively beside Lilith. He didn't seem any happier about this little reunion than I did. Somehow that made me feel better. Like I wasn't completely irrational. For her part, the redhead, who I'd mentally dubbed Jessica Rabbit due to her insane curves and overt sensuality, didn't seem to be paying attention at all.

I'm not bad. I'm just drawn that way.

I didn't know a thing about the girl, but I was willing to bet that statement was as true for the cartoon as it was for her. There was something about the way she held herself—her ducked chin, the waterfall of ruby-red hair shielding her face, the way she clung to the wrist of one arm as if trying to hide behind herself. It all spoke of someone who was terribly uncomfortable being the center of this kind of attention.

As I watched Cain leave, Kai gripped my nape a little harder, tension radiating off him. I didn't like knowing my mate was uneasy. He was typically a rock.

"Are you okay, dragon boy?"

"I'm . . . Fuck, lass, I'm trying not to be affected by them."

"What do you mean?"

"Can you not feel the power they're putting off?"

It took a moment as I let myself sit in the space, feeling the atmosphere. "What is that?"

Oz groaned and shifted in his seat. "Lust. Bru's break isn't for another hour. Goddammit."

"I thought you were shipping yourself and the new American hottie," Sorcha teased.

"The two things are not mutually exclusive, Blackthorne," he hissed, eyes never leaving the sun-bleached blond who looked like he'd be as at home on a surfboard as he was in that white coat.

"No wonder they sent her here," Kai mused. "A succubus who cannae rein in her lure is potentially lethal. We'd do best to give her a wide berth."

The newcomers continued chatting among themselves as they moved around the room, the doctor's assistant smiling as Lilith nodded in response to whatever he was saying.

"How is Swiftie managing her proximity so well?" Oz asked. "Unless he's a Ken doll?"

"Ken doll?" Kai repeated, not understanding the reference.

"You know, nothing below the waist."

Kai blinked, still not understanding.

"For Christ's sake, he doesn't have a penis," Sorcha blurted.

"The new guy?"

"Ken! Oh my fucking God, do you live under a rock? How do you not know about Ken and Barbie?"

"I've never met either one of them."

Sorcha looked like she was ready to tackle him.

"I'll explain later, Kai. Promise." I rested my palm on his thick thigh and squeezed.

"I don't understand why she's so upset," Kai murmured. "It was just an honest question."

"I know, sweetie."

It was times like these that Kai felt like a dragon out of time. For his inked-up bad-boy exterior, he was still fae and had spent most of his life sheltered from the sort of pop culture references we took for granted.

Oz cast him a dubious look. "You were homeschooled, weren't you?"

"Aye, what does that have to do with it?"

As a cult-schooled person who spent her formative years struggling with agoraphobia and anxiety when forced into the public education system, that one stung. "There's nothing wrong with not knowing about something like this, Oz. Leave him alone."

Oz immediately picked up on the defensive note in my voice and blinked quickly. "Sorry," he murmured.

"Miss Moore? A word, please?" Taylor called, startling me out of the conversation I'd been having.

"Me? Why? What did I do?"

"Nothing," he assured me, a dimple flashing as he smiled. "Dr. Masterson is awake and well enough for visitors. She asked for you."

"Uh, okay. Did she say why?"

"No, only that she needed to see you right away."

"That's not fucking ominous," I muttered.

Kai gave me a reassuring squeeze. "Want me to go with ye?"

"No, it's okay," I said, faking a smile of my own. "I'll be fine. I'll meet up with you after, okay?"

He studied me for a moment before giving me a slow nod. On instinct, my eyes dipped to his neck where the head of his dragon tattoo peeked out of his shirt, those violet eyes pinned on me. Something told me Kai and his dragon were having a bit of a disagreement on the letting me go off on my own front.

In the days since he claimed me, I'd noticed the dragon making an appearance more and more. Not just through the tattoo, but also slipping into his voice. Making demands and declarations that were far more . . . primal than what I was used to.

"Come to me when you're done. I'll be waiting." Kai squeezed my hand, and my heart gave a little flip at the urgency in his tone.

"Promise."

"Don't worry, Dahlia. We'll keep him entertained," Oz teased.

"Oh, I'm sure you will."

I knew I'd already been dismissed when Oz slapped both palms onto the table. "Right, where were we? Sorcha, it's your turn. Try this one . . ."

I'd only been to the medical ward once, back when my period had snuck up on me and I needed to grab supplies. It was located on the east side of the grounds in a separate building, which meant I'd have to cut through the greenhouse unless I wanted to brave this torrential downpour.

The weather here was unpredictable, to say the least. Cold and windy one moment, sunny and sort of warm the next. This storm had come out of nowhere, but that wasn't unusual either. I'm sure if I waited ten to twenty minutes, the weather would change again.

Shivering, I opened the greenhouse door and welcomed the burst of warm, humid air as it hit me in the face. The scent of fresh dirt, fertilizer, and blooming flowers filled the space, and I welcomed the change. I was more of a predictable temperate weather girl, not the four seasons in one day type.

"There you are, Polly. Just settle yerself here on this orchid and put yer feet up, lamb." I recognized that voice. What was her name? Tawny?

Coming around the corner, I found the two female pixies flying from one plant to another. Once they landed, Tawny helped a very pregnant Polly sit down on the petal of a large white orchid. The poor pixie woman could barely move, and I was pretty sure she had to stretch out because her belly was too big for her to sit comfortably. I was no expert on pixie biology, but apparently their gestation periods were way shorter than that of human women. Polly looked near to bursting.

"Are you two okay?" I asked, unsure how I could help.

"Och, Dahlia, aren't you a dear one?" Polly panted. "I'm not okay by any stretch. Damn pixie breeding season. I let those cocksure beasties put their spawn inside me, and now I'm paying the price." She rubbed her swollen middle. "I didn't think all four would catch at the same time."

For a second, I was sure I misheard her. "All four . . ."

Tawny nodded, sparing me a glance before resuming the foot rub she was currently administering. "Jax thought he'd up the chances of success by slipping them a fertility potion. Idiot."

"No wonder we were so insatiable. It was fun at the time. You can go next, Tawny. I doubt my pixie bits will be recovered by the next breeding season."

"How often do you—" I cut myself off, realizing that it was none of my business. "I guess if you're okay here, I'll leave you to it."

"Come by and see us again soon. No one comes into the greenhouse. We miss the gossip," Tawny called as I made my way toward the back door.

The last thing these pixies needed was to get caught up on all the terrible things that had happened. They'd lost their home once already. They didn't need to know how close they were to losing it again.

With a noncommittal wave, I hurried along, eager to get my visit with the doctor over with. It didn't take much longer to reach the healing ward, and just like the first time, I was hit with an overwhelming sense of calm the second I stepped over the threshold. It had to be some sort of sedation spell. It was like Xanax but better because my senses didn't feel muddled.

"Ah, Miss Moore, welcome back. Doctor is waiting to see you," the plucky English healer said as she bustled up to me. "We have her in a private room at the end of the ward. Please feel free to ring if you need anything at all."

"Thank you," I murmured, heading off in the direction she'd indicated. Logically, I knew she wasn't going to look like she had when Dr. Temperance had carried her out after the attack. Magic healing was, well, magic. But there was still a part of me that worried what I would find when I entered her room.

I should have known better than to worry. The room was nothing like any hospital room I'd ever seen. If anything, it was like a cozy bed-and-breakfast. Fireplace crackling in the corner, velvet pillows on the beautifully made bed, the guest of honor sitting up in a stylishly upholstered chair with a thick blanket over her lap. Though honestly, the thing that really set it apart was the lack of beeping machinery.

"Oh, Dahlia, good," she greeted as I stepped inside.

I gave her a quick once-over, relieved that there wasn't a bloody bandage in sight. As I'd assumed, the worst of her injuries had been tended to, and now it seemed she was just making the most of her recuperation in a peaceful environment.

"You look like you're on a holiday," I blurted, like an absolute fucking idiot.

Blackwood's chief administrator smiled at me. "I suppose in many ways I am. Won't you take a seat and join me," she said, gesturing to the plush ottoman in front of her chair. "Tea?" she asked, reaching for the small pot on the side table next to her.

"I'm good. Thanks."

She shrugged. "Suit yourself. Nurse Hatchet makes a brilliant cuppa."

"Why did you want to see me?" I asked, trying to get to the point. I wanted to be with Kai, helping Tor find his way back to me and making sure Cain was nice to Asshole. I really didn't want to be here where I knew she'd make me hold myself accountable like she always did.

Her knowing gaze held mine. "Why do *you* think I asked to see you?"

"Is this a therapist trick? Turning everything back on me and forcing me to be introspective?"

"Indulge me. I did just narrowly escape death, you know," she said with a small grin.

"You're not playing fair."

"That's why I usually win."

"I think your doctor buddy reported that I'm not going to my sessions with him."

She tapped her index finger to her nose. "Right on the money." Then she leveled me with another of those all-seeing stares. "And why is that, Dahlia? We were making such great progress. Don't you want to continue that?"

"That's exactly why. *We* were making great progress. You and me. Now I have to start all over with a stranger. He doesn't know my history."

"Yes he does. You know I record all our sessions and take copious notes. Nate knows everything I do."

That made me squirm. "Is that ethical? Aren't I entitled to doctor-patient confidentiality or something?"

"He was your doctor first. And technically those sorts of rules go out the window once someone is admitted to Blackwood."

"That's just great."

"Sarcasm? Not your usual weapon of self-defense."

It really wasn't. I knew someone else who used it, though, and his name started with a C. Well, shit, both of their names started with a C. Were those two rubbing off on me?

Not yet, but you wish they were.

As always, it was Kiki's voice echoing in my mind.

Feeling vulnerable, I dropped my eyes down to the sleeve of my shirt, intently playing with the left cuff like it might save me somehow. "I just feel safe with you, I guess. And that's really rare for me. In such a short time, you've helped me recover bits of my past and come to terms with parts of myself that made me feel broken. You've introduced me to this whole other side of my life I didn't even know existed. Dr. Temperance is the guy I woke up to after one of the scariest nights of my life, who sent me halfway across the globe. It's just not the same."

She reached out and touched my hand. "I understand. It's not easy to be vulnerable, least of all with a stranger. I'm sensing men are a trigger for you, and I should have been more cognizant of that."

I had never thought of it in that sense, but as I reflected on it, the truth was impossible to ignore. Which was sort of funny because, with certain men, I felt undeniably safe. Maybe it was just men in positions of authority. Men like my father?

"I was making progress with you. Figuring out my power, learning how to control it. Now I feel like I've gone backward."

She hummed as she considered my words. "Perhaps we can continue our sessions if you come to visit me here? Just don't tell the staff. I'll clear it with Dr. Temperance."

"Are you sure you don't mind?"

"Not at all. It's my life's calling to help people. You'd be doing me a favor."

"Okay, then. I think I'd like that."

"Excellent. We'll reconvene tomorrow morning."

I'd never been a person who sought out therapy—hell, before Blackwood, I'd never sought out human interaction aside from with Kiki—but having this plan in the midst of everything else going on helped me feel settled. I needed to focus on my own swirling thoughts, my abilities, and the hauntings. As much as I wanted my mates, I needed to remember why I was here in the first place.

CHAPTER EIGHTEEN

TOR

Twenty-four hours had passed since I last saw another living being. If it hadn't been for the food trays that were shoved through the slot in the door at regular intervals, I would've thought I'd been left for dead. Monster that I was, I wouldn't blame them. But I couldn't die. Not without getting to her. Dahlia. My mate.

I knew my plan was working as soon as they brought her to me. The point was only emphasized when the feedings resumed. I'd continue playing the tame beastie so long as it got me out of this cell. But once she was back in my arms, all bets were off.

The steady tick, tick, tick of the clock high on the wall seemed to taunt me. Each second passing by reminded me of time I was missing with her. I had to get out of here. I had a strong feeling I could break free if I really tried.

Breaking free was only half the problem, though, because I wasn't leaving without her. And there was no way they'd sit idly by when I took her with me.

So . . . the games.

It went against almost every cell in my body to pretend that they'd won. That I'd been bested. But she was worth it.

"Mr. Nordson, I see you're still awake and going strong. Forgive the silence, but we needed to ensure you weren't going to attempt something drastic like a breakout." The doctor stood at the glass, and I made a point to take in every detail to find a weakness I might be able to exploit. His collar was undone, glasses perched on his nose, hair mussed. He looked like he'd spent the night wide awake as well. Good. If he was tired, he was weak. Weaklings were easier to dispatch. I could get him in a vulnerable position and get to my mate. If he survived, bully for him. If not, he was a casualty of war.

Who was I kidding? He would never survive.

The Beast didn't do survivors. Only victims.

It was the proper order of things.

"Where. Is. She?" I growled, unblinking as I stared at him through the greasy strands of my hair.

"Miss Moore?"

I nodded once, slowly.

"She's somewhere on the grounds. I can assure you she's quite looked after."

By that fucking dragon who wanted her. Rage burned in my blood at the thought, but I forced myself not to act. If I killed him now, I wouldn't get what I wanted.

"You don't like that, do you? That your mate is with another man?"

I snarled, getting to my feet and stalking up to the glass. The sniveling little man took a step back.

"Careful, Viking. I may not be as large as you, but I assure you, I have my own arsenal of defense."

I bared my teeth at him, unimpressed by his threat.

Men who needed words to inspire fear would never be a threat to me.

All I needed to do was rip out their tongues.

One lift of my brow was enough to send most screaming. Or pissing themselves. That was my favorite.

I smiled at the thought. I was a much better monster than this *doctor*.

He must have sensed it too, because he took a step back from the glass. “I’m here to help you, Tor. I want you to be with her just as much as you do.”

Doubtful.

“Let me do my job. Your curse may keep you in this form, but your mind can still be saved. I see the humanity in you, just there, under the surface.”

Taking a deep breath, I balled my hands into fists and stared him down, knowing what needed to be done.

“Good. Your restraint is very promising for what I have planned. Do you think you can maintain it long enough for us to try something?”

I grunted.

“I’m going to take that as a yes. It’s my assertion, well, Lizzie’s actually. She’s the one who gave me the idea, but then that’s neither here nor there, I suppose.” He cleared his throat. “It’s my belief that if I can help you recapture your foundational memories, it may help you restore a connection to your true self. Or rather, your human self.”

“Novasgardian,” I growled.

He cleared his throat again. “Apologies. My mistake. I’m unfamiliar with . . .”

“Novasgard.”

“Yes, Novasgard. It must be another realm, yes?”

I nodded, a twinge in my chest making me long for the clean, crisp air of home.

“All right. That’s good. It’s your home. The place you spent your formative years. Memories were made there. We can latch on to that.” Feeling more confident, he took a step closer. “You have to be willing to participate in this if we’re going to be successful, Tor.

Especially since we're going to have a literal wall between us. If this goes well, perhaps next time we can see about a change of scenery, but for now, this is our safest option."

I blinked at him, not caring for his ramblings.

"Make yourself as comfortable as you can, then we will begin."

I glanced around the cell. Stone. Stone. More stone. There wasn't a comfortable option. So I went to the corner where I'd been passing my time and settled there.

"Close your eyes, breathe in deeply, then exhale. Do this until your pulse slows."

I held his stare, not trusting him enough to close my eyes in his presence.

The doctor blew out a frustrated breath. "Okay, let's try it this way. Match your breathing to mine. In"—he sucked in a large breath—"out." He exhaled noisily.

I followed along. He wasn't going to hurt me. The man was like an eager puppy. Desperate to please and do a good job.

My only option was to play along. So I did.

Besides, he couldn't hurt me more than they already had by keeping me from Dahlia.

"Picture yourself back in Novasgard. How does it smell?"

I could just grasp the memory. A snowy night with the Aurora dancing in the sky, the briny scent of the sea melding with snow.

"Ocean. Snowfall. Clean." My words weren't as gruff when I uttered them, and he continued.

"Snow? Is it winter? Are you cold, Tor?"

"Yes, but Faðir lent me his cloak. It smells like him."

"Excellent. And can you pick up anything specific about his scent?"

"Leather. Storm."

It was harder to put into words the things that came to mind when I thought of my sire. The feelings were too complicated. Love, yes. But also grief and maybe a bit of shame.

I let out a rumbling sound that could have been a whine or a whimper.

"I want you to hold on to that. Let it fill your chest as you take your next breaths. And as you do, I want you to relax your mind. Focus only on your father. Everything else besides my voice can drop away."

Shivering as the remnants of the Novasgardian winter from my past chilled me to the bone, I heard the crunch of my boots in the snow and the waves crashing on the shore.

"Tell me more about Novasgard. Why did you leave?" the doctor asked.

"My brother."

"What about him?"

"He played a trick."

"How did that make you feel?"

A growl was the only verbal response I could give as betrayal and sorrow cut at me. Before I could answer him in any further way, my memory crashed over me like a rogue wave, taking me under.

Novasgard
Two years earlier

My father's large palm clamped onto my shoulder, and it was only years of training that kept me from shrugging it off.

"I know you're angry, mín sønn."

"Angry? Faðir, he took my place."

"You heard what Cora said. Fate is calling your brother there."

"And what of my fate?" I exploded, rounding on him. "How am I to prove myself now? Ravenscroft was my destiny. I am the one supposed to follow in your footsteps. Not Alek. For years I have shadowed you, taking on the responsibilities required to one day take your place. Alek fucked around at every opportunity, and now he gets rewarded? He gets to usurp me without so much as a conversation?"

"It is clear that while we thought your place was at Ravenscroft, it is indeed elsewhere. You are destined for something different."

Disappointment curled in my gut, hot and heavy. Alek didn't deserve this honor. He wasn't the heir, wasn't worthy of the trust needed to represent Novasgard. I had worked my whole life to make my family and my people proud, and this was the thanks I got?

"Calm yourself, Tor. You may not be a Berserker, but your temper is just as hot as your mother's. Don't let it get the better of you."

"What else am I supposed to feel? Grateful? He betrayed me."

"He did not. It is not a betrayal to go where fate leads."

"It is when he robs me of my fate to do it!" I roared, my body shaking with the intensity of my roiling emotions.

"Your fate cannot be stolen! Have I taught you nothing?" His voice echoed off the cliffs, causing a small avalanche to roll into the sea below.

"I am lost, Faðir. I have no purpose."

His eyes, the same color as the glaciers to the north, softened as they held mine. "Your purpose will find you."

"When?"

"When you're ready."

"And what am I supposed to do in the meantime? Molder here in my childhood room while my twin goes off on *my* grand adventure? Babysit my little sister? Act as Strega's training dummy?"

He laughed. The gall of my father to laugh at my misfortune. "Firstly, Astrid needs no babysitter, and Strega has plenty of willing volunteers if she requires live target practice. You will stay until you are called by your true purpose, Tor. Fate always finds a way. Trust in me if you cannot trust in that."

My father, my hero, the man I aspired to be . . . I would trust him with my dying breath. There was nothing I would not do for the man who gave me life. He could lead me straight into the depths of the underworld, and I would follow him willingly. He was Odin's chosen warrior; I'd have to be an utter fool not to.

"Fine. I trust in you and in fate. I just hope I don't have to wait long to seek my own glory."

"Don't be in such a hurry, mín sønn. Glory always comes at a price, and you can only hope it's one you're willing to pay."

CHAPTER NINETEEN

KAI

Family day. The bane of my internment at Blackwood. Or at least it had been before I had someone to fill the time with. They did this once per month and trotted us all out as though we were well-adjusted and fully in control. Proof that our families' money was being put to good use. Or, in the cases of those who were here to fulfill council-imposed sentences, that the treatments were working and we may one day be reintroduced into society.

It was a dog and pony show, no matter which way you looked at it.

My own family wasn't even allowed to see me as my father's dragon put me at risk of losing control. Or so they said.

So imagine my surprise when, for the first time in my year-long tenure, I received a summons to the family room. My heart leapt at the thought of getting to see my mum. They didn't even let me send correspondence home more than once every few months. Something about not having proven myself. It was an absolute crock of shit. I was arguably the most in control of anyone here, seeing that my dragon was safely tucked away.

Or he had been. Before Dahlia showed up and weakened the barrier between us. But no one else knew that save Dr. Masterson, and even that was mere assumption.

Turning down the hall that led to the family room, I straightened my shirt and ran a hand through my hair, a nervous flutter in my belly. Would mum want to meet my mate? How would she take learning Dahlia had more than one of us?

As I stepped through the open doorway, my eyes scanned the clusters of people milling about the room. Of course, Dahlia caught my attention before anyone else, standing there in a pair of butter-soft leggings and a too-big jumper that had an illustration of a woman bent over a desk while reading. The text said *I look better bent over a book.*

Yes, you do, little mate. But you look even better impaled on my cock.

I couldn't disagree with my dragon's assertion. But I could be annoyed by the rock-hard length currently tenting my trousers. I did not need to be hard when greeting my mum for the first time in over a year.

Dahlia's gaze lit on mine, and a sweet smile curled her lips. I couldn't resist; I was a moth drawn to the flame that was my mate, so I shifted course and headed for her. Just a kiss to tide me over before I got her alone this evening.

Before I had a chance to even greet her, a tornado of a woman flung herself at me.

"Ooh, he is strong. God, I think I could live here."

"Keeks," Dahlia groaned.

The tornado, who I now recognized as Kiki, released me and stepped back, one hand still squeezing my bicep. "Sorry, handsome. I just wanted to know what it felt like to be wrapped up in all those muscles. For science."

"I remember you. The editor, right?" I asked, bemused.

"That's me. When I got the email invite last week, I couldn't pass up the chance to check in on my sweet little smut purveyor. Whatever you're doing is working. She looks so much . . . brighter."

My attention turned to the woman in question, her cheeks pink as she tried and failed to hide her discomfort. "She's been working hard on a lot of things. The least of which is learning more about who she is and what she needs."

"I guess there's more to therapy than I wanted to admit," Dahlia said. "Even supernatural therapy."

Kiki ran an affectionate hand over Dahlia's head. "I'm just so proud of you. Sitting here in a crowded room, being able to carry on a conversation without looking like you're ready to bolt, or worse, puke. You've come so far in such a short time."

"Something about being here settles me. Even if I can't hide from the ghosts." Her fingers played at her collarbone as if searching for a necklace.

I took her hand. "It's being near your mates, lass. We're all better for it."

Kiki sighed. "Swoon. Can you find me one of him, please? Maybe a wolfy version?"

"I'm not sure you want to set your sights on any of Blackwood's residents."

"Why not? You did and totally hit the jackpot." Kiki's focus shifted to something behind me, and if I wasn't mistaken, a drop of drool escaped her now open mouth. "Oh. My. God. What about one of those?"

Turning around, I watched in utter shock as two fae warriors entered the room. Two fae warriors I knew. The Shadow Queen's consorts, Jensen and Finn.

As soon as the thought registered, my heart dropped. They were the reason I'd been invited today, not because my parents were finally allowed to visit. Disappointment hit me hard and fast, followed by a tide of potentially misplaced anger.

I didn't yet know why the fae warriors were here, but they were about to regret coming.

"Excuse me, ladies." I dropped a soft kiss on Dahlia's forehead before taking my leave and heading toward the two men I really didn't want to see.

"Does he know them? Do you think he could slip the broody one my number?" I overheard Kiki whisper-shout.

She was barking up the wrong tree, but that wasn't my concern at the moment.

As I approached, Jensen pinned me with his deep hazel stare. I've heard him described as beautiful, but rugged and deadly came to mind when I looked at the broad-shouldered fae warrior. His dark hair curled just under his ears, and he was sporting a new scar on his cheek. I wondered what had caused that. Was there more unrest within the Shadow Court?

"Malakai," he rumbled, brooking no room for a misunderstanding of who he was here to visit. "You're looking strong."

"I feel it, Commander."

"I've told you before, call me Jensen. Your father did us a great service, and now so too shall you."

"The difference between my father and me is that my dragon cannae be trusted."

The huff of dissent in my head was so loud I momentarily wondered if the beast in question had managed to take control of my vocal cords again.

Finn took me by the shoulder in a brotherly fashion I knew better than to trust. He was trying to disarm me. "That's the entire reason you're here. What you're supposed to be working toward."

"No. I'm here to prevent the needless death of more innocents."

Jensen let out a disbelieving laugh. "You are a fool if you think that is the reason you're here. Allow me to remind you of your duty to your queen and court. Your father would be ashamed to know you've abandoned his legacy out of fear."

"Jensen," Finn admonished.

"No, Finn. He needs to understand. Our queen is with child again. *Your* child. Why would you sit by and allow him to waste precious time we don't have?"

"Because unlike you, I've learned that you get more with honey than vinegar."

"Vinegar gets the job done faster and more efficiently."

"Maybe when you're cleaning up dog mess, but not when you're trying to win someone over to your side."

"Did you just compare me to a pile of dog shit?" I asked, brows lifting high.

Jensen rolled his eyes. "I see your ego is the same as Valor's as well."

"Do you have news of my father?" My heart squeezed knowing he'd been separated from Mum because of my own weakness.

"He is suffering without his mate."

My stomach churned at the thought of being parted from Dahlia.

Never.

My dragon's roar within my mind made me stiffen, and this time when he pushed against the ward between us, it hurt.

"What just happened there? Your eyes." Finn stepped closer, leveling his stare at me.

"I'm mated. My dragon didn't like the idea of not being with her."

Jensen and Finn exchanged looks of shock before both breaking out into felicitations.

"Congratulations, Kai! That's wonderful news."

"Where is the lucky lady?" Finn asked, looking around the room as if he could pluck Dahlia out of the crowd by will alone.

The last thing I wanted was for Dahlia to undergo their inquisition. She wasn't fae. They would be less likely to accept her.

"Actually, I have a question for you. Since the two of you are practically my uncles, and I have no one else I can talk to about something as complicated as this . . ."

"Go on," Jensen said, smirking.

"How do you manage? Your arrangement."

"Our arrangement?"

"You know. Multiple partners. Sharing."

"Are you asking for a play-by-play?" Jensen asked with a raised brow.

"No. Goddess, no, I don't need those mental images. I meant more on the 'not wanting to murder each other' side."

"What do you mean?" Finn asked.

I huffed out a breath, realizing I was just going to have to spit it out. "I've claimed her as mine, but she's also mated to another. Both of us are alpha males, and we nearly burned down the castle because of it."

"He's a dragon as well?"

"No. He's the Beast of Novasgard."

Finn paled. "Alek Nordson is here?"

"Alek? No. His twin brother. Tor."

"His . . . twin . . ." Finn repeated, looking like he was about to become ill.

"Finbar? You all right, mate?" Jensen asked.

"I think I may have made a mistake."

"What do you mean?"

Finn turned to Jensen. "I laid down a terrible curse after the events at the Farrell ranch. Someone had to pay. The Shadow Court warriors deserved justice."

"No. You didn't."

"I cursed the wrong Viking."

Dahlia's voice rang out from behind me. "You did what?"

CHAPTER TWENTY

DAHLIA

"C'mon, Dee. Just a wee introduction."

"Wee? Are you British now?" Kiki pouted at my teasing, but just like she held a mirror up for me when needed, I did the same for her.

"When in Rome."

"This is Scotland," I groused as she tugged me closer to Kai and his two visitors.

"Och, aye. You're wasting precious time. Do you *see* them?"

I did. I also saw the wedding bands on their left hands. Were they married to each other? I didn't hate that idea.

"I don't think they're single, Keeks."

"You are such a thief of joy. Come. On."

Sighing, I gave in and allowed her to lead me over to the small group. We were just about in touching distance when the world dropped out from beneath me.

"I cursed the wrong Viking," the tawny-haired man said.

"You did what? You're the one responsible for ruining Tor's life?" I fumed as I closed the distance between me and the stupidly handsome man, ready to knock his fucking teeth out.

I was absolutely aware that I had no chance in hell in an honest to God brawl with the man, but that wasn't about to stop me. I'd get some shots in before he knocked me out, and that would be worth it. Maybe a few scratches and spilled blood. That's all I needed.

Kai's arm was a steel bar around my waist, hauling me back against him as I lunged.

"Let go of me, you bossy dragon." I fought his hold, but it was useless. The man was stronger than me in pretty much every way.

"Nae, lass. If ye know what's good for you, you'll pipe down and let me handle this."

"What about me makes you think that's going to fly in any universe, Kai? I'm not the fainting damsel. Now let me go!"

"This must be your little mate," the other man said, his lips twisting into an amused smirk.

"Oh shit. Wrong move, handsome," Kiki offered, her voice low.

I saw red, and with a renewed sense of urgency, I struggled in Kai's hold. His grip slipped just enough that I was able to bend my knees and duck under his arm. I didn't make it far. He caught the back of my shirt and reeled me into his chest before I could make contact. But the slight widening of the fae warrior's eyes filled me with pride.

For a second, I'd made him see me, the bridge troll writer, as an actual threat.

It felt pretty damn amazing.

"She's fiery."

"She's human, Finn. Of course she's fiery. Remember the hell Maeve put us through?"

"Maeve isn't human."

"She thought she was."

"Are you two done?" I asked, demanding the attention of the two fae men. "You are going to reverse your stupid curse. Right fucking now."

"I can't." Finn's eyes flicked away from me and to Kai. "It's not possible."

"What do you mean? It's always possible. Every curse can be broken. That's how fairytales work, asshole." I struggled against Kai again, but he held me fast.

"Those are stories. This is real life," Finn said, his voice gentle as he delivered crushing news. As if somehow the words would hurt less this way.

"So there truly is no way to bring him back?" Kai asked.

"I'm sorry, Kai, I . . ."

Jensen placed his hand on his friend's shoulder, cutting off his attempt at an apology. "There may not be anything *we* can do. But when it comes to mates, anything is possible. It's in fate's hands now."

"Fate? As far as I'm concerned, she's a real see you next Tuesday," I grumbled.

"Don't be like that, gem. Fate brought us together." Kai's lips were at my ear as he continued, "And I'd be an arse if I spit in the face of that. Don't you agree?"

As much as I wanted to agree with him, fate had handed me a real shit sandwich. First with my cult-leader dad and crappy upbringing. Then the whole being haunted by ghosts thing. My never-ending list of trauma and triggers. And now the chaos of having not one, but two—and likely more—mates, one of whom was cursed. Frankly, I hated the bitch. She could take her help and shove it where the sun don't shine.

"She doesn't hide her feelings well, does she?" Jensen asked, casting a dubious stare my way.

"Dahlia lacks the poker face gene. Me, on the other hand, I can fake it so well you'd never know." Kiki's comment had me laughing lightly, which I knew was on purpose. "So . . . are you two like . . . together? Is there room for one more in the middle? I could be on the outside too, I don't mind. I'm *super* flexible."

"Kiki . . ." I admonished, but there was no heat to it. I was pretty impressed she managed to use such a tense moment to shoot her shot.

"What is she doing?" Kai whispered.

"I'm redirecting this Titanic-sized shipwreck, obviously."

Jensen shook his head. "We are both spoken for and loyal only to our queen."

"Bummer."

Kai squeezed me gently and pressed a kiss to my neck. "Go on, gem. Be with your friend. Don't waste her visit on a pair of fae warriors who cannae turn back time. We'll find another way to help Tor."

I hated that I couldn't fix it right fucking now. Knowing Tor's curse was a mistake made it even worse somehow. He didn't deserve anything that was happening to him, and it broke my heart.

"I swear to you, my lady, if I find a way to break the curse I laid upon him, I will." Finn dipped his head in a courtly bow, and I swear Kiki swooned.

"He's married," I hissed.

"I don't care. I'm just window shopping."

Kai released me, and I hooked my arm through Kiki's. "Let's go see what other kinds of trouble we can find."

"Oh! Can I meet the pregnant pixie? That sounds like a whole adventure."

I laughed. "Sure. The greenhouse isn't off limits. Come on."

AWARE that my time with my best friend was nearly out, I ran down the stairs—okay, jogged. I jogged down the stairs. Okay, fine, I mostly fell down the stairs, but no one was watching, so it doesn't count.

I could have emailed the new chapters over, but there was something so satisfying about being able to plop the fat stack of paper into her hand. Kiki loved to redline anything she could with an actual red pen. Yes, she kept one in her purse at all times. This would be exactly what she needed on the plane ride home.

I skidded to a stop as I rounded the corner that led to the foyer and found her standing with her back to the wall and a ruggedly handsome scoundrel—read: sneaky fucking pirate—leaning over her, one arm resting above her head as she stared into his eyes.

"Oh no, you don't," I growled before storming the rest of the way over to them.

Without preamble, I shoved him to the side.

"What the bloody hell are you doing?" he asked, feigning being wounded.

"What the hell are *you* doing? My best friend, Caspian? Really? Is one adoring fan club not enough for you?" Before he could respond, I turned wild eyes to Kiki. "He didn't blow any dust in your face, did he?"

"Do you really think so little of me?" If I didn't know better, I'd say he was hurt by my suggestion.

"Yes."

"Here I thought you were a sweet treat, but it turns out you've got a bitter side."

"Bitter? You're calling me bitter, Cas? You. Ruined. Everything."

Kiki's eyes were wide as she watched us fight. "I'm equal parts afraid for what's about to happen and turned on."

"You just won't let that go, will you? You're as bad as the rest of them. No, Caspian, don't steal the treasure from the lost boys. No, Caspian, you can't commandeer this ship simply because it's unmanned. No, Caspian, you can't have any fun at all."

"Fun? Cas, you got a bunch of people killed in a riot you initiated and all but pulled the gun on Tor."

"There was no gun, Dahlia."

"Metaphorical gun. As in you are the reason he's currently locked up and falling victim to his curse."

His shoulders slumped. "I don't know how to fix this."

"You can't. Now get out of here. Leave my friend alone and stay out of my life."

"Out of your—"

"You heard me."

For the span of a single breath, I regretted my words, but only because of the shattered look in his eyes. I'd never seen Caspian so vulnerable. Hell, I didn't even know he could be vulnerable. But just as quickly as it disappeared, the mask slammed back into place. His shoulders straightened, and he let out a shuddering breath before raking his fingers through that thick, golden hair.

"Women. So touchy. I'd say it's been a pleasure, Keeks, but . . ." He offered her a dramatic bow before turning and walking away, putting as much swagger in his step as he could.

"So that was the pirate," she mused as she watched him leave.

"That was the pirate."

"Oof."

"Yup."

"You know he's in love with you, right?" she asked, pinning me with eyes that saw far too much.

"He doesn't love anyone but himself."

"So is that one," she murmured, ignoring my protest completely as she jutted her chin toward something behind me. God, what now?

Before I could turn around, a little yip announced Asshole's arrival, followed by his tiny paws on my calf as he begged for me to pick him up. I scooped the dog into my arms and finally followed Kiki's gaze.

"That man could drag me to hell and I'd go willingly," she whispered, taking in Cain's tall form as he watched us from the shadows at the end of the hall.

"Careful, knowing the people who come here, he just might."

"So what's his story?"

"What do you mean?"

"Well, the pirate betrayed you, so he's got an epic grovel to plan before you let him dick you down. Tor is locked up, and you're plotting his jailbreak so you can dick *him* down."

"Keeks . . . that's not how that works."

She raised a hand. "Just go with it."

I sighed but nodded, knowing the only way out of this conversation was through.

"And then with the dragon, I mean . . . he's dragon dicking you down regularly. As he should." She waved her hand at me again, this time silently requesting a high five which I begrudgingly gave her. "So . . . how about Mister tall, dark, and deadly over there?"

"He hates me. I think?"

"You think?"

"He's so hot and cold. Most of the time I think he hates me, but then he comes in and dry humps me until he comes all over himself. I'm just . . . he's a conundrum."

"Ah, the holdout. He's in denial. Don't worry, he'll come around. No one can resist temptation forever. And you, my darling Dahlia, are the sexiest little cookie on the platter."

"I hate you," I grumbled, completely unable to hide my blush or my smile.

"Well, I love you."

The beep of a car horn from outside pulled her attention from me. "That's me. I have to get going."

"Okay. I still can't believe you came all the way out here for such a short time."

She pulled me into a tight hug, Asshole between us and wriggling in my arms. "Like I said, I love you. Let me know when you walk that pirate's plank. The broody hottie too. There's something to be said for hate sex."

"Why would I bother with hate sex when I could have *love* sex? With my mates, plural?"

I thought it was a brilliant point well made. But Kiki proved that she'd get the last word. As usual.

"Why settle for chocolate cake when you can have the whole dessert bar?" she countered, tossing up one hand in a wave as she walked away. My gut twisted when she called down the hall, "Hey, sexy shadow daddy! You're wasting valuable time being all grumpy. You'll never find better than this woman right here. Not in a million years."

I'd deny it in a court of law, but in that moment, I would have sworn I heard Cain's uttered, "Don't I know it."

SESSION TRANSCRIPT: NOVEMBER 28TH

Dr. Temperance: This is Dr. Nathaniel Temperance, standing in for Dr. Elizabeth Masterson. The date is November twenty-eighth at . . . eleven-oh-two a.m.

Cain: Well done, Doc. Much smoother dismount this time around.

Hook: *snickers*

Dahlia: Asshole.

<<dog barks>>

Dahlia: Sorry, not you, sweet boy.

Hook: So you are talking to me. Lovely. I knew you couldn't stay away for long.

<<beat of silence>>

<<rustling of clothes>>

Merri: You named your dog Asshole?

Cain: He's not hers. He's my dog.

Merri: Then why is he sitting in her lap?

Cain: *grumbled* Because he's a fucking traitor.

Kai: Are ye going to reel this in at any point, Doctor? Or is this just a free-for-all?

Dr. Temperance: *clears throat* Right, let's all welcome our newest group member, shall we? Miss Meredith Deveraux, all the way from America by way of London. How are you settling in, Meredith?

Merri: My name is Merri. No one calls me Meredith unless I'm in trouble.

Hook: Oh, darling, you are trouble.

<<clothes rustle>>

<<chair creak>>

Hook: You don't like it when I call her that, do you, Dahlia? You can't have it both ways. You can't tell me to stay out of your life but get mad when I give other women my attention.

Kai: That's enough, Caspian.

Merri: *whispered* I didn't mean to get between the two of you.

Dahlia: You didn't, trust me. There's nothing to get between.

Hook: Liar.

Merri: This sort of thing happens to me a lot. I'm a bit of a magnet for toxic men. I don't mean to be.

Dahlia: Well, he's all yours if you want him.

Hook: *gasps* I beg your pardon? I'm not some bit of chattel to be sold off because you're bored with me.

Kai: Dr. Temperance. Seriously. Are ye leading this session or not?

Cain: I believe the answer you're searching for is . . . not.

<<chair scrapes across the floor>>

Cain: If it's all the same to you, I have hours of staring at the ceiling ahead of me, and that's far more interesting than listening to the two of you.

Dr. Temperance: Sit down, Cain. This session isn't over.

Cain: Oh? Does that mean you're actually going to attempt to be a doctor now? Or are you still playing at being a substitute teacher, letting your class run roughshod all over you?

<<pocket watch clicks open and closed repetitively>>

Dr. Temperance: I'll thank you to let me be the judge of how this session progresses. My style may differ from Lizzie's, but that doesn't make it less effective.

Kai: How can ye possibly think this is at all a productive use of our time?

Dr. Temperance: Well, in the handful of minutes we've been sitting here, I've learned that four people in this room are entangled much deeper than they're willing to admit. Two of whom are currently on the outs, another who is clearly in denial, and the fourth who feels a compulsive need to control the situation. Hook employs indifference as a defense mechanism, while Cain prefers avoidance. Oh, and Merri carries a heavy sense of guilt over simply existing.

Merri: Harsh, but not inaccurate.

<<silence>>

Dr. Temperance: Did I miss anything?

Dahlia: Just my crippling social anxiety.

Dr. Temperance: No, I clocked that the moment I met you.

Dahlia: Okay, then.

<<pocket watch clicks open and closed repetitively>>

Dr. Temperance: Right, shall we carry on? Brilliant. Let's discuss this week's homework.

<<static>>

End of transcript.

CHAPTER TWENTY-ONE

CAIN

"Stop looking at me like that," I groused as I paced back and forth beside my bed.

Asshole gave me a little yip, which I translated as *"You're the one lookin' at me."*

Did I give my dog's fake voice a Brooklyn accent? Yes. Yes, I did.

"I don't always have to go to her. If Dahlia wants to see me, she can damn well come find me."

My dog's head tilted as he stared at me, then he huffed, turned in a circle, and plopped down on the nest of pillows I'd made into a bed for him.

This I interpreted as *"Sure, buddy. Keep telling yourself that."*

"You are a real pain in my ass. You know that? She isn't a fucking princess. You might be caught in her web, but I can see she's trouble. I have since the day I got here."

Asshole continued to pant, his tongue hanging out the side of his mouth. His ears pricked and he sat up a little straighter, then yawned before settling again. *"You're just mad because you're on the outs. I get to be in her lap whenever I want while she says how handsome I am. Who's the loser in this situation?"*

"You sure are mouthy for something that isn't even seven pounds dripping wet," I muttered, fully aware I was the one insulting myself.

And no, that didn't make me crazy. I considered this one of Dr. Masterson's exercises. Holding a mirror up to my shadow self, or whatever the fuck she called it.

"Fine. Fine, okay? I'll go get her. It's not like I can't control myself around her anyway. I'll just go to her room, stay off her fucking bed, and we can do these stupid tasks Doc assigned us."

Asshole stood, prancing in place excitedly. *"Now you're talking sense."* Instead of pawing at the door like he usually did, he froze in front of my desk, staring intently at the tin of treats I kept there. *"Now give me a fucking treat for being a good boy and helping you work through your issues."*

Sighing, I opened the tin and plucked out one of the artisanal dog treats I'd convinced the cook to make for him.

"Sit," I said.

Asshole looked at me like I'd just asked him to moonwalk.

"Sit."

An indignant huff left him. *"Fucking prick."* His voice in my mind was unamused.

"Asshole, sit."

Instead of sitting, he peed while he stared me down.

"I'm going to shave you bald, you little shit. Then we'll see how cute she thinks you are when you look more like a naked mole rat than a dog."

He jumped up, stole the treat from my hand, and sprinted to the far side of the room. *"Try it. I fuckin' dare you."*

His sharp little barks were like taunts as he scrambled up onto my bed while I cleaned up the piss and grumbled to myself.

I'd just finished washing my hands when a knock sounded on my door.

"Fuck off," I shouted, still annoyed at the bundle of fur happily drooling all over my pillow.

"Um . . . aren't we supposed to be working together?" Dahlia's tentative voice came through the door.

I hung my head. Fuck.

"Yeah, dammit. Hang on."

I gave myself a once-over in the mirror, running my fingers through my hair so it would be artfully tousled. Why did I care what I looked like? She knew exactly what she'd find. A moody prick with a chip on his shoulder who didn't want to touch her with a ten-foot pole.

Asshole's mocking laughter floated through my mind. *"You are such a godsdamned pussy-whipped liar."*

"You shut your mouth when you're talking to me."

"Seeing as that's exactly how this imaginary conversation is going . . ."

"Cain? Do you have company? Who are you talking to? I can come back."

I flung the door open. "Just Asshole."

Her eyes shifted behind me to where the pup was lounging like a damn prince. "Do you uh . . . always talk to him like that?"

I shrugged. "I was testing something out."

"Uh-huh," she said, clearly not believing me. "Does he . . . talk back?"

"No."

Asshole harrumphed, and I glared at him.

"Okay. Well, we don't have to drag this out. I just figured since you seem to want to avoid me like the plague, I'd better extend the olive branch."

"I don't like olives."

She huffed, eyes rolling. "You know what I mean. God, why are you so contrary? Do you do it on purpose to piss me off?'

"You sure think highly of yourself, don't you?"

"Me?" she sputtered.

"I mean, you're over there thinking I've designed an entire personality based on your existence, so yeah. You." I reached out and poked her in the chest, fighting a smirk as she took one tiny step backward.

The fire in her eyes was so enticing. She liked this game we played. "Are we going to stand here all day? If you don't want to do the exercises, that's fine. I have plenty of other things I could be doing."

"Like what?"

Before she could answer, Kai's name raced through my mind, followed by Tor's. She had lots of options to occupy her. The least of which was me.

A distant part of my mind registered that Hook was still on the outs with her. I took entirely too much pleasure from the reminder. At least I wasn't the only one on the sidelines.

Dahlia swept into the room, brushing past me.

"Sure, make yourself at home," I mocked, borrowing her line as I closed the door behind her.

"Thanks, I will." She didn't even glance my way as she perused the sparsely filled room.

Her fingers trailed over the spines of the handful of books I'd pilfered from the library, stopping when she found one of interest.

"Oh, *The Claiming of Sleeping Beauty*? That's one I read way too young."

"Oh? Had an extensive book collection on the cult grounds, did you?"

This earned me another glare. "No. I found it at the library. You know, where the books live."

"They let you check out a book like this one?"

"Nope. It was one of the only places I could go and be comfortable, no matter which foster home I was in. I'd snag a book and curl up in a secluded chair for some escapism. It's how I fell in love with the written word and where I decided writing romance was my calling."

"Reading and writing aren't exactly the same. How'd you know you'd be any good at it?"

She turned to face me, her hands on her hips. "Calculated risk."

"You don't seem like much of a risk taker, baby doll."

"And you don't seem like a guy who'd give his pillow to a tiny puppy, but here we are."

Asshole yipped, and I knew it was in protest of her description. Without prompting, that same rough-and-tumble voice from earlier floated through my mind. *"Who you callin' tiny, sweet cheeks?"*

She moved on, picking up the knickknacks I'd left scattered about, touching my discarded button-down shirt from yesterday where it lay draped on the back of my chair. Why the hell did my skin tingle as her fingers brushed the fabric?

"You're kind of messy," she murmured.

"And you're nosey."

I couldn't help myself; I followed one pace behind her, that delicious pomegranate scent wafting over me. What was it? Her shampoo?

"Fuck her already, man. I'm fixed, and I still have blue balls over here."

My head snapped to where Asshole was napping on my bed. Was I mistaken, or was that a doggy grin curling his lips back? I scrubbed a hand over my face as I turned away from him, wondering for the first time how much of this telepathic conversation was actually imagined.

I was so distracted by the way she smelled and her proximity I almost didn't catch her in time when she began to open the leather journal on my desk. Quick as a flash, my hand slapped hers away.

"Not that."

Her brows lifted with interest. "Why not? Is it your diary or something?" I didn't even need to answer before she crowed, "It *is*! Aw, c'mon, Cain. We're supposed to be revealing our deep, dark secrets. Why not give me a little look-see?"

"It's private. I wouldn't expect you to understand. You have no boundaries."

"Ex-squeeze me? *I* have no boundaries? This coming from the guy that showed up to my room uninvited multiple times?"

"The second time doesn't count. I saved your life. You should be thanking me."

"Honestly, *you* should be thanking *me*. I let you dry hump me until you came in your pants while moaning my name, and I didn't use it against you."

Fuck. Why did hearing her say that make me hard?

"Bazinga!"

"That's enough out of you."

Dahlia's eyes flew wide.

"Not you. Asshole."

She reached out and placed her palm on my forehead. "You feelin' okay? Asshole didn't make a peep. Look at him. Sweet little baby is sound asleep like the angel he is."

"Angel with horns holding up his halo," I grumbled.

"Cain, I get it, okay? You don't like me. But this is ridiculous."

"What is?"

"The way you're treating me. I haven't done a damn thing to you, have gone out of my way to give you a wide berth unless we're shoved together for something like this, but you seem to be even frostier than ever."

I cocked a brow and stared at her. Really letting myself look at the enthralling woman in my room. Dammit, I couldn't want her. I was a married man. I'd found my soulmate—if my memories weren't lying to me. So I was going to push her away. I *had* to.

"Your point?"

"Why?"

"Maybe you should ask yourself why you care so much. What's with your need to be liked by everybody?"

"Don't turn this around on me. Answer my question, Cain. Why do you avoid me?"

Huffing out a frustrated breath, I raked my fingers through my hair and paced the small room. How could I explain this to her without showing her all the cards in my hand?

"You unsettle me. Something inside you feels . . . wrong." *Or right*, my mind corrected. *Too right.*

She stiffened at my assessment. "Wrong how?"

Goddammit, of course she wouldn't leave it at that.

"You opened the box, big guy. Might as well see it through."

Once again, my eyes slid to the mouthy little fucker on my bed. What was going on with these intrusive thoughts? I wasn't even conscious of constructing them.

"Cain!" Dahlia snapped. "Wrong how?"

Swallowing hard, I pulled out the most harmful answer I could. One shrouded in truth, but nowhere close to *my* truth. "Everywhere you go, death follows. Why would I want to be around you?"

She looked stricken, and I immediately wanted to recall my words. To do anything to take that pained look out of her storm-cloud eyes.

"You know I can't control that," she whispered, her gaze dropping to her toes. "It's not like I do it on purpose."

"Maybe that's worse."

Fuck, I hated myself. Hurting her felt entirely too much like kicking a puppy. I'd rather flay myself than endure another minute of this.

"Is this because of the Banshee thing?" Her voice wobbled, but she didn't fall to pieces. I had to give her credit; the woman was strong. "I saw the look on your face when you said it."

"Yes," I said, latching onto the only thing I had. "They can't be trusted. You can't be trusted."

"Why not?"

"Would you trust one of Death's messengers?" I countered. I didn't even know what I was saying anymore. I was making shit up on the spot in a desperate attempt to maintain the walls I was trying to erect between us.

"If the message was truthful, yes."

"Even if they were heralding the death of someone you loved?"

She sighed and shook her head. "We're not getting anywhere."

Taking a seat in my desk chair, she crossed her legs and stared me down. “We don’t have to like each other, or even interact past this moment, but we have an assignment to do.”

“Fine,” I huffed, more relieved to change the topic than anything. “Do you have the envelope with his task?”

“Right here.” She pulled the white envelope out of her back pocket and waved it at me.

Grabbing the hourglass off my desk, I flipped it over and sat across from her. “Well? What’s it say?”

“He said our powers are aligned, whatever that means. We need to sit here, make eye contact, and be . . . vulnerable with each other until the timer runs out.”

I snatched the paper out of her hand. “Surely he was more specific than that.”

She crossed her arms and stared at me. I could practically feel her eyes shooting laser beams at me as I scanned the handwritten instructions.

While he had not elaborated on how exactly our powers were aligned, he had included step-by-step instructions for the vulnerability exercise he wanted us to use.

I didn’t want to look into her gray irises because I knew I’d fall into them.

“This is stupid. How will he know if we don’t do it?” I asked.

“Magic asylum. I’m pretty sure he’ll know.”

“Fine. Look into my eyes. Tell me the thing you are most afraid to say right now.”

“It says we need to settle into the connection with each other first.”

I rolled my eyes. “You are such a godsdamned goodie two shoes.”

“Yes, I am. You should try it sometime.”

The sigh I heaved couldn’t have been more long-suffering. But I leaned forward and locked eyes with her. We breathed slowly, our rhythm synching almost instantly and the air around us becoming heavy with tension of a very different kind. Our souls were gazing into one another, I could feel it. A strange sort of tugging around my husk of a heart.

I almost broke the connection when she said, "The thing I am most afraid to say right now is that despite how mean you are to me, I feel safe when I'm with you."

A kick to the balls would have been less painful. "What about me makes you feel safe?"

"I don't know. Maybe it's the ghost thing. You see them too. You help me banish them."

I nodded once, just a jerk of my chin to show her I understood. But then she kept going.

"As cold as you can be, I don't think you'd let anything hurt me."

Fuck.

"Can't you feel the pull between us, Cain? Fuck, maybe I'm an idiot for admitting it after everything you just said about me, but there's something undeniable here."

My tongue felt too thick in my mouth. I couldn't have formed words even if I knew what I wanted to say.

"Your turn," she pressed.

I didn't say a damn thing. I couldn't.

"Cain?"

My chest was tight; breathing seemed almost impossible. Shit, was I dying? Could I die?

Dahlia didn't notice. No, she thought I was ignoring her, not having an existential crisis. She stood, frustration pouring off her in waves.

"Look, if you're not going to participate, I'll just go."

"Wait," I choked out, standing and taking her by the wrist. I hadn't processed anything beyond that. I just knew I couldn't let her walk out of here believing that I was purposefully avoiding the exercise. She gave me raw honesty. I owed her that much in return.

She went to turn, but I managed to keep her back to me so when I spoke, my lips were at her ear, my breath rustling the little hairs at the base of her neck. I was so close I could see the goosebumps erupt along her skin as I whispered, "The thing I'm most afraid to say right now is *I feel it too.*"

Her sharp gasp of surprise had me rock hard, and I tightened my hold on her wrist as my lips feathered along the nape of her neck. She smelled so fucking good. I wanted her. I craved her.

She is mine.

Dahlia turned around, and on instinct, I walked her backward until she was pinned against the door.

"Cain," she breathed.

Her lips were right there, plump and perfect, begging for me to claim. All I had to do was give in and take her. She wouldn't say no. I could have her and end this torture.

No. No!

Your heart is not your own. You are vowed to another.

With a roar of frustration, I pulled away. "I . . . I need to get out of here."

"Cain," Dahlia said, confusion and hurt thick in her voice. "This is your room."

"Then you need to leave. Right now. Please," I added when it looked like she was going to protest. "Please, Dahlia. I can't."

"But—"

"Go! You've got plenty of men ready to fuck you at a moment's notice. Get out of here."

With a misty-eyed look over her shoulder, she opened the door and bolted. I slammed it closed behind her, both palms flat against the wood as I hung my head, hating myself with every heaving breath.

There wasn't so much as a huff of warning before the dog's voice sounded in my ears. *"Do blue balls feel different for you? Or do you get off on denying yourself all the damn time? Cause I don't get it, man. She was right there. You could have mounted her and put yourself out of your misery."*

"Asshole," I ground out as I cast my gaze over my shoulder. The little ball of fluff was sitting patiently, tongue lolling as he watched me with his beady, dark eyes. “I will personally rid you of your balls if you do not shut the fuck up.”

“Too late. I don’t have any.”

Going to the bed, I sat and rested my head in my hands. “Lucky you. I think she just left with mine.”

CHAPTER TWENTY-TWO

HOOK

"Well, Caspian, my boy, you've really shit the bloody bed this time," I grumbled, bringing the bottle of rum to my lips for another swig.

I'd been parked here for well over an hour, drinking deep and nursing the metaphorical stab wound Dahlia had left in my chest. But after a week of the cold shoulder from her, I finally sat down and examined the truth of my situation. I deserved it. Every single steely glance, every snub, every disappointed sigh. I'd earned her rejection.

And fuck if I didn't know how to feel about that. I wasn't familiar with emotions such as guilt and remorse. I was a pirate—*the* pirate. I took what I wanted when I wanted and never broke a sweat. Regret? I didn't know the word. But I was starting to.

"What does she want from me? I'm a scoundrel. A scallywag. A blackguard, even. She deserves a hero. Not a villain." My words were slurred and sloppy, but I took another deep pull of the alcohol, hissing as it burned down my gullet.

"But I wasn't always such a failure. I used to be a prince. A hero. Maybe I could be again?" A hiccup interrupted my musings, and the world tilted slightly. “But do I even want that? Heroes never get to have any fun.”

Was I whining? Maybe a little. Thank the goddess no one was around to hear it. My reputation would never survive. And what was a pirate without his reputation?

A sorry excuse of a sailor. That’s what.

Bah.

“Oh, my curvaceous sea nymph, please don’t forsake me. I’ll do better. I’ll be the man you need. I’ll hang my hat and become a sailor if that’s what you want. I can’t . . .” I stood and swayed so severely my hand shot out so I could brace myself. “Pfft, if the turret is a rockin’...” Shaking my head to clear my mind, I took a deep breath and continued my thoughts. “I can’t be without the warmth of your gaze for much longer. I’ll wither. I’ll be nothing but a husk. Unrecognizable as the handsome pirate made famous in stories.”

I was no longer sure if the sea on the horizon was rocking or if it was me. Either way, there was a sliver of comfort to be found in the oneness with my true home. My first and forever love.

Without warning, the bottle slipped from my fingers and hit the ground, shattering on impact, the sharp bite of the rum filling the room as it seeped into the wooden floorboards.

“Oopsies,” I said, dropping to my knees as I attempted to suck the liquid up before it was all gone. “Blast. You dastardly porous slats. No one said you could have a drink.”

“Caspian? What the hell are you doing?”

I snapped my head up, finding my voluptuous goddess standing over me. “Da-dah”—hiccup—“Dahlia-darling.” Her name came out as one continuous slurred disasterpiece.

She laughed even though I was sure she didn’t want to. “What was that?”

Instead of answering her, I crawled toward her, not stopping until I had her ankle in my grasp and my lips were pressed to the top of her foot.

"Gah, Caspian, ew. Stop it!" She kicked me away with a gentle nudge of her toes.

"Please, tell me what to do," I begged, sitting back until my bum rested on my heels. I looked up at her in supplication, palms upright on my knees, eyes locked on her face. Or I hoped they were. The room was still pitching side to side. It was hard to focus. "Don't leave me in the cold of your shadow, my sweet girl. I can't bear it."

"Cas," she whispered, with a soft shake of her head. "It's not that easy. I can't trust you. You're only saying these things because you're drunk. You don't mean them and you clearly don't have my best interest at heart."

"I know! That's where I went wrong. I was jealous. A jealous prick with nothing but his own needs in his mind. I don't understand why I am so drawn to you. Never before has a woman had such a pull over me. Love has always been a game. One where I could manipulate the rules to best suit me. They fell hard for me, and I let them. But that's as far as it went. One-sided devotion. A tumble in the sheets that wouldn't last more than a night or two." I clutched at my chest, fingers digging into the mess of my shirt. "And then I met you, and it's like the rules don't make any sense. Everything is upside down. I've capsized in the sea of my love."

Her eyes were wide as she took in everything I'd just blurted at her. Had I done it? Was she mine once more?

"Caspian, stop it. You don't know what love is. You wouldn't know if it bit you on your ass."

All right, fine. Time to pull out the big guns. "Darling," I whispered. "You have bewitched me, body and soul."

She laughed. The vixen who owned me *laughed*. "Oh please. That's from Pride and Prejudice. Get better material if you're trying to win me over. I. Am. A. Romance. Writer. That's like my gateway drug."

"What? No, those are the words etched in my heart."

"Cas . . . stop this. Please. I can see that you're hurting, but it's not my fault. I am not the one who did this to you."

"It is, though. You do it every moment of every day. I'm without you, and it hurts me."

"God, you still don't get it."

Clambering to my feet as she turned to leave, I launched myself at her. "I made a mistake, Dahlia. It cost me everything. Punish me for it if you must, but then, I beg of you, forgive me. Haven't you ever made a misstep? Made the wrong choice? Done something you wish you could take back?"

Indecision flickered in her eyes—or was that just wishful thinking on my part? Either way, I pressed on, dropping to my knees before her. "I'm begging you, sweet girl."

"I'm . . . not sure. You hurt a lot of people, myself included."

"I admit it. I did wrong. The last thing I intended was for you to be harmed in any way. Jealousy made a fool of me."

"You made a fool of yourself."

"Fine."

She looked torn, on the cusp of caving. I knew this was it, my only chance. If I couldn't sway her now, I never would. "I owe you a confession," I blurted.

"What?"

"A confession. You won it from me during our date."

"And you think now is the time to give it?"

I swallowed past the lump in my throat as the words worked themselves up to the surface. No one, not even my crew, knew the truth I was about to share. The one secret I'd kept more closely guarded than any other. "I am descending into madness. Day by day. Hour by hour. One day I won't be myself at all."

"Is . . . is this another one of your tricks?" she whispered, eyes scanning mine as if searching for a hint of a lie.

"No. It's why I'm here. Why I allowed myself to be captured."

"I don't understand."

Sitting back on my heels, I groaned as I threaded my fingers through my hair and tugged. "What more do you want from me? I've given you so much already."

"Cas, maybe now isn't the time to have this conversation. You've been drinking—"

"No. Honesty is the only way this will work between us. I see that now. If we don't have truth, we don't have anything. I am trapped here."

"Aren't we all?"

"No. Here. On this plane. I can't get home to Ravenndel. Not until I find the key, and soon, I'll go so mad I'll forget what I'm looking for and why."

"So, being away from home drives you insane?"

I shook my head. "No, darling. I can be gone as long as I want, as long as I have a piece of my home with me."

"That's the key you're searching for? A piece of Ravenndel?"

"Yes."

"You lost it?"

"It was stolen from me during the chaos of the hellmouth opening and that blasted Apocalypse." Bitterness coated my words.

"You really are losing it, aren't you?"

"If you don't believe in the Apocalypse, Dahlia, you'd better open your eyes. It's nearly come to pass twice now. Once within plain sight of me, the other I learned of in stories."

Instead of acknowledging she heard me, she held out a hand. "Come on, let's get you to bed."

Bed? Oh, okay then.

I accepted her hand gladly, stumbling as though I was walking along the deck of a ship caught in a storm rather than an old castle nestled safely in the Scottish Highlands.

"You believe me, right?" I pressed as she led me down the hall toward the residential wing.

"I believe that *you* believe."

I loosed a heavy sigh. It was a start, I guessed. Bloody hell, she smelled nice. I leaned in and allowed myself to sniff her thick blonde locks. Sweet and innately . . . her. Unfortunately for our *to-bed* plan, my cock didn't perk up.

"Whiskey dick, of fucking course," I grumbled.

"What did you say?"

"Nothing. Give me five minutes and I'll be ready for you."

Somehow we'd reached my room already. I needed to pull myself together so I could give her a night she'd never forget. Make-up sex was supposed to be legendary. I'd never stuck around long enough to experience it, but I was sure Dahlia would blow my mind. No. *I* would blow *hers*. No. She would blow me.

Wait. What was I talking about?

I tumbled into bed, the room spinning as I watched her. "Come to bed, darling."

She sighed and tucked me in, leaning over me and giving me an excellent view of her cleavage. "Sleep, Cas. We can talk in the morning."

I tried to grab her as she pulled away, but she easily ducked out of my clumsy hold. "Wait," I slurred, my eyelids already heavy and mostly closed. "Stay. I don't want this to be a dream."

"It's not. I'll talk to you tomorrow, Cas. I promise."

I opened my mouth, intent on saying something perfectly charming and important. But all that came out was a little snore before I was dragged under by the irresistible pull of sleep.

CHAPTER
TWENTY-THREE
TOR

My mate was near. I could feel her, a tether between us pulling me close even though I was still here, chained once more. They'd slipped something in my food, drugged me so I was out long enough I could be restrained again. Even now I was sluggish, my eyes not tracking as well as they should.

"Tor? Are you awake? It's me."

As if I needed the warning. I'd scented her the second she turned down my hall, and felt her long before that. The core of me was attuned to the heart of her. Her soul was a map I'd been created to read. There was nowhere she could go that I would not follow.

"Tor? Did they do something to you? Why is he chained? Bru, he wasn't in chains last time. You said he was getting better."

Her voice was everything I needed. A balm to heal my jagged edges. She pressed her palm up against the glass as I turned my head so I could finally see her. My mate. So beautiful. So perfect. Made for me. And *he* was keeping her from me.

I yanked on the chains, snarling as I fought to get to her.

"He's a risk to the staff. They don't trust him yet. But that's why you're here. If our suspicion is right, you will be able to soothe him."

"How is his being chained going to prove anything to anyone?"

Bru shrugged. "I don't make the rules, love."

I growled, low and deep. A warning.

Bruno rolled his eyes and lifted both of his hands. "I mean no offense. It's a simple endearment, nothing more. Trust me, pretty as she is, I have no interest in your mate, Beast."

"Mine."

"Yes, yes. We all understand. Dahlia is yours. And—oof!"

Dahlia cut off whatever he'd been about to say with a sharp jab of her elbow to his gut.

"Was that really necessary?" he wheezed.

"Yes," she hissed.

"He's going to find out eventually. Best it happens in the safety of—"

"We'll deal with that later. Today we have other matters to attend to."

"Are you sure? Isn't it better to rip the plaster off now? While he's chained?"

Dahlia pressed her palm to her chest and stared at me with a need I knew all too well. "You wanted me to help you prove that Tor is in control, that he isn't some mindless beast. So let me do that. Let me free my mate, and then he and I will deal with private matters *in private*."

I let out a rumble of approval. Not so much for the words themselves, but at the thought of being alone with her. Mounting her. Painting her womb with my cum. Leaving my mark inside her.

My cock throbbed at the idea. I needed to fuck my mate.

"Dahlia," I groaned, desperate for her to speak to me. Not him.

"I'm here, Tor. We'll get you out of here. I promise." She glanced from me to Bruno. "Let me go to him. Please? I need to touch him."

Yes. Gods, yes. I wanted nothing more than for her skin to be on mine.

"You know I can't, Dahlia. The doctor was very clear in his instructions. No one goes in or out of the cell. I know you trust him, but if something were to go wrong, if the monster took over and tried to escape with you, no one is strong enough to stop him. Blackwood cannot be responsible for an out-of-control Berserker roaming free. It would destroy our sterling reputation, and that is the very last thing we need mere weeks before the Donoghues' annual visit." He sighed and ran a hand through his hair. "But more important than all of that, I won't have your blood on my hands. If it were to go . . . badly, I'd never forgive myself."

"I would never hurt my Dahlia," I growled, less beast and more Tor than I'd been since they'd locked me up.

Bruno looked at me curiously. "Tor? What did you say?"

"I said I would never hurt her. She's my mate."

Relief flooded Dahlia's face as she looked at me. "See, he's there. He's in there, Bru. Look at his eyes. They're changing. Can't you see it?"

He nodded, his brow furrowing as he assessed me. "This was a good visit. I think we need to wrap it up for now, but I'll report all of this back to the doctor. It gives me a lot of hope."

Dahlia pressed her palm to the glass separating us, her expression crestfallen. "But I just got here."

"I find that in times such as these, it's best not to press our luck. We had a breakthrough. Let's leave on a high."

Instead of acknowledging him, she locked eyes with me. My blood roared with the need to go to her. To break free of my chains and smash through the glass separating us. I was strong enough; it wouldn't take much. But it was the plea in her voice that held me hostage.

"I'll come back for you. I won't give up until you're free of this place. So don't give up on me, okay?"

"Never."

She swiped a hand over her cheek, brushing away a tear. My protective instincts wanted me to put Bruno in the ground for being even partly responsible for her sadness. But I was aware enough to know that if I made any move to that effect, I'd ruin everything.

"Kærasta," I whispered. "Go."

Her lip quivered, and two more fat drops rolled down her cheeks.

"C'mon, Dahlia. Let's go get you a nice cup of tea."

"You can take your cuppa and shove it. We're in a fight."

"We are?"

"You're the one keeping me away from my mate," she grumbled, her voice growing quieter as he led her away.

"Not intentionally. If I could do anything differently, you know I would."

Dahlia's sigh echoed in my heart. She sounded so weary. "I know, Bru. But it's easier to be mad at you right now."

"Okay then. I'll be your villain for as long as you need."

The door creaked as it opened and then closed, separating her from me as much as possible. I didn't want to be here any longer. Trapped in this hell where I could see my mate but not touch her. Reaching for the water I knew contained a strong sedative, I knocked back the contents of the glass and waited to be dragged under. I knew a place I could go where the beast wasn't in control. A place I could still be the man I'd been destined to become. The man Dahlia wanted. A respite offered only in my dreams.

"Are you certain you want to do this, Kærasta? Our ways are different from yours."

My bride leaned into my side, a smile evident in her whispered reply. "Would it surprise you to learn I'm kind of turned on by the idea?"

I dipped my head to her ear as she slid her hand under my fur cloak. "Not in the least. My wife is perfectly made for me, a bit of an exhibitionist, and she puts her dirty mind to good use whether on paper or between the sheets."

"What can I say? I'm a giver."

This earned her a mostly feral grin. "Me too. I'm going to make you come until you beg me to stop. And then I'm going to make you come again. I want you boneless, sobbing, your mind not even acknowledging the rite we're performing."

"Sex as a rite. Who knew Odin was so kinky?"

"The rite is not Odin's doing, technically speaking. But it is a way of inviting the gods to bless our union."

"Uh-huh. Seems to me some Viking got his rocks off doing the dirty in front of his buddies and got real creative in explaining it to his missus."

A deep laugh rumbled from within my chest, echoing off the stone walls as we continued down the corridor that led to the temple's main ritual chamber. "What's good for the goose . . ."

"Does that make you the goose? Or am I the goose? I think you're the gander. That's the male, right?"

"Does it matter?"

"Well, no, but I do appreciate a well-placed knowledge bomb in the middle of my smut. It's like Reading Rainbow, but for good girls."

"And by good, you mean naughty."

"Exactly. The goodest of the girls."

"You're my good girl. And now you're my wife."

She made a happy purring sound that had my cock swelling beneath my leather breeches. "Mmm, say it again."

"Which one?"

Her nose crinkled, and she deepened her voice. "My wife."

I held her tighter and pressed a kiss to the top of her head. "*My* wife."

She swooned, leaning hard into my side as if she'd lost the ability to stand on her own. Unable to resist the opening she'd just given me, I swept her up into my arms and carried her bridal style the rest of the way down the hall.

Once we reached the double doors, I didn't let her down. Instead I kicked the right side open and barreled into the chamber, our laughter ringing out and drawing the attention of all five of the masked witnesses.

"They look so somber," she whispered as I placed her in the center of the enormous bed that had been assembled in the middle of the chamber. The view was unobstructed from any angle.

"I would be somber as well if I had to watch and not participate."

"Good thing you get to participate, then." She parted her thighs and crooked one finger at me. "I'm glad they're wearing masks. That way I don't ever have to know who saw me naked."

"It's for their protection, not yours. I'd likely have to murder any man who saw you in that state, and they know it. Which is why I plan to hide you as much as possible by burying my face in your cunt."

"Mmm, I like this plan. You're so smart, husband."

Pride washed over me at my newest title. And coming from her, the compliment meant more than she knew. Dahlia had a brilliant mind filled with creative energy and inspiration. Her words hit me in the chest, and I wanted to do anything I could to hear them from her always.

The crash of a gong rent the air, making Dahlia flinch. I locked eyes with her, and a feral growl escaped before I could stop it.

"It's time, my love. Open for me."

"I can part my thighs all day long, but it's not going to do anything about this dress."

Without a word, I grasped the neck of her bodice in both hands and tore the lace and satin gown in two.

"You were saying?"

She held up a palm. "Give me a second. I think I just came."

I laughed. "I told you, wife. There will be no mercy tonight. Your pleasure is mine."

I didn't wait for permission; she'd given me that by agreeing to be here tonight. Instead I laid between her legs, hitching her thighs over my shoulders and grabbing her by the hips so I could hold her in place. She writhed as I blew a stream of air over her already glistening pussy, then tilted her pelvis in search of what I was withholding.

I was close enough that the vibration of my chuckle rolled across her sensitive skin, and she moaned. "Christ, stop playing with it and eat it."

"You asked for it. Remember that when you beg me to stop."

"Do your worst."

"Mmm, have I mentioned I love it when my little wife is a brat?"

"Have I mentioned I need you to make me come?"

I brushed my beard across her thighs, and she shuddered. "Ticklish, Kærasta?"

"You know I am. You're being mean."

"No. Never mean. I only want to make you feel good. I want to worship you until the sheets are soaked with your pleasure."

Her hands fisted in my hair, and she yanked until I was forced to look up at her. Fuck, her body was made for my attention, soft and pliable, rounded in all the right places. "Stop. Teasing. Me."

My grin was pure sin. "Never. Not when it gets you this wet."

To prove my point, I slid the tip of my finger through the center of her folds, parting her and watching more of her sweet nectar dribble out. I traced her lips before giving in and sinking one digit inside her heat. She was already so soft and open, her walls desperate to clench around me. But I had all night to make her mine, and I was going to take every single minute I had, forcing these witnesses to watch until they couldn't stand any longer.

She writhed against me, desperate for more. I was just as desperate to give it to her. Lowering my head once more, I flicked my tongue across her swollen clit, making her cry out and fist my hair.

"More, please. Oh God, Tor."

I hummed my approval, loving how her walls squeezed my finger in response.

"They're watching us," she panted. "They're watching you make me come."

"Are they hard for you? Are they tenting their robes as they pray to Odin to take my place?"

"I . . . I . . ." She wasn't able to finish her sentence as I began eating her in earnest.

I sucked her and continued fucking her with my finger before adding a second. The flood of her arousal around my fingers told me she was close to her first orgasm of the night. Using my teeth, I nipped her most sensitive flesh as I curled my fingers and pressed hard on the perfect spot within her.

"Oh fuck," she cried as she came around my hand, a gush of liquid coating my beard and making me so fucking hard I had to thrust into the bed to ease my need.

"Come here, please. I want to taste myself on you."

"Not yet. You're going to come again."

"I can't."

"Yes you can. And you will."

Throughout her climax, I continued to gently fuck her with my fingers, doing what I could to help it last. At my growled promise, I renewed my efforts, pumping in and out more quickly while making a beckoning motion inside of her. Her mewls of pleasure had me grinning.

"Give me more, my beauty."

"I . . . fuck."

"I promise you'll get that too."

I continued to work her over through two more orgasms, one right on top of the other. Her skin was the flushed pink of a woman well loved, glistening with sweat, but it was her nipples that betrayed how much she still needed me. They were tight little buds, begging for my mouth.

"Tor, please. I . . . oh God, please . . ."

Her pleas were nearly incoherent. It was clear she didn't know if she was begging for more or begging me to stop.

There was no way I was about to stop.

I worked her through three more climaxes, not stopping until the sheets were soaked with her cum and her thighs trembled as she tried in vain to close them. Tears streamed down her cheeks, but she writhed, begging for more.

"I need you. I need your cock, elskan mín. I am so empty. Please come into me."

The way she used my mother tongue made my dick jump. Fuck, it sounded so good coming from her mouth.

"Soon, beauty. Soon."

"Now. Please. Gods. I need it."

Pulling back, I stared at her swollen cunt, her clit standing like a ripe berry. I couldn't help but appreciate the mess I'd made of her. She was my masterpiece, splayed and boneless, drenched in her cum. Crying for me to fill her. But I still wasn't finished with her. I would never be finished with her.

"Spread your legs wider, Kærasta."

"I can't," she panted, thighs shaking.

Reaching down, I slapped her needy pussy hard enough she came on contact, her arousal leaving her in a rush.

"You made such a mess."

"You did."

"I know," I said, not bothering to hide my pride.

"Are you proud of yourself? Are you proud that you reduced me to this in front of an audience?"

"Yes. Now all will know that I have ruined you for anyone else. None will ever fuck you like I can."

Her eyes found mine and the love shining in them made my chest tight. "Then show them. Show them how well you fuck your wife, Tor."

"With fucking pleasure."

There was no resistance when I notched myself at her entrance and slid straight home, filling her to the hilt.

"Allfather above, you're more perfect than Valhalla. I could die here and never leave."

"Maybe finish what you started first."

Her chuckle was barely more than a rasp, but it still filled me near to bursting with love.

"Oh, I intend to."

I wasn't going to last, not after all the times I'd made her scream my name. Glancing up at the glass dome above us, I grinned at the dove-gray sky, a scant few stars still visible. It was nearly dawn, and I'd made good on my promise to my wife.

Grabbing her ankles, I placed them on my shoulders while I lifted her hips and slipped a pillow under them. She cried out as I sank as deep as I could inside her.

"Are you ready?"

"For wh-what?"

"All of me?"

"Yes?"

"Are you asking me?"

"Yes?"

"Nervous, my love?"

"It's just that you're very large and very strong. You might break my pussy."

"Don't forget that fate gifted you to me, which means you are my perfect match in every way. You were born to take me."

She bit her lower lip and nodded. "Okay."

I pulled out and watched her beautiful face as I slammed home. Nothing but pleasure raced across her features. So I did it again and again until the bed creaked in warning and my balls drew up tight. The way her full tits bounced with each thrust was mesmerizing, and I couldn't help but cup them as I drove into her. That was the end for me, the moment I knew I couldn't pull back even if I wanted to. My climax barreled forward, hurtling me over the edge as she clenched around me and called my name.

My roar of pleasure ricocheted off the walls, so loud it shattered the glass dome above us and let in the cold air of my homeland. If not for the quick reactions of the witnesses who threw up a magic shield to protect us from the falling glass, we would have been killed.

I fell onto her, my face nestled against her neck, cock still mostly hard and inside her. Warm cum leaked from her, mine and hers combined. Part of me wanted it to stay where it belonged. I never wanted to leave this place.

"I guess it was a good thing the witnesses were here, huh? Talk about bringing down the house."

A low laugh escaped me at her wit.

"I love you, Kærasta."

"I love y—" Her words cut off as a door slammed open, and I was ripped from the blissful dream of a future I could never have.

Dr. Temperance stood only feet from where I was still chained. Still a beast. Still without my mate.

"Oh, good. You're awake."

CHAPTER TWENTY-FOUR

DAHLIA

Have you ever felt like someone was watching you? Like if you opened your eyes, you'd see a horrible figure standing over you, waiting to pounce or to drag you to hell? Me either.

Until this moment.

I couldn't say what exactly it was that woke me up or even precisely when I realized that I'd made the transition from sleeping to waking. One minute I'm riding a Ferris wheel at some sort of annual hog-tying competition—where Caspian and his partner Notorious P.I.G. won the blue ribbon—and then I was back in my bed staring up at the ceiling. Except my eyes were closed. I could feel them. It was the strangest thing. Even through my lids I could see the crack in my ceiling, the water spot, the shadow of the light fixture.

I wanted to sit up, to clear my head of the heaviness making everything slightly fuzzy, but I couldn't. I could barely breathe.

And through all of this was an underlying sense of dread.

Dread, because I knew beyond any doubt I wasn't alone.

Something was in here with me. Standing over me. Waiting. Watching. Angry and threatening.

I whimpered, my fingers finally able to move the barest inch. If I could get free of this paralysis, I could run. Would I have time? Would it give chase?

Something told me the answer was a resounding yes. The spirit was growing bolder, more demanding—because surely this was the same entity that had nearly made me piss myself twice now. I couldn't bear the thought that it was something else. Something worse. One vengeful spirit was enough, thankyouverymuch. It had to be the same.

Right?

Cain wasn't here to rescue me this time. What would happen when it finally hurt me?

I was finally able to force out one word, weak as a feather in the wind, but still there. "P-please."

My eyes peeled open, even though the last thing I wanted was to see the truth in front of me. She hovered there, inches from my face. Her curtain of long hair hid her features, the cold strands brushing my cheeks. My breaths came in shallow pants as my heart threatened to burst from my chest.

Icy fingers wrapped around my ankle, distracting me from the pulsing mass of angry ghost hanging above me.

"Wh-wha—"

My word cut off on a scream as I was pulled out of my bed and flung onto the floor. I was mostly in shock about what just happened, but thanks to the impact with the floor, I was able to regain full control of my body. Racked with bone-deep shivers, I stared at my bed, no trace of the entity remaining. That didn't mean I was staying here, though. I was getting the fuck out of Dodge.

I ran.

Well, I shambled.

I didn't stop until I reached the sanctuary of Kai's room. I hammered on his door, praying he was here and not in his tower. For once, luck seemed to be on my side because I'd only just started a second round of hammering when a sleep-rumpled dragon shifter appeared in the doorway. Shirtless, of course.

"Dahlia? What's wrong?" Much more alert, he peeked out into the hall, as if searching for some sort of assailant, before tugging me into his room.

"Ow," I winced, stumbling as my ankle protested the movement.

"Who hurt you?" Kai snarled, grabbing me and inspecting every inch of me.

"I-i-it." My teeth were chattering so hard I couldn't get a word out. Kai wrapped me in an embrace and pressed a kiss to my forehead.

"It's all right, gem. Come on. Let's get you warmed up, and we can talk about it when you're put to rights."

I nodded, unable to do more than that as he lifted me and carried me into his bathroom. Another time, I would have appreciated how effortless of an act it was. It was swoony when the hot guy could carry the fair maiden. It was far more so when said maiden was built like a linebacker. But right now, I was just glad I didn't have to think. Kai was in charge, and I was happy to hand him the reins.

With the devotion of a lover, he slowly stripped me until I stood before him nude and unashamed.

"Into the tub with ye, lass. You're shaking like a leaf."

I stepped into the hot water, and my handsome dragon settled next to me, his large palms caressing my back and shoulders. "Tell me what happened?"

"Sh-she was . . ." I swallowed down a sob before finally working up the courage to relay everything to him.

"She?"

"The g-ghost."

"The one from my tower?"

"N-no. The m-mean one."

Understanding crossed his features. "The spirit Cain banished?"

"Yes."

"She's back?"

The water worked its magic, and soon I was no longer shivering from a potent cocktail of adrenaline and fear. "Yes. And this time she grabbed me. I think she really wants to hurt me."

"What do you think she wants with you?"

"Fuck if I know. Maybe she wants to suck out my soul. Or worse, maybe she wants to possess me and wear my body like her very own meat suit."

Kai growled at that.

"She cannae have you. Any part of you. Yer mine."

My lips hitched up at the possessive fury in his tone. "I don't think she cares, sweetie."

"I care."

He washed my hair, then used his bar of sweet-smelling soap on my skin, cleaning every inch of me until he reached my tender, bruised ankle. "Oh, lass. What did you do to yourself?"

"It wasn't me. It was her."

"The ghost did this?"

"Mm-hmm. She dragged me from my bed. I thought I wasn't going to get away."

He made an unhappy musing sound. "It sounds like she's growing more powerful."

I turned that over in my mind, comparing the different encounters I'd had with her. To date, the first one on All Souls' was by far the biggest display of power, but given that the veil between realms was thinnest, that made sense. Since then, though, each visit from her had been exponentially worse than the one before it. First with the mirror, then shoving me out of my chair, and now being woken up and pulled out of my bed. Who knew what was next. She'd already left physical evidence of her strength on me twice.

"I don't know what she wants."

"Have ye asked her?"

My stomach clenched at the thought. "No, why would I? She's done something to harm me pretty much every time I encounter her."

"She's coming to you for a reason, lass. It's your job to figure out why."

"Well, it's not a job I want. I didn't apply for it. I quit."

"Callings don't work that way, love. You cannae deny who you are."

I raised both my eyebrows and gave him my most deadpan stare. "Really, Guy with the Dragon Tattoo? You want to run that by me again?"

"Can ye deny that you are called to me? That we're meant for each other even though you've already got a mate? In a sense, I am yer calling too. Denying your ability to see spirits would be like casting me out and ignoring destiny."

"What about you ignoring your dragon? Or is it okay for you to ignore your calling but not me?"

He grumbled and averted his gaze, pretending to busy himself with folding and unfolding a fluffy white towel.

"Uh-huh. That's what I thought. Nice to meet you, Pot, I'm Kettle."

Kai huffed. "It's nae the same at all."

"It's exactly the same and you know it. It's why you can't even meet my eyes right now."

"You don't get it. My dragon is . . . wily and not to be trusted. You have yet to grasp the full extent of your power. Until you do, you are a danger to yourself and others, mostly because you are bound to find yourself in situations you dinnae know how to get yourself out of. Or, even more likely, you'll attempt something in a moment of panic, and it could go terribly astray. The difference between us, lass, is that your situation is something you can control with time. But me? No amount of time will ever change things. Dragons cannae be controlled. He is and always will be a danger. Locking him away was the safest route for everybody."

I rolled my eyes. "Kai, what happens when he finally breaks free and you lose control because you wouldn't work with him? Because that's what happens in every story ever written about something like this. Remember Ghostbusters, when they locked all the ghosts in their big ol' trap, and that stupid EPA guy came around and shut it down? Boom, NYC was flooded with powerful, dangerous spirits, and that Gozer lady got out of hand. And don't get me started on the Marshmallow Man. If they'd just befriended him, maybe the city wouldn't have turned into a giant s'more."

"What?" he asked, his bewilderment making it clear my thoughts had gone clear off the rails and I wasn't making sense.

"Okay, so maybe that was a bad example. I just mean, 'with great power comes great responsibility' is a saying for a reason. Right now your dragon is fighting you, even with your wards. What would happen if you two worked together?"

He shook his head and stood, holding out the towel for me, a silent gesture that made it clear bath time was over. "It's not a risk I can take. The last time I let him out . . ." Kai sucked in a harsh breath, his face paling. "There is so much blood on my hands, gem, I'll never get them clean. When I make a mistake, people die."

A bone-chilling realization skittered through my brain at his words. The cult. That night, I was a sacrifice. I screamed like the banshee I was proving to be, and they all died. All of them. But I survived because . . .

"It was me. I killed them."

"Who?"

"The cult. I screamed, and they died so I could escape. Kai, you're not the only one who has blood on his hands. How can you tell me to harness my power and turn around and lock yours away?"

I would have sworn his dragon tattoo gave me a little nod, as if urging me to continue.

"I get that you're scared. Trust me, I am too. Clearly. But knowledge is power, right? And our gifts are something neither of us can run from. You said so yourself. So I'll try to master mine if you will try to master yours."

Indecision flickered in his eyes. "Let my dragon loose?"

"Maybe not fully free, but loosen the reins a little?"

"I don't know how, gem. The last time he had any control, he took it all."

"Well, maybe we need to incentivize him a little." My fingers went to the top of the towel I was wearing.

"What do you mean?"

"You know, give him a reason to behave. A little tit"—I dropped the towel and flashed a little nipple, trying not to grin when Kai's pupils lengthened into slits—"for tat." I poked his dragon tattoo right in the eye.

Laughing, he reached for me and tangled his fist in my dripping wet hair, pulling me close enough I could feel his erection press against my belly. "Ah dinnae ken what you're talking about, but if your tits are part of the equation, count me in."

I fucking loved it when he went all Scots on me and his accent thickened. And that even when he didn't understand a word I said, we still somehow ended up on exactly the same page.

Maybe there was something to this written in the stars, fated mates thing.

"Unleash the dragon, Kai. The dragon *dick,* that is."

"Oh, my pretty wee mate, you asked for it," he said, but his voice was all dragon now, and his eyes weren't just slitted pupils, but glowing purple fire.

I definitely hadn't intended on getting railed when I fled to Kai's room, but I sure was happy at the unexpected turn of events. If I had to be woken up in the middle of the night, I'd much rather it be for orgasms than ghosts.

Unless the ghosts wanted to give me said orgasms, but that was neither here nor there. I'd leave that to Rebel. I was much more interested in riding the Dragon Express straight to O-town.

Dropping my towel, I stood before my dragon mate and waited for him to make his move. Anticipation danced in my veins, making my nipples tight and my thighs clench. I wanted this for so many reasons. One, because I wanted Kai. He made me feel safe and worshipped. He gave me an escape from my own head, which wasn't easy to do. He saw me. Two, because Kai and his dragon were one and the same, he just didn't want to accept that yet.

"What if I hurt you?" Kai asked, his voice softer, eyes back to his natural color.

"You won't. I'm your mate."

Those eyes went dragon again, and I swear to God my arousal was running down my thighs.

"That's right, wee one. Ye are. Now come here to me and let me fill you until I'm dripping from you."

It was on the tip of my tongue to say something saucy, but the words evaporated under the heat of his stare. The man was looking at me like he'd been trapped on a deserted island for over a year and he'd just found himself an all-inclusive resort. Namely: my vagina.

I had a feeling my pretty kitty might not survive the experience. Sorrows, sorrows, prayers. But also? #worthit

I pressed my palms to Kai's warm chest, loving the way the ink of his dragon was tangible under his skin. With gentle fingers, I traced the tattoo, and Kai rewarded me with a deep, pleasured growl.

"My wee mate is teasing me."

"Not teasing. I'm admiring you. It's my turn."

"Well then, admire me a little lower, mate."

Biting my lower lip, I did as he instructed and slipped my fingers beneath the waistband of his joggers, gasping when I found him hard and straining. He hissed, and his hips jerked at the contact, but I didn't stop. I ran my thumb over the weeping tip and flicked my gaze to meet his.

"Is that more your speed, dragon?"

"Aye. Now do it again wi' yer tongue."

A little flutter of nervousness broke through my lusty haze.

All right, Dahlia. While you've technically never given a blowjob, you've written about a hundred of them. Breathe through your nose. Don't use your teeth—unless he asks for them. Play with the balls. Your hand is your best friend. Get sloppy. Sound effects show your enthusiasm. He'll

probably like it if you cry. Shoot, I didn't wear any mascara today or lipstick.

"Are ye okay, gem?" he asked, taking my chin between his finger and thumb.

"Yeah. I'm fine. Just . . . strategizing."

This earned me a quirk of his brow. "Strategizing? Are ye planning a hostile takeover or something?"

"I have a feeling you'll agree as soon as you hear my terms."

"Go on, then."

Shit.

He called my bluff.

Reaching for the pillow on the bed, I avoided answering back and made myself a little cushion for my knees. Then I assumed the position. He seemed even more enormous from this vantage point. He towered over me, his sizable bulge intimidating but also sending a thrill through me. I was going to taste him. I licked my lips, earning a low hum of arousal from him.

"You sure look pretty on your knees for me," he said, his voice a husky rumble as he wove his fingers through my hair.

His approval sent another delicious wave through me, and I was eager to see if I could earn any more strokes to my ego while I was down here.

With no warning, I bunched the fabric of his pants in both hands and yanked until they were around his ankles, his cock springing free and nearly hitting me in the face. It was swollen and throbbing, the tip purple and glistening with precum. The runes ringing the base of him seemed to shimmer and move. I wondered what would happen if I touched them.

Kai sucked in a breath. "Careful. A few more of those, and I'm likely to go off like a rocket."

I tucked that info away to take advantage of later.

It's now or never, Dahlia.

Reaching one hand out, I lifted his thick shaft and ducked my head, taking one of his heavy balls into my mouth and sucking deep, catching him off guard.

"Good fucking gods."

Pleased with my opening salvo, I lavished the same attention on the other before pulling back and using my free hand to cup and roll them.

Balls. Check.

The sounds he made only spurred me on. Confidence growing, I leaned in and licked a line from base to tip, savoring the burst of his salty essence when I reached the crown.

"Where'd you learn that?" His fingers tightened in my hair, and his hips moved in shallow thrusts as though searching for more.

"You should know. You've read my books."

"Dirty girl," he panted, but given his tone, it was clearly praise, not censure. "Show me what other tricks ye have up yer sleeve."

"I can hold my breath for a really long time."

"Ye donae need to do that. Just breathe through yer nose, lass."

"Okay." Wrapping my hand around his shaft, I psyched myself up to swallow him. Fuck, he was big. And ridged.

Opening wide, I tested out sucking his head into my mouth, savoring the velvet softness of his tip, tracing his frenulum with my tongue, loving the little shivers he responded with. Then I swallowed him down to the root, and his shocked grunt was everything. Ev-er-y-thing.

I released him with a wet pop and smirked. "Did I mention that I don't have a gag reflex?"

"Oh lass, I dinnae know if you should have told me that. Now I'm going to have to bury myself in your throat to make sure you're telling the truth."

I opened my mouth wide.

"Fuck. Me."

"I'm trying to, but you keep talking."

I put him back in my mouth, sucking him over and over until my jaw ached and his thighs trembled. His grunts and growls got more animalistic as time went on until he began swelling in my mouth.

The fingers knotted in my hair grew more insistent as he tugged me away from him. I was just as insistent in my efforts to get him off. Now that I'd learned firsthand what it was like to be in control of someone else's orgasm, I couldn't get enough.

"Lass, I need ye to stop. Fuck. I cannae control it much longer."

I wanted to taste him as he came down my throat. The last thing I was going to do was stop. Not when I could feel him pulsing in my mouth, feel his balls drawing tight.

"Gem, stop. I . . . Gods. I cannae . . ."

I backed away, realizing there was genuine panic in his words. "Are you okay? What's wrong?"

As I watched from my place at his feet, his body began to transform. First it was the rippling of scales randomly up his arms and over his chest. Then it was his hands, as they turned black and his nails lengthened to razor-sharp claws that dug into the flesh of his thick thighs.

"Your dragon," I whispered.

"You said you wanted dragon dick. I'm just giving my wee mate what she wants." His voice was deeper, rougher, and his eyes had gone reptilian again.

"You always do. You're such a good mate."

He made a rumbling sound in his chest that wasn't quite a purr but not exactly a growl. Either way, I knew I'd pleased him.

"So . . . do I get to suck this dragon dick, or . . ."

Kai took his length in one of his claw-tipped hands. "Or."

He didn't need to explain his choice. I had to swallow at the sight of his transformed erection. Kai was already blessed in the man meat department, but this? Fuck, I must have been a very good girl because this was a fucking gift.

Not only was his entire shaft larger, but those ridges that felt so good were more prominent. Where it curved down toward the base was twice the size it had been, meaning that when he was inside me, he was going to press against every possible erogenous zone. I, for one, couldn't wait. I ran my fingers down the length, stopping at the bulbous swell near the base.

"What's that?" I asked, my mouth watering.

"That's my knot. We won't use it until I breed you."

Breed. Me.

Fuck.

Why was that so hot?

With four words, he'd all but reduced me to a sopping mess.

"My wee mate likes that, does she? Do ye want me to fill you so full of my cum there's no doubt you'll carry my child when we're through? I can."

"Th-the spell."

He held up a clawed hand. "One slash of my claw across the place I inked you, and I could undo all that protection. Just say the word."

"Um . . . no. I think we save the babies for later. Like . . . way later."

"Are you sure?"

"Yes?"

I knew I didn't want a child right now, but fuck if he didn't paint an enticing picture.

"Maybe we just practice the breeding? You know. Do all that cum filling, but save the sex trophies for another time."

"I like to practice. Now, bend over the bed, lass. You've got me in a state, and I need to do something about it. I can also smell how needy you are for me. I want to make you scream my name."

I think I set a personal record in how quickly I got to my feet and into position.

"Arch your back for me and spread those cheeks. I want to look at what I've done to ye."

The fanny flutter that sent off rippled through my entire body.

The man was beyond potent. He could get a nun knocked up with a single crook of his finger.

"Like this?" I asked after I did what he wanted, my face pressed into the mattress.

"Exactly. Look at you. Soaked and swollen for me."

"Yes."

"Are you ready to take me?"

"I am. So ready."

"Are ye sure? I haven't prepared you yet."

"Fuck, Kai. I couldn't be more turned on if you tried. Please. I'll tell you if I need you to stop."

He folded himself over me, his chest pressed against my back, his lips at my ear. "That's the thing, my wee mate," he growled, his dragon fully in control. "I dinnae think I'll be able to stop once I'm inside you." Then he nipped my earlobe as he began pressing into me.

"Ah," I moaned as the stretch burned in the most delicious way. "Slowly."

"I'm going as slow as I can. I swear."

"Good. Oh fuck. It's so good."

He sank in so slowly I thought he'd never be sheathed fully inside me, inch after inch, his labored breaths my only indication he wasn't done yet. My eyes rolled back in my head as those ridges I loved rubbed against the walls of my pussy. I felt so full, so stretched, but also so completely turned on. A couple flicks of my clit and I'd go off like a damn sparkler at a Fourth of July parade.

"Dahlia, I need you to stop squeezing me like that. I want to make you come first."

Oh, I loved the tightness in his words. Every one punctuated with tension.

"I'm close."

"Then come fer me, mate. Let everyone in this bloody castle know who ye belong tae."

That was all I needed. Permission. Apparently, I *was* a good girl. And I was going to shut up and take that dragon dick.

He slipped his hand up my spine and didn't stop until he

wrapped it around my throat as he pounded into me so hard my teeth clattered. My cries were nearly incoherent at this point as he fucked me through not one, but two orgasms.

With my second shout of his name, he followed me over the edge with a feral roar, his thick cock pulsing inside me, those ridges rubbing every oversensitized nerve I had. Another mini shockwave of pleasure hit me as his hot cum flooded my womb.

It was a while before our breathing slowed, but once it did, I couldn't help but chuckle.

"What's so funny?" he asked.

"I was just thinking that as far as trial runs go, that was pretty damn good."

"Oh, I don't know. I'd say I passed with flying colors."

"Does that mean we get to do that again?" I teased, turning my face to look at his.

His pupils lengthened and his eyes flashed. "Sure we can. As soon as you explain to me exactly what sent you running to my room."

"I already told you—" I protested, not wanting talk of my stupid poltergeist to ruin a perfectly good afterglow.

"Nae. You said there was a ghost. Not what happened. We need to understand these hauntings if we're ever to get to the bottom of them." He smacked me on the ass as he pulled out of me. "You want to take me for a ride, lass? Then ye better get talking."

CHAPTER TWENTY-FIVE

KAI

Though it pained me to leave Dahlia's side, after hours of her peacefully sleeping nestled on my chest, the need to patrol the grounds and ensure her safety won out. I kept one eye on her as I dressed, hoping my bustling around the room wouldn't disturb her. I needn't have worried. She was fast asleep. The multiple orgasms I'd given her saw to that.

"We saw to our mate's needs. And this is one of them. She just dinnae ken. The dragon should be her first line of defense, not the last. Ye cannae stop the threats before they reach her door."

Nodding, I pulled on a hoodie and cast a longing look over my shoulder. Dahlia was splayed out in my bed, the sheets barely covering her full tits, hair a mass of tangled white gold, lips still swollen from taking my dragon cock. She looked perfect there.

"Our nest is where she belongs."

For once my dragon and I were in complete agreement. It seemed that Dahlia's little challenge hadn't been a total catastrophe after all. In as long as I could remember, I'd never felt this . . . at peace with the creature inside me.

"That's because yer accepting me. Like ye were meant tae. We weren't destined tae be foes."

"Then why did you burn down a whole fucking village and nearly have me executed?" I muttered aloud while quietly stalking through the hallway.

"Because ye were denying what ye are. What we *are. I cannae be locked away to molder and rot. I need tae stretch my wings. I was never meant tae be caged."* He shifted under my skin, the tattoo almost itching as though the ink was trying to escape my skin. *"We were never supposed tae be separate. Until ye shunned me, I was a part of ye. I dinnae have a voice until ye gave me reason to find it. All this is yer doing."*

I swallowed convulsively, not sure what to do with that lightning bolt to the heart. If I'd felt guilt over what happened to that village before, I felt it a hundredfold now. To know that my ignorance and fear led to such a slaughter . . . it was unforgivable. Dahlia was right. I could no longer bury my head in the sand. Doing so would risk unleashing far worse than I ever dared to imagine. I had to accept him fully, but the idea terrified me.

"Dinnae be scared of yer destiny. Ye were born to fly. My fire pumps through yer veins. Together we are the protector our mate needs. Ye cannae serve her the way she requires as a mere man, but as a dragon? There's none who could ever stand in our way."

"And what happens when you slip up and kill her?"

Rage filled my veins, coming directly from him. He didn't even respond. I knew the truth in my heart, though–that could never happen. He would protect her just like I would. We would die for her.

"I can't yet. I don't trust myself to be able to pull you back."

The sensation of roiling smoke filled my mind. As if he'd huffed in his dragon form. But, for once, he didn't push me. Perhaps he could tell what a concession I'd already made, that what I really needed was time. And truly, I didn't know if I had it.

Mind heavy with those thoughts, I wasn't truly aware of my surroundings again until I found myself outside, already on the path to my tower. The scent of cigar smoke curled in my nostrils, forcing my attention to the dark silhouette of the man leaning against the nearest battlement wall. I wouldn't have known it was Cain except Asshole trotted up to me and grabbed onto the cuff of my joggers, growling and tugging with surprising force.

"Asshole, down," Cain grumbled.

The dog didn't listen. Instead he yanked harder.

"Get yer wee beastie off me."

"I'm trying. He's got a mind of his own. What are you doing out here anyway? I thought you had your little princess all wrapped up in your bed."

I cocked a brow. "How the fuck did you know that?"

He shrugged. "I don't get a lot of sleep."

"It may be an asylum, but stalking is still frowned upon."

"You say stalking, I say listening. From my room. Four doors down the hall. Someone should have a talk with you about what 'quiet hours' means. Honestly, I'm surprised you haven't gotten a noise complaint."

I raised a brow, not sold on the bullshit he was selling. Then again, I had told her to scream for me and make sure everyone knew who she belonged to so . . . achievement unlocked?

"Careful, Cain. Your jealousy is showing."

He made a flustered sound of denial and flicked the ash off the end of his cigar, the smoke curling up around his face in the moonlight. "There's nothing you could do to make me jealous."

"Shall we place a wager on that?"

He glared at me, a rebuttal written across his face. Before he was able to say anything, though, the new . . . well, I wasn't exactly sure what he was, but the American came stalking up to us, a stormy expression on his skinny face.

"What the hell are you two doing out at this time of night? There's a curfew. Hasn't anyone told you a serial killer is on the loose? God, you Englishmen. You don't take anything seriously."

"Excuse me? I. Am. Scottish." If I could control my fire, smoke would've escaped my nostrils. "Call me an Englishman one more time, I dare ye."

"Wrong move there, champ. What did you say your name was again? Harlan?" Cain drawled, pushing off the wall and stubbing out the cigar in the center of his palm like an absolute badarse.

"T-Taylor."

"Well, Taylor. I'd say you made a grave error in judgment just now. Maybe next time you try to approach a couple of grown-ass men, you show some damn respect, puppy."

Asshole yipped, like he was agreeing with his master. Although, perhaps he was objecting to being lumped in with the interloper. It was hard to tell with this pup. He conveyed a lot of emotion without having to say a word.

"You two should get inside. They have the road leading to Blackwood closed, and everything is in lockdown. The Ripper killed Marge, the barmaid at The Hag's Tooth. She only stepped outside a moment, and he struck. Her blood was still steaming when they found her."

I had no trouble at all picturing the salty old woman. Her ruddy cheeks and ample bosom, hair wiry and streaked with gray. I was sure she'd once been a great beauty, but life had not been kind to her. Nor death, it would seem.

"Wait, wasn't Marge a human? I thought the Ripper only killed magical folk."

Taylor's Adam's apple bobbed as he nodded. "That's what's so concerning. The police say he's devolving, which could indicate a full spree killing. Thus the curfew, so again, if you two wouldn't mind going inside . . ."

"If he's on the loose, I should be out here, patrolling. I'm a dragon. I can take him down if need be."

Taylor shook his head. "I'm under strict orders to ensure you're all safely inside. The tracks he left indicate he headed into the Black Forest. He could already be here."

"Who's to say *you're* not him?" Cain asked. "You sure came upon us in a hurry, Taylor. Where were *you* coming from? The Hag's Tooth. Do you have blood on your hands?"

"Why would I even bother to say anything to you about it if I were him? I'd just kill you. I could've come up behind you both and slashed your throat."

"Ye could have tried."

Apparently, my dragon spoke out loud because Taylor paled and took two quick steps back.

"And I thought my fire hands were impressive. Your eyes fuckin' glow." That may have been the closest thing to a compliment Cain had ever given me.

"I'll show you impressive . . ."

Thankfully, this aside remained safely in my mind. I wasn't ready to start navigating a world where both of us were free to speak at any time.

"I'm not staying out here and debating with you. If you two want to get yourselves sliced open, go ahead. Don't say I didn't warn you."

Taylor stormed off, his red scarf blowing in the breeze behind him.

"Good help is so hard to find these days."

"He's not the help," I said.

"May as well be. At best, he's Temperance's errand boy. That's barely a step above butler."

"Have a lot of butlers where you come from, Cain?"

"Sure," he said in his most deadpan tone. "From what I can recall."

"Which is a fat lot of nothing?"

"There've been a few flashes."

"Involving butlers?"

"Sure," he said again, giving me nothing.

"Well, since I have ye . . ." I gave him a level look. "We need to talk about Dahlia."

"And this is where I leave you," Cain said, taking a step toward the main building.

I stopped him with a palm on his chest. "I know she's being haunted, and I know you helped her."

As expected, that got me his full attention. Making the most of it, I filled him in on everything Dahlia had shared with me about her most recent attack.

"Do you understand now why I need your help? Hook cannae be trusted to watch over her. Tor isn't available. As much as I want to, I'm not capable of being in two places at once, and my skill set is best served keeping watch out here. She needs you. I've seen your fire. You're the only one who can see what she sees, and as far as I know, you're the only one who has banished this creature."

"Much good that did, since it just came back."

"It's still more than I can do."

Cain rolled his eyes. "Get her a protection spell, a fucking Ouija board, a circle of salt, I don't know. I'm not her damn husband or her daddy. I've got too much else to do."

Asshole growled, then released a series of sharp, disapproving barks.

Cain's gaze shot to the dog. "Are you kidding me? You don't think finding out who the fuck I am is important? I can't sit outside her door and listen for every moan and whimper."

The dog yipped some more.

"Asshole, we're not having this conversation. She's not mine. You might think she is, but you're dead wrong."

"Uh. Do you want me to leave you two alone?" I asked, curious if he was really talking to his dog or if this was a side effect of some new medication.

Asshole growled and pawed at the ground a few times before Cain sighed. "Yeah, you're right." Then he looked at me. "Fine. I'll take the night shift. It's not like I sleep anyway."

"Perfect. You can start tonight."

He sighed, his eyes straying to the castle behind me. "Can't wait."

CHAPTER TWENTY-SIX

CAIN

Bodyguard. I never thought that'd be my title, but here we fucking were. What I'd assumed would be me sitting outside her room, watching like some kind of stalker, turned into something completely different. Part of me wanted to be in there with her, watching over her as she slept and keeping the darkness away. The other part wanted to be anywhere else. The urge to run and avoid how she made me feel set me on edge, but Asshole had made his point earlier during my conversation with Kai. I needed to be in the room. It was the only way to help her fight off the malevolent soul if it returned. Or the Ripper if the murderer found a way to scale the wall and climb in through her window.

I blamed Kai and the stupid American for worrying about either of those possibilities. But now that they'd planted the seed, I couldn't ignore the threats either.

If something happened to Dahlia, something I could have prevented . . . as much as I'd swear otherwise, the truth was I wouldn't forgive myself. She'd gotten under my skin. Attached herself to me like a damn parasite, leeching away my self-control. And it seemed these days I had very little of that to begin with.

Before I could knock, Asshole hit the door with his paw in rapid succession. Dahlia opened it and stared me down, a confused sort of annoyance on her pretty face. It took everything in me not to let my eyes sweep down her body and appreciate her curvaceous figure in that little nightgown.

"What?" she sniped.

"I'm here for the night shift."

"Come again?"

"Kai sent me. To watch over you. In his place."

She crossed her arms and gave me a dubious once-over. "Did he now?"

"Yes."

"He never mentioned anything to me."

"Maybe he was too busy putting his dick in you."

"Jealous?"

I didn't bother answering, so she rolled her eyes. "Well, I don't care what weird deal you two made. You can sit outside. I don't want you here."

"I can't help you out in the hall. Not fast enough. I saw what that spirit did to you, and by the look of your ankle, it's only gotten worse." The bruise ringing her bare ankle was an ugly, mottled green and purple, and it sent unmitigated rage through me. "Why didn't you come to me when it happened?"

She sighed. "Because we. Are. Not. Friends. Cain. Most of the time you treat me like I'm invisible. Except for the few moments you give me a glimpse of the man behind that mask of indifference. You're exhausting."

She thought *I* was exhausting? She should try living in my head for a while. See how it felt to be consumed with thoughts of nothing but *her*. And my past. And how they went together. Or didn't go together. I was walking a tightrope, and if I fell, it would be into infidelity or misery.

"We're friends," I finally countered.

Her series of slow blinks said everything. "You have a severely warped understanding of friendship. Friends do not treat each other the way you treat me. The hot and cold. The back and forth. The . . . meanness. What you are, Cain, is a bully."

"I am not."

"Are too."

"Am not."

"Oh my God!" she shouted, throwing her hands in the air. "You are such a petulant child."

Frustration burned within me. I needed her to understand how ragged and broken my spirit was, but if I told her, that would mean I was voicing something I didn't dare admit aloud. It would make me the one thing I knew in my core I didn't want to be. Unfaithful.

I'd married the woman in my memories. Promised my heart to her. My love and devotion. I was clinging to the vows I'd made by the skin of my teeth.

What I needed was answers. Who was the woman in my dreams? Or rather, *where* was she? Was she even alive? Given my memories of the banshee, perhaps not. But, and it was a big but, if she was, she was the one my heart belonged to. Not Dahlia.

Not while my true bride lived.

"Let me in, little flower. It makes no sense for both of us to go without sleep tonight. I can see how tired you are, and there's no disguising the fear in your eyes. You know the ghost could come back at any moment, and unless you want to spend the night curled up on my bed, you need to make space for me in your room."

She stared at me hard, a war raging behind her eyes.

"Please. It's what Kai wanted. He's standing guard outside, and the only way he can handle being away from you is knowing I am here watching you while he cannot."

Was it a low blow? Yes. That's why I knew it would work.

I may not remember much about myself, but one thing I knew with absolute certainty was that I always won.

Dahlia heaved a sigh and pushed her door open wider. "Fine. But you can sleep on the floor. No humping me in your sleep or trying to spoon me." Her eyes shifted to the puppy zooming inside and diving onto her bed. "Same goes for you."

"You'd be lucky to have me in your bed, and you know it," I muttered as I walked inside.

"What was that?"

Instead of repeating myself, I jutted my chin toward the rumpled sheets and the little dog who'd made himself at home on her pillow. "Good luck with that one. He's not very well trained."

"Don't be a poor sport, buddy. Just because I'm getting what you're too scared to take. God, she smells so good. I bet she'll cuddle me all night."

I glared at the dog, who hadn't shut up since our chat the other night. Without investigating why that was too closely, I'd simply accepted it as another riddle that was my life.

And it wasn't the only new development in the last few days.

My power was growing by the day, but I had no clue what that meant. And by power, I didn't mean my fire.

My eyes slid to the corner of the room that was cast in shadow, and with the smallest mental tug from me, part of the shadow detached like a wisp of smoke and slithered across the floor. The second I released it, the shadow fragment returned to the mass of darkness. This was an interesting addition to my toolbox, one that I'd barely begun to crack open.

"You know," Dahlia murmured as she slipped beneath the covers. "With you sitting in the dark, I probably won't know you're even there. Except for your scent. I'll know if I can smell you."

I smirked as I took up a seat in the dark corner and trained my stare on her. "You can smell me?"

"Yes. I do have a functioning olfactory system. I haven't gone nose blind."

Unable to stop the chuckle from escaping, I covered it with a cough and adjusted my cuffs. "And what do I smell like? I assure you, I showered today."

"Good. You smell good."

"Describe it for me, baby doll. I want to know."

"This isn't helping me sleep."

Reaching up, I turned off the light and waited for my eyes to adjust to the only illumination in the room coming from the moonbeams through the window. How was she even more alluring in the silver glow of the moon? Fuck.

Her eyes fluttered closed. "Mmm, let's see. If I were describing you like the villainous love interest in a novel, I'd say . . . leather, moss, and misty evening walks under the trees."

"Flowery descriptions get you pretty far, don't they?"

"That's why I have an editor. She reels me in. It's true, though. You remind me of warm nights in a grove of trees scattered with Spanish moss. There's a heady quality to your scent. I like it."

Dammit, I loved listening to her talk. It was doing nothing for the way my cock was tenting my pants. I'd never been so thankful for the dark in my life. I needed her to stop talking before I lost myself and did something stupid. Like climb into bed with her.

"You're never going to get to sleep if you keep talking to me."

"You're the one who wanted to know."

"Go to sleep, Dahlia."

"Fine." She huffed and rolled so her face was hidden from my view. Then, only a moment later, she said, "Cain?"

"Yes."

"What do I smell like to you?"

My stomach knotted with fierce hunger. I had to clear my throat and shift my position on the floor before I could find my words. "Nighttime walks in a garden. Sweet and lush with a hint of tartness, like ripe fruit. Not citrus though, more like . . . pomegranate."

She sucked in a breath and then a shaky laugh. "And you say I'm flowery. 'Nighttime walks in a garden,'" she mocked.

"Hush now. I'll tell you a story so you can fall asleep." I don't know why I offered. I just . . . wanted to soothe her.

"I do like the sound of your voice when you're not annoying the ever-loving shit out of me."

"Be quiet or I won't give it to you."

"I didn't take you for a Daddy."

Instead of Dahlia's husky voice, it was Asshole's gruff rasp in my ears.

"I'm not a Daddy."

"What? Who said you were?" Dahlia asked, confused. "Actually, no. I could see that. You're definitely strict enough. Maybe a stern brunch daddy. Or . . . a stern cotillion daddy, even."

"What the fuck do you mean by that?"

"I bet you're frowning disapprovingly right now. Your palm is all twitchy because you want to whip me into shape. Ooooh, Cain, are you a brat tamer?"

I immediately schooled my expression to smooth out the frown lines and then curled my fists into hands to ignore the sensation that had been building in my palm. Everything she said sounded absolutely appealing. And I hated that. I also hated that it made me harder than stone.

"Is that something that interests you?" I asked hesitantly. I didn't really want to know, did I?

"Do I seem like a brat?"

"Yes." My answer was immediate, and I had to adjust my dick.

"Hmm . . . I never really thought about myself that way, but I guess I am. I never saw myself as a girl in need of a Daddy, but . . . it makes sense, doesn't it? I wasn't ever good enough for my actual father, and any scrap of love I got was only because I'd proven my worth. I've only ever known love with conditions. So obviously I need someone who will let me lash out and love me anyway. I have the daddiest of daddy issues. Of course I would want to push back and challenge a man to see if he could really handle me. If he was worthy of my trust and vulnerability. If he'd take me as I am and not make me earn a drop of his affection."

"I can fucking handle you."

Gods above, why couldn't I stop talking?

"Can you? It doesn't seem like it to me."

"Yes, Dahlia. I can. Now stop talking. You're giving me a headache."

In truth, I was lightheaded, horny beyond belief, and about two seconds from crawling in that bed with her and proving exactly how well I'd handle her. She was becoming my bad habit. Needing something to distract me, I called the shadows to me, darkening the corner so she couldn't see me at all.

Asshole's laughter floated through my mind. *"Smooth move, shadow Daddy. She'll never know you're there now. You really fooled her."*

"I hate you," I grumbled.

"What was that?" Dahlia's sleepy voice floated to me.

"You shouldn't ever have to earn love. It should be freely given. No conditions."

The rustle of her sheets as she snuggled deeper under them was punctuated by a yawn, then a soft, "Goodnight, Daddy."

I barely swallowed back the groan her sleepy words caused as I palmed my aching length. Hearing her explanation and the yearning in her voice had me longing to be that man for her. I didn't want to be her actual father, but a man who gave her everything she needed to feel safe. I never wanted her to have to question her worth or whether she was loved. It was the height of foolishness. She had two fucking mates already, and yet the pull I felt was undeniable.

She called to me in a way I'd only experienced once before. With my wife.

And I hated myself for it.

It felt like betrayal, but also . . . fate.

Why did that word strike such a chord in me?

"You're on to something, boss. Won't be much longer now at all."

"Quiet," I growled. "You'll wake her up."

He couldn't possibly. I was the only one who seemed to hear him, but still.

A few silent moments passed before she sighed in her sleep, then moaned. Fuck, that sound. It was going to be my undoing.

"God, yes," she rasped, eyes still shut. "Touch me."

That wanton plea ripped through me like a bullet. She arched her back, and pleasure crossed her sleeping face. If she whispered another man's name right now, I thought I might die.

"Mmm. So good. More, Cain."

Well, hell.

I'd thought I wouldn't make it through her dreaming about someone else. Turns out there was no fucking way I could sit here while she had a sex dream about me. I'd be inside her before her eyes could open, turning her fantasy into a reality.

Kai would have to understand. This temptation was simply too much.

"Stay with her," I ordered, fleeing from my corner of the room.

Asshole's laughter chased me out. *"Some Daddy you are. It's okay. I'll stay here and keep watch for you."*

I didn't answer him. All I knew was my control was perilously close to breaking, and I owed it to Dahlia to find out the truth. She deserved more than a cheater in her bed.

She deserved a man who could give her everything.

And I desperately wanted to be that man.

CHAPTER TWENTY-SEVEN

DAHLIA

Dr. Masterson's office looked exactly the same, even after her long absence.

"I'm so glad you're back, Doctor."

She tossed me a smile as she continued to riffle through the pile of paperwork on her desk. The only clue she'd been injured was the Hermès scarf tied around her throat, disguising her most obvious scar. "Me too, Dahlia. I was growing restless in the healing ward."

"Even with our sessions?"

Her eyes twinkled as she lowered herself into her chair. "It's no exaggeration to admit you were the highlight of my days. Well, you and Trisha's sticky toffee pudding." We shared a laugh, and then she hit me with the real question. "So what's on your mind, dear? You seem troubled this morning."

"Troubled. That's one word you could use. Distraught. Despondent. Frustrated. Forlorn."

Dr. Masterson laughed and held up a hand. "I think I've gotten the gist."

"It's Tor."

"Your mate."

"Yes. He's still locked up. What if he's never released?"

Her eyes were sympathetic as they held my gaze. "I could lie to you and say that isn't a possibility, but we both know that it is. Instead, what I can promise is that I will do everything in my power to help you both avoid that eventuality."

It should have been reassuring, but it wasn't. "I'm not sure there's anything you *can* do."

"Perhaps not . . . but maybe *you* can."

I frowned, my fingers plucking at the hem of my sweatshirt as I processed her words. "How? I can't even touch him. He needs me, and instead of fighting for him, I'm hiding from ghosts and fucking a dragon."

Her surprised cough had me lifting my gaze to her again.

"Sorry. TMI."

"There's no such thing in therapy. It's what we're here for."

"I thought we were here to figure out my shit."

"Isn't that what we're doing?"

"No, my ghost shit. You know the screams, and the haunting, and the . . ." I sighed. "Why am I such a fucking mess?"

Her gentle smile didn't ease my frustration. "Dahlia, have you ever considered that all of this is connected? Your power unlocking, finding your mates, remembering your past, accepting your destiny. The universe has a funny way of putting us exactly where we're supposed to be."

"So Tor is supposed to be in chains? The universe is an asshole."

"Maybe. It's a test of sorts, is it not? And what the two of you learn by undergoing it could be the difference between a life together or alone."

Alone? That broke something inside me. "Help me get him out, Doctor. He doesn't deserve this."

She shook her head. "I can't. But, as I said, you can."

We were going around in therapy circles.

"What do you propose I do?" I burst out, my frustration unwilling to be contained.

She made a soft, considering sound, tapping her forefinger on her chin. “Well, we know that your presence soothes him.”

“Call me Valium.”

She smiled, but continued with her train of thought. “What the board needs in order to revisit the terms of his incarceration is proof that he can control his baser urges.”

“Okay, so how do we get them that?”

Her eyes turned back to me. “I think you need to put on a show for them. Something irrefutable. You need to work your magic and prove that Tor will listen to you no matter what. Tame him.”

“And if I can’t?”

“Then use your scream. It’s your best line of defense, and we already know he’s not immune to it. You saved us all from him once already.”

My gut churned at the thought of letting the scream out again, but she was right. I could stop him if I needed to. “They won’t let me inside. I’ve tried more than once.”

“Leave that to me.” Standing, she walked across the office to her desk before picking a phone receiver up from its old-fashioned cradle. Who still had phones like these? Supernatural psychologists, I guessed. Except I didn’t remember seeing it with its shiny black details and gold handle in any of my other sessions.

“I’m sending Dahlia down to see Tor. No interference. Give her full access and privacy.” Her expression went stormy. “Don’t argue with me, Joffrey. She is to be given full access. Period.” There was a beat of silence as she waited for his answer. “That’s better. I guess I won’t be interviewing for your replacement after all.” There was one more beat, and then she smiled, hanging up the phone. “Prickly little pear, isn’t he? I have so much fun winding him up.”

I shook my head, surprised at her admission. She wasn’t one to let her personality slip. I guess we were becoming friends or something.

“You said privacy? I thought we were supposed to prove he could be tamed. How can I do that if no one knows?”

"When you emerge with all your limbs intact, that'll be proof enough."

Something told me that wasn't the whole story. I held her gaze and raised a brow, waiting for the rest.

"And every cell is monitored via video feed."

My cheeks heated, realizing that our first time had likely been caught on tape. Oh God, I had a sex tape. For some reason, the thought didn't fill me with dread.

Nope. I was a class A freak because it turned me the fuck on. Who did I have to bribe to get my hands on a copy?

"Go on. The arrangements are made. Help him."

I didn't wait for her to ask me again, and I must have been in some sort of daze, because I didn't recall the walk to his cell at all. I was just there. His door cracked open, Tor in chains, eyes locked on me.

"Mate," he pleaded, his voice rough and hungry.

Rolling my shoulders back, I contemplated my next move. Masterson said I needed to put on a show. That I needed to tame him.

It was a blessing I didn't know exactly where the cameras were. It prevented me from giving myself away by searching for them. If this was going to be believable, Tor couldn't be in on the plan. It had to be authentic. Which meant his submission had to be real. Taking the reins didn't come naturally to me, but I'd written my fair share of dominant characters. All that research was about to come in handy right now.

"Yes. Mate." I pressed my palm to my chest and approached him. The beast thrashed and jerked on his restraints, reaching for me, but I stayed back. "No, Tor. You need to listen to me. Do you understand?"

His eyes narrowed, and a needy growl escaped him. "Mate."

"Do you want to touch me, Tor?"

Recognition flashed in his expression, some of the black receding from his eyes. "Yes." It was a long, drawn-out groan.

I'd be lying if I said my panties weren't soaked. Good thing no one asked.

"Say please," I demanded, a little thrill going through me at being the one to take control.

"What?"

"You heard me. If you want me, beg me. Give me your obedience."

If I'd expected resistance, I would have been sorely disappointed. Because that wasn't his reaction at all. Tor's lips twisted up in a primal grin.

"You want me to beg?"

"Yup."

"Do you need to hear how badly I desire your sweet cunt?"

My breath hitched. Fuck, that was hot. He was sexy when he was all beast, but dirty-talking Viking was my catnip. God, I'd missed him.

"I'm waiting."

Dropping to his knees, he settled his hands on his huge thighs, head bowed. "Please, Kærasta. Please end my suffering. Can't you see how hard I am for you?"

My eyes shifted to the generous bulge in his pants. "I can. But if you want me to do something for you, then you're going to have to do something for me first."

"Anything."

I crooked one finger. "Crawl."

The clink of his chains as he maneuvered himself onto his hands and knees only emphasized the carnal beauty of the moment. Tor was one of the biggest, baddest alphas I'd ever met, and right now, he was on his knees. For me.

"Good boy," I purred. There was a fine line between degradation and submission. I only wanted to prove he wasn't the monster they feared. Or if he was, that he'd be mine to command.

He stopped a few inches from where I was standing when his

shackles ran out of slack, his head tilting so he could look up at me. "I can go no further."

"That's all right. You did so well. I'm so proud of you."

A purr rumbled in his chest.

"You like to please me, don't you, Tor?"

"You're my mate. I would die if you asked me to."

I took his chin in my hand as I tipped his head further back. "Right now, all I want is pleasure. For us both."

"I have missed you, Kærasta. Craved you."

"So have I. I ache for you, Tor. Touch me. Make me feel good."

"You're wearing too many clothes." He reached for me but couldn't close the distance.

"So are you. I have an idea. You take care of those pants of yours. I'll take care of mine."

He didn't need telling twice. It was easier for me to shed my leggings than it was for him. He had to scoot back to give himself enough slack in his chains to tug the cotton joggers down his long, thickly muscled legs.

It was no burlesque show, but I was panting all the same. A naked Tor was a beautiful sight. So was a bound one, if I was being honest. It was giving me all sorts of filthy ideas. Just as he shifted to get back on his knees, I stopped him with a bare foot to his chest.

"Stay there. Lie back."

The way his abdomen rippled as he got into position made my mouth water. Even in his beastly form, Tor was a sight to behold. A deadly creature made for killing with a face carved by the Norse gods. My thighs clenched as a flood of arousal pooled between them.

"Tell me what you need, my beauty. Please let me serve you."

"First I want your mouth. Then I want your cock."

"Yes," he growled. "Sit on my face, mate. Ride me and use me for your pleasure."

"You don't give the orders this time."

"Please sit on my face and use me for your pleasure?"

I giggled. "That's better."

He grinned up at me, looking like an angel, even with those curling horns. The tips were wicked sharp, so there was no way I could safely lean forward, which meant I'd have to face the other way. No hardship there.

Walking alongside his stretched-out form, I stopped when I reached his shoulder, then pivoted so I was straddling his head and facing his feet.

"I could stare at your perfect cunt all day, but I'd much rather taste it."

"Good, because you're about to." In a brazen move I'd only ever written about, I sat on his face just like he wanted, moaning as soon as he began licking his way to my clit.

It felt so good, I momentarily forgot the role I was supposed to be in and whimpered. "Fuck, Tor. That feels amazing."

His answer was lost as he continued to lap at me, but the vibration of whatever he was trying to say was a welcome treat. I had to return the favor.

Stretching myself out along his body, I took the tip of him into my mouth and gave an approving hum.

He released a garbled groan before sucking my clit hard enough that I jolted. God, I wasn't going to be able to do this for long. I'd forget what I was doing to him because I was coming so hard. That wouldn't be fair to him.

"Sit, Kærasta. You're hovering. I can't reach where I want you most."

The way his lips feathered over my pussy sent little sparks shooting to my clit. I didn't even care that he was ordering me around. His hands came up to my hips as he pulled me lower and settled me onto his mouth. A satisfied moan from him had me grinding down, my palm wrapped around his throbbing dick since now I couldn't reach with my own mouth.

His hips rocked, thrusting his cock into my grip while I whimpered and approached the precipice. He knew exactly how to top me from the bottom, and I was here for it.

"Tor," I sobbed when he started fucking me with his tongue.

There was no way that was a regulation-length tongue. It was curling inside me, lapping at my inner walls with the same dexterity as his fingers. He was going to make me come. I could feel that build, the desperation gathering. I needed just a little more friction. As though he could read my mind, Tor pulled his tongue from me and concentrated on my swollen, throbbing clit. His teeth scraped it just hard enough that I exploded, coming all over his face to the sound of his pleasured grunts.

I'd barely caught my breath when his hands grabbed my hips and lifted me off him.

"Oh, I—"

Whatever I'd been about to say was lost as he bodily moved me down and impaled me on his massive cock.

I wasn't even sure the physics of it were possible, what with the chains and my body weight, but as always, Tor made me feel delicate. There was a lot to be said for a man built like a truck.

The sounds I made as I rocked on him in this position would have been alarming to the casual passerby. They were somewhere between animalistic grunts and the wails of a feral cat. He was so deep like this. I braced my hands on his legs and closed my eyes as I rode him hard, knowing his view was of my round ass and slick pussy taking his dick.

"Yes, beauty. You take me so well. All the fucking way. Use me. Take your pleasure. Fuck—"

His grunts of pleasure drowned out my own. He was loud, and it only ramped up my own need. I loved knowing that I'd reduced him to this.

A rough grip tangled in my hair, yanking my head up as Caspian's voice crooned, "Naughty vixen. Why didn't I get an invitation to the party? I love a good ride."

My eyes snapped open. "Cas . . . how . . ." It was hard to form words as Tor continued to thrust into me. "How did you get here?"

Cas loomed over me, his expression dark, dick already hard and in his other hand as he lazily stroked the thick length. He smirked. "You left the door wide open, darling. Begging me to come see what all the fuss was."

"I've missed you," I admitted on a groan as Tor thrust up hard.

"I'm right here, love. I'm never leaving you." He winked and tipped my head up a little more before rubbing the head of his cock over my lower lip. "Now open wide. Show me exactly how much you missed me."

"Cas," I moaned, the thought of sucking him while fucking Tor doing all sorts of things to my insides. Not to mention Tor rearranging them.

Fuck, I was close.

Holding Caspian's gaze, I opened my mouth as wide as it would go. It was all the permission he needed to slide in deep.

CHAPTER TWENTY-EIGHT

HOOK

Of late, it would seem I spent my nights standing in the shadows, watching other men leave Dahlia's room. I wasn't a fan. When would it be my turn to do the leaving? Cain could watch and deal with this burning pit of jealousy in his heart instead of me.

Truth be told, once she allowed me into her bed, I wasn't convinced I'd be able to make myself leave. I'd likely have to be bodily removed. I certainly wouldn't be bolting as though the hounds of hell were on my heels like the broody man already halfway down the hall.

"My, my, sweet girl. What is it about you that sends grown men fleeing for the hills? Do they not know how to handle you? Are you insatiable? No worries. I'm sure I'm more than up to snuff."

I snuck toward her door, anticipation humming in my veins as I pulled out the skeleton key I'd pilfered, ready to do a little breaking and entering. I stopped short, however, when I saw the door was ajar.

"Oh, Cain. Such bad manners. You rushed off so fast you didn't even make sure to close the door after you?" I tutted.

A low moan came from within the room, drawing me inside like a siren to a sailor. Except this one wouldn't kill me. But I'd give my right hand for a chance to let her try and ride me to death.

I crept in like a thief in the night, though it was not her belongings I was interested in. If anything, it was her virtue. A soft snicker left me at the thought.

A tiny growl sounded in response, and my eyes went wide at the sight of the fierce little dog standing at attention at the end of her bed.

Well, this wouldn't do. The bilge rat would sound the alarm before I was able to have any fun at all.

"Now, now, furball. Don't go making a scene when you don't need to. I'm not the one you need to be protecting her from. Pirate's honor." I held up a hand in a semblance of a salute.

Asshole yipped, and Dahlia sighed in her sleep, shifting under her covers.

"Mmm," she moaned.

The pup tensed, and his lips peeled back, readying to bark again, but I whipped out a pinch of pixie dust from my pocket and sprinkled it over his snout.

Instantly, the animal calmed, his face taking on a blank expression, tongue lolling, eyes blinking heavily. While used as a stimulant and aphrodisiac by humans and supernatural creatures alike, pixie dust didn't have the same effect on those belonging to the animal kingdom. Thank the goddess. Just a sprinkle was enough to sedate a mastiff. Asshole wouldn't wake up until well into the afternoon.

"Much better," I crooned to myself as his tiny snores filled the air. "Now, where were we?"

I rubbed my palms together in anticipatory glee. I'd been meaning to pop by Dahlia's room, though tonight was the first night she'd actually been alone. The last thing I wanted to see was Kai stuffing her full of his dick. That was my job.

Speaking of, my darling was breathing heavily, her palm skating up her soft belly until she cupped her breast. Touching ourselves already? Don't mind if I do. Watching her writhe was as big a turn-on as stumbling upon an orgy. And those breathy little moans? I couldn't have asked for a better soundtrack as I pulled my throbbing length out and gave it a few cursory strokes.

"Mmm, my wicked little darling is seductive even in her sleep," I murmured, even though she couldn't hear me. "Is this your fantasy? The one you talked about with the doctor?"

But then she whispered Tor's name, and the sound sent a spike of frustration through my chest. Dreaming of him, was she? I could fix that. The subconscious mind was a suggestible thing. With the right amount of finesse, I could redirect her thoughts.

Leaning down, I gave her a hair a soft tug and moved until my lips were close enough to graze her ear, whispering, "Naughty vixen. Why didn't I get an invitation to the party? I love a good ride."

She moaned and arched into me. Goddess, she smelled divine. My dick was so hard I was sure it was about to punch a hole through my trousers.

"Cas . . . how . . ." Her question startled me, too coherent for someone who was lost in a dream.

I went with a version of the truth. A shade of morally gray, really. "You left the door wide open, darling. Begging me to come see what all the fuss was."

Confusion swept across her face before it cleared, and she sent me reeling with her whispered confession. "I've missed you."

Fuck.

I hadn't expected that, but now she'd said it, I wasn't going to let it pass me by. I missed her too. "I'm right here, love. I'm never leaving you." Cock straining as her eyes fluttered, threatening to open, I rubbed my weeping tip over her lips. "Now open wide. Show me exactly how much you missed me."

I'd expected to find her lost to her slumber, body boneless and pliant, the perfect fuel for my fantasy. Little could I have known she'd become a willing participant in what I'd assumed would be an epic wank.

Her tongue darted out, brushing the head of my aching dick and making me hiss with the nearly uncontrollable urge to shove my cock down her pretty throat. But her teeth looked strong, and the last thing I wanted was to catch her off guard and end up losing a few inches after this.

I contained myself. Barely.

"Cas," she moaned, the sound delightfully wanton and impatient.

It was more than I could have hoped for. But then she truly shocked me and opened her mouth wide, silently begging me to give her the skull fucking we both craved. I was but a mere pirate; how could I resist such exquisite temptation?

Answer: I could not.

Pirates were not in the habit of denying themselves anything. It was a direct contradiction to everything they—we—stood for.

"Gods, sweet girl. Your mouth." I groaned as she wrapped her lips around me and sucked. My eyes rolled back in my head as pleasure already, embarrassingly, began to build at the base of my spine.

She moaned around me, and I tangled my fingers in her hair, rocking my hips in shallow thrusts. I was going to wake her up for sure if I didn't keep it down. I forced my eyes open to glance down at her face, only to falter. Her dove-gray irises met mine.

Dahlia was staring up at me.

"I . . ."

Was at a complete loss for words, is what I was.

Talk about being caught with your pants down. What was the proper decorum in this situation? Did I pull out? Continue? Say hello? Dahlia saved me from having to do anything.

She blinked a few times, then grabbed my arse to hold me in place as she bobbed her head and sucked me harder.

"God's teeth," I cried. "You're the devil, aren't you, love? Sent to seduce me away from my goal."

She hummed in response before grabbing my balls and tugging so hard I trembled.

A garbled moan was the best I could manage as my orgasm came barreling at me.

"I'm going to come," I gasped, feeling that she deserved at least a little warning.

That only spurred her on. Fuck, had I ever been sucked off this well? It was like she'd been born to do it, taking my shaft until I slid down her throat, and she swallowed around me. I was seeing bloody stars, and my godsdamned knees were weak. I think I was about to swoon.

Or come harder than I ever had in my life.

I wondered what she'd think about becoming a pirate's wife?

There was absolutely no fucking way I was ever letting her go after this. A man didn't taste nirvana only to go back to an ordinary life on the seas.

Her nails dug into the flesh of my arse as she gave me one last hard suck before I went off like a cannon. I had to hold myself up on the wall. It was that or collapse on top of her with my dick lodged in her throat. That felt like bad form after what she'd just given me.

Pulling out of her delectable mouth, I took a moment to compose myself, my vision returning from its blurred state and focusing on her. She lay there, a string of her saliva and my cum connecting us still before she licked her lips and broke it.

"How did you know?" she rasped.

There was no judgment in her tone. No anger.

I was completely out of my depth here. I never counted on being discovered. So I did what I did best. Brazened it out.

"I'm a pirate, love. Nothing remains a secret for long around us."

Sitting up, she frowned momentarily but then reached for my hand, threading our fingers. "So this was about giving me something I was too afraid to ask for?"

"Would you be cross if I said yes?"

"No. It's you. If anyone was going to give me my fantasy without judgment, it would be my pirate."

Her pirate.

"Does this mean I'm forgiven, then?"

She narrowed her eyes at me. "More like you're on probation."

"How many more nocturnal emissions will see me free and clear?"

"I'll let you know when you get there."

I hesitated to ask and risk ruining my good fortune, but I did want to be clear on this point. "Does that mean I get to come to you like this again?"

She bit down on her full lower lip and nodded. "I really hope you do."

"Shall we say you'll leave the door open for me?"

A shadow crossed her face. It didn't take me long to decipher it.

"You prefer not knowing when it's going to happen."

Her eyes slid to mine as she curled protectively in on herself. "Is that weird?"

"No, my darling. It's the sexiest fucking thing I've ever heard. Look, I'm hard again just thinking about it. But before we go any further than me waking you up with my dick, we should have a proper discussion about what it is you want to explore. Scenarios that excite you as well as the things that are absolutely off limits. I need to know the rules so I don't stray into dangerous territory or make a serious blunder we can't come back from. After all, this is about pleasure. I'm only interested in that which is sure to get us both off."

"I thought pirates didn't care about rules."

"We don't, generally speaking. But these are the kind that will have you screaming my name, so consider me your star pupil."

Her cheeks turned a soft shade of pink, visible even in the dim light flooding her window. Gods, but she was alluring, and she didn't even know it.

"How can we know what we'll enjoy until we try it?"

"We won't, but I have it on good authority that fantasy doesn't always translate to reality, so we should probably also have some sort of ripcord in case one or both of us isn't enjoying ourselves."

"Like what? A safe word?"

"Hmm, perhaps. Though if you're choking on my dick, you can hardly use one can you. No matter, I'll sort it out, love. Leave it to me."

I dragged a hand through my hair, not wanting to leave her but knowing I shouldn't stay for fear of confessing my undying devotion to her and losing every single pirate point I'd ever earned.

"Goodnight, sweet girl," I murmured, turning toward the door.

"Wait. Don't leave. Please?" The raw vulnerability in her voice had me turning back in an instant.

"You want me to watch over you?"

She patted the space beside her. "You can sleep with me if you want."

My eyebrows shot up.

"Sleep," she emphasized.

"I'm handsy in my sleep," I warned her.

"I just woke up with your dick in my mouth. I think I can deal with a wandering hand or two."

"Well then, love, scoot over."

In moments, I was wrapped around her like her very own sexy octopus. My legs twined through hers, one hand cupping her ample breast.

I'd never felt so at ease in my life. The closest I'd ever come to this sense of rightness was at sea, but even then, it didn't quite touch the comfort of holding Dahlia in my arms.

For the first time since I'd lost my piece of Ravenndel, I felt settled. At home.

And that scared me as much as it soothed me.

Because if I could lose something as vital as my compass, I could easily lose her as well. I almost had.

"Goodnight, Cas," she said with a sigh as she snuggled into me.

I squeezed her tight and layered kisses along her shoulder. "Goodnight, my darling."

CHAPTER TWENTY-NINE

DAHLIA

I still didn't like being in my bathroom alone after what happened with the ghost the first time Cain had been in my room. It took every ounce of my willpower to even look in the mirror, heart pounding because I couldn't help but anticipate the spectral finger scrawling a message on the glass again.

A shriek of fright bounced around the small room when the ding from my laptop went off.

"Sonofamotherfuckingwhore," I panted, hand on my chest as if I could somehow slow down the gallop of my heart.

I'd been so sure the ghost would make an appearance, the electronic chime had caught me completely off guard. In other news, if this writing gig didn't pan out, I could explore a career as one of those scream queens. My lungs were impressive. I paused for a second, my brain snagging on the thought. Was this because of the banshee thing? Or was I overthinking it?

Careful, Dahlia. Any second now, a big, burly dragon is going to smash through that door because you can't handle getting an email.

Shaking my head and muttering to myself, I moved back into the main part of the bedroom, angling for the laptop I'd left open on the bed. My heart gave a little pang that it was empty. Not just of Hook, who'd snuck out with the dawn, but because Cain hadn't stayed *and* because my dream of Tor had been just that. A dream.

Leave it to my subconscious to come up with a whole-ass therapy session as a means of foreplay. Jesus.

I knew it had to be because of my guilt that Tor was still locked up while we were all out here, free and clear.

Huffing, I sat down and pulled the laptop into my lap. I knew exactly who sent this email, and I knew exactly why. I hadn't been pulling my weight on the professional front lately, and Kiki wasn't going to let me slide.

Sure enough, a one-sentence email that could've been a text stared back at me.

It simply read, *where are my pages?*

I typed out a quick reply, wincing as I did. *In my head.*

As if on cue, my phone rang.

I answered the video call and sat back on the bed, braced for a tirade.

"In your head? What kind of answer is that?" Kiki was at her desk, big black-framed glasses perched on her nose, brow stern.

"The truth. I've been busy."

"Yeah, busy getting railed. Your lips are swollen. Why are they swollen, Dee? What were you doing?"

Oh God. She was like a bloodhound with this stuff.

"Why are you still awake? What time is it over there? Midnight? One?"

She waved a perfectly manicured hand. "Stop deflecting. Whose dick were you sucking? Was it the dragon? The yummy shadow daddy? God, this game is so much more fun now that I've seen them live and in color."

"I wasn't—"

"Show me the roof of your mouth. I used to be a dental hygienist. I can see it if you gave head within the last twenty-four hours, you know. Bruises on the soft palette never lie."

"You're making that up," I said, horror overtaking me at the thought. Were we really all just walking around with our mouths advertising what we'd been up to the night before? Christ, add yet a new thing to the list of shit I'd never get over.

"Hand to God, it's true. There have been studies published and everything. Dicks do damage."

"I kind of hate you for telling me that."

She shrugged. "Just over here sharing the facts, Dee."

"Unshare it, please. Scrub my brain."

"So . . . who was it?"

"Caspian," I muttered.

"The *pirate*? Wow, I really thought it'd be the grumpy one. He seems like the type to hold your hair back while he makes you choke on his—"

"Okay, that's enough," I interjected, needing her to stop because I was picturing exactly that scenario and not hating it at all.

Just like I hadn't hated waking up to Caspian filling my mouth. As it had the night before, heat surged through me. Having my fantasy brought to life in such an unexpected way was ah-may-zing. I'm sure I should be mad at him, maybe a 'normal' person would be, but the truth was I wasn't. Not even a little. He'd given me something I'd been too afraid to ask for. Something I'd secretly dreamed about for years. And it was even better than I could ever have imagined.

Even now I blushed. I couldn't picture asking Tor or Kai to give that to me. But my devilish and depraved pirate? He was the perfect person to engage in a little CNC.

"And? How did it go? Is your jaw sore? I have this great massage trick I can teach you."

My cheeks burned. "It was really sexy. And yeah, I feel like my jaw was unhinged just so I could fit him. Does that get easier?"

"Not really. It's all about the stretches. You're a clencher, right? You need to do a little pre-head prep."

"Pre-head prep . . . like gargling?"

"That's for after." She pushed her glasses up the bridge of her nose and grinned at me. "My little girl, all grown up and going through her epic ho phase."

"Hey, we don't slut shame."

"I'm not. Everyone should have a ho phase. Some people never want to leave it. More power to 'em."

"I just want to go on record that it needs a better name. Women who embrace their sexuality are always labeled as hoes or whores. Men are just men. We need to do better."

"Noted and seconded. Motion carries."

"Great. Productive call. Go to bed." I almost got away with it. Almost.

"Whoa there, hang on, miss. Where are my pages?"

Dammit.

"It's been hard to write much more than a scene or two with everything going on here, Keeks."

"I'm sure it's hard finding time between your meditation sessions and enthusiastic dick sucking."

"You do know what's happening here, right? Serial killers. Ghosts. Attacks on the grounds. For a place meant to relax and rejuvenate me, Blackwood hasn't been successful. Instead, I think I'm more tired than I was when I got here."

"Fuck. Now I feel bad. I was about to give you shit for trying to tell me that Asshole ate your homework."

"Asshole would never. He's a good boy. And he knows I would shave him."

"At least you wouldn't have to bleach him too."

"Ew, Keeks."

She laughed, then went back to business. "Have you sent me everything you've put down so far? What about an outline?"

"You've read every word I've typed. I have some handwritten scenes but they're not fleshed out yet. And I'm working on an outline. I can put that in our cloud drive if that helps?"

Her eyes lit up. "Yes. I just need something to give to the higher-ups so they see proof of progress and know another book is actually coming. They're panicking a little because the last time they had a writer take a hiatus, he never finished his series, and the TV network had to come up with a plotline all on their own for the last season. Disaster."

"And the chapters I already sent you aren't proof enough?"

"Like I said, they want proof of *progress*."

"Maybe I should start holding chapters back, then."

Kiki's jaw dropped. "Don't you dare."

I lifted a shoulder unrepentantly. "Serves them right. Maybe they should try to be creative while in the middle of a quarter-life crisis. It takes me days to write what they devour in a matter of minutes. They can fucking wait."

"I love you, but you know that's not how this works. They gave you an advance for this series. You owe them a book."

I sighed and grumbled, "I should've kept self-publishing."

"Just think about the movie deals."

"Like the one that landed me in this place? Yeah, hard pass. I'm never going to a premiere again."

"Okay, bad example. Think about the money you can swim around in, Scrooge McDuck."

"Germs."

"Well, now you're just being ornery."

"Give me a week, and I'll have an outline to you. I am guaranteeing you right now that I won't stick to it even a little, but you'll have it."

She grinned. "That's my girl. Now, go do some jaw stretches before you sprain it. You don't work well when you're in pain."

I hung up with her and, instead of stretching like she'd suggested, opened a new document. She wanted an outline, that's exactly what I'd give her.

It was time for me to get serious about revisiting Rebel and the Haunts. I just had no idea where their story would lead.

SESSION TRANSCRIPT: DECEMBER 5TH

Dr. Temperance: This is Dr. Nathaniel Temperance, standing in for Dr. Elizabeth Masterson. The date is December fifth at nine-thirty a.m. I'm here with Tor Nordson in his isolation cell.

<<chains rattling>>

Tor: *growls*

Dr. Temperance: Now, Tor, we won't get very far if you try to break your restraints again. You've been making such progress.

<<chains rattling>>

Tor: You must feel very brave stepping inside my cell. But you forget that I know the truth.

Dr. Temperance: What truth is that?

Tor: I can smell your fear. You're sweating, Doctor.

<<pocket watch clicks open and shut repetitively>>

Tor: Enough. Bring me my mate. I need her. You taunt me with her over and over.

Dr. Temperance: Subject shows significant progress with his verbal communication. It is of note that with every interaction he has with Dahlia Moore, his cognitive functions grow stronger. There is also marked improvement in both his social skills and control.

Tor: Where is she?

<<chains rattling>>

Dr. Temperance: She is in a session with Dr. Masterson. Not to worry. We are taking great care with your mate, Tor.

Tor: Lies. If you were caring for her, you would bring her to me. She needs her mate.

Dr. Temperance: If you want to get out of here and back to her, then you need to prove you can be trusted.

Tor: Have I not already proved that by allowing you to live?

Dr. Temperance: *nervous laugh* I was thinking of something a bit more trying for you. A true test of your restraint.

Tor: Oh, trust me, Doctor. It's very trying.

Dr. Temperance: You are not doing yourself any favors taunting me.

Tor: *sighs* I'll go mad without her. Eventually even the small distance between us will drive me insane. Then where will you be?

Dr. Temperance: I am aware. But we cannot allow you to roam free with the rest of our residents until you've proven your ability to restrain yourself in even the most triggering of situations.

Tor: Go on.

<<pocket watch clicks open and shut repetitively>>

Dr. Temperance: It may seem a bit unorthodox, but since your mate isn't yours alone—

Tor: *growls menacingly*

Dr. Temperance: Exactly. Since Berserkers are notoriously possessive, and she has more than one mate, more than one partner, it would be prudent for us to test your control when faced with witnessing her being cared for by another.

Tor: You want my mate to perform for you?

Dr. Temperance: N-no. *clears throat uncomfortably* That's not what I'm suggesting at all. This would not be s-some kind of s-sex show.

<<chains rattling>>

Tor: *series of heavy breaths* I will have your tongue.

Dr. Temperance: Now, Tor. Be reasonable.

Tor: Reasonable? You want to watch my mate get fucked by another man. It is a mercy I don't take your eyes as well.

Dr. Temperance: Who said anything about . . . *whispers* fucking?

<<uncomfortable silence>>

Tor: *sighs heavily* Kai.

Dr. Temperance: Pardon?

Tor: Have her bring Kai. I will prove to you beyond doubt I can contain my rage. No one else looks at her but you. When Kai walks out of here with his dick still attached and his heart functioning, you release me.

<<pocket watch clicks open and shut>>

Dr. Temperance: Are you sure?

Tor: It was your idea, wasn't it?

Dr. Temperance: Well, in theory . . . yes. But—

Tor: If this is the only way to prove myself, I will do it. But then, Doctor, you *will* release me.

Dr. Temperance: Your chains remain intact. Not a scratch on Kai or Dahlia.

Tor: *snarls* I would never hurt her.

Dr. Temperance: Even so, do you agree to my terms?

Tor: Bring them.

<<shuffling footsteps against concrete>>

<<door opening and closing>>

Dr. Temperance: *fighting to catch his breath* Good heavens.

<<static>>

End of transcript.

CHAPTER THIRTY

DAHLIA

Damn, this place is pretty.

My heart swelled with the overwhelming sense of contentment I felt any time I let myself bask in the beauty of the Highlands. Usually when people waxed poetic about a location, they were full of shit or biased as hell. But not this place. The Highlands were every bit as magical as they said. Was I a romantic? Yes. Did I care? No. Scotland had always been a dream locale for me, and I'd never had the chance to visit until now.

Good job. You had to get locked away in an asylum to get here.

A sharp gust of wind sent my hair flying into my face.

Note to self: no more walks without a hair tie.

I was so absorbed in the task of collecting the unruly strands that I didn't immediately notice the telltale prickling along my skin.

"Motherfucker," I growled, not remotely happy about my alone time being interrupted by a ghost.

As much as I loved the attention of my men, I craved time to myself. I was an introvert, forced to interact with people more often than I chose to. And now it seemed like we were adding ghosts to the mix. Turning on my heels, I faced the spirit who so clearly had something they wanted me to know. My chest tightened at the familiar visage only inches away. Tor's relative.

Confusion slammed into me. The last time I'd seen Alistair, he'd been hot on Tor's heels, following him around, but that was over a month ago. Had something happened to bring him back? Or maybe there's some kind of ghostly barricade in No Man's Land, and he's wondering where Tor is.

"Uh, Tor's not here, man."

Internally I snickered at my not-so-accidental Cheech and Chong joke.

"I'm here to speak to you, my dear."

The warm and resonant voice that came from him reminded me of a favorite actor of mine from nights spent up past bedtime as I peeked around the corner and watched Star Trek in secret. I'd never been caught by my foster family, but let me tell you, Patrick Stewart had me in a chokehold.

"Look who learned how to talk. Good for you, Pat Stew."

Amusement briefly flickered across his face. "You remind me of my niece. She was an irreverent little shit at times too."

"Tor's mom?"

"Just so."

"I love her already."

"She certainly won't love you if things continue as they are."

My belly twisted. My own parents hadn't thought much of me, so you'd think the words wouldn't cut, but they did. "What? Why?"

"Tor needs you, yet you're outside in the cold, staring blankly at the water instead of helping him."

"Firstly, you're a bit of a dick. Secondly, you must not have been paying attention because I have been working my ass off trying to get Tor out. You try and convince a bunch of shrinks that an unhinged Berserker isn't going to go on another rampage. It's not exactly an easy task."

He let out a chuckle before reaching out and running his spectral fingers over my cheek, the strange bite of cold causing me to step back with a gasp. "What are you doing?"

"I seem to be stronger when we speak to each other."

I wasn't sure how to feel about that. Was he trying to say I was some sort of spiritual battery charging him up? Or was he feeding off my energy? Either way, I wasn't sure I liked it.

"Um . . . good for you? Maybe don't touch me without permission, though."

"My apologies. I didn't intend to overstep. I was just caught up on how Evalina had been right about so many things. It never ceases to surprise me how much there is still to learn, even after being dead all this time."

"Mmm," I hummed noncommittally. This interaction was freaking me out. Not because he was scary—as far as ghosts went, it was a bit like hanging out with Mr. Rogers—but chatting up a ghost in general was sincerely off-putting. Every now and then, he'd flicker in and out, like a channel with static. And even at his strongest, I could see Blackwood's main building through him. It was messing with my head.

"Well, like I said, Tor isn't here. Do you want to leave a message?"

"Not for him, no. I'm here to speak to you, Dahlia. It's very important."

"Because Tor's mommy is going to be mad at me? Tell her to get in line."

"Because you are the anchor, and without you, he will be lost. He hasn't got much longer before madness overtakes him. He's been separated from you too long, and a soul bond so newly forged requires near-constant connection in the first few weeks."

"So no pressure, then." I huffed and crossed my arms for good measure, but honestly, he wasn't saying anything I hadn't already tried to convince the doctors of myself. Tor's continued incarceration was a constant pain point for me.

"He needs you, his mate, to soothe his lost soul and bring him back. He won't survive once he gives in to the insanity. We'll lose him."

Anxiety turned my veins into ice. "What part of I'm trying do you not understand? They won't let me stay long enough to do anything."

"Your first mistake, my dear, is believing that they are allowed to control you."

"Did you miss the part where I'm committed?" I shivered as a particularly cold gust of wind skated its way over my throat.

"Only because they fear you. Tap into your power. Become who you were destined to be. Only then will the path become clear."

"I'm sure that sounded like sage advice to you, but it was about as helpful as a bucket of dog shit. Unless you have a concrete method on how I'm supposed to discover said power, you're no help."

He sighed forlornly. "Youth is wasted on the young."

"And wisdom is wasted on the dead and asshole-ish," I grumbled.

"Go to him, Dahlia. Now. You have to admit to yourself that you are stronger when he's with you. The bond between a Berserker and his mate doesn't happen lightly. Or to the unworthy. Fate has something in store for you. Something that requires you to have a partner like him at your side. He cannot help you if he's locked away."

I narrowed my eyes. "How do you know? Are you some kind of oracle?"

"No, dear one. I'm dead. I see a great deal from beyond the veil. Secrets are for the living."

My breath left me in a dejected whoosh. "I didn't ask for any of this, you know. The ghosts, or the weirdo banshee screams, or any of it."

"We never do. That doesn't change our purpose."

"How can I possibly have a purpose? I don't even know what I am yet."

"So figure it out. But first, save your mate."

"You say that like I haven't been trying," I spluttered.

"He needs you to try harder. Help him. Bring him home to you. Trust me when I say none of you will survive what's coming if you're apart."

"I'm really starting to hate you. I have enough random shit I panic about on a daily basis, and now you have me adding spontaneous annihilation to the list. So thanks for that." My skin broke out in a rush of goosebumps as he began fading ever so slightly. Message delivered, I guessed, but it wasn't enough. Before he left, I wanted to make sure he was as frustrated by our encounter as I was. "One more thing before you go wherever you are when you aren't harassing me. Do me a favor?"

He cocked a brow. "Yes?"

"Say 'make it so.' Just the once."

Rolling his eyes, the well-dressed ghost vanished without granting my request.

"God, spirits are so touchy these days."

But even as I said the words, I knew he'd won our little face-off. As soon as I left here, I'd be doing exactly as he'd suggested. Tor and I needed to take a stand and prove we could be together, and the thought of him dying had panic lancing my heart. The only person who could help him was me.

"Ms. Moore, you're just the person I was looking for."

I skidded to a halt before momentum would send me crashing into Dr. Temperance. It had been harder than expected to track the handsome doctor down. He hadn't been in his office, group room, or in any of the common areas. I'd finally cornered his new assistant and was told he had a two o'clock appointment and should be in his office. Which sent me back where I had started.

"Funny," I muttered, blowing a few loose strings of hair out of my eyes. "I've been looking for you."

He took in my flushed cheeks and wind-swept hair, but to his credit he didn't comment on my appearance. "Well, we found each other. Any chance Mr. Nash is with you?"

"Does it look like I'm hiding a dragon shifter in my pocket? Or perhaps one of his heretofore unmentioned skills is invisibility, and I have the power of sight."

"Ah, yes, there's that razor-sharp wit I've been hearing about. Not to worry, I will summon him." The doctor's gaze settled on someone behind me, and he ordered, "Collect Mr. Nash. Bring him to No Man's Land. No argument."

My brow furrowed at that, and my heart kicked up a notch. "You're not going to lock up another of my mates, are you, Doctor?"

He blinked at me. "No, of course not. Well, not without good reason."

"Then why do you need Kai in No Man's Land?"

"If you recall, I said I was looking for both of you." His lips curled up in what I think was supposed to be a reassuring smile. Mostly, it just made me think he farted. We were a long way away from when I used to think of him as the hot doc. Now he was the flatulent dude keeping my Tor locked up.

"I need to see Tor."

"And you will. Once Kai joins us. I'm not your enemy, Miss Moore. Not by half. I'm trying to help."

"Don't you think Kai being with me will set him off?" The thought of Kai being anywhere near me while I tried to talk to Tor was anxiety-inducing. Just like it had been the last time. We'd gotten lucky, but if what Alistair had said was true, Tor was closer to the edge than any of us suspected. What if we didn't get as lucky this time?

Unbidden, my dream from the other night returned to me. The one where I'd had an impromptu session with Dr. Masterson and then a mini orgy in Tor's cell. Had that been some sort of omen? Something told me Tor wasn't a sharer, especially in his beastly state. I should have realized it was a dream straight away when my beast didn't bat an eye at Cas joining us. But maybe there was something to my dream doctor's idea.

"Is this a test?" I asked, gaze flitting from him to the hallway.

"Of sorts, yes. Tor has agreed."

"And what happens if he doesn't pass?"

"He stays where he is. Or . . . we send him back to Novasgard where his jarl can see to him."

"So banishment," I said, reading between the lines.

Nate shrugged. "It's better than the alternative."

Execution.

I shuddered. There was no way I could let that happen.

"And if he passes, that's it? No more imprisonment, he'll be released?"

"That's the idea."

"I want your word, Doctor. If we do this, you let him go. No more hoops."

He leveled his stare on me and nodded. "No more hoops."

My back stiffened as I felt Kai's presence before he made a sound behind me. This wasn't just Tor's life being put at risk. In his beast form, he could tear even the strongest creature limb from limb. I'd witnessed it firsthand.

"I don't know if thi—"

"I'll do it, lass."

"You don't even know what you're agreeing to."

He turned me to face him, purple irises locking on mine. "Aye, I do. He's important to you. You need him, and I'll do whatever is required of me to make sure you get him back."

I reached for his hand, something in me settling at the warmth of his skin pressed against mine. This was absolute madness. The epitome of waving a flag in front of a raging bull, but if it meant freeing him, then it was our only choice.

Still holding on to Kai's hand, I leveled my gaze back on the doctor. "Take us to him."

My Tor stood in his cell, chained to the wall just as he had been in my dream. Only this time, Kai was directly behind me, the door was locked, and there was no possibility of Cas joining in. Tor's obsidian gaze had locked on me the moment I'd stepped into the room. His nostrils had flared as he'd sucked in a sharp breath, but other than that, he'd remained still.

It was as if we were all poised on the edge of a cliff and knew what waited for us in the depths below.

"Do or die, Dahlia," I muttered.

"What?" Kai asked.

"You heard what the doctor said. We have to challenge Tor's control. Make him show them he's stronger than they give him credit for."

"And nothing is a bigger threat than another man touching his mate," Kai finished.

I bit down on my lower lip, nodding. Again I was struck by the parallel of this moment and my dream. Had my subconscious pieced together what I was supposed to do? Or was it something else, like a vision, perhaps? Could that be another part of my hidden identity I'd yet to uncover?

There was no time for me to dwell on it now, but I knew once Tor was free, I'd have to circle back to that piece of the puzzle.

"Dahlia," Tor grumbled, a strange tightness in his broken voice. "Please."

"He won't harm you, gem. I willnae let him." Kai's palm slipped around my waist, pulling me against his chest.

"I need her." Tor's voice was a rasp of gravel, but his eyes weren't on me any longer. He focused on Kai and where he was touching me.

"Then prove you can bloody handle yourself, Viking."

A low growl rumbled in his chest, but Tor gave Kai a slow nod. He wasn't happy, but he was on board. For now, anyway.

I hated that we had to do this. That I knew there were cameras somewhere in this room and strangers watching what should be a private moment between me and my two mates. But . . . I also loved it.

I loved the way Tor's eyes blazed as he tracked the movement of Kai's fingers over my skin. How his breaths were shallow pants, and each caress of his eyes echoed in my core.

"Make her want you." Tor sounded more like himself than he had in a long time, but he also pulsed with a dangerous energy.

"I didn't realize you were the one in control here." Kai's lips brushed my neck as he spoke, and shivers raced down my spine.

"Isn't that the point?"

I moaned, more of a whimper, really, and leaned back into Kai's hold. "Take off my shirt," I whispered.

Kai stiffened for a second and then melted against me. "Are you sure?"

I knew he was referring to my being topless and on camera, but at this point, I'd let him fuck me here and now if that's what it took. I had no scruples when it came to saving Tor.

As soon as he removed the fabric from my skin, my nipples pebbled in the cold air. I'd never been more glad I hadn't worn a bra. Tor groaned from his position near the wall, his cock already straining against the pair of joggers they'd given him to wear.

"Touch me, Kai. Please?"

He rested his chin on my shoulder, and even though I couldn't see him, I knew he was looking at Tor. "Where should I touch her, Viking?"

Tor was all grunts and growls, his eyes flashing with lightning as he worked to keep himself under control. "Make her cry out."

I could feel Kai's lips curl into a smile against my skin. "Your name or mine?"

"Kai," I panted as his fingers tweaked my nipples, pulling and twisting them until I was riding the edge between pleasure and pain.

"Ah, mine it is."

He nibbled my neck, large palms cupping the weight of my full breasts, and the chains rattled as Tor responded to the sight before him. His harsh breaths only added to my arousal. As did the wet spot growing on his light gray sweats. My Viking was dripping for me, just like I was dripping for him. For both of them.

Fuck, I wasn't supposed to be enjoying this so much . . . right?

"Tor," I whispered when my fingers went to the waistband of my leggings and dipped inside.

He growled, his muscles trembling and swelling as I toyed with my clit. "Mine."

"Ours," Kai corrected.

Tor's jaw flexed, but he didn't argue. Kai grabbed my jaw and turned my face toward him, dipping his head and claiming my lips.

I was swept away on a sea of sensation as Kai's tongue tangled with mine. His large hands continued to plump and play with my breasts while I toyed with my clit. Kai's smoky scent filled my nose, but it was paired with the wild winter storm that was Tor's. It was my new favorite fragrance, an instant aphrodisiac. I was drunk on it. On them.

My mates.

The unmistakable sound of chains breaking stopped us, Kai's hold on me tightening as I turned my attention to the mountain of a man looming inches from me.

Tor stood before us, unrestrained, trembling with rage as Kai continued touching me.

Kai's lips were at my ear. "It's okay, gem. This is what they need to see. He's still in control. He just wants to be closer to you."

"He can touch me too. I'm not stopping him."

"Tell him that," Kai whispered. "We can both make you feel good."

His teeth sank into the muscle at the base of my neck, and I cried out, the noise making Tor snarl louder.

"Tor," I whispered. "I'm okay. He's not hurting me."

Eyes never leaving Tor's, I waited as the fury left his face, and he reached for me, clawed hands terrifyingly beautiful. But his eyes were no longer pure black. Midnight now ringed his irises. It wasn't the beast looking at me. It was Tor.

My Tor.

"Kærasta," he whispered, his voice thick with longing. And then his lips feathered over mine in a kiss so sweet it could have been written about in a fairy tale. In that one kiss, I tasted him, his heart, his love, his pure devotion. He wasn't a mindless beast, but a man cursed to terrify all who encountered him. I'd do anything to get him out of this cycle and into one that would appreciate everything he brought to the table.

"That's quite enough of that," Dr. Temperance's voice crackled over an intercom speaker I couldn't locate for the life of me.

Tor's lips feathered over mine a final time before he stepped away. Submitting to the doctor's command. Proving, beyond all reasonable doubt, that he could control himself.

"You're free to go."

"All of us?" I asked the disembodied voice, hope making my voice break.

"Not yet." Before I could protest, the doctor continued speaking. "Tor needs to be properly discharged, but as soon as the paperwork is complete, then yes. We've seen all we need to see. Tor passed his test."

CHAPTER THIRTY-ONE

KAI

Threading my fingers through hers, I walked alongside Dahlia in the dim light of dusk. The loch was blanketed by a layer of mist, the air heavy with the promise of rain. In a setting like this, the grounds of Blackwood appeared every inch the Gothic horror movie set people would expect from a supernatural asylum. But with my mate by my side, it seemed more a gothic romance rather than the former. Goddess knows they certainly had their share of ghosts and creepy crawlies in them as well. Two sides of the same coin, really.

"Earth to Kai. Come in, Kai."

I blinked, realizing I'd been lost to my musings and missed what she'd said.

"Rutting fool. There's a murderer on the loose, and yer getting distracted? Have I taught ye nothing?"

Ignoring that, I smiled down at my beautiful little mate. "Sorry, gem. My head was somewhere else."

"Anywhere fun?"

"Actually, I was thinking the two of us could find a nook somewhere out here and finish what we started earlier."

There was no missing the arousal flooding her scent. "Is that so?"

"Mmm."

"Just right here in the open, where anyone could stumble upon us?"

"Seems tae me ye prefer it that way."

Her cheeks flushed a delectable pink. "It depends on who might see. And who might . . ."

"Join in?" I finished for her.

Biting her lower lip, she nodded.

"That might happen sooner than ye think."

The warning was all I needed to start scanning the horizon. There. It didn't take more than a flash of his clothes to recognize him.

Caspian, the little bugger. Skulking around and spying on us.

"What about him? The pirate?" I asked, jutting my chin toward where Hook lurked.

Her shoulders stiffened, a strange sense of arousal and unease radiating from her. "We have an uneasy truce, I guess, but I haven't forgiven him fully for what he did to Tor. He can't be trusted enough to be in our group."

"He's a tragic creature, living outside the warmth of your gaze."

"He's not outside it. Just not fully encompassed by it. You, on the other hand . . ."

My dragon preened. *"If it's warmth she's after, I'm more than up for the task."*

Her head quirked to the side, eyes scanning my face. "Your dragon is speaking to you, isn't he?"

"How can you tell?"

"You get this faraway look in your eyes. Like you're listening to music no one else can hear."

I smirked, loving that she was so attuned to my expressions. "He is a constant buzzing in my brain at this point. You've all but freed him, and he won't let that go."

"Me? I didn't do anything."

"You dared me to unleash him. It was hard enough keeping him in line, but a dragon could never resist the lure of his mate."

"Is that why you were inking yourself? That time I caught you in your tower?"

Clenching my jaw against the dragon's pressure in my head, I nodded. "Aye. My spell has been weakening ever since your arrival. I was trying to fortify it."

"And then we basically played sexy chicken and sent what was left crashing down," she surmised, her blush deepening as she recalled the night my dragon took center stage in her bed.

"I wouldnae have it any other way."

"Really?"

Even my dragon perked up to hear my answer. I could feel him, like a prickle inside my skull. "You were right. I cannae deny what I am. And now that we are mated . . . I need to know that I can keep you safe from any threat."

"Does that mean I get to meet him?"

The smug bastard was gloating. *"She wants me, see? Let me out to play with our wee mate."*

Stay in yer lane, ye terrible great lizard. Ye ken the rules.

To Dahlia, I said, "You've talked to him."

"No, I mean, like, will I get to *meet* him." Then she flapped her arms like a great winged bird. "In the scales, you know?"

I couldn't help myself; I laughed. "You are adorable. You know that, right?"

"So are you."

"No, I'm not. I am fierce and terrifying."

*"*I *am fierce and terrifying. Yer a meat suit."*

She likes my meat.

"She likes mine *better."*

Dahlia interrupted what was surely about to devolve into a petty game of one-up-manship, stealing our attention as she leaned into me and dropped her voice. "You're a kitty cat. And I know just how to make you purr."

Fuck me, I was trying to turn this ship around and stop focusing on the sexual aspect of our relationship, but she made it nearly impossible. If I had it my way, she'd never leave my nest, and we'd already have a dragonling on the way. But I couldn't. Not with everything still hanging in the balance. The Shadow Court was going to pull me back as soon as I'd proven to have the control needed to defend them. That meant I'd have to leave her, no matter how much it hurt to do so. She wouldn't survive in Faerie, and there was no way Tor would ever let her go, even if she could.

Dahlia cupped my cheek. "He sure is chatty tonight," she murmured, incorrectly guessing where my thoughts had wandered.

"He never shuts up," I said, not wanting to weigh her down with the heaviness of my thoughts. There'd be time for that later. Best to let her enjoy the return of her Viking before presenting her with yet another hurdle.

"I know one way to shut him up," she said, stepping a wee bit closer to me.

My palm immediately went around her waist, pulling her in. "I'm all ears, lass."

Lifting onto her toes, she presented her lips for a kiss. I dipped my head and met her mouth with mine, sighing at the contact, not realizing just how much I truly needed it.

A gust of wind sent fallen leaves and twigs scattering, bringing with it the scent of an oncoming storm. I stiffened, forcing myself to pull away from my mate.

"We should get inside, gem. It's not safe for us to remain out here much longer."

"I thought you wanted to finish what we started."

"Aye, I do. But a storm's coming."

The rumble of thunder rolled across the sky, a warning of what was to come. Then it happened again and again, until it was constant. Dahlia stiffened in my arms, her attention trained behind me.

"Tor," she whispered, pulling out of my hold.

Turning around, I saw the Berserker standing at the crest of the hill which led to the castle. By all rights we shouldn't have been able to hear him, but what I'd mistaken for thunder hadn't been the gods fighting in the sky. It was the Beast. He'd been freed, and he was coming for his mate. He was unnaturally still, his hair a wild tempest flying in the wind. He took one step toward us. Then a second. By the third, he was running, his long strides eating up the distance between us.

"Dahlia, I need you to listen very carefully," I urged.

"He won't hurt me, Kai."

"Just do what I tell ye. When I say so, run as fast as yer legs will carry ye. Do ye understand?"

He was close now, close enough I put myself in front of her and prepared to do the thing I'd promised him if it came to this.

"Get ready," I pressed.

Unleashing what I could of my dragon, I stood my ground as Tor closed in on me.

Planting my feet, I counted his steps.

Three.

Two.

One.

"Run, Dahlia! Run!"

CHAPTER

THIRTY-TWO

TOR

They thought I was in control. They were wrong.

As soon as I caught her scent on the wind, I was lost to the primal urge to find my mate and bury myself as deep inside her as possible. Everything else was in the way. White noise. A thing to be ignored or disposed of.

Including him.

"Tor, no!"

A beastly growl ripped through me, saliva dripping from my fangs as I bared my teeth at the man standing between me and the woman who owned me. He sent her away. He told her to run from me. Me. Her true mate. As though I'd harm her in any way.

There was nowhere she could hide that I would not find her. My instincts were honed, and the pull between us was undeniable. I'd find my Kærasta if she was an entire world away. Not even death could keep us apart. I'd stalk her through this life and the next.

She. Was. Mine.

With ferocious strides, I closed the distance between my adversary and me. Dragon fire blazed within his irises, his pupils slitted, hands shifted to deadly claws. He was no match for me. A Berserker in search of his other half.

We locked eyes as the fool started running headlong toward me. I threw my head back and laughed. He thought he could best *me*? Pathetic.

Standing firm, I timed his steps, sweeping my arm across my body and out. I swatted him away as if he were no more troublesome than a gnat. But gnat or not, I was still a Berserker. The entire brunt of my strength was behind the hit, and he went flying straight into one of the castle walls. The old stones were no defense against Kai's bulk. The wall collapsed, burying him beneath the rubble. Was he dead? I doubted it. But I wasn't going to stop in order to find out. My beauty was out there, alone, unguarded, and I was meant to be her protector.

Tipping my face to the sky, I inhaled deeply, drawing in the scent of the forest, and, more importantly, my Dahlia.

Just one hit of her, and my dick was hard.

I strode unerringly down the path she'd taken, not bothering to rush. There was no question whether or not I'd find her. Let her tire herself out; it only made my job easier. Because once I caught her, I was never letting her go again.

It wasn't long before the sound of crunching leaves and snapping twigs reached my ears, followed closely by a low string of curses.

"Ow, dammit. Stupid tree. These tits were not made for running."

I couldn't help myself. I laughed. I loved everything about her, including the way her human body worked against her. Especially when it was for my benefit.

I found her in a clearing, hands on her knees, breaths coming in gasps. The way she looked up at me through the curtain of hair that had escaped her bun made me smirk.

"Are . . . you . . . going . . . to . . . eat . . . me . . . now?" she asked through harsh pants.

My grin was all beast. "Yes."

And then I was on her.

She let out a sharp scream as we went down, but I protected what was mine in all things. I cradled her and rolled us so when we met the ground, I took the brunt of the fall, but before she could wriggle free, I had her under me again.

"You ran from me," I accused.

"Kai told me to," she wheezed.

I lifted my head just long enough to hold her gaze. "I liked it."

"You did?"

"Mmm," I hummed, burying my nose in her neck again. "Chasing you is my new favorite game." Then I nipped her, not hard, just enough to leave my mark.

"And you like biting me too? And holding me down?"

"Yes, Kærasta, I do." I rocked my hard length against her hip. "Can't you tell?"

"You mean that's not a tree trunk in your pocket?"

"I don't have pockets."

"That's a real design flaw in those pants. Pockets are essential."

A laugh rumbled from deep in my chest. "I guess I'll just take them off."

"Good idea. That'll teach 'em."

"Who?"

"The pants-maker people."

"Pants-maker people?" I repeated with a chuckle. "I thought you were a writer."

"Who can be smart and wordsy when *you're* lying on top of them? It's a wonder I remember any words at all."

My fangs retracted bit by bit as our banter continued, the beast still present and begging for his mate, but my consciousness much more my original self.

"What's that look in your eyes, Tor?" she asked, reaching up and brushing my hair away from my face.

I fucking flinched as she touched me, knowing I didn't look like the same Novasgardian prince she'd first met. I may never be him again. Where my hair had once been blond like my twin's, it was now inky black and crowned by horns. Not to mention the rest of me. I was monstrous. Beastly.

Thanks to this curse, I might always be.

"Do you . . . do you think you can love me like this?" I asked, my heart crawling up my throat, voice breaking and turning to a rasp.

"On the floor of the deep, dark woods?"

Mischief shone in her eyes. She was trying to pull me away from the hard question I'd asked. But why? Because she didn't want to answer me? Or because it didn't matter to her? Either way, I needed to know. So I pressed.

"Dahlia, I may never be myself again. I might look"—I took a shuddering breath—"this way. Forever."

Sensing my despair, her smile faded. "Do you think so little of me that you really believe any of this"—she waved a hand at my body—"matters to me?"

"I'm not the prince any longer."

She took my face between her palms and forced me to look at her. "I see you, Tor. The man I fell for. You're in there right now. I can see you looking back at me. The rest is inconsequential. I've learned a lot about acceptance in my life. Being built the way I am . . . living in LA, it's not hard to get caught up in what we look like. But I'll let you in on a secret."

I couldn't look away from her. "Go on."

"Physical beauty is fleeting. One day we're all going to wake up wrinkled and old. And that is not a bad thing. It's a privilege to age, you know? One that was almost stolen from me. It's a gift I don't take lightly. So no, Tor, I don't care if you look like a Norse god or have horns and scales and eyes that swirl like galaxies. All I care about is that you're in there looking back at me."

She kissed me then, her lips desperate and frantic as she changed the course of the moment. I didn't worry about what she thought of me anymore. I couldn't. Not after what she'd said. It was me she wanted. Me she craved.

I never should have doubted her. She was made for me. My perfect match in every way. A gift from fate that I didn't possibly deserve but would spend the rest of my life attempting to.

"I need you."

At first I thought the words came from me because it'd been exactly what I'd been thinking, but the breathless plea was hers.

"I'm a beast, Dahlia. It won't be the same."

She took my hand and placed it over her breast, eyes dark with lust. "I've already been fucked by a dragon. How much different can it be?"

Jealousy blazed to life within me, the monster taking center stage at the challenge in her question. A growl worked its way up my throat. "Oh, I'm going to show you. Put your hands over your head, and don't fucking move."

"Ooh, growly Tor is back. Yay me."

I snatched her by the wrist, forcing her to do as I said and arranging her so I had her arms pinned above her head and her body at my mercy. It was all I could do not to tear her clothes off her body so I could drive in here and now.

"How're you gonna fuck me with those pants on, big boy?"

A snarl ripped out of me, but I slashed the fabric down one side and let it fall free, releasing my straining cock in answer.

"Oh, I see," she whispered, squirming beneath me.

Before she could say anything else, I did the same to hers, shredding her shirt and leggings.

"What if I liked those?"

"I'll get you new ones."

The scent of her arousal flooded my system, short-circuiting my brain. It was impossible to think beyond my need to sink inside her.

"I thought you were going to eat me," she teased, but the breathless quality of her voice betrayed her.

My mouth watered at the thought, but I'd already taken myself in hand and was rubbing the swollen head of my dick between her slick folds. She was hot and wet, the perfect welcoming sheath for my aching length. My arms trembled with the effort to hold back and not drive inside her.

"Oh, Tor. I see it in your eyes. You can't stand it, can you?" she asked.

"What?"

"Waiting. You're all . . . filled with primal need."

"I am."

Those two words cost me more than I cared to admit. I'd only had one night with her before she was taken from me. One night of utter bliss before I'd become something inhuman. What if I hurt her? What if I lost control? It was taking everything I had not to give in to the instinct riding me. I'd heard the stories of Novasgardians who'd found their mates. Weeks spent in uninterrupted euphoria, near constant fucking until they had to stop or die. All of that had been stolen from us.

"You see," she whispered, reaching up and taking my face in her hand again. "This right here is the reason I will love you no matter what. Because even now, as lost to your beast as you are, you're putting my needs above your own. You call yourself a monster, Tor, but you are good and kind, honorable and gallant. You are exactly the man your father raised you to be."

"I want to be the mate you deserve."

"You are. Now take what you want. You can have your dessert later."

"Dahlia . . ."

"Give in, Tor. I want it, and we both need it."

There was no arguing with that. Not that she gave me a chance.

She parted her legs wider, rocking her hips up and seeking me out. "Don't be gentle with me, Tor. Let me have the beast."

With a harsh groan, I shoved into her to the hilt, her whole body moving up the slight hill we'd been resting on.

"Yes, like that. More, Tor. I want you. All of you."

Her impassioned cries tore through the last of my resolve. I couldn't deny my mate anything, least of all me.

"Hold on to me, Kærasta."

Her fingers dug into my back, legs wrapping around my waist as she did what she was told. I pistoned into her, each hard thrust driving her farther up the hill. I wanted more, though. I needed to be as deep inside her as I could get.

"On your knees," I growled in her ear.

"O-okay."

Pulling out of her, I flipped her over impatiently, giving her round arse a sound slap as she positioned herself. Her hair was a wild mass of tangles, with twigs and leaves stuck in the strands. Somehow, that made this even hotter. She was a mess—for me.

Gripping her hip in one hand, I took myself in the other and then slammed in with enough force to knock the breath from her. Her groan of absolute pleasure had me pulling back and doing it again.

"More," she begged. "Harder."

Before I knew what I was doing, my fist was in her hair, and I was thrusting as hard as I could, the slap of our flesh meeting filling the air.

"Fuuuck, beauty. You take me like you were made for my cock."

"I was."

"Fuck yes, you were. You're mine, Dahlia. Forever."

"Yes. Yes."

Her walls were tight and hot around me, but I wanted to feel that perfect fluttering, the squeeze that told me she was coming all over me. Reaching down, I slipped my hand across her belly until I found the bud of nerves I knew would send her off like a rocket.

"No, I don't want this to be over yet," she protested, trying to wriggle away.

I tightened my hold on her hair, yanking her back. "Who said anything about this being over? You and I will never be over, beauty."

"I j-just meant the s-sex," she panted, her entire body shaking as her climax started to rise.

"If you think I'm going to let you go after one orgasm, you don't know me at all. I've been without my mate for days. I want everything you have. I want you spent and dripping with my cum. I'm not going to stop until you beg me to stop."

"God, Tor. I . . ." Her words cut off on a thready cry as the pleasure took her.

Unfortunately, I didn't get to bask in her climax because my attention was torn from her as a large figure stepped out of the shadows, his gaze intent on us.

CHAPTER THIRTY-THREE

DAHLIA

I was going to die right here while being railed in the forest by a beast. That was possible, right? To die because the pleasure was too intense? I was sure I'd heard of it happening. If not, I might be the first.

Maybe they'd put up a monument for me right here. It could say something like *Here lies Dahlia Moore. She flew too close to the sun.* Or maybe *In memory of Dahlia Moore, she died doing what she loved.*

"God, Tor I . . ." Jesus, I was coming again.

But he stopped, his whole body tensing—and not in a good way.

I couldn't quite form words or get my body to obey because I was still mid-climax, but I knew something had changed. When he started growling low in his throat, I realized we were no longer alone.

Well, shit. I really was going to die impaled on Novasgardian dick.

"You look beautiful like this, gem." Kai's voice instantly soothed me as he stepped out of the shadows, his eyes glowing amethysts in the dark. "But I think you need a little more attention, don't ye? You have two mates, after all."

Tor's hands dug into my skin so hard I knew I'd be wearing his bruises. I didn't hate the thought. They were like a parting gift. Sex-mentos, if you will.

"She's mine," he snarled, rutting deeper into me as if to drive his point home.

I groaned and dug my fingers into the dirt to keep myself upright. God, it felt so good.

"She's . . . ours." The confidence in Kai's voice made my pussy flutter, but as he drew closer, the clearly disheveled state of him was cause for concern. His shirt was torn, his body caked in gray-white dust. There were bits of rubble in his hair, and flecks of dried blood peppered his skin.

"What happened . . . to you?" I gasped as Tor continued to rut into me. Later, I was definitely going to revisit this moment and laugh about how I was trying to carry on a normal conversation mid-fuck. What even was my life? Maybe I was dead already and this was all just a dream.

"Just a bit of an obstacle. Don't worry about me, lass. I'm a dragon. I'm not easy to kill."

"We're busy," Tor grunted, wrapping his hand around my throat and pulling me up until I was pressed against his chest as he continued to fill me. "Aren't we, Kærasta?"

Kai didn't flinch; instead he strode forward, ripped off his shirt, and began opening his fly. "She wants us both. Look at the way her body responds to me. I'm her mate too, Tor. You know it's true."

Tor snarled, his fingers clenching tighter around my throat. "Is it true?" he growled into my ear.

"Y-yes," I stuttered.

"He's yours?"

"Y-yes. Just like y-you."

"You want us both to have you now?"

The way my cunt clenched around him, the flood of arousal coating his cock, and the way I squirmed on him should have been enough of an answer. But I managed to choke out, "Please."

Without warning, Tor adjusted us so he was sitting on his heels and my thighs were splayed over his. I didn't hate it. This position had him a little less deep, but in a way, I felt more stretched than before. Fuck, he was girthy.

"Ride me, Kærasta. Take your pleasure from your mate." The way he hit the T on the last word, I knew he meant it for Kai.

This fight for dominance between them had me practically feral. Maybe later, when I wasn't getting absolutely railed, I might worry about them fighting for the top spot in the lineup. But right now? It was only benefiting me.

For his part, Kai just laughed. He wasn't fazed by Tor's alpha posturing at all. He was assured of his place in my heart. As he should be. He'd just spent the last week warming my bed and fucking me silly. My dragon had nothing to prove.

"Open up, gem. Suck my dick like I taught you. Let's show your Viking what you've learned."

The way Tor grabbed my tits said he didn't like knowing Kai had taken that first away from him.

"Just remember, dragon. I had her first. She's been mine since the moment she walked through Blackwood's doors."

"You didn't have her mouth around your cock first."

Tor rocked into me, and I whimpered. "No, but I filled her before you did. I claimed her first. I will always be her first."

"Be her first, then. I'll be her last."

Fuck. Me.

"Do you two want me to leave you alone? My fingers and I can take it from here if you'd rather work this out together." It probably would have packed more of a punch if I hadn't been panting and moaning through the question, but I really needed them to stop fighting and start really fucking me.

I'd been fantasizing about both of them—honestly, all of them, but we'd work with what we got—taking me for weeks now. I didn't want to miss my big moment.

"The hell you will, mate. This pussy is mine," Tor growled.

Kai skated his hand over my head, tangling his fingers in my hair. “The only orgasms you’ll get tonight, gem, are the ones we give you.”

“You make so many promises, but your dick still isn’t in my mouth.”

Tor let out a low chuckle. “Ah, so you’re a brat then, are you?”

“When the occasion calls for it. Someone’s gotta make sure I get what I want.”

“No, Kærasta, it's our job to give you what you need.”

“Look at that. He’s a fast learner.”

Tor let out a growl of annoyance at Kai’s baiting.

If I didn’t do something to stop them, they’d eventually end up actually fighting. I really didn’t want that. Tor promised me endless pleasure. I was going to take him up on that. So, I reached up, grabbed Kai’s length, and took him into my mouth, effectively putting an end to their argument.

When in doubt, suck his cock, right? Problem solved.

“Oh fuck, lass. Just like that.” His fingers dove into my hair and tangled in the thick strands.

Can I just say there was something magical about being used like this? They had me completely at their mercy, could do anything they wanted, and yet, I’d never felt more adored in my life. These beautiful men held me in a way that was damn near worshipful, and I was here for it.

“Goddess, gem. Your mouth. I cannae describe how much I love it.”

“Oh, brilliant. He’s a talker,” Tor grumbled as he layered kisses down my neck. “I can talk too, remember? I can tell you how tight your cunt squeezes me. How slick and hot it is around my dick. Oh gods, beauty. I could stay here seated deep inside you forever.” He groaned and rolled his hips upward, spearing me deeper. “You take my cock like it was made for you. Such a good girl.”

I whimpered around Kai while my pussy fluttered around Tor.

This was even better than I’d imagined. And as a smut writer, I’d imagined *a lot*.

Kai's fingers ran along the side of my face, trailing over the tears that had already escaped my eyes from the way his cock slid down my throat.

"Swallow around my dick, gem. I want to feel your throat tighten on me."

The rasped order, combined with the tenderness of his caress, had me desperate to obey. I wanted to give these men everything they were giving me.

"She fucking loves that. Her cunt is fluttering around me. Fuck." Tor's hands were everywhere, cupping my breasts, squeezing my nipples, frantically tightening around my waist and then hips.

I'd just come, but was well on my way to detonating again.

Tor's lips were at my ear, teeth grazing the lobe as he whispered, "Give me another, my beauty. Give me as many as you can."

His fingers went to my swollen, aching pussy, touching everywhere but my clit, and I thought I might kill him if he didn't actually touch me.

I moaned in protest, not wholly surprised when Kai's pleasured groan joined mine. "So fucking good."

If I wasn't preoccupied by the two dicks filling me, I'd feel like I needed to be doing more, participating in the action, but they held me in place and there was nowhere I could go. Kai's gentle grip kept me still so he could rock into my mouth, while Tor's more than capable hands positioned me exactly how he wanted. I'd never found the term fuck doll particularly appealing, but now that I was basically living it, I had to admit it was pretty amazing. It forced me to exist in the moment and fully experience everything they were giving me. There were no intrusive thoughts. No worries about how I looked or what my body was doing. Only pleasure. Pure, mindless pleasure.

I let out a garbled moan around Kai's length as Tor finally grazed my clit with the tip of one finger. My hips rocked, but he held fast and drove up into me.

"No, you stay where I put you. Suck him hard while I make you come."

Yes, sir.

I never took myself as a submissive, but something about Tor and Kai taking charge and bossing me around was doing it for me big time. Maybe because I was always the one orchestrating these sorts of scenes, and them taking control gave me freedom I didn't know I craved. Or maybe it was just fuck hot, and I didn't need to overthink it.

"Fuck, keep going like that, and amnae going tae last."

Kai's brogue seemed to get stronger the closer he got to his release. I loved it. It meant his dragon was close to the surface.

The knowledge made me suck harder. Stretched around his girth as I was, I couldn't do much more than that, but it didn't stop me from trying every trick I could think of. I slid my hands up his strong thighs until I cupped his balls with one and used the other to tease his taint.

"Fuuuck, lass."

Oh yeah. That was exactly what he needed. My own pleasure was building as Tor continued fucking me and toying with my clit. Kai spread his legs a little wider, and my finger ran along his ass, searching for my target.

"Yes, gem. Touch me."

I didn't have lube at the ready, and while I wasn't experienced, I was a romance writer. I knew exactly what my obstacles were in this territory. Penetration might be off the table, but I could still play with him a little. Internally I was smirking as I pressed and circled his tight pucker, dragging sounds out of him that sent sparks shooting straight to my already needy clit. Oh yeah, I was definitely going to come again.

"Whatever you're doing to him, keep doing it, Kærasta. It's making you squeeze me so tight. Are you going to come all over my cock?" Tor's beard brushed my nape a second before he scraped his teeth along the sensitive skin and shuddered.

I tightened around him in answer, and he let out a ragged groan.

"She's close," Tor grunted.

"So am I," Kai rasped.

Together.

Obviously I couldn't verbalize the order with my mouth stuffed full of Kai's dragon dick, but I think they got the message.

Tor picked up his pace. "Come for me, Kærasta. Be my good girl and come so I can."

I was lightheaded and so fucking close. I slurped around Kai, adding pressure to the finger playing with his ass.

"Goddess, I'm there," Kai groaned, his shaft pulsing in my mouth.

Tor rubbed my clit as he fucked me, his breaths tense and harsh. My God, he was good at this. Then he took away the friction on my sensitive nub, and I almost cried in frustration. Until the sharp slap of his fingers against my pussy sent me over the edge. I came almost painfully, swallowing my cries and Kai's dick all at the same time.

Kai's cum poured down my throat as he thrust into me and roared his pleasure. Tor bit down on the tender place where my neck and shoulder met as he found his own release, the thick length inside me swelling even further as he filled me.

My dragon pulled out of me as I rode the rest of my climax, a little of his cum escaping my mouth. Using his thumb, he pushed the dribble back between my lips.

"You know the rules, gem. Every. Last. Drop."

Obediently, I licked his finger clean, my breaths coming hard and fast as I drifted down from my high. I went completely limp, my body well and truly spent. Tor's cock began to soften inside me, his cum already leaking from me. I didn't want to lose any of it, but I knew it was inevitable.

"That was . . . really fucking hot." I barely recognized my voice, raspy as it was. "A threesome wasn't on my list of things to do while in Scotland, but I'm not going to complain."

"Maybe next time we can try it in a bed?" Kai asked, moving to pull me off Tor, but my Viking held tight, so Kai gently plucked a leaf out of my hair instead. "Your body pressed between ours . . ."

"Mmm, sandwiches. Best enjoyed in a bed."

"That is, as long as Tor here is game."

"Not every time. We may be sharing her, but I will need her to myself as well. My beast will demand it."

"As will my dragon."

"So I'll just draw up a pussy schedule then, shall I?" I hoped they heard the smile in my voice.

My mind went to Caspian and the way I needed him even when I was angry with him. And then there was my elusive Cain. How was I going to rotate between them all when the time came? They got one night a week each, with Friday as my sandwich day and the weekend free-for-all? My pussy throbbed just thinking of it.

I guess I'd just have to ride that dick when the time came. Or I did.

Ba-dum tsh.

CHAPTER THIRTY-FOUR

HOOK

Naughty, naughty. A spit roast, right here in the open? How utterly, sinfully depraved. But where was my invitation, love? I would've been happy to be included, even if I only watched them rail you while I had a wank. But no, instead I'm reduced to being nothing more than a peeping Tom rather than having the pleasure of eye contact with you while you come apart.

Did our night together mean nothing to you? Am I to be punished forever for one thoughtless misdeed? Someone needs to learn the meaning of forgiveness.

My thoughts continued on in this fashion, spiraling uselessly while jealousy warred with my arousal. Fuck, she looked beautiful like that. Cock shoved up her cunny, another down her throat, tears streaming down her cheeks and her nipples so hard they could cut glass. My palm skated over the bulge in my trousers, itching to take out my straining length so I could relieve the pressure in my balls. I'd leave the forest floor painted with my cum so she could find it on her way back to the estate.

"He'll find her out here."

"He's watching you."

"He's coming for her."

Without warning, three frantic whispered voices spoke at once, their words whipping around me like gusts of wind.

"The woods aren't safe."

"He's in the trees."

"Don't turn around."

My heart thudded like a caged beast. I wasn't easily scared, but this was disorientating at best. I couldn't get my bearings with their rapid-fire warnings flying at me. Were they spirits? Wood sprites? Mischievous pixies? Or something more ominous?

"Save her!"

The raspy voice was a shout this time, different from before, and loud enough I nearly jumped out of my skin. Save who? Dahlia? She was doing just fine with her two male companions. Neither Tor nor Kai would let a damn thing happen to her.

"Go! Now!"

The warning was accompanied by a ripple in the trees, a brief gust of wind that seemed to part the shadows just long enough for me to catch a glimpse of something out of the corner of my eye. What was that? A cloak?

"Say your prayers, cowardly knave. You picked the wrong woman to spy on." Silently, I added, *It's only okay when I do it.*

Reaching for my cutlass, I groaned when I came up empty-handed. Blasted doctors and their *safety concerns*. How was I to dispatch this threat with nothing more than my cutting wit? Good thing I wasn't a fan of rules and always kept a dagger in my boot. Rushing footsteps across dead foliage had me following the perpetrator's trail easily. Whoever this was, they weren't blessed with the soft-footedness of the fae. I'd catch him and present him to Dahlia as a sign of my devotion. Tor wasn't the only one who could lavish her in bloody gifts. He might be the beast, but I was still Captain Fucking Hook. I was well-versed in making my enemies cower before me.

My prey zigzagged through the forest, but it was easy enough for me to follow, especially with those infernal whispers encouraging me.

"There. Just ahead."

"Stop him before he kills her."

"Don't let him escape."

Bloody hell, I needed these voices to stop rasping in my ear. It wouldn't do to die of a heart attack in the middle of the woods.

I ran for it, chasing after the man I'd come to realize must be the Ripper. Why else would he be skulking about the woods?

Perhaps a better question was why the spirits in the woods were talking to me, but now was hardly the time for introspection. Through a break in the boughs overhead, I could just make out a plague mask covering his face, the eyes an eerie, glowing red.

He stumbled over a tree root, and I saw my opportunity. I rushed for him, weapon in hand, and we collided with a grunt. My dagger made purchase with his thigh, causing him to roar in pain and fight to free himself of me. I pulled the blade free and went in again, but my target knocked the steel out of my hand with a sharp blow to my wrist.

That wasn't good. While I'd gotten the drop on him, I was more crafty and cunning than physically formidable. I was a lover, not a fighter, if I'm being honest. I did my best work in the shadows before my opponent ever saw me coming. But this opponent was more than aware of me now, meaning the tide had definitely turned.

His legs curled up, and before I knew it, booted feet slammed into my stomach, sending me flying off him and clashing with a boulder. With the wind knocked out of me, I had to work to catch my breath. Every inhale felt like knives stabbing my lungs. He'd broken my pissing ribs. The arsehole was stronger than I'd given him credit for.

He was quicker to his feet than me, soon looming over me with my stolen blade held threateningly in his hand.

"Stand up," he growled in an unnaturally deep and raspy voice. I'd seen enough horror movies with Kai to recognize a vocal changer when I heard one.

"Of course . . . you'd . . . be . . . an American," I wheezed as I pushed to my feet. We were almost the same height, though he had a couple inches on me. It didn't make me feel any better about my odds.

"You supernatural freaks disgust me. Fae scum are the worst of them all."

"Now, now," I teased weakly. "That's not very nice."

Burning pain cut through my side as he shoved the dagger in while his red glowing eyes remained trained on me. "If I was nice, I'd make this fast, like I did the others."

That was all the confirmation I needed. This was definitely the Ripper. Which meant there was no way I was getting out of this alive. He'd kill me and then use my body for parts. I was a dead man, which meant I might as well make the most of my last seconds on this plane.

"If it's my hook you're after, it's in my pants," I spat, determined to brazen this out to the bloody end. If he wanted me weeping and begging, he was in for a world of disappointment.

I reached up, attempting to knock the bird-like mask from his face so I could see who this fucker was, but he stopped me with a gloved hand around my wrist. I'd already lost enough blood to make me woozy.

"Go on, then," I forced out. "Do your worst."

"I intend to."

He raised the blade again, the bloodied steel glinting in the moonlight. But before he could drive it home, an unearthly roar filled the air, the sound almost on top of us. He faltered, head snapping in its direction. I recognized the roar as one of Dahlia's men finding their completion, but it was obvious from the way he tensed above me that the Ripper thought someone was hot on his heels. I could have laughed. I knew the truth of these woods, and it was clear my attacker didn't.

The Black Forest played tricks on you. Made you see things that weren't there. Believe they were closer than they appeared, or vice versa. In sum, it was one massive mind fuck. I knew it. The residents of Blackwood knew it. But *he* didn't. And I was damn well going to use that to my advantage.

I smirked, breaths coming in shallow rattles. "You . . . didn't think . . . I was alone . . . did you? We caught you."

My eyes drooped, my vision going blurry from blood loss, but I worked to stay standing as he dropped the knife and abandoned me. As my hold on consciousness faded and I slid down the big boulder, I could have sworn I saw him disappear into the ground. But then again, I knew better than to trust anything I was seeing right now. All that truly mattered was that, against all odds, I'd survived.

Speech sluggish, I still managed to get the last word in. I always did.

"And Captain Hook lives to fight another day."

CHAPTER THIRTY-FIVE

DAHLIA

I kind of loved working in the greenhouse. The scent of loamy earth, the warm, damp air, the beautiful blooming plants, all grounded me in a way not much else could. I'd thought I was a plant serial killer, but maybe I just wasn't working in the right environment.

Sorcha, on the other hand . . .

I bit back a smile as the vampire took another bloom in her long, elegant fingers and ripped it from its stem, adding it to the graveyard at her feet.

"You know, you're supposed to be pruning, not destroying, right?" Oz said as he deadheaded a rose bush.

He looked strangely amazing in his 'gardening chic' outfit. The man was wearing a pair of cropped shiny silver pants, a black sweater, and hot pink Crocs, all pulled together by a set of pink and black gardening gloves. How it worked on him, I'll never know.

"Does anyone else think it's weird that we were suddenly given assignments this morning?" I asked, interrupting what was sure to be a long-winded argument that went nowhere.

Oz shrugged. "Maybe Dr. Masterson is just trying to keep us busy while she's out of commission. Idle hands and all that."

"I have to admit, this feels like a distraction. But I suppose it's another way we can work toward proving we're ready to return to our lives. Step one, care for plants. Step two, care for ourselves."

"Since when is killing plants caring for them?" Oz asked.

Sorcha snickered. "If you think anyone is getting out of here, you're delusional."

A chill ran down my spine. "What? It's rehab. Of course we're getting out."

Oz chuckled darkly but didn't say anything. Sorcha's unnerving topaz eyes turned on me, a vicious gleam in them.

"This isn't rehab. It's not a mental hospital. They're not trying to help us. This is a prison with pretty window dressing to disguise its truth."

A series of sputtering denials was the best I could manage. "Wha . . . but . . . no. You're lying."

Sorcha arched a brow. "Am I? You can see ghosts. Go ask any one of them wandering the grounds. They'll tell you themselves. No one ever leaves Blackwood."

"But they have to! I mean . . . people would notice if no one ever left. For starters, this place would be crawling with people."

Tossing another innocent bud to the ground, Sorcha pouted at me. "Poor sweet summer child. Have you ever heard about parents taking their pets to the *farm*? It's the same thing."

"No. There have to have been people who left."

"Oh, they left all right. They're buried in a secret tomb somewhere on the grounds," Oz offered.

"This has to be against the law."

Sorcha shrugged.

"And . . . you have to be wrong. I left! I went with Cas and Tor into town."

One brow lifted as she assessed me. I was really starting to hate that judgmental fucking eyebrow. "And you returned, obviously."

"Of course. I needed to," I admitted, my voice weakening with every word.

"Why did you need to, Dahlia? You were free of the grounds. You could've escaped. Why would you willingly come back?"

Ice ran through my veins.

"B-because," I answered lamely. To be fair, it hadn't been my choice to come back. I'd been drunk and Tor carried me, but I knew that even if that hadn't been the case, I still would have returned.

I could argue that it was because I didn't feel *stuck* here. I had my mates, and I was learning things about myself, finally coming to terms with the secrets of my past. Why would I try to escape from a place that was helping me get well? But knowing that Blackwood was a prison in disguise . . . Well, that changed things, didn't it?

"You won't be able to leave. The moment your name was added to the register, you were doomed. When you set foot over the threshold the day you arrived, a compulsion spell was set. I should know. The Donaghues have immense power, and the seal created for the spell was infused with their blood. Every few years, they bring in one of the Belladonna witches to renew it. Usually under the guise of the donor benefit."

"Why?" I asked, bewilderment making my voice shake.

"For the good of all," she said solemnly. "We are dangerous."

"But this is supposed to be about rehabilitation. About making it safe."

"We will never be safe. Not in the eyes of the Council, or our families. Blackwood is a life sentence. Or in some cases, a many-lives sentence. Welcome to the club, kid."

"Why didn't you mention this before?"

Sorcha and Oz exchanged looks.

This time it was Oz who answered. "Why bother? Most who get sent here don't last more than a month or so. Those of us who do . . . well, ignorance is bliss, right?"

"Oh God." Did Kiki know what she was sentencing me to? No. She couldn't have. She'd never lock me up and throw away the key.

What about Kai? Tor? Did they know the truth? I was pretty sure Cain didn't; he didn't know much of anything. But Caspian? Did my pirate know what he'd gotten himself into?

"I think I'm going to be sick," I groaned, my stomach knotting painfully.

"Oh, please tell me when you're finished. I'm a sympathetic puker," Oz said, grimacing.

Taylor chose that moment to join us. He took in Sorcha's mound of decapitated flowers, my hunched-over position, and Oz taking off his gloves and quickly running his fingers through his hair.

"Uh, sorry to interrupt, but I need to speak to you, Miss Moore." Taylor's voice was low and hushed, similar to the tone you'd use when delivering bad news.

Oh hell. What now?

Not even an hour ago, I'd been riding the high of my reunion with Tor in the woods. I was sore in all the best ways and had left him snoring happily in my bed when I'd been summoned down here for my new work assignment. Now I could barely remember what it felt like to be happy.

Hello despair, my old friend.

"Dahlia?" he prompted.

"Rip it off, like a Band-Aid."

"Excuse me?" he asked, his handsome face scrunching up in confusion.

"Whatever horrible news you're about to deliver." I tensed, gritting my teeth as I said, "I can take it."

"Caspian Hook was found on the edge of the Black Forest early this morning."

Found? He'd been found. In the forest where a known serial killer was roaming free.

"Oh God, no," I moaned, my knees giving out.

Taylor moved fast, catching me before I could hit the ground.

Sorcha scoffed. "Found how? There are lots of ways one could be found. Found dead? Found eviscerated? Exsanguinated—my personal favorite—mindlessly babbling to himself while wandering naked?"

"Oh, that's a favorite of mine," Oz piped up.

"He was stabbed and badly beaten."

I swallowed thickly against the bile crawling up my throat. One by one, every plant in the greenhouse withered. Oz and Sorcha exchanged looks while Taylor paled.

"Stabbed? Who would stab him?" I knew that question was ridiculous before I finished asking. The man was begging to be punched in the face on a daily basis.

"He's been asking for you."

I latched on to the meaning behind the statement. "He's alive."

"Well, yes. Obviously."

"Obviously?" I repeated with a hysterical laugh, the plants instantly perking back up. "I think you need to take a refresher course on delivering news, Swiftie."

Taylor cast a wary gaze around the greenhouse before stuttering, "M-my name is Taylor."

"Whatever. Take me to him."

"Are we not going to mention the plant thing?" Oz loudly whispered to Sorcha.

"I think we tuck that nugget away for another day."

Ignoring both of them and the sense of foreboding settling in my chest, I snapped, "Now!"

Taylor gave a curt nod, and I followed him out of the greenhouse, not daring to look behind me.

I must have entered some sort of fugue state, because I couldn't recall anything about our journey to Caspian's room. One second we were in one place, and the next I was standing outside his door.

"Go on in. He's stable and waiting for you. But um, before you do, Dr. Temperance mentioned that he's been a little . . . out of sorts."

"You just said he was stable."

"He is. Physically. Mentally . . . well, if he says anything odd or perhaps sees things that aren't there—"

"He's hallucinating?"

Taylor held his thumb and forefinger an inch apart. "Just a little."

Worry gnawed at me. "Did he hit his head or something?"

"Not that we know of, but between you and me, he's been losing his mind bit by bit since he arrived here."

"How would you know? You just got here," I snapped, feeling unexpectedly defensive on Cas's behalf.

Taylor stepped back just a fraction. "I've read his file. Dr. Masterson noted it from his very first session."

Caspian's voice echoed in my mind. *"I am descending into madness. Day by day. Hour by hour. One day I won't be myself at all."*

"Oh, Cas," I whispered. He'd told me and I hadn't listened. I trained my focus on Taylor and gave a curt nod. "Let me see him. Alone."

Taylor opened the door and stepped out of my way. The second I crossed the threshold, my pirate's eyes locked onto me.

"My Wendy bird. You came." There was a strange, childlike innocence in his voice.

I cleared my throat, fighting against the sudden spring of tears in my eyes. "Of course I did."

The soothing sound of waves crashing filled his room, and I couldn't see it to be sure, but I'd bet everything I owned that there was some sort of scent diffuser in the room because it smelled like we were on a beach somewhere.

"What happened to you, Cas?" I asked as I sat on the side of his bed and took his hand.

He blinked, his eyes clearing and losing their dreamy cast. "I saw you."

"Me?"

"In the forest."

He didn't need to elaborate. My cheeks burned, but not with shame. "Did you watch?"

"For a while. Naughty bird, not inviting me to play," he murmured, tapping me on the nose with his index finger. Expression darkening, he continued, “But then I saw something. The trees were talking. Warning me.”

“The . . . trees?”

“Whispers, always whispers.” He lifted one hand, waving it about as if trying to stave off gnats.

My heart clenched. God, it was worse than I thought.

But then he gripped my hand tightly and pulled me in. “He was there. I stopped him, but he got away.”

“Who?”

“The Ripper.”

My voice stuck in my throat as fear clutched it. “Y-you saw him?”

He smirked. “I stuck him with my dagger.”

“And he just let you go?”

Cas chuckled, and it had the little hairs on the back of my neck standing on end. “He heard the screams in the trees.”

“W-what?”

“We weren’t the only ones in the forest.”

“What the hell is that supposed to mean?”

Cas stared into my eyes, his ocean-blue irises so deep I could’ve drowned in them. “You know. You know, my little rabbit. I know you know.”

It was so frustrating not being able to get a straight answer from him, but if the size of his pupils was any indication, the man was high as a kite.

He crooked his finger, beckoning me closer, and I couldn't deny him. Leaning in, I didn’t stop until his lips were at my ear.

“I know where he lives,” he whispered. “I watched him crawl into the bowels of the earth.”

Then he laughed, and that was perhaps the scariest thing of all. He sounded absolutely unhinged.

“Those are some good pain meds, huh?” I said, forcing the words through a strained smile.

“Wendy bird, Wendy bird,” he crowed, “would you like to fly with me?”

"I'm not Wendy."

His expression went serious. "Oh, but you are. I feel it." He grabbed my hand and pressed it to his chest. "Right here."

"I'm Dahlia, Caspian."

His brows furrowed in consternation. "I know that."

"So I can't be Wendy."

"Yes you can. You *are*."

"Jesus fucking Christ," I muttered, squeezing the bridge of my nose.

The door swung open, revealing Dr. Temperance and a uniformed police officer, and the mood in the room instantly changed.

"No visitors," Cas bit out. "I'm with my Wendy bird."

"Mr. Hook, I'm Detective Inspector Chisholm. I'd like to speak to you about the events of early this morning."

"No."

"I'm afraid you don't have a choice," she said, her smile firmly in place and her voice brooking no argument.

"I'm not sure he's up for it," I offered.

"That's for us to decide, Miss . . ."

"Moore. Dahlia Moore."

"Are you his girlfriend?" she asked, eyes sharpening with interest.

"Girlfriend?" Caspian scoffed. "What an insignificant word for the depth of our connection. Her ancestors were meant for mine. The Darlings and the Hooks. Twin flames through every lifetime. She's the reason my heart continues to beat. The wind in my eternal sails . . ."

I placed my palm over his mouth to stop his rambling, my cheeks burning. Where the hell had *that* come from? The Darlings and the Hooks?

"Uh . . . see what I mean?"

The DI laughed softly. "I do." She gave me a meaningful look.

"You can stay if you want, but this is going to take a while, and I can assure you, it won't be pretty."

Dr. Temperance cleared his throat. "Miss Moore, some privacy, please? This is not something you should be involved in."

I didn't appreciate his trying to kick me out, but I hadn't intended to stay anyway. I needed to tell the others what happened. Tor and Kai would be furious that the Ripper had been out roaming nearby while we'd been busy doing . . . other things. Not to mention the bomb Sorcha and Oz dropped this morning.

"You can't kick her out. It's my ship, you scurvy—"

"It's fine, Cas. I have to go anyway. But I'll be back to check on you later, okay?"

"Okay, my darling. Give us a kiss before you go."

He puckered up, making obnoxious smacking noises with his lips until I leaned down with an exasperated huff.

"I'm still mad at you, you know."

"I know. Kiss me anyway, love."

So I did. And the moment our lips collided, I knew I'd never be able to let him go. No matter how mad I was. Maybe there was something to that twin flames thing after all.

CHAPTER THIRTY-SIX

CAIN

The comforting sound of my pen scrawling across paper as I wrote in my journal usually sent me into a zen-like state. It helped me—gag—center myself, just like the doctor said it would. Not tonight.

Tonight my mind was too crowded with everything I'd been avoiding the past few days. Namely, her. Despite my arrangement with Kai, I hadn't been back to her room since the first night I was tasked to watch over her. I couldn't. Not when with every tense second that passed, every sigh or moan that fell from her lips, I was one snap decision away from fucking her with the kind of abandon reserved for fantasies.

This madness had to stop. I was bound to another.

Which was why I'd holed myself up in here, hiding from everyone, desperate to uncover the truth of my past. If I could just remember, I'd finally be free from my obsession.

At least, that was the plan.

My memory had other ideas. It was still doing a world-class impersonation of swiss cheese.

My magic, however, was growing by leaps and bounds. I held my hand out in front of myself, watching the shadows escape my fingertips just like my fire did. Still rolling the shadows through my fingers like a magician might a coin, I lifted my other hand and called a ball of blue flame into my palm.

Curious, I moved my hands until they were parallel to one another, my shadow and flame now touching. I half expected the shadows to dissipate as the flame consumed them, but instead the two elements merged, creating something new. The new flame was so dark as to be almost black, but there were hints of plum and indigo within.

The name for this transformation came to me unbidden: shadow fire.

Interesting.

I'd tuck that away for future use. I knew from my few memories the fire could kill, but I hadn't fully realized what my shadows were capable of. Mostly I just used them as an extension of my hands. Right now, to Asshole's extreme delight, I had a shadow-formed hand dedicated to petting him. Spoiled little pup.

Lifting the thought from my brain, he attempted to nip one of said fingers. *"Don't you dare stop. I've finally got you right where I want you."*

After the night with Dahlia, I realized the dog really could speak in my mind. Unsettling? Yes. Strangely, though, I wasn't surprised. Our bond was just another piece of the puzzle.

Returning my attention to the journal, I frowned down at the circular scribbles in the corner, frustrated beyond belief that I couldn't muster a single word tonight. How was I supposed to learn anything else about myself if I couldn't tap into my memories?

"Bashing your head against a wall might work better."

"Oh, you're an expert now?"

Asshole huffed. *"It doesn't take an expert to see your way isn't working. When have you ever been able to recover a memory on demand? That's not how this works, you giant dummy."*

"You're one to talk, you stuffed toy."

The puppy growled. *"Keep that up, and I'm gonna start biting things off in your sleep."*

"You could try. It wouldn't even fit in your mouth."

"Doesn't have to fit for it to hurt."

The temptation to smother him with my shadows was strong.

"Oh please. You'd never hurt me. I'm your best friend."

"Friend is a strong word."

"Lifemate? Do you like that one better?"

"No."

"Call it what you want, but you're stuck with me, pal. I followed you here, didn't I?"

"I might like you more if you told me where you followed me *from*, since you're so fucking knowledgeable."

"Can't. You might play fast and loose with the Fates, but I know better. I follow the rules. I'm a good boy, remember?"

I sighed, gripping my pen so hard I nearly broke it in two. This wasn't working. And if the last few days had taught me anything, forcing it would only serve to leave me with a splitting headache.

"Fuck this," I grumbled, abruptly standing and heading for the door.

Asshole trotted along behind me, tongue lolling to one side. If I were truly evil, I'd kick him in his fluffy, adorable face. So, I suppose I wasn't Lucifer, then.

Hmm.

Opening the door, I strode confidently into the hall and collided with a frantic Merri. My shadows caught her before she hit the floor, righting her as she panted for breath.

"Oh, Cain, thank you. I'm so sorry. I should look where I'm going." She glanced behind her down the long, empty hallway.

"What are you running from?" I asked. It didn't take a rocket scientist to figure out she was trying to get away from someone.

"It's Logan. He . . . I think I triggered his rut. He's more aggressive than I'm used to, and I don't want to hurt him."

The unmistakable sound of rushing footsteps came from the far end of the corridor, a low snarl accompanying them. Well, shit.

"Get behind me," I growled, tugging her up. That was my first mistake. I touched the succubus with my bare hands. Chivalry ruined everything.

I didn't know if I had much experience with the species, but it was common knowledge that a direct touch from one of the sex demons was the equivalent of a bottle full of Viagra. The more powerful the creature, the more painful and desperate the arousal.

From the feel of things, Merri was one of the most powerful of her kind. And since she was here, she was clearly not in control.

"Fuck, Cain, I'm sorry. I-I didn't mean to." Her apology was effusive and immediate as she pulled herself free of me.

"It's fine. Just go." I had to bite the words out before I groaned and tried to hump her instead.

It didn't ease even after she ran, and there wasn't a damn thing I could do about my raging hard-on until I saw her safe. Logan was nearly here. Sending my shadows forward, I cloaked the hall to disorient him. He floundered around in the darkness—which I had no trouble seeing through—muttering to himself in frustration before ultimately spinning around and going back the way he came.

I wasn't going to make it back to my room, not with the way this arousal was pulsing through my veins. My cock throbbed as I adjusted it to make space, but even that amount of friction had me hissing in pained pleasure. In a snap decision, I stumbled back into the library, closing the door and throwing the lock as I tore open my pants with my free hand and fisted my rigid length. I'd deal with the mess later. If I didn't come right now, I thought I might die.

As always, thoughts of Dahlia filled my mind.

I was helpless to resist her in this state. I welcomed the memories of her writhing beneath me, moaning my name, running her hands down my back.

"Fuck. Fuuuck," I grunted, spilling into my hand shamefully fast.

Breaths coming in shuddering gasps, I hung my head and stared at my still straining cock. "Godsdamned fucking succubus."

Thankfully some of the urgency had vanished with my orgasm, but I could still feel the arousal riding me. If Dahlia had been here, instead of only in my mind, I would still be thrusting inside her, working on climax number two. Making her whimper as her cunt clenched and milked my dick for all it was worth. Gods, what would she feel like? Slick, tight, hot. Like velvet squeezing me until I filled her to the—FUCK.

"Get it together, Cain. This is succubus magic, not you. You don't want her."

My cock had other plans. He didn't give two shits whether it was Merri's pheromones or Dahlia. He wanted to get off again. Soon.

I couldn't go out there like this. If I ran into my sweet baby doll, I'd have her bent over the nearest flat surface so I could sink inside her and then watch my cum drip from between her slick folds. I'd fall to my knees and clean up the mess I made with my tongue.

"Oh fuck. Dahlia!" My entire body shuddered as another orgasm tore through me. I hadn't even touched myself this time. Just the thought of fucking her had been enough to send me over the edge.

The hold she had on me was insidious. The harder I fought it, the deeper she burrowed her way inside me. Maybe I should just fuck her. Give myself room to be the villain I'd been told I was. Villains weren't faithful. They took what they wanted. They had no remorse. They fucked the woman who had them obsessed until she couldn't walk straight, and then they stole her away to their beds and chained her up, never letting her go.

"No. No!" I gritted out, fury and guilt twisting me up inside.

I slammed my palm down onto the glass-top table beside me, the unexpected sound of shattering glass cutting through the sexual fog I'd been lost in.

"Ow, dammit," I grunted, realizing shards of the table had torn through my skin.

Something about the drops of blood smeared across the glittering glass tugged at my mind.

"*Now* you fucking remember?" I muttered, but the words were lost as I fell into the past.

"Are you certain this is what you want, my lord?" the old crone asked.

"It comes with a terrible price," the maiden added.

"One you cannot come back from," the mother said solemnly.

I gritted my teeth, annoyance simmering in my veins. A terrible price? This was an easy price to pay. A bargain, even. "I will not give her a child. You have my word. She will be mine, and there will be nothing my wife will want for."

"It will not be so easily done. She is willful." This from the crone, who stood to the right.

"You cannot ever understand the urge to be a mother. It is something, that if present within her, will not die out." The mother gazed at me with an almost pitying expression.

"Infatuation will only get you so far," the maiden added, her innocent visage drawn into sorrowful lines. "Love is not something you can manipulate or force."

"I will have her as my own. I would give anything in my power to have her."

The old crone tutted. "Obsession is a dangerous thing. The earth will tremble and quake with his wrath."

The mother held out an athame. "We will grant you this bargain, my lord. It must be sealed in blood. From the moment your sacrifice is made, your union will be fated."

Bowing her head, the maiden intoned, "Persephone will be yours."

"Fine." I snatched the blade from her hand, slashed a deep line across my palm, and held the bleeding appendage over their altar.

The first drop of blood to hit their golden chalice filled with two twined strings sent a burst of magic into the air. It rushed toward me and slammed into my chest, leaving a painful ache in my heart. I knew, then and there, it had worked. I would have her as my bride, and I'd never let her leave me.

The images in my head swirled and rearranged themselves until I found myself in the same chamber with the same three women, but it was obvious time had passed. The wound in my palm was long healed, but the ache in my heart was now a gaping hole.

"You took her from me!" I shouted, tears burning my eyes and blurring my vision. "Return my love. I'll give you anything. Name your price."

"You've made your deal, my lord," the maiden reminded me.

"You knew the price," the crone said coldly.

"You didn't heed our warning," the mother offered.

"I gave her a child, and you killed them both."

"You killed them." The maiden stared boldly as she spoke.

"You broke your word." The crone was more dismissive in her judgment.

"A child born of death cannot be allowed to exist." The mother's words were barely a whisper on the wind.

"Why not?"

"Who are you to question fate?" the crone shouted.

"We are beyond the gods." The mother's voice was no quieter.

The maiden nodded. "We are ruled only by the universe itself."

"She was my wife. All she wanted was to bear my child. Is that really so much to ask?" I whispered, my voice breaking.

"Death cannot create life. It is an anathema," the crone replied, her voice gentler now.

"The realms are separate for a reason," the maiden murmured.

"Trying to join them will only tear them both apart." A tear slipped down the mother's cheek, and I knew it was for my loss. She, better than her sisters, understood what they'd taken from me.

"I understand. Just return her to me, and I will never give her the baby she wants. I will bear the burden of her sadness. It's better than never having her in my arms again."

As one, they shook their heads and said, "It cannot be undone."

Despair hit me like a tidal wave, and I fell to my knees, but a spark of hope lit inside me. She was dead, but not gone. She'd return to me as a soul in the River Styx. I could have her again, simply in another form.

"No, my lord. She will not return as a soul for you to command." The old crone's words were like a dagger to my hopeful heart. "The life you stole was reclaimed."

"What do you mean?"

"Her soul was returned to the heavens," the maiden ventured.

"To be reincarnated at a time unknown even to us." The mother lifted her chin, as if in defiance. "Balance has been restored, my lord Hades."

SESSION TRANSCRIPT: DECEMBER 7TH

Dr. Temperance: This is Dr. Nathaniel Temperance, standing in for Dr. Elizabeth Masterson. The date is December seventh at . . . one forty-five p.m. We are in Caspian Hook's quarters as he's been recently injured.

Hook: Is the formality really necessary?

<<soothing ocean sounds fill the room>>

Dr. Temperance: Can you please turn that down, Caspian? I can hardly hear myself think.

Hook: *slightly unhinged laugh* Some pirate you are.

Dr. Temperance: I am not a pirate, Caspian. I am your doctor.

Hook: That's *captain* to you, you scurvy knave. You'll bloody address me properly while on my ship, or you'll walk the plank.

<<soothing ocean sounds dim>>

Dr. Temperance: We're not on a ship, Caspian. We're in your room at Blackwood.

<<papers shuffling>>

Dr. Temperance: *muttering to himself* Did they forget to update your chart? I don't see any meds listed.

Hook: *snort of laughter* You're ridiculous. Can't you see the way we're swaying? I'm surprised you have your sea legs, you lily-livered codfish. Did that brat Pan send you? Is this a mutiny? I swear I never looked twice at Tinkerbell. She's not even my type.

Dr. Temperance: *heavy sigh* Caspian, we've been over this. I must say, I'm incredibly disappointed by your lack of progress. Out of everyone in your peer group, you're the only one who seems to be going backward. These delusions of yours are out of control.

Hook: How very dare you, Doctor. Delusions. *scoffs* I know what I saw in the forest.

<<soothing ocean sounds continue>>

<<pocket watch opens and closes repetitively>>

Dr. Temperance: And what did you see, Caspian?

Hook: I am bored with you and this conversation already.

<<rings a bell>>

Hook: Get me my sexy nurse. And some rum. And maybe a sandwich. I'm famished.

Dr. Temperance: *long-suffering sigh* You don't have a sexy nurse, Caspian.

Hook: Don't I? Shame. You may leave. I'd very much appreciate it if this conversation was over.

Dr. Temperance: Well, that's too bad because you nearly died, and we need to get to the bottom of what happened.

Hook: That detective inspector already questioned me. I told her everything.

Dr. Temperance: Yes, but given your mental state, they've asked me to get to the bottom of whether these were the ramblings of a madman or a credible witness.

<<sheets rustle>>

Hook: *pained groan* Need I remind you of the beating I took? Who did that? The bloody trees? No. It was a man. He bled like a human. I saw him dive into his hidey-hole. I got a good slice in on his leg too.

Dr. Temperance: Where's the dagger? How did you even get one? You're not allowed weapons at Blackwood.

Hook: Ah, but I'm a pirate, mate. I always have something up me sleeve.

Dr. Temperance: Caspian, we searched every inch of the forest. There was no hidey-hole, as you called it. The only blood at the scene was yours.

<<soothing ocean sounds stop>>

Hook: *drops voice* Are you calling me a liar, Doctor?

<<pocket watch opens and closes repetitively>>

Dr. Temperance: I'm telling you what we found. Nothing. Your delusions are getting worse, and this time you ended up hurting yourself, spinning a cockamamie story about the Ripper. I'm telling you, the police don't think there was a human dressed in a costume in the woods plotting his next target. They think you were the one plotting. They think *you* are the Ripper.

Hook: I know what I saw.

Dr. Temperance: Do you? How can you be sure of anything when you're so clearly going mad?

<<bottle breaks>>

Hook: Get out!

Dr. Temperance: Now, Caspian, control your temper.

Hook: OUT!

Dr. Temperance: There's no talking to you when you're like this. We'll have to reschedule for when you're feeling better. Session terminated at one-fifty-four p.m.

<<static>>

End of transcript.

CHAPTER THIRTY-SEVEN

DAHLIA

I gave the pixies a wave as I traipsed through the greenhouse on my way back from spending time with Dr. Masterson. She was doing so much better but hadn't officially been cleared to work for another week. I personally couldn't wait. Dr. Temperance looked at me just a little too long, smiled just a little too widely, and there was a glint of attraction in his eyes I couldn't ignore. I'd grown accustomed to what that look meant with the four men who'd been vying for my attention. And I wasn't afraid to admit that I much preferred the Scottish doctor's methods.

Somewhere in the last week or so, our sessions had gone from feeling like a therapist and her patient to more of a meetup between old friends. I'm not sure how it happened, and if you'd told me that's what would happen when we first met, I'd have said you should stop getting high on your own supply, but here we were.

Maybe it was the way our conversations felt less one-sided. These days she was more prone to giving me answers than strictly asking me questions. I couldn't help but replay the last of them in my mind, wondering if her theory had legs.

"Why do you think the spirits haven't been as loud lately?" I asked. "Am I losing my power already?"

"I don't think so. The farther we get from All Souls' Day, the thicker the veil. And you said yourself that last visit was a doozy."

"So you think the spirit is recharging or something?"

"Well, it's a spirit, not a battery, but yes. Something like that."

"Which means she'll be back."

"With the way she's attached herself to you, I think it's safe to say she won't stop until she gets what she wants."

"And what's that?"

"You tell me. You're the one who can talk to ghosts."

And that's where our conversation had wrapped up. I'd been ushered out by a helpful healer who never failed to remind us about the restrictions of visiting hours. What did the ghost want? Part of me was convinced it was to scare me to death. The other part thought there was more to it. This haunting was purposeful, trained on me, and with such hatred, there had to be a connection between us. I just couldn't figure out what it was. Not that she—something about it made me feel like the energy was feminine—stuck around long enough for me to ask.

My musings carried me through Blackwood's halls and up the staircase until I reached the door to my room. I stopped a few feet from it when I saw a familiar box wrapped with a ribbon waiting on the floor.

"Oh, Tor, please tell me you didn't."

I hesitated, nose crinkling in disgust, before I took the last few begrudging steps to my door. I didn't even have to open the box to spot the trickle of blood leaking out from the bottom. My shoulders sagged.

"You did."

With a grimace, I kicked the corner of the lid up, knocking it back so I could steal a peek at the contents without having to touch it.

An ear. He'd given me a fucking ear.

"Jesus Jones and the apostles," I hissed. "It's only been a few days since you were released. When did someone piss you off enough to warrant this?"

I stooped down and picked the box up using just my thumb and one of my fingers, fighting the urge to lose my breakfast as I carried it with my arm stretched out in front of me.

The hike to Tor's room gave me time to rack my brain. He and Kai had carried me back to my room after our night in the forest, one acting as lookout while the other snuck a naked me back upstairs. We'd only just made it inside when Tor started going at me again while Kai drew a bath. I vaguely remembered Tor growling something at somebody before the door slammed hard enough that the walls rattled, but I was in too much of a sex haze to pay it any attention.

God, my fanny fluttered at the memory of the way he'd held me up with one hand while he filled me against my wardrobe. Then Kai came out of the bathroom and just . . . watched with a grin on his lips.

It wasn't until Kai called my name that I realized I'd stalled mid-trek and was just standing in the hallway with a freaking ear in a box.

"Gem? You all right?"

"Have you seen Tor?" I asked, the question tight in my throat.

He shook his head. "Not since the gym this morning. Why? What's in the box?"

I gulped. "You ever see the movie Seven?"

"No," he said slowly, confusion drawing his eyebrows into a V.

"You never *ever* ask what is in the box. Trust me. It doesn't end well."

"Is it that bad?" He reached for the package and I jerked it away, my stomach rolling when I felt the ear shift inside the container.

God, it was like Tupperware for body parts. He couldn't keep doing this. I'd put up with a lot of things, but not a mate acting like a feral cat.

"Tor left me a present."

That seemed to be all Kai needed to know, familiar as he was with the previous gift. "More fangs?"

"An ear," I croaked. "A pointy one."

"Wonder what the poor faeling did."

"I think they were eavesdropping."

"Ah, that tracks." He winked at me. "Dinnae be too hard on him. His claim on ye hasn't been secure long. And he could've done a lot worse to the poor bastard."

That was true enough. As far as restraint went, it was something. Not sure what Dr. Temperance would think if he found out, though.

"Here, let me take that and dispose of it for you," he offered.

This time when he reached for the box, I let him take it from me. "Thanks."

"Tor's room is two doors down from mine. In case you havenae been for a visit." He dropped a kiss on the top of my head before turning on his heels. "I'll save you a seat beside me in group."

"Shit, that's today?"

He chuckled. "Aye. In ten minutes, lass. Better shift it and go scold your beast so you don't arrive late."

His palm connected soundly with my ass before he sauntered away, fucking whistling.

These men of mine were going to drive me bonkers.

I hurried off toward Tor's room a second time, only to stop short as I rounded the corner and nearly ran into yet another broody bastard who drove me nuts.

"Cain! God, you guys need to wear bells or something."

He flicked his piercing gaze up to meet mine but returned it to the floor before we could form any kind of connection. "Or maybe you need to just watch where you're fucking going."

I snapped my head back as if he'd slapped me. "Ouch."

I figured he'd been avoiding me since the night he'd forced his way into my room and then snuck out before I woke up, but I hadn't been prepared to go back to this. He was as cold and distant as he'd been when we first met.

His posture stiffened, and then he took a sharp breath before reaching out and grabbing my wrist. "You're bleeding. Who fucking hurt you?"

"What? No, I'm not." I followed his gaze and found a smear of—yuck—ear blood on my hand. Swallowing, I weakly explained, "It's not mine."

A muscle feathered in his jaw, and his fingers spasmed around my wrist before he let me go. In the second before he released me, I caught something in his gaze. Something I hadn't noticed before. It looked like . . . despair. Before I could fully clock the emotion, his mask was back in place and his eyes trained on the ground.

"Are you okay?" I ventured, thinking that asking him to punch me in the nose would probably be less painful. How many times did I need this man to shut me down before I got the hint?

He says one thing but then does another, like stand guard while you sleep, or hump you into submission. It's not your fault you're confused. It's his. And his big dick.

"Of course I'm okay. I . . . fuck, leave me be, woman."

Shadows spilled down the hall, sending my heart rate skyrocketing at the possibility my malevolent spirit had returned, but Cain closed his eyes and took a deep breath before I realized he was calling them back into himself. Oh shit.

What was it Kiki had called him? Shadow Daddy? Looks like she'd been onto something.

"Uh . . . that's new."

When he didn't say anything I looked around, realizing his other shadow, the tiny furry one, was missing. "Where's Asshole?"

Cain blinked, as if the question confused him. "Oh, he had a late night. Met a lady friend, I guess. He's sleeping it off."

Go Asshole. Get it, buddy.

My lips twitched even though I was annoyed as hell at his owner.

Cain made to step away but didn't make it far because Tor walked out of his room, freshly showered and looking edible as all hell. "You two having a party in the hallway or something?"

"Or something," Cain muttered.

Tor leaned against the wall and gave me a lascivious grin. "Did you get my present?"

Shudder.

"About that."

"Don't worry, it'll grow back. Eventually."

"Not the point. I appreciate that you want to give me things, but maybe we stick to flowers and leave the body parts to other people."

"Flowers wilt. You can't make a necklace of the body parts of your enemies with flowers."

While I appreciated the sentiment, it took everything in me not to puke on his ginormous feet. "I don't want a necklace made of . . . that."

Cain was trying in vain to get around us, but even with his attention locked on me, Tor didn't miss anything. "Hold on, we'll walk together."

"Lovely," Cain gritted out, his hands balling into fists at his sides.

"We aren't done talking about this, Tor. I mean it. No more limbs."

"An ear is not a limb," he said breezily.

"Appendages, then."

"I suppose I'll stick to teeth and eyes."

Cain sighed heavily. "Way to miss the point entirely, Viking."

"What was that?" Tor snarled.

"She doesn't want your creepy souvenirs. She's not a monster like you are. There's nothing appealing to this perfect creature about teeth and bloody ears being given as presents. Give her gifts all you want, but for fuck's sake, make sure they're things she loves."

Cain's fingers began sparking with blue flames, and he broke away from us both, muttering a litany of curses as he walked away.

Tor watched him disappear and then looked back at me, as if considering what he'd said. For one perfect second, it seemed like Cain's advice was about to take, but then Tor laughed and shook his head. "What does he know?"

My shoulders slumped in defeat. More boxes dripping with blood waited for me in my future.

Tor's palm rested on the small of my back as he and I walked down the hall toward the stairs. We took a couple of steps in silence before he asked, "Do you really not like the gifts, Kærasta?"

What could I say when he sounded so genuine and a little hurt?

"I'll get used to them. It's just . . . not common in my world. We're more chocolate and flowers kind of people."

His lip curled. "But where's the romance in that?"

"I think, and tell me if I'm wrong, it's in what happens after you give them to me." I rose on my tiptoes and beckoned him to meet me halfway. "Like when I thank you for the flowers with my mouth around your—"

"Ah, there you two are. Come on, we'll be late for group. I don't want to miss my first one back after my near-death experience. So much to talk about. Stories to tell. Ah, it's almost like I'm back on my ship, regaling the kidnapped lost boys with tales of my many adventures."

Caspian stood at the top of the staircase, all swagger and guyliner. You wouldn't even know he'd been injured by the look of him.

"Cas! I didn't think you'd be joining us. How'd the interview go?"

He rolled his eyes and waved his ringed fingers. "The same as they always do. They didn't want to hear what I had to say, so they created a story that better suited the narrative they preferred."

The carefully crafted reply was such a stark difference from the man I'd left blathering about Wendy birds in his bed, that I couldn't resist the urge to hug him.

Cas grunted from the impact of my body colliding with his. "What's all this, then?" he asked, belatedly wrapping his arms around my waist and squeezing. I had to admit, I loved it when he was tender with me.

"I was just worried about you."

"Is that all it takes to earn your affection? Perhaps I'll have to see about getting into another scrape sometime soon."

"Please don't. I don't think my heart can take too much more right now."

For the first time in weeks, it felt like everyone was safe and where they should be.

My gaze drifted back to Tor. He was still wearing the evidence of his curse, with his horns and the scales running up his arms, but his face had lost some of its edge. He no longer seemed quite as wild. Maybe it was the eyes that had returned to his midnight blue or that his cheekbones no longer looked sharp enough to cut. Or maybe it was just the fact that his lips were curved in a slight smile.

"I'm fully forgiven, then?" Cas asked, nuzzling into my hair as we walked down the staircase and made our way toward the group room.

"Don't do it again," I whispered.

"On my honor as a pirate."

Tor snorted. He actually snorted. "Fat lot of good that is."

"Fair," Cas conceded, making us both laugh.

"You coming?" Kai asked, sticking his head out of the room. "Cain and Merri are already inside."

"Merri?" Tor asked suspiciously.

"Ah, you haven't met the newcomer yet," Caspian said with mock sympathy. "I do hope you've drained your balls recently, or this will be a bumpy ride."

My cheeks burned at the look Tor gave me. I personally saw to the draining of said balls this morning before he left to work out. Twice. Pinned by his gaze as I was, I didn't miss the way his eyes roamed down my body or how they lingered on the place where Caspian's hand still clutched my hip. Our time with Kai in the forest had been good for him. He was still possessive as hell, but he was learning how to share. At least his first instinct was no longer ripping someone's arm off and beating them with it.

Isn't it? He just *left you an ear.*

Okay, so maybe he wasn't as evolved as I thought.

Joffrey appeared like a thief in the freaking night from around the corner, his shock of red hair and sallow expression mildly terrifying. "Mr. Nordson. Mr. Nash. I'm afraid your session has been canceled. Dr. Masterson has requested your presence."

"Now?" Kai asked.

"She said it was most urgent. Follow me."

Kai looked at me with a frown.

"Don't worry, gents. I'll see to our girl," Caspian offered gallantly.

"That doesn't fill me with comfort," Kai muttered.

"Touch her and die," Tor growled.

Caspian swallowed hard, but to his credit, he didn't back down. "I'll only touch what I'm asked to touch."

Tor didn't like that. I could tell by the visible shudder that worked its way down his muscled body. Swallowing, he closed his eyes and breathed deep, his nostrils flaring as he sucked in air.

"It's okay," I whispered soothingly, my hand hovering just above his bicep. I didn't want to touch him while his eyes were closed and accidentally set him off. "I'll be fine. You can come find me when you're done."

"Not a hair will be harmed on her head, pirate. Not if you want to keep your lungs inside your chest where they belong."

Caspian didn't shoot back a snarky comment this time. Instead, he gave Tor a terse nod and simply said, "You have my word."

"We're trusting you," Kai said, danger woven through his words. "Don't make us regret it."

Why was that so hot? The posturing and the striking of an accord. All over my safety.

I discreetly fanned my face. Who needed succubus pheromones when they had these guys strutting around and giving them away for free?

As I watched my two mates walk away with Joffrey taking the lead, I had a vague thought that he was taking my favorite sandwich with him. But then Caspian's lips were at my ear and his fingers threaded with mine.

"Come on, love. Let's get this over with so I can steal you away for a day of debauchery while your keepers are busy. We have so much lost time to make up for."

There went my fanny. Fluttering all over the place. Again.

"What makes you think I'm interested in that?"

Cas's laugh washed over me. "Oh, darling. Did you forget? I know all your tells. I know what your face looks like when you want to come. What you sound like when you come for *me*. There's absolutely no way you don't want to make up for lost time. Not after the greedy way you sucked my cock the other night. If you can want me that much while you hate me, you must be fucking dripping for me now that you love me again."

"I-I never loved you."

"You wound me. And you're lying to yourself, but no matter. We'll get there in the end. Our course is set. It's really only a matter of time before we reach our inevitable destination."

"Where's that?" I asked, more than a little breathless.

"Happily ever after, of course. Isn't that where all lovers end up?"

I had to push him away just so I could draw in a full breath. "Jesus, who are you, and what did you do with Cas?"

"Oh, my sweet darling, I am Captain Hook. And I'm not giving you up without a fight."

I had no comeback for that. I wasn't sure I wanted one, to be honest. But it was a good thing, as it turned out, because a very frustrated Dr. Temperance stormed into the hall.

"Do you two have any intention of joining us, or are you going to continue to waste everyone else's time?"

"Someone's crabby this afternoon. Missing your Lizzie? I know how aggravating it can be when you're forced to *abstain*."

If smoke could come out of the doctor's ears, I was pretty sure it would. "Sorry, Dr. Temperance. We're coming in now."

"Good. We're already ten minutes behind schedule. As it is, we won't have time to do at least half of my exercises."

"Then I guess it's a good thing we're short a few members."

"What? Why?" Temperance looked from Cas to me as if checking the validity of the statement.

"Joffrey came for Tor and Kai. Said that Dr. Masterson needed them urgently."

"Bollocks. Well, I guess we'll make do. Come on."

He spun on his heel and went back inside, leaving Cas and I to look at each other like a couple of guilty school kids.

"Go on then, love. After you."

I narrowed my eyes at him. "You just want to stare at my ass."

"Of course I do. It's one of my favorite sights."

Instead of scoffing or rolling my eyes, I walked into the room, putting a little extra sway in my step for his benefit. The strangled groan he let out sent a thrill through me. I could get used to teasing Captain Hook.

CHAPTER THIRTY-EIGHT

HOOK

If I could have skipped through the halls of Blackwood without looking like a complete arse, I would've after the attention I'd gotten from my darling. However, I kept my cool. I didn't let her see that my heart was soaring like I'd been thinking happy thoughts. I was a dastardly pirate. Not a lovesick fool.

"She's too good for you."

"You'll ruin it."

"You'll be the reason she dies."

Those bloody whispers attacked my senses as I lounged in the dayroom and plotted how I could get her alone so we could seal our bond with our bodies. Now that Tor was loose, I knew sneaking into her room in the middle of the night for some more nocturnal fun time was going to be hard, if not impossible, to manage. Which meant I had to go back to the drawing board.

"Are you going to continue this assault on my senses indefinitely?" I hissed, not even caring if the residents around me heard me talking to myself. I wouldn't be the first.

As if mocking me, they remained silent.

"Bloody nuisances," I muttered, heaving a sigh as I glanced idly around the rec room. It was fuller than usual. Everyone seemed to be loitering around today. With our dear Lizzie out of the picture, things around this place were far less structured than usual, leaving us with nothing to do but sit around with our metaphorical thumbs up our arses.

Or not so metaphorical, as the case may be. I wasn't one to judge.

Needless to say, I actually missed her rigid schedule and asinine therapy sessions. It gave me so many opportunities for mischief while the others were occupied. Now, I couldn't make heads or tails of the staff rotations or the availability of spaces I needed to creep through. It was a bloody thorn in my side, if I'm being honest.

Heaving a sigh, I let my gaze sweep across the occupants of the room, taking in the usual suspects. Sorcha and Oz were playing chess in the corner, Kit, Drax, and Cain were playing cards—it didn't escape my notice that I was not invited—while Dahlia sat alone with a notebook in her lap as she furiously scribbled on the paper. Oh, to be inside her wicked mind right now. Just the look on her face said she was writing something deliciously naughty.

The new girl, Merri, was curled up in the chair next to her, reading some sort of bodice ripper. A few shifters I wasn't as familiar with sat around another table nearby, piecing together a puzzle. I couldn't help but snicker as I recalled stealing one piece out of every box during my first week here. They'd never have the satisfaction of achieving its completion, and I loved it. What could I say? A pirate's life was the life for me.

And there were even more folks gathered in front of the telly watching an old black-and-white movie. Dracula, if memory served. Ah, yes, there he was in all his glory. Shoe polish widow's peak and all. *Snort.* It was about as accurate as Captain Jack Sparrow.

A bead of sweat trickled down the back of my neck, and I shifted uncomfortably in my seat as I swiped it away. All these bodies were making it decidedly balmy in here today. I wondered if the windows were painted shut? Would they care if I broke one?

I opened the third button on my shirt, revealing more of my chest in an attempt to get a little air. Someone had switched on the furnace or started the fires burning a little early. Scanning the room, I caught sight of Dahlia—because of course I'd always find her first—and grinned at the sight of her flushed cheeks, the way she bit her lower lip, and the . . . oh yes, the hard nipples poking at her thin camisole. When had she removed her jumper? I'd missed it. Damn.

I wanted to suck them into my mouth. Lavish her breasts with the attention they deserved. Pepper her body with bite marks and lay claim to her.

Fuck me, she was a temptress.

And I was on fire.

"She's theirs, not yours."

"She wants them."

"She doesn't need you."

Those godsdamned wanker sprites needed to stay out of my head. I didn't need their intrusion on my already flagging confidence. Dahlia had forgiven me. She said so herself.

Didn't she?

Technically all she said was, *'Don't do it again,'* but that counted . . . right?

Except she'd sat with Merri and Cain during the group session, leaving me alone on the other side of the semicircle of chairs, so perhaps I'd heard what I wanted to hear.

I tore my gaze from the torture of her being so close yet so far and took note of the rest of the residents spending their afternoon in here. Clothes had begun to be stripped because of the heat, but there was a decided undercurrent of sexual tension thick in the air as well. The lust-filled expressions on some of the shifters had me swelling in my trousers.

Those on the couch had started to caress one another. One had his hand gliding down another's neck while the person on his other side was working on his zipper. Bloody hell, were they in rut? I'd always heard shifter ruts and heats were intense and came out of nowhere. I never thought I'd bear witness to one.

Their heavy breaths told me that was about to change. The burliest one, who'd been caressing the man in the middle, stopped his gentle ministrations and instead gripped him by the nape and crushed their mouths together. All this while the group working on the puzzle devolved into a sex-addled trio. One of them swept the puzzle pieces off the table to make space for the wild fucking we were all about to see.

Eyes wide, I looked around to see if anyone else was paying attention to the shifter sex-a-thon that was about to take place.

Oh no.

It wasn't just the shifters. It was everyone.

Kit had his dick out, and a sultry siren was sucking it down like it was her favorite popsicle. Drax was nowhere to be found. And then there was Cain. Manspread, eyes burning blue fire, hands clenching his thighs so hard his knuckles were white as he stared across the room at Dahlia.

What the devil was happening?

But then I realized the truth as my cock throbbed for release and my body fought against my will. Merri sat unbothered, her face serene, skin practically glowing with health as she flipped the pages of her book. Every now and then, she'd giggle, or her eyes would flare wide. She was feeding on us all, and she didn't even know it.

I had to get the fuck out of here before I did something Dahlia would never forgive. She didn't want me yet, and if I took her, or anyone else right now, there wouldn't be a way to unring the bell.

It was the travesty of my existence that I couldn't take advantage of this moment. The Hook BD—before Dahlia—would have without an ounce of remorse. But not now. I've learned my lesson. I actually cared what my darling thought of me. Which meant even though she was sitting there, biting down on her lip and squirming in her seat, begging for relief, I wasn't going to be the one to give it to her.

Damn it all to hell and back.

Being a hero was exhausting.

While I was busy eye-fucking her, the gossip had found their way over to me. The three merfolk were on their knees in front of me, hands sliding up my legs, clothes nowhere to be found.

"Hook, you're straining. Let us take care of you," one of them said, her wavy pink hair barely covering her nipples.

"Use us however you need. You know we always take care of you," the merman said, much bolder in his exploration as he reached for my cock.

The third one stood and offered her cunt to me, one leg planted on the chair so I could see how wet she was. "You haven't tasted me yet. I'm ready for you."

"No thanks," I grunted, pushing to stand. "I'm a carnitarian. I don't eat fish."

"Since when?" the pink-haired one shouted after me.

"Since Dahlia," I grumbled to myself, storming from the room.

I should have alerted Temperance to what was happening in there. But I wasn't in any state to have contact with anyone with an orifice I could fuck. I needed to get off, but more than that, I needed to stay true to my sweet girl. The only way she'd ever be mine is if I proved my devotion.

As I said, being a hero was exhausting.

And not very much fun.

CHAPTER THIRTY-NINE

DAHLIA

I ran through the darkened halls of my aunt's abandoned home, knowing he'd catch me if I faltered, not sure if I wanted him to. This stranger had been stalking me, masked and deadly, for weeks. He would kill me if he found me, wouldn't he?

My inner voice said that was a lie. He'd had every opportunity. I'd woken with him standing over my bed two nights ago, and instead of sinking his blade into my chest, he'd stroked himself to completion all over it.

P*hew.* Was it hot in here, or was it just my steamy fucking scene? There was no way my publisher would let this new plot bunny fly, but if I showed Kiki, she'd go to bat for me. I'd had to put it on paper once it came to me. If it got me this hot and bothered, my readers were going to love it.

I looked up from the notebook I'd been scribbling furiously in since claiming my seat in the corner. Oh.

Maybe it wasn't me.

I took in the lingering glances, stolen touches, and flat-out orgy that had broken out in the room.

Was there a memo I missed? Group sex in the rec room. Party starts promptly at two. Pants optional.

Cas strode out of the room with his hands clenched into fists, eyes focused on the exit and never wavering. That seemed out of character for a pirate. Shouldn't he be all party all the time? I briefly considered going after him, but my gaze caught on a pair of intense blues from across the room. Cain stared at me—only me—and the heat in his eyes was enough to make my breasts ache with the need for his touch.

As if he was plucking the thought straight from my mind, his eyes drifted down, landing on my chest. I followed his gaze, letting out a little gasp when I noticed how my nipples were straining against my cami. They were so hard they looked like they were standing at attention. Or *begging* for attention.

My nipples were totally needy little whores and not good little soldiers. I could practically feel his mouth sucking on them. I wondered if he was a boob man. Kai was definitely an ass man. Tor was an every-part-of-me guy. The jury was still out on Cain and Cas.

Cain pulled his lower lip into his mouth, biting down and dragging a moan from me. Wait, was I jealous of a fucking lip? Shit, I was. I wanted to be the one he was biting on. Any part of me he wanted. We all volunteered as tribute.

Leaning forward, I gave him more of my cleavage to look at, the tops of my breasts nearly spilling out of the tiny top. The way he shifted in his seat and the hunger in his expression made me clench my thighs in response. Yeah, he was definitely a tits guy.

Good thing I had those in spades.

Not caring about the rest of the people in the room—they were distracted with their own bedroom games anyway—I ran my palms up the sides of my body, taking my breasts into my hands and giving them a playful squeeze.

Cain leaned forward, eyes locked in on what my hands were doing. Daring me to keep going. I wanted to see what I was doing to him, to find out if he was as affected physically by this as I was. Because more than anything, I needed the answer to be yes. It wasn't a one-sided attraction, even if he tried to deny the truth.

Well, I guess he didn't deny his attraction to me. He was the one who kept bringing it up. It was more like he was trying to repress it. So maybe all he needed was a little nudge.

As the idea flirted with my mind, I bit down on my lip. Was I really going to do this? Here? In front of all these people, just to see if I could force Cain to lose control?

Swallowing nervously, I crooked one finger into the top of my shirt and started to slowly tug it down.

I guess I was.

Before my nipple was exposed, Cain shot to his feet, his movement so fast he nearly flipped the table in front of him. God, he had a tent in his pants big enough to fit a three-ring circus. Good for you, Cain. Good. For. You.

And me.

I couldn't help the wicked snicker that accompanied the thought.

Shooting me a murderous and really fucking sexy glare, he adjusted himself, eyelids fluttering at the contact in the most tantalizing way. Then he stormed out of the rec room with his jaw clenched so tight I could see the muscle popping low in his cheek.

That's your cue, baby girl. Go get your man!

As always, the voice of my inner cheerleader sounded like Kiki. She was my biggest enabler, always encouraging me to step outside my comfort zone, and *this* was way past anything I'd ever dared. I was doing that a lot these days. Yay for personal growth.

Without sparing a look for what anyone else was doing—there were just some things you could never unsee, and I didn't need to carry certain people's O faces in my memory banks—I went after him.

We needed to talk this through and figure out what it was we were dancing around, or I'd go truly insane. The tension was too thick between us.

Talk. Yeah, that's totally what you have in mind.

This inner voice was all mine. I was such a snarky bitch when I was calling myself out.

One way or another, something had to give. I was tired of the hot and cold, will-they-won't-they BS. It was exhausting. I wanted him to exhaust me in another way. One that was much more fun.

And sweaty.

A mental image of me licking beads of sweat off Cain's chest had me nearly combusting then and there. His thick fingers curled in my hair, tugging me up so he could kiss me hard and shove me up against the wall.

Oh God. There were moments it paid to be a romance writer. I think this was one of them. My mind was *full* of ideas. Very naughty, delicious ideas.

I caught sight of Cain's tall form as he rounded a corner and I upped my pace, needing to catch up, look into his eyes, and make sure he saw how much I wanted him. His long strides were eating up the ground. By the time I made it to the foyer, he was already climbing the main staircase that would take him to the residential floors.

I won't say that I ran, but a bitch was breathless by the time she reached the stairs and started up after him. In a move one could only call a superhuman burst of speed, I caught up to him and snagged the man by the wrist so he couldn't ignore me. Truthfully, all he'd needed to do was shake me off him, but he didn't. Cain turned and stared at me, a strange mix of grief and lust dancing in his eyes.

Now that I'd caught up to him, some of my bravado fled. I didn't want to force this. He had to choose.

So I didn't say anything. I just held his stare, both of us breathing hard. Him due to his inner battle, me for my daring display of athletics. Well, athletic for me.

The moment stretched. And stretched.

I parted my lips, not sure if I should speak and break the moment, but dying for something to happen.

The grief in his expression melted away and was replaced by a feral hunger I'd only ever seen on Tor's face. Oh yes. It was on.

He yanked me to him, my soft curves colliding with his hard body. Then he let out a low, rumbled growl a breath before his lips slammed down onto mine.

Cain's kiss was everything I'd imagined and more. There was an undercurrent of punishment to it that only made it hotter.

"Finally," I breathed into his mouth.

"Your room. Now," he growled back, nipping my bottom lip.

CHAPTER FORTY

HADES

Everything was different now that I knew my truth. So why did I still feel a strange sense of guilt over wanting Dahlia so badly? But my Persephone was dead. The return of my memory gave me so much clarity and somehow none at all. It was as if my reasons for keeping my distance no longer mattered, and yet I was weighed down with so much guilt for being the reason she died that I didn't trust myself. All I was good at was destroying the things that I loved.

My cold heart was broken. But right now, Dahlia was the sun, warming me in her gaze. Sunshine breaking through the darkest storm clouds, lighting the way to my salvation. Or perhaps it was damnation.

All I knew was that I was done fighting her lure. I didn't have any more fight in me. Resisting Dahlia was like refusing nightfall. It was impossible. She was a force I was helpless to deflect. I should know, I tried.

But the instant my lips touched hers, I knew I'd thrown myself off the cliff without a safety net to catch me. I would have her come hell or high water. She was mine.

"Finally."

"Your room. Now." It was closer, and with the things I intended to do to her, I wasn't interested in prying eyes.

She pulled away just far enough to search my face, her lips curving up in a sinful grin at whatever she found there.

"You taste so sweet," I whispered. "I need more."

Her little whimpered moan had me coming unglued. My kiss this time was deep and rough as I devoured her mouth. We fumbled on the stairs, hands tearing at each other's clothes, teeth nipping, moans ragged and desperate.

Her hands were at my belt, struggling as she blindly attempted to undo it. Mine were . . . everywhere. In her hair, drifting up her shirt, cupping and squeezing her ass. Now that I'd given myself permission, I wanted everything all at once. I was a kid in a candy store, and I fully intended to gorge myself on her pleasure.

"I need you," she moaned.

"You'll have me," I promised, breaking free of our kiss long enough to check how far we were from the door.

I needed to touch her and feel if she was as affected by this as I was. My cock throbbed with the insistent pulse of desire to fill her. Was she wet for me? Her cunt swollen and slick? Clit a hard nub aching for my attention? Gods, I hoped so. I would bury my face between her thick thighs and worship at that bundle of nerves until she gave me her orgasm to drink down.

Dipping into her leggings, I cupped her warm center and groaned at the slickness that immediately coated my fingers.

"You're dripping for me, baby doll."

Her laugh was a husky rasp as she cupped and stroked my cock through my pants. "You want to talk about the two-by-four in your pants, buddy?"

"Fuck, Dahlia. As much as I love your hands on me, I am dying. I need inside you, and if you make me come in my pants again, I won't be able to do that."

The brat didn't release me. In fact, she used that opportunity to squeeze a little before working my fly open.

I jerked backward and immediately grunted in pain.

"Did I hurt you?" she asked, quickly releasing me.

"No," I said, swallowing through the ache blossoming across my lower back. "Doorknob," I explained.

To her credit, she at least tried to hide her laugh. "Oops."

"Enough of this," I growled, scooping her up and tossing her over my shoulder.

Her delighted squeal made me grin, a rare thing for me. I had to admit, I liked it. She made me feel whole in a way I hadn't experienced for . . . eons.

"Open your fucking door, baby doll. Unless you want me to have you up against it out here in the hall for Joffrey and the ghosts to watch."

The lock clicked and the door swung open. I didn't take the time to turn on the lights; instead I used my shadows to shut the door behind us as I closed the distance between the door and her bed.

Even upside down over my shoulder, Dahlia continued to torment me. She ran her hands along my thighs and ass, squealing when I spanked her for daring to reach between my legs. Not because I didn't want the touch, but because I didn't want to drop her.

"Behave."

"Make me."

"You're going to wish you never said that, brat."

"Guess we'll find out . . . Daddy."

Oh fuck. I nearly came on the spot.

Thankfully the bed was within reach, allowing me to toss her down and watch her bounce.

Gods, it should be a crime to do the things she did to me just watching those glorious breasts move in a mockery of what they'd do when I pumped her full of me. I had to close my eyes and breathe deep just to avoid embarrassing myself.

I did not make it this far just to come in my pants. Again.

"Why are you standing so far away?" she whimpered. "You can't touch me from over there."

"Yes I fucking can."

To prove the point, I summoned the shadows and made quick work of her clothes. Those discarded, I used the shadows to hold her spread open for me and another to whisper over her skin, discovering her with my magic the same way I was about to with my body.

"Oh God, that's a neat trick." I fucking loved how breathy and aroused her voice was.

"Here's another," I said with a smirk, wielding the shadows like a cock and dipping it between her legs and then pressing it inside of her, filling her.

She didn't speak so much as moan a string of incoherent sounds. So I did it again.

"That . . . has no right . . . to feel . . . sooo gooood."

I felt it too, but not the same way I would if it really was my straining length sinking inside her. But we had all evening. If she or any of the others thought I was letting her go until the sun rose tomorrow, they were delusional.

My shadow tendrils slid over her thighs as I continued fucking her with the thickest one, and with each pump, my own cock wept, eager to do the same. I swept across her clit in time with every thrust, loving the way her tits bounced as she arched into the shadows, seeking more, begging me to let her come.

"Cain!" she cried, and something in me broke. The moment was no longer about me finding release, but her. Perhaps it had never been about me at all. Because this, watching her come undone, was every-fucking-thing.

"Come for me, baby doll. Give me your pleasure. I need it."

Her climax was exquisite. Her face contorted in pained pleasure, and her back bowed off the bed as she rode my shadows, chasing every last drop of her orgasm.

I could only imagine what it would be like when it was my dick she was milking. As she came down from her high, I pulled the shadows back and stepped closer to the bed, my pants open, shirt unbuttoned, breaths tight with the effort it was taking me not to nail her to the bed until she couldn't move.

"Please," she whispered, reaching for me now that I'd unbound her.

"I think you might be my undoing," I murmured, not fully intending to say the words out loud as I crawled up onto the bed. Thankfully she seemed too distracted to have heard me.

"You aren't going to take your clothes off?"

"After," I breathed, my lips brushing hers. "I need inside you too damn bad to waste another second."

I reached between us, pulling my rigid length out and notching myself at her soft, sweet entrance.

"Hold on to me, baby doll. I'm not going to fuck you sweet and slow. Not this first time."

"Good. I don't want sweet or slow. Hard and fast, Cain. Fuck me hard and fast. Put us both out of our misery."

Unable to deny her, especially when her demand so clearly mirrored my own desires, I drove into her in one vicious thrust. Immediate relief flooded me at the way I fit inside her. It was like coming home after a long, painful absence. I didn't stay still for long because she gasped and tilted her pelvis to take me a little deeper. Her heels dug into my ass, nails scored my back, and I realized she wasn't simply taking more of me. She was rubbing her swollen clit against my pubic bone in search of that extra stimulation.

Oh no. That wouldn't do.

I called forth another shadow tendril and sent it to do the work she was failing to complete, grunting in pleasure when she clenched down on my cock as soon as the shadow made contact.

"God, yes," she groaned, a deep guttural sound I felt in my dick. "I'm so close. I'm gonna come again. Can I"—her eyes locked on mine and her lips curled—"Shadow Daddy?"

That word. That. Fucking. Word.

She hadn't missed how I'd reacted the first time, and now she was weaponizing it against me.

"Yes," I gritted out, pistoning into her harder and faster, the sound of our skin slapping together filling the room as my own climax barreled its way forward.

I wanted to make it last longer, to live in this bliss between her thighs, but it was too much. The pleasure, the fulfillment, the soul-deep certainty that this was exactly where I belonged.

"Fuck, baby. You take me so good. I can't hold back," I said, my words groaned and frantic at the same time.

"Fill me up, Daddy," she whispered.

And I was done for. That was it. Toe-curling pleasure raced through me as I jerked inside her.

She was right there with me, her inner walls gripping tight and milking me with each pulse of her orgasm, sending me flying higher.

I couldn't breathe. Could hardly see. Scratch that, I *couldn't* see. The black dots dancing in my periphery clustered together until they blocked out everything but the euphoria. And in that darkness, the floodgates were ripped wide open.

Everything that had been locked away came roaring back. I'd already uncovered my name, but this was the pure, unfiltered truth. Every second of my life, from creation to this moment, condensed into one all-encompassing explosion. And not just my truth. But *hers*.

I sucked in a ragged breath, my eyes flying open and finding her guileless gray depths peering into mine. She reached for me, her hand cupping my cheek, but before she could speak, I did.

"I found you."

Gazing at her, our bodies still joined, I nearly wept at the gift the Fates had *finally* given me.

It was her.

Her eyes.

Her heart.

Her fucking soul.

"Persephone."

CHAPTER
FORTY-ONE
DEATH

I pulled the needle through the woven cloth, grimacing as I pricked my finger with the sharp tip.

"Oopsie daisy!" I chirped as a drop of blood splashed onto the eggshell fabric. "Oh well, you won't mind a bit of blood, right Chaos? Don't you regularly bathe in it?"

The horseman in my brilliant containment cell snarled. "If it's yours, I'll make sure to lavish in it. Let me out of here."

I smiled sweetly at my petulant prisoner. "No. I don't believe I will. But don't worry, I've got a surprise for you."

Tying off my thread, I looked at my handiwork. *Cell sweet cell.* Grinning, I stood and sauntered over to the glass containing him, pressing it against the double-sided tape I'd already placed there. "What do you think? Brightens the place up a bit, right?"

"I am going to tear out your throat when I get free."

"Ooh, I'm quaking with fear. You never did give me enough credit. My sisters have failed, but I'm wiser and more patient."

"How long are you keeping me here?"

"As long as it takes."

"As long as what takes?"

"For the rest of the party to get here. Time is on my side."

As I spoke, a shiver raced down my spine, and I let out a little giggle. It was happening. I could recognize the feeling now that I'd experienced it once before. The next rite was nearly complete.

"Oh, goodie, our next guest is about to arrive. I think you're going to like this one. I know I'm excited. Any guesses who it is?"

He glared mulishly at me.

"Fine, be a spoilsport."

My ears popped as a large domineering figure materialized in the cell next to Chaos's. There was just something about him I couldn't take my eyes off. Grim always had a way about him. Maybe it was the silver hair and the stern expression or the broad shoulders I knew were covered in thick slabs of muscle. Or, you know, the fact that he and I were kindred. The horseman Death stared at me with murder in his eyes.

"And then there were two," I murmured with a wide smile.

"You."

I giggled and waved. "Me."

"What is the meaning of this?"

"If you have to ask me that, my darling Grim, you haven't been paying attention."

"I try to never pay attention to you."

Huffing, I leaned forward and pressed a kiss to the glass surrounding him, my pink lipstick leaving a perfect mark to taunt him. "It's the end of the world, darling. My Apocalypse. Welcome to the table."

"Release me."

"You know I can't. I have big plans for you. Big. Huge." Twirling, my laughter filled the room while the two fuming horsemen stared daggers at me. "Settle in, fellas. Things are about to start picking up. It's too bad you won't be able to see the show. Don't worry, I'll fill you in with the highlights."

"I'll kill you for this, you bitch!" Chaos shouted.

"Not if I get to her first." Grim pounded on the glass, but to no avail. "You won't succeed, Hel. I'll make sure of it."

"Toodles, boys." I skipped to the door and switched off the lights, leaving them in pitch-black silence. "Sleep tight. Don't let the bedbugs bite."

The sound of the heavy door locking behind me echoed through the corridor, followed by the enraged howls of the two horsemen I'd summoned. Two down, two to go.

The Apocalypse was within reach. I could taste it.

And no one had any idea what I was doing.

You think my sisters would have learned by now never to bet against Death.

I *always* win.

Well that sounds ominous. . .

Thankfully, The Mate Games : Death will continue in Hateful Prince.

Want more now? How about a scene from your favorite Asshole?

We thought that might get your attention.

Download your Hunted Beast bonus scene at www.themategames.com/BeastBonus or get the audio version at www.themategames.com/BeastAudioBonus

THE MATE GAMES UNIVERSE

BY K. LORAINE & MEG ANNE

WAR

OBSESSION

REJECTION

POSSESSION

TEMPTATION

PESTILENCE

PROMISED TO THE NIGHT (PREQUEL NOVELLA)

DEAL WITH THE DEMON

CLAIMED BY THE SHIFTERS

CAPTIVE OF THE NIGHT

LOST TO THE MOON

DEATH

HAUNTING BEAUTY

HUNTED BEAST

HATEFUL PRINCE

HEARTLESS VILLAIN

More by Meg & Kim

Twisted Cross Ranch

A dark contemporary cowboy reverse harem

Sinner's Secret

Corruptor's Claim

Deadly Debt

Also by Meg Anne

Brotherhood of the Guardians/Novasgard Vikings

Undercover Magic *(Nord & Lina)*

A Sexy & Suspenseful Fated Mates PNR

Hint of Danger

Face of Danger

World of Danger

Promise of Danger

Call of Danger

Bound by Danger (Quinn & Finley)

The Chosen Universe

The Chosen

A Fated Mates High Fantasy Romance

Mother Of Shadows

Reign Of Ash

Crown Of Embers

Queen Of Light

The Chosen Boxset #1

The Chosen Boxset #2

The Keepers

A Guardian/Ward High Fantasy Romance

The Dreamer (A Keeper's Prequel)

The Keepers Legacy

The Keepers Retribution

The Keepers Vow

The Keepers Boxset

The Forsaken

A Rejected Mates/Enemies-To-Lovers Romantasy

Prisoner of Steel & Shadow

Queen of Whispers & Mist

Court of Death & Dreams

Gypsy's Curse

A Psychic/Detective Star-Crossed Lovers UF Romance

Visions Of Death

Visions Of Vengeance

Visions Of Triumph

The Gypsy's Curse: The Complete Collection

Standalones

My Soul To Take: A Forbidden Love Meets Fated Mates PNR

Also by K. Loraine

The Blackthorne Vampires

THE BLOOD TRILOGY

(Cashel & Olivia)

Blood Captive

Blood Traitor

Blood Heir

BLACKTHORNE BLOODLINES

(Lucas & Briar)

Midnight Prince

Midnight Hunger

THE WATCHER SERIES

Waking the Watcher

Denying the Watcher

Releasing the Watcher

THE SIREN COVEN

Eternal Desire (Shifter reluctant mates)

Cursed Heart (Hate to Lovers)

Broken Sword (MMF menage Arthurian)

~

STANDALONES

Cursed (MFM Sleeping Beauty Retelling)

~

REVERSE HAREM STANDALONES

Their Vampire Princess (A Reverse Harem Romance)

All the Queen's Men (A Fae Reverse Harem Romance)

About Meg Anne

USA Today and international bestselling paranormal and fantasy romance author Meg Anne has always had stories running on a loop in her head. They started off as daydreams about how the evil queen (aka Mom) had her slaving away doing chores, and more recently shifted into creating backgrounds about the people stuck beside her during rush hour. The stories have always been there; they were just waiting for her to tell them.

Like any true SoCal native, Meg enjoys staying inside curled up with a good book and her fur babies . . . or maybe that's just her. You can convince Meg to buy just about anything if it's covered in glitter or rhinestones, or make her laugh by sharing your favorite bad joke. She also accepts bribes in the form of baked goods and Mexican food.

Meg is best known for her leading men #MenbyMeg, her inevitable cliffhangers, and making her readers laugh out loud, all of which started with the bestselling Chosen series.

ABOUT K. LORAINE

USA Today Bestselling author Kim Loraine writes steamy contemporary and sexy paranormal romance. **You'll find her paranormal romances written under the name K. Loraine and her contemporaries as Kim Loraine.** Don't worry, you'll get the same level of swoon-worthy heroes, sassy heroines, and an eventual HEA.

When not writing, she's busy herding cats (raising kids), trying to keep her house sort of clean, and dreaming up ways for fictional couples to meet.